JASON ANSPACH

NICK COLE

# LAST CONTACT

SEASON 2

BOOK 5

GALAXY'S EDGE

Paperback ISBN: 978-1-949731-72-9
Hardcover ISBN: 978-1-949731-74-3

Edited by David Gatewood
Published by Galaxy's Edge Press

Cover Art: Tommaso Renieri
Cover Design & Formatting: Kevin G. Summers

Website: www.GalaxysEdge.us
Facebook: facebook.com/atgalaxysedge
Newsletter (get a free short story): www.InTheLegion.com

# WHO'S WHO...

What follows is a summary of some of the characters found in this book, and their stories up to this point. More characters will appear in this volume but listing them up front would kind of spoil things. If you find yourself lost, consider joining one of the Galaxy's Edge fan groups listed at the end of the book. There is no shortage of fellow leejes who love talking about the story of Galaxy's Edge (and speculating and theorizing about what comes next).

**Aeson Ford**—See Aeson Keel.

**Aeson Keel** – See Wraith.

**Andien Broxin** – A Nether Ops operative who worked closely with Legion Dark Ops (*Kill Team*). Broxin's military career began as a Republic Marine (*Forget Nothing*). She was selected for an experimental Legion training program (*Forget Nothing II*). Presumed dead at the hands of the Cybar (*Message for the Dead*), Broxin was saved by a dissenting Cybar named Praxus and is currently working with him.

**Archimedes** – The head of a peculiar Savage mini-hulk that gathers lost star-farers and pits them against combat simulations. Archimedes made a deal with an ad hoc alliance composed of Prisma, Ravi, and members of Goth

Sullus's elite strike force, allowing them to leave the ship if they would restore control to Archimedes. He awaits a final solution to a high-value scenario... one that requires the help of Wraith.

**Bear** – Dark Ops captain who oversees Kill Team Victory. No longer regularly involved in direct action due to injuries suffered in the Second Battle for Utopion (*Retribution*), he fills the role once held by Major Owens.

**Bombassa** – Senior NCO for Kill Team Victory. Former legionnaire who sided with Goth Sullus's Black Fleet (*Attack of Shadows*). Following Article Nineteen, was sent undercover as "Lashley" to determine Nilo's motivations and capabilities (*Takeover*).

**Casper** – Also known as Admiral Sulla, Casper Sullivan, and a host of other aliases. A friend of Tyrus Rechs and Reina who shared their experiences at the hands of the Savages and was given exceptionally long life (*Imperator*). Sulla was the mastermind behind the galaxy's war against the Savages, convincing Tyrus Rechs to found the Legion and bringing about the unification of the galaxy through the forming of the Republic (*Savage Wars* trilogy). Casper's thirst for a power that could fully defeat the enemies of humanity led him to study under Urmo, and ultimately to his betrayal and murder of Tyrus Rechs as Goth Sullus (*Imperator, Galactic Outlaws*).

**Crometheus** – A Savage marine who lived in a simulation on the edge of madness (*Gods & Legionnaires*). Part of the Savage tribe known as the Uplifted, he was presumed deactivated. The reasons for his reappearance and the subsequent change of his reality are currently unknown.

**Crash** – See KRS-88.

**Cybar** – A species of mechanical, non-biological life. Created by unknown causes in one of the Temples of the Ancients (*Legacies*). Discovered by the Republic and recovered by Kill Team Ice (*Legacies*, again). Given the planet Khan Sakh (*Legionnaire*) as a home world, while also used to construct a doomsday fleet (*Message for the Dead*).

**Death, Destroyer of Worlds** – Psychopathic and homicidal Nubarian gunnery bot originally acquired by Tyrus Rechs (*Contracts & Terminations* series). Now the property of Aeson Keel.

**Donal Makaffie** – Eccentric, existential genius. The inventor of H8. An expert on many things Savage, possesses an ability to intuitively comprehend what they're attempting. A member of Kill Team Ice and veteran of the Savage Wars.

**G232** – Admin and protocol bot originally acquired by Tyrus Rechs (*Contracts & Terminations* series). Now the property of Aeson Keel.

**Garret** – A technical wizard and savant. Was a former slave of Lao Pak, "liberated" by Aeson Keel, and now serves as a crewmember on the *Indelible IV*.

**Goth Sullus** – See Casper.

**J-316** – A very old "missionary" bot meant to evangelize and/or proselytize humanoid species. Programmed in multiple faiths, J-316 has been receiving "new revelations" concerning the worship of Oba.

**Jack** – A Repub Navy spy who went independent following Article Nineteen. He was hired by Nilo to obtain Savage artifacts only to be double-crossed and left for dead by a Tennar Nether Ops agent known as Honey (*Takeover*). He remains in the employ of Mr. Nilo.

**Kill Team Ice** – A team of volunteers, formed by Tyrus Rechs and Admiral Sulla during the Savage Wars, taking from the best of the Legion. Its members agreed to remain in cryo-stasis until a military application arose that required their unique talents.

**Kill Team Victory** – Dark Ops kill team founded shortly after the Battle of Kublar. Active team members: Bombassa, Pina, Neck, Nix, Nobes, "Toots," Wello.

**KRS-88** – Psydon-era war bot (*Tin Man*). Was repurposed to serve as a bodyguard for the Maydoon family and was specifically tasked to protect Prisma (*Galactic Outlaws*). Though it is a capable killing machine, it prefers a life of peace.

**Lao Pak** – He pirate king.

**Leenah** – Endurian "princess." Exceptionally skilled mechanic. Former MCR rebel. Keel's main squeeze. A surrogate mother to Prisma for a time.

**MakRaven** – A living legend within the Legion and the self-proclaimed premier donk fighter in the galaxy. Roped into one more enlistment by Cohen Chhun, in order to oversee the rebuilding of the 131st Legion into a "Savage-ready" fighting force.

**Masters** – Quite possibly the sexiest man in the galaxy. Definitely the best abs in the galaxy. Screenwriter. Heartthrob. Dark Ops legionnaire. In considerable trouble at the moment.

**Nilo** – A genius-level intellect who controls a vast corporate empire. His shadowy past involves parents who were apparently lost to Gomarii slavers, though he believes his father is alive and trapped somewhere beyond galaxy's edge. He is desperately seeking as much Savage technology as possible, despite it being illegal to possess such artifacts.

**Praxus** – A member of the Cybar collective who dissented from the directives of MAGNUS and CRONUS. He was the lone Cybar to oppose aligning with those discovered beyond galaxy's edge. He accepted exile in order to save the life of Andien Broxin, whom he saw as the next evolutionary step for the Cybar—the perfect blend of machine and humanity.

**Prisma Maydoon** – Juvenile girl whose father, Kael Maydoon, was murdered by Goth Sullus. She hired Tyrus Rechs to seek her revenge (*Galactic Outlaws*) and found herself swept up in the rise of the Cybar and the fall of the Republic. Has a preternatural ability to use what Goth Sullus called "the Crux."

**Ravi** – One of the Ancients, left behind to help humanity resist the destruction coming from beyond galaxy's edge... if such is even possible. See also *Urmo*.

**Reina** – A Savage prisoner who helped free Tyrus Rechs and Casper Sullivan (*Imperator*). She later disappeared, though she seems to have had some communication with Casper before the man became Goth Sullus (*Gods & Legionnaires*). Trained in what Goth Sullus called "the Crux," she has returned to the galaxy, revealing to Prisma Maydoon that she is her mother (*Legacies*).

**Skrizz** – Wobanki smuggler who briefly co-piloted for Tyrus Rechs (*Galactic Outlaws*) before joining the crew of the *Indelible VI*. "Tamed" by Prisma, Skrizz sought the girl out on his own before turning to piracy. He was enticed by Donal Makaffie into resuming the hunt for Prisma, this time by leading Makaffie to Aeson Keel.

**Surber** – Nilo's right-hand man. A no-nonsense enigmatic human who seems more suited for the boardroom than the sort of violent situations Nilo and Black Leaf continually encounter (*Takeover*). His name was given to Wraith as the source behind the termination contracts (*Legacies*). It is unclear if he is the same individual.

**The Dark Wanderer** – A mysterious and evil entity tied to whatever darkness is looming for the galaxy. Currently holding Ravi as prisoner.

**Tyrus Rechs** – The founder of the Legion (*Savage Wars* trilogy). Given immortality by Savages while their prisoner (*Imperator*), Rechs escaped and dedicated his life to destroying them. Rechs has lived multiple lives, primarily serving as a soldier on the galactic stage. When the House of Reason sought to assassinate him (*Legionnaire*, Epilogue), Rechs went underground, living a new life as a bounty hunter (*Contracts & Terminations* series, *Galactic Outlaws*). Plagued by a degenerating memory, Rechs was killed by Goth Sullus and Kill Team Ice.

**Urmo** – Urmo. Urmo Urmo. Urmo! (*Imperator*)

**Wild Man** – A tortured soul and exceptional sniper. Savage Wars veteran and member of Kill Team Ice (*Savage Wars* trilogy).

**Wraith** – Former legionnaire turned Dark Ops deep cover operative who developed a fearsome reputation as a bounty hunter and mercenary. Former member of Kill Team Ice. We'd talk about what happens in *Savage Wars*, too, but if you haven't read it... spoilers.

**X** – A Nether Ops department head whose machinations led to the wholesale slaughter of friend and foe alike. A man accustomed to playing all sides, he ultimately aligned with Goth Sullus and the Black Fleet's imperial takeover of the Republic. He was killed by the legionnaire Exo (*Retribution*). While deceased, his plans are still being carried out by a deep state network of operatives.

**Zora**—The bounty hunter daughter of former Dark Ops legionnaire Doc. She was brought in by Doc to help train Aeson Ford to better serve in deep cover. Hired by Nilo to convince Keel to work for his corporation, Black Leaf.

# 01

"How's it look?" Aeson Keel held out his hand and made a short, sweeping gesture at the *Obsidian Crow*'s instrument panel before him and the wobanki Skrizz. They had just made the jump to hyperspace and were racing through the folding spirals of faster-than-light travel to meet with several other interested parties for a rendezvous safely away from the ears and eyes of information brokers or spies—including those on the mining colony they'd left behind.

Skrizz, with his eyes half-shut as though drifting to sleep, slowly scanned the cockpit as if taking it all in for the first time now. This was his considering, thoughtful look.

"About the same as the one you used to co-pilot?" Keel prompted, because that was what he truly wished to know.

When Keel had first met Skrizz, the large predatory catman was serving as Tyrus Rechs's first mate—at least temporarily—on a different *Obsidian Crow*. A ship that was now long-since destroyed. And yet here it was again. Or close enough, Keel hoped—hence his desire to get the wobanki's stamp of approval, his confirmation that this really was a reasonable facsimile of Rechs's old ship. For ever since Keel had put on Rechs's armor—something he'd done merely for expediency at the time—he'd felt an affinity bordering on kinship for the old bounty hunter. He'd barely been acquainted with Rechs in life, yet the dead man now seemed to shape so many of the paths Keel was traveling.

Skrizz finally gave a purring judgment that was steeped in admiration. This version of the *Obsidian Crow* was a *little* different than the one he'd flown on before, but mostly the same. The wobanki told Keel that this was a very old freighter. An antique.

Something Keel already knew.

The smuggler nodded. "Yeah, it's practically ancient. Stands out like a lone bunt'tah. Seems the old bounty hunter was partial to this particular make and model. He put together more than just the two you've been inside. Got a whole hangar full of 'em."

Keel side-eyed Skrizz to see if that elicited a reaction, but the wobanki merely stared at the old console as though he hadn't heard a thing. He flipped a thrust/repulsor decoupler, listened, and then decided that Keel was correct to have it where it was.

It was then that the little Nubarian gunnery bot, Death, Destroyer of Worlds, rolled down the corridor to sit just outside the cockpit. It had been listening to the conversation from afar and now beeped out its assessment of the wobanki for Keel to hear. The smuggler turned around to see the bot suggestively opening the compartment where it kept its blaster pistol as it informed "New Boss" that it didn't trust the wobanki. New Boss, it said, should probably, just to be safe, kill Skrizz during one of the frequent naps the wobanki were known for. The species were embarrassingly lazy in between bouts of their admittedly impressive violence.

Keel gently swatted Skrizz's muscular arms with the back of his hand and then tossed his thumb in the direction of Death. "You ever see this bot before? With Rechs?"

"*Natu.*"

This seemed to frustrate the little bot, who must have felt that his credentials were being called into question. He stated for the record that *he* had never seen Old Boss with this wobanki. Something for New Boss to consider.

"Take it easy," Keel soothed. "Didn't mean it like that. Just... trying to get a better idea of the guy whose fleet, armor, and weapons collection I've inherited."

Death helpfully offered that Old Boss was good at killing. New Boss fit in well so far.

"Thanks for that," Keel said. "I could say the same to you. I can't see myself taking a job without you now that I know the kind of help you can bring me."

The gunnery bot chirped appreciatively.

Keel leaned back in his chair and spoke into the cockpit, addressing himself and no one as much as he did Skrizz. "I dunno. It's almost like the old man forgot he had these bots or something. He was losing it at the end, I think."

Skrizz nodded and swished his tail in agreement. The wobanki had heard the same stories that everyone else who knew him had. The fearsome, nearly unstoppable bounty hunter Tyrus Rechs had been an old man living in the advanced stages of an untreated kind of dementia. Or perhaps he'd simply forgotten that such diseases of the mind could be cured. Maybe Tyrus Rechs couldn't remember enough about his problem to address it. And no longer fully knowing all the things he'd done or truly grasping the things that still needed doing—maybe that had driven him into becoming what he was: the most brazen and fearless bounty hunter in the galaxy. A man who recklessly and repeatedly threw his life on the line, always trusting that his sharp skill set and his even more powerful armor would save him.

Until one day it didn't.

He looked to Skrizz and let out a breath. There wasn't anything the wobanki could tell him about the bounty hunter that he didn't already know. Keel changed the subject to something more useful.

"So this guy, Makaffie... Do you trust him? You gave up the start of a new life to put us all in contact."

Skrizz said that he trusted a man—any human—inasmuch as he believed he was being told the truth. He thought Makaffie was telling the truth about Prisma. Anything beyond that, though... *"Pachuca totakka pachuca ten nay."* Which was an old wobanki saying best translated as, "Do not sleep before hearing the snores of the other."

"I don't trust him either," said Keel. "But I'm willing to go along if it means finding out what he knows about Prisma."

Then Skrizz asked if Keel trusted Nilo and Jack and Zora and all the other new faces who had so recently crashed their appointed meeting on the mining colony.

"I trust Zora," Keel said. "She's in the same category as you are—someone who saved my life when theirs wasn't at risk. Someone like that, I owe trust until they give me a reason not to."

Skrizz gave a firm growl of consensus. It was the same with any wobanki. Matters of life and death were matters of honor. Those who acted honorably should be treated with honor—unless they had since dishonored themselves. Then... it didn't matter if they lived or died.

"But just because I trust Zora," Keel continued, "doesn't mean that she couldn't be tricked, if you know what I mean." The smuggler let his gaze rest on Skrizz, communicating that the wobanki could just as easily be fooled by Makaffie. "As for Jack, he's one of those navy spooks. Not quite Nether Ops and maybe no better. But... he got into a fight with Nether and I don't think it was a simple family feud. You never really know with them, though. They wanted him dead either way. Probably still do.

"And then there's Nilo. I know about as much as you do. Maybe a little more but not enough to give me any firm opinion. Can't say I'm sorry about what he did to the donks and the Reason loyalists on Kublar, though."

Skrizz said that he'd heard a rumor that Nilo and his Black Leaf corporation was going to try something similar on Kima. Only this time, they'd help the MCR to overthrow the legitimate—or at least current—Republic rule. The wobanki asked Keel if he'd heard the Legion invaded the planet.

"Yeah, I heard about it."

The wobanki was watching Keel closely, looking for any unspoken clue that Keel was somehow involved with the Legion's latest plans for war. Serving aboard the smuggler's ship with Prisma had been one thing, but when Skrizz had seen how close Keel was with the Legion and its Dark Ops operators... There comes a point even for a wobanki when the risk isn't worth the reward. Skrizz had no interest in getting swept up in another war.

He just wanted to find Prisma. And then... and then...

He wanted to find Prisma.

The nav-computer began to sing its warning that the ship was preparing to dump out of hyperspace. The wobanki gave a slight yelp and raised his whiskers. This was sooner than he expected. He looked curiously at Keel, seeking an explanation.

"I had our rendezvous point jump toward us. Cuts down on travel time. Everybody else is probably recalibrating their jump drives right about now, trying to keep up with its beacon."

"*Tenchu gabba job?*"

"No, it's okay. I want for us to get there first and still have some time to prepare."

Skrizz squinted his yellow, feline eyes as he peered out of the forward viewport. He saw a dark gray speck in the distance that rapidly grew larger as the *Obsidian Crow* raced toward it.

"Let me enhance that for you," Keel said. He drew his mouth into a lopsided smile and tasked the old ship's relatively new holocams with the job of visual magnification. A holographic window superimposed itself over the main cockpit view—another feature not original to the old ship—showing the strong, fierce prow of an old-model early-Republic light attack carrier cruising silently toward them as the stars twinkled brightly in its wake.

Skrizz gave a soft growl of appreciation. "*Tenchu namcha?*"

"Called the *Battle Phoenix*. Another one of the old man's forgotten treasures."

It's said that all wobanki are naturally curious. Intergalactic evolutionary biologists, publishing and reviewing one another's papers from within the towers of academia, hold that this is due to their evolution from predatory big cats some twenty thousand years before. But whatever the origin of this curiosity, it manifests in a manner that doesn't blend well with the academic pursuit of knowledge. One would not find a wobanki in a lab coat, its claws tapping on a table as it sips a cup of steaming tea and reviews a colleague's work.

The academics have a reason to explain this reality as well: wobanki are solitary creatures for the most part. They tend to roam alone on their home world, only coming together to mate or to fight off some threat to a larger geographic region or the species as a whole. That doesn't mean they are incapable of sharing space with other humanoids, even among the tight confines of cities. But a wobanki's inner thoughts and personal life are rarely shared with others. They hold their own counsel and do not feel less for it. Indeed, they see the need for community shown by some other species—especially the hated moktaar—to be a weakness.

Therefore, even when a wobanki wishes to dedicate its life to discovery, it does not file into the expected gates that lead to the writing of peer-reviewed papers. Such a wobanki are typically wanderers, jumping from one end of the galaxy to the other and tolerating others only as much as is necessary to allow them to satisfy their own internal drive to find answers. To satisfy their curiosity. Quite often, such a life requires the use of honed hunting and fighting skills, the way of tooth and claw needed to survive whatever they might encounter and uncover.

Keel knew this about the species. He knew it specifically about Skrizz.

When his former crewmember had been a captive aboard the Cybar mothership, it was no accident that rather than staying with the other survivors—Garret and the killer, Hutch—he instead spent his time roaming the ship. Prisma and the other prisoners had been found by Garret at that time, and so perhaps Skrizz could have told himself he was seeking an unexpected way of rescuing them. But the truth was, he was roaming simply... to *see*. To see what mysteries the great war ship contained. To delve all the way into its deepest darkest heart and then to know it.

Because his curiosity demanded that it be known to him.

They might have left Skrizz wandering on that ship. Wandering, but not lost. They *would* have left him were it not for Prisma's insistence that Keel go and find him. Find her lost, killer catman.

Now Keel was worried that the same curiosity might lead to Skrizz getting killed while on the *Battle Phoenix*.

"Listen," he said as the pair walked down the *Obsidian Crow*'s ramp to step foot on the *Phoenix*'s massive hangar bay. "I haven't had the time to really look into this ship. But knowing its previous owner, I wouldn't be surprised if there are some traps still set up meant to kill anyone who's not him. Ran into something like that at one of his old hideouts as a matter of fact."

Tyrus Rechs's "Doghouse" had been guarded by a wicked auto-turret defense system capable of ripping Keel, Exo, and Bombassa to shreds had Ravi not somehow known how to pass its security check.

Skrizz growled disappointedly. Then, perhaps feeling that his abilities as a scout and hunter were being challenged, he issued killed another wobanki saying: Are you the father of my litter?

Keel gave a lopsided grin. "I think Masters is the only human I know who could probably answer that question with certainty. No, I'm not. And I'm not gonna tell you what you can or can't do. I'm just asking you to be careful."

Skrizz sniffed the ship's recycled air. There was too much dust. He sneezed to clear his nostrils and then sniffed again. Then he looked at the assortment of ships in the hangar.

"The old man named them all *Obsidian Crow*," Keel said. "Someone else must've named the carrier."

Skrizz remarked on how the ships were the same model, but not identical. Each ship seemed to have been modified to a sort of specialty role. One looked to be little more than a fast approach craft with an ample cargo hold. Massive battery cells added above and on its sides were likely meant to give extra power to its shields or engines. In and out. Hit and fade. Another was so heavily armored that it was without the standard crysteel viewports. It was all thick hull and stubby sensors with multiple shield arrays. A ship meant to take a beating and survive, whether in combat like an armored command shuttle or while traveling through the harshest zones the galaxy had to offer. The early jump ships—the expensive ones anyway—had been like this, nothing but metal tombs with a sensor suite. But those who owned them survived gravity wells and other astronomical disaster zones during the mad dash to settle the galaxy following the discovery of FTL technology.

And there were more still. Including, of course, the all-purpose craft that Skrizz and Keel had just disembarked from. That one seemed the most like the ship the wobanki had briefly served on, what felt like a lifetime ago already.

Skrizz was just wondering whether Keel might be willing to part with one of the ships, when the high, prissy voice of an admin protocol bot began shouting its greetings from further inside the carrier. The wobanki flattened his ears in displeasure at the sound.

"Master Wraith! Master Wraith! I am *so* happy that you have returned."

Keel nodded. "Skrizz, this is G232. Rechs's butler, I suppose."

"Well," the bot replied, "I wouldn't put it quite so—"

"Everything okay on the *Phoenix* while I was away? No boarders? Nothing caught on fire?"

"I'm sure I'd remember something like that happening, Master."

"Good." Keel strode past the bot, motioning for Skrizz to follow. Down the ramp behind them both rolled Death, Destroyer of Worlds.

G232 tilted its head to the side to watch the bot. "Oh. I see you've returned... how... good."

The little bot swore some foul oath in its digital Signica language so fiercely that G232 actually straightened upright—as though the figurative stick the Nubarian gunnery bot had threatened its counterpart with had actually been rammed into the suggested spot.

"Three-Two, I want you to meet Skrizz," Keel called over his shoulder, summoning the admin bot and not bothering to hide the amused grin on his face. There was something about the little gunnery bot that felt right to Keel. It was like... like being on the teams again. That's what it reminded Keel of. He had never desired to own a bot, but Death was different. It was an odd feeling for the smuggler, one he thought he might tell Garret about. He was starting to understand the young code slicer's affinity for bots a little bit more.

"I am certainly pleased to meet you," G232 said. The bot bowed, put its arm behind it, and made it swish like a tail as it yammered something in the wobanki language. Then G232 turned to Keel and explained. "That is the expected greeting of honor for a wobanki, including the proper respectful tail motion. It should put him quite at ease, Master Wraith. You see, I am pleased to inform you, Master, that I am capable of sensitively communicating with over two hundred thousand different —"

"Great," Keel interrupted. "Sounds like you understand wobanki. Skrizz is going to want to take a look around. Go with him. Show him anything he wants, tell him anything he asks. If there's someplace you can't or won't access, tell me so I can see what we can do. You know this ship and—"

G232's hands went up in the air in jubilation. "I know this ship very well, Master!"

The bot was so eager to be helpful that it elicited an odd mix of annoyance and pity in Keel's stomach.

"Fine. Go. Give him the tour."

"I will, Master Wraith! I certainly will!"

Skrizz yammered something about how he wasn't a cub. Keel could tell the wobanki didn't mean it, but it was best not to question a wobanki, even if you considered one a friend. There is a certain delicacy that needs to be upheld in dealing with the cat-men, particularly when in front of strangers. Even if those strangers were just bots.

"Take him or leave him," Keel said as he gestured to G232. "I'm just saying that he'll make a better tour guide than me. I've got to get ready for everyone else's arrival."

Keel looked to the center of the docking bay. A small number of automated freight tugs were stacking and gathering crates and laying them out to form a large table and benches. "This the staging area I asked you to set up?"

G232 turned around to look. "Yes, Master. It was the best I could do given your parameters and the circumstances. If only I had more time! I'm sure something more comfortable could have been arranged. And perhaps you could have stopped somewhere in the core to acquire better stores than our meager pantry now possesses."

"It'll do." Keel checked his chrono. "Won't be long before the others arrive. If you're gonna take a look and still be back to hear about Prisma, you'd better get going, Skrizz."

The wobanki stood defiantly, and then his resolve broke and any pretense of feline disinterest evaporated as he hurriedly moved to explore the ship.

G232 shuffled off behind him, imploring the swift predator to, "Wait! Please! Slow down!"

# 02

It was Makaffie who next arrived aboard the *Battle Phoenix*. As his small shuttle assault set down, Keel noted the Black Fleet markings under its wings and sides. The ship could have been stolen, but Keel didn't think so. Something about the unhealthily slim man suggested to Keel that he was likely to have been involved with Goth Sullus and his empire. But then, Keel had had friends on both sides of that war. It didn't necessarily mean anything.

Still, as the ramp lowered and Makaffie began to march down, Keel kept his hand close to the Intec blaster at his hip.

To the side and out of sight, Death waited in the wings. The little gunnery bot was ready with his own blaster and probably praying to the robotic gods for a reason to use it. Skrizz and the servitor bot were still exploring the ship.

"First one here," Keel said once Makaffie had stepped onto the deck. He looked past the scrawny, slight man into the yellow-lit shuttle's entryway. No one else was there.

Makaffie let out a tittering laugh. "Well now technically I am the *third* person here. Because you're here and I assume that you did not kill our wobanki friend during the jump nor did he die of natural causes. Therefore, he is most likely around here somewhere. In the fresher, perhaps, but still here." He held up three fingers. "So... three.

I am third. Unless of course we were, you and I, to pose as those enlightened fellows who count a bot's personhood as on par with our own. In which case I would be the fourth one here. I can see your Nubarian peeking at me from behind the strut of that ship."

Death chirped a digital curse and then rolled into view, probably praying even harder for a chance to kill the man in front of him.

Makaffie smiled and waved his fingers at the bot. "Hello! And, of course, Sergeant Fast—Captain Keel—my being the third or fourth one here is entirely dependent on the assumption that this big old ship doesn't have a pre-existing crew, or at least more bots stationed. So, am I really the third one here? The fifth? Fifteenth?"

Keel give a flat, annoyed frown and then motioned for Makaffie to follow him to the staged meeting area. "This way. I'll give you the one-credit tour."

Makaffie smiled grandly. "Oh, there's no need for that. I'm familiar with the *Battle Phoenix*." The man giggled and watched as Keel turned around, unable to fully hide his surprise. "Yes, I've been here before. Same as you. Not a lot of times, mind you, but I *have* been here before. To be honest, I'm surprised this ship is still in working order. It's seen more than its fair share of action. But I suppose that's just the general's way. He didn't like things to go to waste. Ships. Equipment. Soldiers. I think the entire Kill Team Ice project was almost as much about him being angry at losing a good man to the Savages as it was about finding an equalizer for how long those kelhorned ghouls lived compared to his legionnaires. You lose a lot of knowledge in a generation. More than you'd think possible."

By the time Makaffie had finished talking, Keel was already walking a few steps ahead of him. "Well, since you know the place, make yourself comfortable until the others arrive."

Now it was Makaffie's turn to frown. "Oh, that's not the answer I was hoping for, Aeson. Sergeant Fast. It was my hope that by freely revealing to you my familiarity with this ship belonging to the later Tyrus Rechs, that you might be induced to open up and trust me... just a little bit more."

Keel gave an exasperated smile. "It didn't work."

"Well now, I trust *you*. I trust you completely! In fact I can think of perhaps only one other person alive with whom I would rather entrust my life than you. Did you know that, Captain Ford?"

"Can't say I care much either way."

Makaffie tapped his lips with his finger. "Oh, but you *do* care. You care a lot. You want to know all about Kill Team Ice. Don't you? That's how I got your attention before. And I can see that you know some of the story, but you don't know all of it. It's just the two of us around. Nothing to do but wait. Let's chat about Kill Team Ice, shall we?"

"And you can tell me everything," Keel said skeptically. "Fill in all the blanks."

"Oh, no. Not *all*. I just know my part of the tale. But you see, when two people who know some of the story, but not all of it—when they get together and one tells his part and the other tells his... well, at the end of the thing sometimes both walk away with more of the truth than they had before. Shall I begin?"

Keel didn't say anything, so Makaffie continued.

"I was asleep, and when I woke, my leader stood before me. But my leader was also gone. Does that make sense to you as a military man? How your leader can be right there in front of you, addressing you, briefing you, but your leader can also be gone at the same time? It sounds like I'm speaking in riddles and I confess I am. Sometimes it strikes my fancy to do that sort of thing. What I mean to say plainly, Sergeant Fast, Captain Ford, is that when I woke up from that sleep my *commander* was present, but my *leader* was gone. *You* were our leader, Aeson. Where did you go?"

Keel felt a swirling sense of dread in his stomach over the question. Unrest from having encountered a clue to the truth that seemed to promise nothing but a more complicated life. Wasn't life complicated enough?

The smuggler balled his fists and squeezed his thumb against his forefinger at the knuckle. He'd been Captain Ford of the Legion, then Dark Ops. He'd seen that man become diluted by the years he'd spent posing as Captain Keel and Wraith. And now, he no longer knew where Aeson Ford ended and Aeson Keel began. There was no bright line, no separation; who he was at any given moment was strictly a function of how he chose to behave. He lived as two people, presenting himself according to who seemed to want more of the one or the other. The legionnaires wanted more Ford and less Keel. Leenah had fallen in love with Keel, not Ford.

And Wraith...

Well, perhaps no one wanted more Wraith.

An amalgam of personas swirled in his psyche. Because he at once felt he was all these men. And yet how could that be? He had left his brothers as Captain Ford. He had worked to be Keel. Worked to be Wraith.

But that *work* wasn't work. It had felt natural. Like he'd emerged rather than transformed.

And now Makaffie spoke of yet another life he'd lived. How much more could there possibly be to uncover? How many more lives deserved to be brought into his consciousness? What new burdens and obligations would he find down this path?

And how much guilt?

He had nearly lost the thread of who he was while operating as Aeson Keel—and as Wraith. He was forced time and time again to go up against crooked and fraudulent legionnaires who wore the gleaming, shiny armor that Captain Devers had promised so many years before on Kublar. How many of those false legionnaires, bought and paid for, had he killed? How many dens of thieves and murderers had he ended because Dark Ops no longer could?

But had they *all* been that? He'd nearly broken himself trying to come to terms with the dark knowledge that he'd never be sure if the men he'd killed were enemies rightly executed, or friends unjustly murdered. No matter that those men sought to kill him just as eagerly.

He wasn't keen on uncovering more dark thoughts to grapple with—which seemed a likely outcome if he went down this road with Makaffie? His uncertainty and curiosity had already been waning since working again with Kill Team Victory, and the desire to know what any of it meant started dimming faster still after seeing Leenah's face again.

He could do without creating more complications.

"I went to the Legion Academy," he said flatly. "I remember my old man shaking my hand before I got in the ride to the base. I fought with 131st Legion through hell, and I joined Dark Ops. I went looking for something that none of my superior officers could even identify but were all sure was out there."

Keel pointed at the Black Fleet markings on Makaffie's shuttle. Makaffie turned and looked, and his face lost some of its amusement.

Keel continued. "While I was out there looking I got mixed up with my crew, which got me mixed up with Tyrus Rechs and the girl, which led to me fighting for Article Nineteen. And now I'm here. And until I get Leenah some closure on Prisma, it doesn't matter whatever else happened."

Makaffie put his index finger on his lower lip. For a moment he seemed finished with the conversation. But then the budding, self-assured smile returned. "But Sergeant Fast, you haven't told me what happened *before* your old man shook your hand and sent you to the Legion Academy."

Keel stood still and glowered at Makaffie. Some of the bravado in the scrawny man's face bottomed out, but he wouldn't look away.

"Have a seat." Keel's voice was low—almost angry. A warning that let Makaffie know pressing the matter might very well be an invitation to violence.

As Makaffie sat down on one of the cases that had been set up around the makeshift table and sat down, he wisely said nothing further.

Team Nilo arrived next. A beautiful combat-capable space yacht nearly filled the shield bay as it passed through, gliding just a few meters above and below deck and ceiling. Keel had been right that even a ship so grand and large as

Nilo's could find room inside the *Battle Phoenix*'s hangar bay… but it had been close.

Makaffie let out an appreciative whistle when the yacht's engines were cycled down and it vented its gases. A ramp extended from within the recesses of the ship, rather than dropping straight down and serving double duty as a hatch—a more expensive option, but as it allowed the actual hatch to be nearly impenetrable to borders, it was a wise upgrade for anyone who'd choose to fly in such a ship, as they were often magnets to pirates and other scum seeking quick, immoral credits.

The first crewmember down was a surprise to Keel. Out hopped a peculiar… bodyguard. A Kublaren who had some sort of modified N-4 rifle hanging from its broad shoulders on a strap ornamented in feathers and fragments of bone. Keel couldn't remember the last time he was this close to a koob. But since the creature didn't even have its hands on its rifle, Keel kept his hands off his piece as well. He wondered if he'd need G232 to translate. Keel had learned a little of the koob language while with Victory Company, but that knowledge had faded with time.

It was a relief when the second being out of the yacht was a man and not another koob. Jack, dark-haired and bearded, emerged from the opening and then stopped to look around the *Phoenix*'s hangar bay, a wolfish smile plastered across his face. He sent a casual, two-fingered salute to Keel as he sauntered down the ramp, a medium blaster pistol holstered at his side.

Nilo came next, with Zora on his heels. The tech magnate looked around, impressed. "This is quite a ship you have here, Wraith."

Keel held out his arms. "Well, it's paid for."

"It's called the *Battle Phoenix*," Makaffie loudly announced around a bite of some sandwich he had brought with him. "He got it from Tyrus Rechs."

Nilo raised an eyebrow. "That sounds like an interesting story."

Zora joined her boss at the bottom of the ramp. "Keel can find a way to make it boring." She walked up to the smuggler and raised her eyebrows knowingly. "Or just make it about himself."

"You have no idea how much I missed this," Keel said sarcastically.

Zora fluttered her eyes and kissed the air mockingly, which elicited a choking laugh from Makaffie that left bits of sandwich at his boots.

Introductions were made, and then Keel turned his attention back to Nilo, who stood congenially before him, a warm and well-practiced smile resting comfortably on his face. There was no impatience there. None of the "time is credits" restlessness common to so many of the other rich men of the galaxy Keel had met. Men who wanted Wraith for one problem or another and showed their impatience to Keel, unawares.

Nilo held out his hand, and Keel shook it. The Black Leaf executive pointed to the stacked crates and repulsor containers where Makaffie sat. "I take it that's where we'll be having our discussions?" He quickly added, "Not that they're inadequate. I just want to make sure I have the right spot before I set everything up."

Keel grimaced at Makaffie, who sat sucking each finger behind the last mouthful of sandwich. "That's the place. You plan on treating us to some kind of holo-presentation?"

Nilo chuckled. Not nervously or with annoyance. A warm-hearted sound of enjoyment that suggested he was older than he was. "No. And I imagine that you got your fill of those while still an officer in the Legion, Captain. But I do have some holo-chits I'd like to set up that I think will make our shared situation more easily understood."

Keel didn't ask how Nilo knew of his time in the Legion. Zora had probably blabbed while trying to stall for more time in Keel's extended absence. He had to admit he was partly to blame for that, so he didn't bother looking to see if she showed a guilty conscience. Instead he looked back to the yacht's ramp. No one else had followed Zora down during the time they'd all been talking.

"Where's Leenah and the kid? Still on board?"

"I have a small crew on board," Nilo said. He kept his face fixed on Keel. "But Leenah and Garret aren't with them. They decided not to come with us."

At once the atmosphere around Keel darkened. The very air around him seemed to pop with unspoken accusation.

Zora quickly stepped in to defuse the situation. "They're still coming, jump jockey. Just not on the yacht."

Nilo compressed his lips into a flat look of resignation. He dropped his head for a moment and then brought it back up with a grin. "They wanted to surprise you. And of course, my telling you that gives the surprise away. Doesn't it?"

Keel didn't need Ravi's help to determine the best odds for what Nilo was alluding to. Leenah had told him in their brief reunion about how the *Indelible VI* was *not* lost, but repaired and better than ever. He should be happy to see it—and her again; he should be thankful for the surprise and all its considerations. But instead his mind whirled with calculations and plans that figured in the well-being of his crew and what he would do should this all go bad.

Only seconds passed between Nilo's explanation and the *Phoenix*'s proximity alarm alerting everyone of a ship coming to dock. Once upon a time, that alarm would have led to crew members, technicians, and assorted bots to hurriedly get clear of designated landing zones capable of sizing themselves to contain shuttles, freighters, star-fighters or any other number of star craft. But the *Battle Phoenix* currently had so much open deck space that there was no need for personnel to scatter to make room for the *Indelible VI* as it floated through the wide horizon of the shield array and glided to an open docking berth.

In the cockpit, Keel could see Leenah smiling at him so brightly that her white teeth and deep pink lips were all that he could take in from her face.

Home.

She was home.

# 03

The *Indelible VI* set down on its landing struts and vented its gas as its ramp lowered softly to the deck. On first impression, everything about the ship seemed the same as the last time Keel had seen it—it was as if he'd awoken from a nightmare and, heart racing, slowly discovered that all was as it should be and nothing disturbed.

But as the smuggler forced himself to examine the ship, he began to see the differences. The comms array had been upgraded to something newer, a design he didn't recognize. That was probably Garret's doing. The landing struts looked the same, but freshened, the lubricants clean, not yet carrying the dust and grit of a hundred different worlds. The glow of the *Six*'s power engines, powering down, seemed brighter and clearer cast against the *Battle Phoenix*'s dock plates and inner hull.

Nilo and Zora had stood behind Keel and watched the ship as it landed. Zora wore no expression, but Nilo smiled lightly at the sight. Makaffie stood up and brushed the crumbs off his clothing with noisy sweeps of his hands as though expecting to meet whoever was set to come down the *Six*'s ramp and not wanting to give a slovenly impression. Jack's and Pikkek's eyes were also on the arriving freighter, although the Kublaren warrior seemed just as interested in the rest of the ship; he licked alternating eyeballs as a sort of subconscious tic, and each time his tongue darted out, his frog-like head swiveled between the *Indelible VI* and another point of interest.

Once the ramp gently touched the deck, Keel took a step forward, the anticipation of seeing Leenah again driving him to speed up time. The shortness of their reunion on the mining colony seemed a tragedy now that they'd been separated again. Those standing behind him took some unspoken cue to step back and fade into the background where they congregated around Makaffie, who searched the folds and pockets of his clothing for unwanted sandwiches to share.

The *Six*'s ramp was angled away from Keel, so he could hear the footsteps coming down before he could see anyone. He moved around to look straight on and saw… Garret clomping down in his oversized boots.

The code slicer looked about the *Battle Phoenix* with his mouth hanging open. He closed it, looked some more, opened it as if he was about to say something, and then closed it again. Finally he noticed Captain Keel striding in his direction.

Garret held out his arms for the hug he seemed to think was coming. "The *Six* is better than ever. You're really gonna—" Keel patted the young code slicer on the shoulder as he stepped around the hug, not even hearing the kid's words. "… like… it."

Keel's gaze was fixed on Leenah, who now lingered at the top of the ramp, waiting for Garret to move along. Waiting for it to just be them. Her and Keel.

At the foot of the ramp, everything became crushingly, joyfully real to the smuggler. So many others he'd known and loved had died. Leenah, somehow, was still alive. And the *Indelible VI*, his home for the last many years of his life, was returned. Love lost and found again. Home left and restored.

Leenah rested her hands over her stomach, almost regally, becoming to Keel an *actual* princess. Even a queen. "Are you happy?" she asked. "Do you like it?"

Keel's trance was broken by the question. He looked at the ship, reached up and caressed its underbelly, watched his fingers as they traced impervisteel panels once destroyed and now miraculously regenerated. This ship *was* his ship. Not a replacement. Old spacers will tell you that no two ships are exactly alike, and a practiced hand can feel the difference in the way the hull is fast-fused to its frame; the curves are as varied and distinct as a woman's, and a man knows his ship from feel as much as sight. This ship was Keel's. Beyond the notable upgrades—which Leenah had been doing anyway ever since she first joined the crew—it was the same as it had always been.

Finally, the smuggler's attention came back to Leenah. He smiled. "I don't know how you manage to do all the things you do."

"Most times I wonder the same about you, Aeson."

In time, Leenah and Garret would take Keel through every cubic centimeter of his resurrected and revitalized Naseen light freighter. Leenah would explain how much faster its engines were and how the jump drive had been upgraded to a point that there was almost no distance the ship couldn't travel, and quickly. All this achieved at as-tronomical expense, paid for by Mr. Nilo. While Keel was appreciative, someone else's credits being involved al-ways raised his suspicions. But Garret would assure his captain that there were no tricks. No tracking beacons or malicious worms. He'd checked it all.

"The AI and flight systems are as much my creation as the hardware is Leenah's," Garret would say. "It all went through me. It has an updated AI, but I still ported and partitioned the old, funny one just in case you ever miss it."

Keel doubted that would ever happen.

The *Six*'s shields were supposedly four times stronger and ran on their own dedicated power supply kept completely separate from weapons, which ran on a grid of its own, and the primary flight functions, not to mention the standard redundancies for life-support and the other niceties of a modern starship. And yet each system could be coupled to serve as a redundant fail-safe at so many points that the ship would practically need to be atomized before all of its systems could fail. And should Keel ever choose to route *all* power from one system to another—shields in favor of weapons, for example—the *Six* would perform at levels that went far beyond the limitations the various engineers and manufacturers of the ship had ever believed possible.

Or at least it would for a time. Until it broke itself.

"Best not to try that until you need it," Garret would say, stating the obvious.

After Keel and Leenah's all-too-brief and public reunion, with Garret lingering as an uncomfortable but happy witness, Keel led the two last arrivals to the staging area. Skrizz was waiting for them, and he engulfed both Garret and Leenah in a rare and furry hug that went contrary to the species' usual studied indifference.

Then the wobanki drifted back to sit near Makaffie, perhaps feeling that since the mercurial little man had been paramount in bringing about the meeting, he owed him the honor of his presence. G232 shuffled and fussed about, lamenting the deplorable lack of refreshments and other luxuries owed to its guests. The *Battle Phoenix* had never been stocked as it ought to have been, but Master Rechs never had visitors.

"I must say, Master Wraith," G232 gushed as the smuggler took a seat next to Leenah. Keel noted that Garret sat by Nilo. "You have surpassed both of my previous masters' records of hospitality by percentages reaching the hundreds! Unless of course you count the brief stay of humanoids captured by Master Rechs in exchange for their... bounties... was it called?"

Death, Destroyer of Worlds now thought itself something of a personal guard for Keel. His use of a blaster, that blessed instrument of personal defense, to destroy the double-crossing Honey had written the role into his code. The little bot thought of the weapon it kept hidden inside its upper compartment regularly. It looked vigilantly for opportunities to use it, and when none seemed ready, it fantasized about the others in the room breaking its probability models and ruthlessly attacking the others. And then the gunnery bot would make the kelhorn pay in blood.

The bot now daydreamed scenarios that featured Jack, then the Kublaren, then Nilo each playing the role of aggressor. Sometimes they killed New Boss's Endurian, making Death's own kill shot that much sweeter and appreciated... in the purely imaginary situation, of course. Death wouldn't kill anyone without reason. Probably.

The gunnery bot's dreams were interrupted by G232's incessant prattling. And when the protocol bot feigned not to remember that Old Boss took in contracts and terminations in exchange for bounties, the Nubarian bot trilled and bleeped in anger at its counterpart's showy pomposity.

G232 looked as stern as possible for an impassively faced bot. If its face were a malleable holoscreen, as some of its kind possessed instead of a fixed and molded head, it would be glaring right now. "I was *not* trying to impress them with my civility, you clanking little ratchet," it said. "Although I do acknowledge the possession of such—unlike you, you psychopath. Your memory crystals should've been sharded a long time ago."

The admin bot seemed to realize that its outburst was done among company, which was most improper. Sheepishly, it said, "I do apologize. This little one excels at driving me almost to madness. He takes a sadistic joy in tormenting me, though I'm sure I don't know why I deserve it."

Leenah tilted her head to whisper in Keel's ear. "This a new thing you're doing here? Adding bots to the crew?"

Keel gave a fractional shake of his head. "Not exactly. I'm gonna keep the little one, but I'm not so sure about Fancy Pants over there."

G232 straightened; its audio receptors had no problems picking up the master's voice. This was a troubling development for the admin bot. A bot its age would likely have its memories analyzed and then be sold for scrap. Oh dear.

If any of the gathered biologics noticed the bot's unease—which would be a very unlikely occurrence; indeed, nobody ever noticed the travails of a bot—they were soon distracted from it by Nilo.

The Black Leaf magnate cleared his throat and gathered the group's attention.

"Two thousand years ago, the first of what we call Savages left a planet that most of us gathered here acknowledge as our original home: Earth. They disappeared into the deepness of space, considered lost by those who discovered faster-than-light travel only a generation or so after the last of them departed.

"Their return marked the beginning of what would become known as the Savage Wars. A war that raged for centuries and ended only a few generations ago."

Nilo had arranged holochits on the several tall crates shoved together to form a table much too long for what was required, and now they glowed to life. An assortment of lighthuggers and other Savage hulks appeared as though an enemy armada had been set on a sand table. They winked in and out in simulated destructions, and those gathered wondered if the display was only for show, or if Nilo had somehow traced back the history of that long and sometimes mythical war and was now showing them actual glimpses—moments in time.

Nilo continued. "The war flared and faded until reaching a period where a Savage collection, called the Savage Nations by the Republic, conquered nearly half the galaxy, splitting it with the Republic. These Savages were a unified collective held together by something alternately called the Uplifted, the Pantheon, or Maestro. At this time a Savage victory seemed not only plausible, but inevitable. And then Republic worlds began to form peace treaties with the Savage Nations, most notably Sinasia, which was heavily punished for the act until very recently."

In the small audience, Makaffie raised his hand up slightly over his head. "I assume you'll be coming to a point where you'll provide information of a sort not readily available in the most elementary of children's books on the subject?" There was an air of indifference in the man's voice, as though he didn't really care either way, but was just asking the question for the sake of it.

Nilo nodded politely.

"The Savages," he said, "who had long prided themselves on evolving past humanity, went from a seemingly inevitable victory to the realization that a Republic victory was as likely as their own. Thank the Legion for that, because indeed, the Legion achieved that victory for the Republic. But by that time, the Savages had initiated plans to achieve an ultimate victory, even from the ashes of defeat."

Makaffie crossed his arms, but didn't speak further.

"Their goal was to destabilize the Republic," Nilo went on. "But to do so effectively meant that the Savages must pass as humans, as distasteful as that might be to them. These Savages inserted themselves into planetary, and eventually Republic government. They were distributed on every world the Legion liberated, often fighting alongside the Legion and against the very Savages they covertly represented.

"As these agents slowly infiltrated the Republic, they consolidated their power, forming a secret oligarchy known amongst themselves as Mandarins. That oligarchy became the dominant and controlling power of the Republic, and its emergence coincided with the renaming of the House of Liberty to the House of Reason. It was these Mandarins who were finally overthrown by Article Nineteen."

Nilo paused as though he expected questions or a buzz of conversation, but none present spoke beyond a low, rumbling croak from Pikkek.

Keel had never heard any of this. Not in all his time in Dark Ops or while bleeding intel from information brokers spread across the farthest corners of the galaxy. He'd been to Sinasia on countless smuggling trips. He'd worked among the underground crime syndicates on Utopion and had gotten cozy with just about every rebel and insurgency group out there, revealing them to Dark Ops and then watching with growing frustration which ones the House of Reason protected and which ones they allowed to be destroyed. And yet he'd never caught the slightest whiff of this. Savages in human form. Infiltrating the government.

It absolutely felt like something Keel would have heard about in sketchy rumors, at least. Conspiracies fell apart because people talked—they always talked. The bigger the conspiracy, the more likely a leak. But he hadn't even heard someone like Masters spin that sort of a tale.

He looked around the room. From the looks on everyone else's faces, this was the first time any of them had heard it, too. Even Garret, who regularly swam through the various conspiracy theories on the dark corners of the holoweb.

Makaffie might have been the exception. He didn't appear shocked, and like Keel, he was seeking the expressions on the others' faces in the hopes of reading there some recognition or shared confusion. Finally, he slapped his hands on his knees and stood. "Well, I'd say that qualifies as new information then, Nilo. Yes."

Nilo gave a single nod and pointed his finger at Makaffie, shaking it gently as though he'd just figured something out about the man. "You knew this already."

Makaffie closed his eyes, slowly reopened them, and nodded. "I did."

Zora shifted in her place uncomfortably. There was always in her a burning desire to know what went on around her. Her patience in waiting to be dealt information was short, and so her question to Nilo sounded more like an accusation than anything else. "That's what you've really been after this whole time? What happened on Kublar... you took down the House of Reason loyalists—the Mandarins?—where they were holding out?"

There was no anger in Nilo's face. The thought of dressing down his employee for so stringently questioning him never crossed his mind. "The Mandarins, I'm afraid, are no longer the Republic's primary worry. Which isn't to say that they're not a threat. They were in control of most of the paramilitary intelligence unit known as Nether Ops, and the remnants of that group have provided more complications than I had hoped for."

Jack muttered into his hand, "You can say that again."

Pikkek swelled his air sac in reply and licked both eyes.

"I can assure all of you," Nilo held out his hands before those seated about him, "that my intention here isn't to hijack the conversation. I know how much the girl Prisma means to many of you. Her importance to you makes her important to me as well." His gaze settled on each person present, individually. "I need the people in this room as my allies." Finally he turned to Wraith. "Especially you. So if you'd prefer we stop here to address the girl, I'll sit down."

Leenah crossed her legs and her arms and looked to Keel. He gave a slight nod, communicating in the moment that it was all right. They could wait to hear about Prisma. This was important.

"Don't let me stop you," Keel said.

Nilo bowed slightly in appreciation. The holo-chits set on the makeshift table shifted in a zigzag stretch of static and then changed their displays from a loop of Savage hulks engaged in battle into busts of senators and House of Reason delegates who blinked and breathed and swallowed, as though standing by to speak. They were all recognizable, had all been towering figures in Republic life. Chief among them was Senior Delegate Orrin Kaar, first among equals in the House of Reason.

"The Mandarins. For years they gathered their power. At first just a few, who set out to make sure their planets or galactic districts would keep them in power continually as more were slowly brought to the growing collective on Utopion. That collective became a controlling interest, and soon the only semblance of dissent was either from an old dissident or a young upstart elected against odds—and both of these types were eliminated through concentrated election campaigns, bribery, or in later years, assassination."

Jack looked annoyed. "I wasn't exactly runnin' the show for the Navy on Utopion, but I seem to recall plenty of dissent and fighting inside and between the House of Reason and the Senate."

"An orchestrated show," Nilo said, causing Garret to nod enthusiastically. That was exactly the kind of conspiracy he'd read plenty of in his time. "An illusion to give the populace a sense that what was happening was not predetermined by the powerful. The Senate was easily bought. House of Reason delegates were either playing roles, or themselves being played by the Mandarins."

Jack's face remained skeptical, but the hardness faded. There were no saints on Utopion. It had been bad—maybe it still was. But the shock of it being worse than you imagined was strong. Things only got *that* bad when people accepted what they should not accept, when they were fooled and willingly stayed fooled. The corruption was as much their fault as it was those who sat at the head of the table.

*What can you do?* was the rhetorical question, easily repeated to justify such betrayal of the Republic's purpose.

*What did* I *do?* was the very real question the galaxy must confront upon seeing the results of what they tolerated for so long. And when the answer was "nothing" or "I helped them along," well… that was hard.

Nilo continued. "The Mandarins' purpose was to weaken the Republic. They began by controlling its institutions, its elections, universities, and culture. But the death blow was the destruction of its military—a force that had once stood against the monstrous Savages and prevailed. One by one, each branch was cowed and brought under the Mandarins' influence, until finally even the Legion itself allowed corruption to enter its ranks through a coordinated campaign that introduced House- and Senate-appointed officers.

"The Savage Wars were long and horrible. The galaxy wanted peace. And perhaps, so did the Legion. So they tolerated the intrusion. Those who did not or would not do so were targeted for assassination—either their character or their lives. Removal from the Legion was the goal in both events. Take away the Legion officers deemed too dangerous to the Mandarins' regime."

"Like General Rex," said Makaffie. Keel had been thinking the same thing.

Nilo nodded. "Among many others. My team's research provided evidence that many conflicts dating just prior to Psydon were instigated by the Mandarins not only to increase the Republic's grip on a post-Savage galaxy, but also to eliminate legionnaires they believed most likely to call a preemptive Article Nineteen." He looked coldly about the room. "It's much easier to easier to kill a man through warfare than to end him through shame or 'accidents.' And people get suspicious of character assassinations. They wonder why random crime strikes the troublemaker now that they're making noise about Utopion. But no one thinks twice about a man killed on some faraway planet. Is that not so, Jack?"

Jack cast his eyes down. "That's so," he said, and he sounded as though he hated the words.

Zora was following Nilo with consideration. She gestured to the holographic images of the senators and House of Reason delegates slowly rotating in 360-degree arcs on the table. "Everyone here is dead," she said. "I can appreciate learning what was once going on behind closed doors, but I'm not seeing what you need us to do about it now."

"Knowing what led us here is as important as any plan we'll put together," Nilo replied. "I need you all to see the galaxy as I've learned to see it."

He readopted his professorial tone as he resumed his lecture. "A systematic weakening of the Republic's defense and the removal of the Legion as a threat to Utopion was followed by a massive misappropriation of funds. All the Republic's pomp and prowess—its many fleets— were proved to be illusions once Goth Sullus attacked. But credits had been taken to build these non-existent fleets, to keep these illusory armies trained and equipped. And that funding had to go somewhere."

Skrizz, who had been swishing his tail lazily as though not fully listening, took note at the mention of credits. He asked where the money went, and Keel wondered whether the wobanki was dreaming of some fantastic adventure that ended with the recovery of a stolen galactic treasury.

"The credits went everywhere imaginable, and always for the benefit of the Mandarins. Recall that they did build a fleet with the help of the Cybar race, whom they kept hidden from the galaxy—at considerable expense. But even more of the treasury went into loyal corporations which in turn worked to launder the money, either back into the delegates' pockets or into the darkest corners of Nether Ops. The *true* Nether Ops, which didn't exist on any books anywhere.

"They diverted credits to land conglomerates who would purchase entire planets—after the House of Reason sent zhee colonists in to drive down the values, of course. The Legion would then be sent in to quietly eliminate these zhee insurgents, liberating the terrorized denizens of that world and, more importantly, allowing the conglomerates to achieve fantastic returns. These lands, purchased at a fraction of their worth, were then used to bribe others, perhaps to perform some clandestine military operation on the Republic's behalf.

"The process played out again and again, varying only in the details. Send in zhee, humans, anyone who would cause the trouble that needed to be caused. Away from the violence, bribe individuals with the opportunity to own massive portions of a planet and its resources. These individuals often became senators who were compliant to the House of Reason, thankful for the opportunity to turn on friends, family, and countrymen for instant wealth and a place at the table.

"I began to see that much even while navigating Black Leaf through the corporate mire."

Something that Nilo had been preaching didn't sit quite right with Leenah. She furrowed her brow and turned a question over in her mind. "You said they purposefully weakened the Legion and the military. Why would they do that when legitimate threats to their power, like the MCR, were growing?"

Leenah had once been part of the Mid-Core Rebellion. She'd gotten swept up in its talks of revolution, popular on her home world, which had suffered too long the callous neglect of its representatives. Though not a warrior, she had wanted to help put an end to the blatant and bloated hypocrisy that festered on Utopion. In a way, she'd done that by linking herself to Keel, and indirectly, the Legion itself.

And yet, what she somehow knew deep down, even before Nilo confirmed it, was that it had all been a lie.

"The MCR was a Republic-initiated insurgency started by Nether Ops. Their purpose was to commit war on planets where the Republic could or would not do so, usually to strengthen that planet's loyalty to the Republic itself. It was also a major avenue for smuggling weapons into Nether Ops. That said, for a time the MCR *did* grow beyond what even the Nether Ops could control. And that led to one of the few legitimate uses of the Legion by the government during our lifetime: they performed a necessary check against the sort of terrorists, opportunists, and killers who flocked to the Mid-Core Rebellion. But the Legion couldn't keep up with the flow of these new 'recruits.' And when there were more criminals in the MCR than revolutionaries, Nether Ops was once again in position to steer them where they wanted them."

Leenah nodded, a little sorrowful, but accepting. She was glad to have been captured and stuffed into the smuggler's hold aboard the *Indelible VI*. Glad to have escaped that life, though she hadn't been sure of it at the time.

Nilo held out his arms. "What was the end game then? The Mandarins had control of the House of Reason and the Republic. They used that control to systematically weaken it."

Jack rocked on his heels. "From some of the things I saw, they were clearing the way for Goth Sullus to do what he did."

Keel nodded. "The Legion has plenty of intel showing that the House of Reason, Nether Ops, and appointed officers in all branches were working together to build the Black Fleet's power."

Makaffie shifted uncomfortably in his seat.

"Goth Sullus, however," Nilo said, "proved to be an unexpected complication. I can assure you of that. He was thought to be the force who could crush the Legion entirely—and then be controlled by the Mandarins from his seat in Utopion. Instead he proved to be the catalyst that got the Legion to finally declare Article Nineteen. You can't know how close the Legion was at that point to having forever lost its ability to do so."

Keel gave a lopsided smile. "Yeah, well, Goth Sullus also executed all these floating corpses displayed on the table."

Nilo smiled. "The two heads of the dragon didn't know what the other was doing, and each head seemed to have planned secretly to devour the other. Yes, Goth Sullus largely destroyed the problem of the Mandarins when he executed most of the House of Reason and disbanded the Senate."

Keel looked over to Makaffie, who sat back and stroked his chin thoughtfully. The wiry man looked concerned about something.

"You got something to say, Mak?"

The question seemed to jolt Makaffie from a daydream. He shook his head and smacked his mouth as though it contained the unpleasant texture of a night's sleep. "Nothing... nothing this man is saying is a lie. I know. I was there for more than you can imagine. I worked for Sullus. I was part of his... well, let's just say he *relied* on me and my team. The markings on that assault shuttle aren't an accident. Now Goth Sullus, he told us what had happened to the Legion, and he told us that the House of Reason had been compromised and needed to be done away with. None of us minded that. Didn't have problem with any of it.

"But what he did to the Legion... that was never part of the plan. The end game was never supposed to be him taking over the galaxy and setting himself up as emperor. The man who did that... I never knew that man."

Garret was leaning forward, his neck strained as he listened in anticipation. "What *was* the end game supposed to be?"

"The Savages," Nilo answered, his voice soft and solemn. "The very first of the Savages. First to leave Earth for the darkest depths, seeking to make for themselves a reality where they never died. Where none of the lesser people could question them. Challenge them. Oppose them. These Savages used what we know as the Uplifted or the Pantheon and their Savage marines to do their deep and long work. And they've been communicating out in the deep darkness through a Savage artifact known as the strand."

Makaffie's eyes lit up.

"And if we have the strand," Nilo continued, "then we have everything. The full sum of these first Savages' knowledge and all their communication, all their plans, is in that strand. It's all stored and verified through a host of nodes—the different strands—that partitions and rejects anything outside of itself. Once we have it, we'll know where they've been, where they're going, and what they intend to do. And we can stop them."

Nilo looked to Makaffie, whom he seemed now to consider a fellow expert on the subject. "Isn't that so?"

Makaffie squeezed his bottom lip between his fingers and stretched it out, revealing small, crowded lower teeth. He let go and made a little *click* with his tongue. His obscure, self-assured persona seemed to grow. "Well I suppose that's part of it, yes. Those Savages are out there, and in fact I once tangled with them, took out a few of their worlds and hulks before we lost the trail leading back to the numeral alpha. Then the Uplifted showed back up and things got busy for another few hundred years, you see."

All around, the faces of those present took on looks of confusion at the seemingly impossible things Makaffie was reporting. He was crazy. But then again... maybe somehow he wasn't. And Nilo didn't seem to think the man was lying.

"Something dark is on its way," Makaffie finished. "That's what Goth Sullus woke us up for. To try and stop it. Death is coming. Not even the Savages can compare with it. And unlike the Ancients... none of us can run from it."

# 04

The jungle teemed with so much life that every breath Prisma Maydoon inhaled seemed to have just been exhaled by a myriad of other creatures. The air was warm and carried with it diverse and constantly changing scents dripping with odors sometimes sweet, sometimes rank, and sometimes indistinguishable. And that was only when she breathed through her nose. Whenever she sucked in air in her mouth during the strenuous climb up a great hill that flatlanders might have called a mountain, she could *taste* it. It had a sweet, decaying flavor. Had she been an experienced drinker—her father had never allowed her so much as a taste—the flavor might have been familiar. But to Prisma it was strange and unpleasant.

"I am detecting several life forms," rumbled KRS-88 as the repurposed war bot pushed aside large fronds of a native palm with razor-sharp tips.

Prisma had cut herself on one several hours before when the party at first began to push through the jungle. The pain was so severe and intense that she had cried out. Her mother, who led the expedition, had stopped and come back to her, and Prisma at once hid the bloody wound, embarrassed at seeming weak or childish.

"Let me see it," Reina had said, before frowning at it and gently blowing on Prisma's fingertips. "These hurt.

I know." She brushed away Prisma's hair and the small tears that hadn't been there when the girl only had the pain to deal with.

It was nice. To have a mother... it was nice.

Prisma usually hated that sort of doting attention. Adults didn't fawn over one another just because of a skinned knee or a sliced finger. But this felt like... lost affection now come due. A payment for all the tender cares she'd missed growing only under the care of her father. Prisma became enamored with her mother all over again.

Now, hours removed from that moment and with the pace remaining steady but feeling faster due to the cries of Prisma's muscles and feet, the pain had returned. Her fingers throbbed and stung where the palm blade had sliced the layers of skin apart with all the precision of a surgical laser. The wound was a thin red line, and the skin on either side pushed it closed, puffy and slightly discolored. Nothing alarming, nothing deep purple or black, colors Prisma associated with poison or illness. Just a bright, swelling pink.

Prisma didn't know whether it hurt so much because she couldn't stop thinking about it or if she thought about it so much because it hurt. Either way it shortened her temper.

"You don't have to keep saying that, Crash," she spat out, quietly at first but then finishing with boldness and volume when she realized that the bot would hear her mutterings no matter what. "This place is nothing *but* life forms. It would be more helpful if you just told us the next time we're alone."

"I apologize, young miss." The bot's booming voice, even when kept to a relatively low level, was enough to send beautiful orange-and-green-feathered birds flying from their hidden perches to display a variegated beauty in the brief glimpses of flight seen between trees.

"KRS-88 is only doing what we have asked it to," said Reina, her rebuke gentle. "If the manner of the machine's response is inadequate to us, doesn't the blame lie with those who gave it instructions and not with the machine itself? Your protector is a tool, and how well any tool is wielded depends on its user."

Prisma didn't agree that Crash was a *tool*. He was more than that. He was special. And not just because Prisma and the war bot had grown so close together. Crash wasn't like other machines. His programming said one thing, but he wanted other things. His own things. He thought freely even if he always obeyed in the end, and Prisma chose to believe that was out of love and loyalty to her rather than some slavish devotion to code. In fact, if something ever happened to Prisma, she was sure that Crash wouldn't take an order from another living thing ever again.

But of course she didn't say that to her mother even though she knew it to be true, the feeling firm and strong within her heart. She knew the words to properly express that feeling wouldn't come when she needed them, and then she'd be forced to admit that her mother was right, and that Crash was just a bot, just a tool. Even though he wasn't. She would lose, and not because she was wrong. She would lose because she lacked the technical ability to argue and use the right words and paint the right pictures.

But she knew the truth about Crash.

"But you are right when you say that life is all around us, Prisma," her mother said, finding a way to make the discussion somehow encouraging. "But how do you *know* this? Is it something that you heard and saw? A simple matter of deduction?"

It was a surprisingly short time before the jungle reverted to its throbbing, humming state, its contentious clamor having been only temporarily halted by Crash's voice. It was almost as though the place collectively viewed the three walking through its midst as guests and not predators. And Crash's loud voice had caused all the living, teeming things to pause and look silently on these guests in annoyance, as though a drunk had stumbled his way into a dinner party and scandalized everyone with his loud, apologetic bellowing.

"I guess it was that. Deduction," said Prisma, knowing that her mother's question would only be a preface to another, deeper question. But she couldn't sense what that might be. Perhaps her mother was looking to teach her more of the strange abilities that Ravi had uncovered in her and that her mother seemed to have mastered. "Also... it's a jungle. I've been on worlds with jungles before plus I've seen the nature holos and they all say a jungle is a place where lots of things live."

"That's true. But this place, Prisma, this place is unique. There is no holoprogram that can unravel its mysteries. No explorer who found it, examined it, or began to understand it would ever think to leave and reveal it to the rest of the galaxy. Those who find this place, even in error, become something else. Always."

"But you knew it was here."

"And I knew what I would find."

Something about her mother's words caused Prisma to shiver. But still she tried to please her. So she opened up further.

"It wasn't just deduction. I could... *feel* it too. Like when you had me close my eyes on the Savage ship. I could feel it and see it in my mind and it was just everywhere."

Reina stopped long enough from her spot at the front, leading the expedition up the green and mist-swirled hill, to turn and let Prisma see her approving smile. "Very good. The life contained on this planet is so strong and abundant that even one without your gifts would be able to feel it. They would have no way to understand the feeling, no way to adequately describe it... but they would feel it as truth inside themselves all the same." She looked around. "This place is more than what is now."

She began to undertake the climb again, and Prisma and her bot followed. The girl expected some elaboration to come after so cryptic a sentence. Instead they walked in silence for another five minutes.

The mist now sat heavy on the jungle hillside, and it seemed to seep its way into Prisma's bones. The dense fog felt tangible, spilling over the tops of her boots and squeezing its way inside, where it slicked her feet. It poured down the front of her shirt and parted her hair to climb down her back whenever she turned her head to look at something. The mist brought with it an unusual, damp warmth, as though it were a lungful of hot breath blown from a giant.

After taking a series of easy, meandering switchbacks, they at last reached a clearing. Prisma's mother had led them to the top of the hill, and they stood now on its bald head, a place invisible from below. The trees and broad-leafed vines of the thick jungle terrain avoided this place. Only slender grasses fluttered softly against Prisma's boots, and despite the pain of the palm fronds still in her fingers, Prisma felt compelled to bend down to feel them. She found them to be as delicate as scorpion silk, and she let go for fear of destroying them.

At the center of the clearing were two benches made of uncut slabs of stone. Prisma's mother sat on the longer of the two and shucked off the pack she'd carried up the mountain. Prisma thought the smaller bench was for her, but since her mother hadn't called her, she just stood and looked around, more curious about her surroundings than she was in need of a rest. She was tired, but she could rest on her feet just fine.

The two benches formed an L-shape, and set before them was a ring of sharp black rocks that looked as though they had been darkened by fire, only there was no ash or charred wood. The slender grass had grown up in the center of the ring of rocks, its delicate blades nearly hiding the stones. Another growing season and they would be out of sight completely.

A refreshing wind blew across the top of the hill. It drove away the warm and lingering mist, and Prisma's skin no longer felt moist or sticky, but neither was it cold.

"Where are we?" she asked.

Her mother's face was thoughtful. "We are at a place that few have ever been. And many who have are still here. Their bones lay beneath this delicate field."

Prisma looked down at her boots, lifting one foot and then the other, half expecting to see the manic smile of a skull staring up with gaping empty eyes. But she saw only grass, laid down by her weight.

"This is where I learned the use of the same power that has been awakened inside of you," her mother continued. "And here, you will be trained to do the same. You must learn it, Prisma. To stop what happened to your father—to my husband—from happening again. The galaxy cannot endure another Goth Sullus."

Prisma turned in a slow circle. She felt as though her mother had bidden some ancient teacher—perhaps whoever had trained *her*—to come forward and reveal itself. But when she finished her slow spin, only Crash and her mother were there. Not even the sounds of the teeming jungle life below seemed to reach this bald spot at the top of the hill.

Prisma understood. Her mother would be her teacher. "Well I guess you know what you you're doing, since *your* bones aren't under my feet."

She smiled at the delivery of her joke, but her mother's face was sober.

"No, Prisma. I died many times in my training. And unless your own abilities exceed what I believe to be possible... so will you."

Prisma swallowed, and Reina closed her eyes for a long moment. A very long moment.

"Yes, Prisma," she said at last, "so will you. I can sense your bones already beneath us. The bones of those who've come to this planet have always been here, even before we first arrive. Yours and mine, the same."

# 05

Before night had fallen on top of the hill, Reina sent Crash to forage for kindling and deadwood for a fire. The bot came back with heavy armfuls, stacked high over his head and somehow not impeding his steps. He dumped the load and quickly stacked it.

"Shall I set the blaze?" he asked.

Reina said that she would and sent Crash to find still more wood. The bot came back several more times until it seemed to Prisma that the cold stone benches were set before a tangle of high wooden walls.

Prisma's mother then started a fire in the middle of the old hidden pit. Prisma watched the grass as it reached a point of surrender, its slender greenness unable to withstand the heat any further. Each tender blade would ignite from stem to tip in brilliant white magnesium sparks that hissed heavenward like a lit fuse before consuming itself and transforming into a slim pillar of ash that buckled and fell among the glowing embers. Prisma's face lit and relit with each of the fire's magnificent conquests over the delicate, silky grass.

It was beautiful. Almost... celebratory.

She caught her mother looking at her warmly. Reina smiled, and it reminded Prisma of a look her father would give—and when given, he often would say, "I remember doing that when I was your age." Prisma wondered whether, the first time her mother had seen these strange stalks of grass flame skyward, she'd had the same sense of wonder. Prisma decided that she had. She didn't want to ask. She wanted it to be—and so she wouldn't risk it not being.

She went back to eagerly looking for the next blade, anticipating its fantastic immolation without feeling as though she was being childish for doing it. No... not even that. She went back to looking without having to worry that someone *else* would see her as a child for doing it. For being delighted by the natural world. With her mother, she could be a young woman... but she could also still be a little girl for a little while yet.

When the excitement in the fire subsided and the flames realized the furthest extent of their conquest, hemmed in by the ancient ring of black rocks, a steady flicker of shadow and orange glow settled in and cast its pallor over the three campers. Prisma wanted the moment of peace and solitude to last forever. She could stay here forever. Whatever peace she'd lacked at Mother Ree's sanctuary was here now. She enjoyed it for a good while before her mother finally spoke again.

"KRS-88," she said. "Shortly, it will appear that my daughter and I are in stasis. We will seem to you as frozen, paralyzed. You will wonder if our bodies can survive so long without food or movement. Accept that what will happen is beyond your ability to grasp."

The bot nodded once while Prisma listened, unsure.

"I ask of you only one thing, faithful machine. You must never let this fire die any lower than how you now see it. Your task, for as long as you can perform it, is to keep this fire tended and burning, both day and night. Do you understand?"

The war bot's eyes shone brightly. He looked from Reina and then to Prisma and back, his neck emitting the whirs and subtle whines of his synthetic parts. "I understand. I think this means I will not be speaking to either of you for some time?"

Reina nodded. "You are correct."

"In such case, allow me to say goodbye. For now."

The bot turned to look at Prisma. He could see tears welling in the girl's eyes. And something in his core ached because he could not do the same, though he wanted to.

"Goodbye, Prisma. For now."

Prisma swallowed a hard and painful lump in her throat—the bot had raised her and knew her better than anyone else—but she managed to keep her voice even. She was proud of how well she controlled her own emotions. It felt like a triumph over some trial. Another proof that she was no longer a slave to fear or any other emotion. But especially fear.

"Goodbye, Crash. Do a good job with the fire. I'm sure it will feel like no time at all has passed."

Prisma looked to her mother for assurance but could discern nothing about how long this training would last.

"I will be thinking of you, Prisma," declared the massive war machine.

Without another word, Crash stood from his squatting position near the fire and set out to find more fuel, beginning the mission he'd been assigned right away. He knew Prisma and her mother did not need him by that fire any longer. And... walking away would be easier.

Prisma felt a tear spill over and run down her cheek. She thought to wipe it away, but then held her arm down.

That would only draw more attention to the fact that she was crying.

Reina must have seen the tear's reflection amid the flames. She got up and sat beside her to wipe it away, but she didn't stay seated next to her. After a moment she arose and returned to her own bench once more.

There she placed her hands on her lap and sat tall and straight, like a queen set to teach her daughter a lesson on how to become... her. Someday.

"The life that you felt around you, Prisma, is all that can be found still living on this world. But now close your eyes and feel with me your way through."

Prisma did as her mother asked. And as her eyes closed, a deep, unnatural darkness fell over her. She reached out and sensed the life around her, which revealed itself to her as small blue orbs of flame. That included her and her mother, spaced apart on the benches, though Prisma could not see their bodies, only their essence of life. She allowed her mind to radiate outward, and as she did so each new life, no matter how small, shone brighter in the darkness until it was as radiant as the celestial heavens.

And then the darkness was almost gone entirely. Life was everywhere.

"And this, Prisma, is only what lives on the mountain. Were you to reach out further, you would see more life still, until the entire planet was mapped out in your mind. Understand that first, my daughter. What you can sense near you, you can sense in the lands beyond, to the ends of this world."

Prisma wanted to ask what the name of the planet was. Reina had brought them here by what seemed like magic.

It had begun with a short jump aboard the very ship Prisma had taken aboard the Savage reclaimer. That jump took them to a planet Prisma had never seen before—not this world, but another. They abandoned the starship on that world, and Reina led Crash and Prisma on a much briefer and less strenuous hike. When Prisma thought now about that planet, she realized that it hadn't revealed itself and the life it contained to her. Not like wherever she was now. This world, before the fire, *sang* to her, whereas the life on that world was... dull, fearful, its living things hiding behind branch and leaf, beneath the stones in the water that babbled along merrily before them, right up to the temple that would take them to their final destination.

In the earliest days of galactic exploration, before the Savage Wars, the temples of the Ancients were once thought to be magnificent. They were revered and held in awe. Whenever a new one was discovered, scientists and curious travelers alike would come to gaze at it. But as more were discovered and the greatest minds and the most powerful technology and all the digging and sensor scans were undertaken—when the realization came that the galaxy could not penetrate the temples and learn their secrets—interest waned. It all but died out once the Savage Wars began. And by the time they ended, the temples of the Ancients were accepted as an unsolvable galactic mystery. Unknowable. Or at best, something for future generations to consider. They would need that. A galaxy without questions and mysteries, a galaxy where all the answers had been found, could do nothing but collapse in on itself.

So when Prisma followed her mother and the gurgling stream to the temple of the Ancients on that world before this one, her heart did not race. It was just another interesting sight on an enjoyable hike with Reina and Crash. No different than seeing the great root structure of a fallen tree or the curious carvings made by erosion on a great and mossy boulder. In fact, the temples of the Ancients had become such mundane wonders that few beyond dedicated hobbyists or adherents of various cults even bothered to travel to witness them. The galaxy had other wonders, better wonders, and perhaps even more importantly, experts who could explain them.

So when Reina approached the temple, Prisma watched her without much interest. She was sitting on a rock near the stream, not tired but enjoying being off her feet. She was about to remove her boots when her mother faced the temple and lifted a hand.

But when the temple began to open, Prisma dropped her partially untied boot from her lap. Her mouth fell open.

Crash was the only of the two who had the wherewithal to speak. "Most unexpected."

"Come, Prisma," Reina said, beckoning her daughter to follow as if she'd done nothing special in unlocking a thing that had been shut and sealed since long before its first discovery.

Prisma stood outside the opening, dumbfounded, her legs trembling in excitement as her mother disappeared within the temple. She looked at her bot for a moment and then hurriedly jogged inside, holding the straps of her survival pack against her shoulders to keep it from bouncing against her back.

The temple was dark inside, and what light did enter from its opening revealed no ornamentation or beauty—only an empty stone room, appearing much the same on the inside as it did without, with motes of dust, undisturbed for millennia, dancing in swirls. The meager light from the door grew even dimmer as the hulking KRS-88 made its way inside. And then the entryway sealed itself of its own accord, slowly cutting off the remaining exterior light.

Then only the glow of Crash's optical sensors could be seen in the darkness.

"I've got an ultrabeam in here somewhere." Prisma shrugged off her ruck.

Reina spoke softly in the dark. "There's no need."

Before Prisma's eyes, soft blue glowing stars appeared, nebulas and swirling clusters of star systems, making her a celestial giant standing in the middle of the galaxy. The twinkling lights filled the darkened confines of the inner chamber with a powdery blue glow. Prisma looked to Crash and saw his sturdy warrior frame cast in the same ghostly pallor. The brightness of these particulate stars illuminated his dull, armored coat until he seemed to disappear in a deep darkness of shadow below the waist.

Prisma looked around in wonderment.

But Reina was focused on her work, such as it was. Her hands moved, and the galaxy moved with them. She looked like she was gracefully dancing, performing some ritual known only to the Ancients and her. A ritual that unlocked this long-sealed mystery and made Prisma feel proud.

And there was something else, too. The presence of that... power. What Goth Sullus had called the Crux. Prisma didn't know what to call it, but she felt it intensely. It radiated from her mother's hands as great sections of stars expanded until it felt like Prisma was inside of them, looking at planets and moons, asteroid belts and great solar storms. Then these systems would quickly recede and the galaxy would spin on in a new direction, as though even now they were traveling from system to system.

"The way is difficult," Reina said cryptically and through much concentration. She seemed now to be pulling the darkness at their feet up from the floor, casting the brilliant canopy of stars high overhead where they grew small and indistinct—clusters of lights, cosmic constellations. She looked to Prisma as though she was pulling something up from the deep by a long and sturdy rope tethered to the very bottom of the galaxy.

A single star appeared brightly at Prisma's feet, shining against her boots and then rising to light up her pants and shirt until it glowed marvelously before her eyes. She wanted to reach out and take it in her hands, but no sooner did the thought come to her than she heard her mother's warning in her head.

*Do not touch it, Prisma.*

This star, pulled from the depth of the chamber, was alone. So great was the distance between it and the others that they seemed not to exist at all, high above them. Their light was faint to the point that Prisma wondered if her eyes were tricking her. She wondered if Crash could see them. She would ask him later.

At last, Reina let her arms relax and walked to stand beside Prisma. "In time, I will teach you to use the temple of the Ancients. You may already be able to open them, I think, but you must never touch what is inside until I have instructed you in the way."

"What will happen?"

"That is always uncertain. The Ancients expected those who used this place to know what they were doing. If you do not, it will still work, only the temple will decide for you. And what it decides may not be according to your liking. Or your safety."

Prisma nodded. She believed it all at once, with no lingering curiosity that wickedly called for her to test the fact of it. Reina had delivered a truth, undisputed and indisputable, and Prisma knew it instantly and unquestioningly.

It was very unlike her.

The war bot also behaved in an unlikely matter. He did not immediately accept the explanation and file it as a source of knowledge. He had questions, and when he asked them, the voice sounded unusual to Prisma's ears. "What... what should happen if *I* were to touch it?" Crash said.

At first Prisma thought the question was scientific and academic. Crash was one of those bots who, when encountering something not already stored in his substantial memories and subroutines, sought a materialistic explanation that it could record and, having done so, consider itself a little more complete than it had been. Coming just a little closer to the relentless perfection ultimately required of a being meant for servitude.

Only the question wasn't like that at all. The way the bot had asked wasn't as though it were seeking an answer from Reina, but rather... it was seeking a truth that might lie in the star itself. Crash wasn't asking for information to download and process. He was... wondering.

Hadn't Reina told Prisma that Crash was a bot, and nothing more? When they'd spoken of KRS-88's desire to live its life in the peace of the sanctuary, Prisma had been sure that Crash had wanted to stay, but mother had dismissed the observation. She said Prisma was casting human emotions on something that did not possess them. That Crash went with Prisma because he was required to.

But it was clear to the girl even now that the gardens of peace on En Shakar were what the machine longed for.

Mother Ree had suggested that Crash was something more than a bot. The opposite view of her mother's. Was that true of all bots, or was it only true of Crash? Was it something that only Mother Ree could determine? The old woman had seemed to know so much, and now Prisma felt a sudden sense of loss for the time she'd had with her; there were so many things she could have asked and had answered, and now that opportunity to learn from the kindly woman was gone—perhaps forever.

The thought brought with it a resolve to not let the same happen with Reina. Prisma looked from her mother to Crash, who seemed to have straightened himself and was standing tall... as if pretending that he hadn't said anything. She wondered what that might mean as well.

Perhaps Reina noted the peculiarity in the way Crash acted as well. If so, she didn't betray it. She looked evenly at the bot and said, "You should not touch it either."

It was at that moment that Prisma realized the bot's powerful arm, which bore equally powerful wrist blasters and micro-rockets, had been slowly rising to grasp the star. In its optical sensors it conveyed a hesitant curiosity, as though wishing to push a finger into it. The arm slid back down to the bot's side.

"I'm going to take hold of the star you see now, Prisma," Reina said. "And when I have done so, we will travel to its location in the way of the Ancients."

"Like Ravi?" Prisma asked, remembering her friend's curious ability to arrive from nowhere and disappear in the same manner.

"Just the same."

Prisma reached out and took Crash's cold, metal hand. The war bot squeezed gently around her tiny fingers, dwarfing her human hand as easily now as it had done when she was a little girl. Then she reached out her free hand for her mother.

Reina looked down at the offering, momentarily confused. She smiled gently. "We do not need to be holding one another. We will all arrive together." But before Prisma could withdraw her hand, Reina reached out and took it anyway.

Prisma wished that feeling of safety and togetherness would last forever.

And then, in the blink of the eye, they were somewhere else. The solid wall of an entirely different temple opened, revealing a jungle under a foreign sky. This planet teemed with life that Prisma could *feel*, though she didn't yet see any of it as her eyes adjusted.

It was then that Reina led them on the long trek up the mountain, to the very seat where Prisma now concentrated, feeling that life once more, sensing it, probing for more of it. All the life on this world that had been, that was now, and would ever be. She could sense it all, growing larger and larger.

Then she heard Crash's voice, though distant, as if speaking to her through a dream. Painful, parting words.

"I shall spend my time thinking of you, young miss."

Prisma felt her eyes wet with tears. She blinked them open, searching for Crash, wanting to tell him how much she loved him.

In that moment, she was struck hard in her chest, and she felt searing pain. Looking down, she saw the protrusion of a long spear buried between her ribs, depriving her of breath. Feathers hung near the hilt, and Prisma somehow knew its point had penetrated through her back.

She fell on her knees and—fearing the pain that would come from falling on top of the weapon—twisted herself sideways to land on her side. There was no air left in her lungs to be forced out from the impact. The fire danced before her, inches from her face, but she could not feel its warmth. Her vision blurred. Her life flowed out of her.

Prisma died.

For the first time.

# 06

"You sure this is a good idea?" Leenah asked as the *Indelible VI* was hauled toward the lone Savage hulk that loomed before them. Makaffie had said the thing would grab them out of hyperspace, so Keel, not wanting to risk the kind of damage that event might cause to a ship he'd just been reunited with, opted to fly in from a different jump point and approach through real space.

"Not particularly, but we're heading toward the thing anyway." Keel had added several hours of flight time for him and his small crew—a strike team, really—as a result of jumping in so short. The time had given him the opportunity to see what the rebuilt *Six* was capable of, and so far he was duly impressed. The sublight engines were every bit as fast as Leenah had promised they would be. Probably more so.

"I didn't mean the whole flying straight into an active Savage cruiser part of it," Leenah clarified. "That much I already knew was crazy. I meant you going in without your new armor."

Keel glanced down at the set of mercenary armor he'd taken from aboard the *Battle Phoenix*. He'd left Rechs's armor with Garret. "That armor is finicky," he explained. "So, yes. It's a good idea. And if Garret can get it working as good as he thinks he can, I'm willing to do at least one op without it. Something tells me I'll need it a whole lot more later."

"Only if we survive what comes next," added Jack helpfully from his seat behind the pilot and navigator chairs.

The spy was wedged in between the bounty hunter Zora and the Kublaren Pikkek, as part of Strike Team One. Makaffie, Skrizz, Nilo, and Black Leaf mercenaries stationed on Nilo's yacht would insert via Makaffie's assault shuttle as Strike Team Two and should arrive at any moment, preferring to take the direct route and be pulled from their hyperspace travel; Keel had left that much earlier in order to coordinate the arrivals as they were.

Together they would board the Savage hulk, defeat this weird Tyrus Rechs simulation Makaffie had gone on about, and then rescue someone called only "the Wild Man." To Keel, each and every one of those mission elements sounded utterly ridiculous, like something out of a bad holofilm. But the annoying little man was dead serious. And in exchange for Keel's help, Makaffie had agreed to tell him how to find Prisma. That was all Keel cared about. Finding the girl. If that meant making a deal with Makaffie and willingly boarding a Savage hulk, so be it.

"Speak for yourself," Keel said to Jack. "I plan to make it out of this."

Pikkek leaned forward and switched off the cockpit's artificial gravity. "What this *k'kik* do?" A persistent and low buzzing sounded. Hair and tendrils began to float from heads, and any bodies not strapped down began to leave their seats.

Keel slapped the koob's hand away while Leenah reactivated the artificial gravity. "Don't touch that," Keel scolded. "Don't touch anything."

The Kublaren pulled his hand back, but he didn't seem bothered by the rebuke. He croaked out a sound of wonder, as though this was the first starship he'd ever been aboard. "Why no—*k'k*—touch?"

Jack smiled, clearly amused by the exchange. "Because, Pikkek, you might go and cause us all to die, you touching the wrong button. Big die."

Pikkek licked his eye and made no indication he comprehended any of that until he finally croaked, "Big die."

After some silence, Zora leaned forward to speak in Leenah's ear, though she was loud enough for Keel to hear, too. "Don't worry about the armor. Jump Jockey over there still has a head hard enough to stop any bolts sent his way."

"I wouldn't put a whole lot of stock into armor anyway," Jack said dryly. "We got Savage 'ghosts' and artificial battlefields and who knows what other kinds of crazy waiting for us. I've seen some of the hell that old Savage tech can muster, seen it up close. Only thing about the armor that might matter is how fast you can run in it. But then again, you never know. You never know."

Makaffie's briefing of what the two teams should expect had painted a bleak picture. Shipboard Savages that seemed capable of existing ethereally at-will and immune to blaster fire. An unpredictable custodian named Archimedes who would need to be relied on in order to achieve the objective. Simulations indistinguishable from reality and every bit as lethal.

"Not exactly a prime vacation spot," Keel said.

The *Indelible VI* emitted an automated warning as Strike Team Two emerged from hyperspace. The high-pitched, warbling *wee-wee-oh, wee-wee-oh* seemed to have sounded the moment the assault shuttle appeared in real space. In truth it had done so split seconds *before* the arrival, a marvelous testament to how quickly the *Six* could now detect sublight anomalies. Most search sensors, including the one previously on Keel's ship, only gave a proximity alarm once the incoming ship was fully materialized in real space. The split-second early warning might seem like a small difference, but it was a huge advantage to be able to flip on the shield array before surprise blaster cannons could ravage Keel's hull. If a jump-based ambush did come up, the detection system Leenah had somehow found could easily be a lifesaver.

But this ship, Team Two's assault shuttle, wasn't ambushing anyone. Already it was being pulled in by the Savage hulk's powerful tractor beam, the same as the *Indelible VI*.

Leenah activated the comm. "Strike Team Two, this is Team One. How copy?"

Keel smiled slightly at Leenah's use of military comm etiquette. The time she'd spent with him and some of the other legionnaires had clearly rubbed off on her.

"An excellent question," answered Makaffie, whose amplified voice inside the cockpit was decidedly *un*-military. "I do have a very solid copy. A solid copy indeed. Or at least, as solid as something can be when transmitted through the ether of a comms relay."

"This guy," mumbled Jack in the back seat. But then, Jack had gotten more than his fill of lazy, unhelpful comms chatter while working for Black Leaf. More of the same in this new ally was hardly a promising sign. Where were all the professionals?

"Tell him we're being tractored toward the hulk," Keel instructed Leenah.

"That makes two of us," said Makaffie. "Wonder which one of us they try to suck into that hangar first. Remember, parking lot is pretty full. Don't doze off. Makaffie out."

Through the *Six*'s front viewport, the Savage hulk grew larger and closer. Its tractor beam was housed in an armored polyp just above the gaping hangar bay itself. Most such devices required an enormous amount of power and could even then only pull in one ship at a time; they were designed to bring in starfighters on rapid approach, eliminating the risk of the fast-movers crashing inside the hangar during the stress of combat. But this Savage beam had no trouble treating the light freighter and assault shuttle as if they were Preyhunters, effortlessly moving them so that the ships were both caught in the powerful beam. Even if Keel chose to fire his blasters, which he wouldn't, any missiles or torpedoes he let loose would instantly be caught in the beam and likely shoved right back down the pipe.

The only disadvantage of the design was that the beam housing would be susceptible to damage from any ship large enough to hit it. But that risk was probably considered worth the tradeoff of freeing up valuable space for other things—like uninterrupted virtual arenas of death.

The comm came to life again as Makaffie spoke. "Looks like it will be age before beauty, Sergeant Fast. We've pulled into the lead. Did you know that I'm actually only six months older than you? It might not look that way right now, we've aged at different rates, but it's true. It is the unvarnished truth. Makaffie out."

"What's that all about?" Zora asked.

"My desire to know decreases with every word he speaks," Keel muttered.

Leenah was watching him. "Why does he call you Sergeant Fast?"

Keel shrugged. "You know all the aliases I do, sweetheart."

Apparently sensing that now was the time for questions, Pikkek, who had been fidgeting nervously in his chair, asked, "When Big Die?"

"Not much longer," said Zora.

It was interesting to Keel that there seemed to be a shared connection among everyone on board except himself. He knew each of them individually except the koob, and the women quite well. But as a group, he was the bystander. There was a bond between the others that had been forged before he'd come into the picture, one that Keel only had gotten snippets of while going over the *Six* during the real-space hop. He knew it involved Gomarii slavers, Leenah nearly dying multiple times, and a whole host of other things that Keel found himself wishing he'd been on hand for so he could have done something about them. That had been the first time he'd truly questioned his decision to go off on his own instead of sticking with Garret at the very least.

"Ain't gonna be the kind of big die you can tell your eggs about, Pikkek," Jack said. "None of it's real."

"But... k'kik... we die, ya?"

"They can kill us, but anything we kill ain't real."

This made no sense to the Kublaren, who licked his eyeball and stared at the approaching vessel from the side of his head.

"When's that big ship o' yours arriving, Wraith?" Jack asked.

"Any minute now," Keel said, not particularly wanting further conversation. It was the countdown before the operation's start, and he preferred to have that time to himself. Time to focus, to make final preparations in his mind for war.

There had been some debate about what might happen when the *Battle Phoenix* arrived. Makaffie was not certain whether the Savage hulk had a functioning hyperdrive. Archimedes had said that they did, and it was the fear of the ship jumping, never to be found again, that had prompted Makaffie to abandon the Wild Man to begin with. That way, at least one of them would still be near the objective if the hulk left its place. It hadn't so far, thankfully, but there was no telling what it might do when the light assault carrier showed up. If it couldn't jump, then the *Battle Phoenix* should easily be able to disable its engines. If it *could* jump...

Well, that would be bad. A thing all parties wanted to avoid. And yet, the only thing they could think of that would be worse than losing the hulk to a jump was to have both strike teams on board with no way to escape the tractor beam should Archimedes decide not to cooperate. So the final decision had been to jump the *Phoenix* in just before the strike teams reached the hangar bay. That would at least give the hulk a difficult choice: to run, if it was capable, or to complete the capture according to the mission parameters that were its primary objective. And while that decision was underway, all parties believed that the *Battle Phoenix* could handle what happened afterward.

The theory went that the hesitation between capture or fleeing, however long it might be, should be enough for the carrier to determine whether or not the hulk was preparing to make the jump. If it warmed up the massive drive needed to propel the ship through hyperspace, the carrier would have enough time to disable it before the leap. At least that's what Garret, still aboard the *Battle Phoenix*, had theorized, along with the help of the *Phoenix's* "unreal" AI. Of course, the code slicer had used many more words than that, but his conclusion was clear, and no one challenged him on it or came up with an alternative. Nilo agreed, citing his research into the Savage hulk's designs.

The light assault carrier would jump in, and then one way or the other, the Savage hulk would be denied escape.

*Wee-wee-oh. Wee-wee-oh.*

The alarm went off even earlier this time, as the arrival of a much larger ship activated it all the sooner. Keel exchanged a quick smile with Leenah to show her how impressed he was with the upgrade.

Several close blaster cannon bolts raced over the top of the *Indelible VI*, filling the small gap between the Naseen light freighter and the assault shuttle as they were tractored toward the hulk and impacting on the beam's armored protective plating. The quick and furious barrage led to a fantastic explosion that rippled against the hulk's shield arrays.

Zora shoved her head forward between Keel and Leenah. "What the hell is that?"

Keel palmed her face and pushed her back into her own row. "A problem. Stay outta my way!"

Another volley of blaster cannon fire slammed into the Savage hulk, overpowering the shields and annihilating the tractor beam's power supply.

The *Indelible VI* hung in place for a moment.

"Tractor's dead," Keel announced as his hands went speedily to controls both physical and holoprojected on the dash before him. "We're flying under our own power again."

It was Nilo who called on behalf of Team Two. "Wraith, why is your assault carrier firing on the target?"

Keel gave a half-shake of his head and mumbled, "Must not be house-broken." He switched the comm to live. "I wish I could tell you. Leenah, get the kid on comms and find out what's going on."

The Endurian went to work.

Nilo sounded like a man whose plans were rapidly slipping between his fingers. Not desperate, but concerned. He was looking to Keel to allay those concerns. "Suggestions, Captain?"

"We try to get inside faster."

Keel increased the acceleration and shot the *Indelible VI* toward the docking bay, overtaking the assault shuttle in a blur. He was only vaguely aware of Jack's and Zora's tight grips on the headrest of the seats before them. Pikkek's air sac inflated to a bright purple and deflated again in rapid, hyperventilating croaks as the blue glow of the hangar's shield array began to fill the forward display.

There were safer ways to test the speed limits of his ship, but Keel took advantage of this one. And though the hangar would be overflowing with derelict and captured starships—not a place to go in full speed no matter how cavernous it might appear from the outside—that just meant it would give him a chance to see how well the ship could slow down, too.

"Everybody hang on!"

The *Indelible VI* swooped down into a direct course for the exact center of the hangar's shielded docking entrance. All the while, more blaster cannon bolts—enormous, energized particles—picked apart the hulk's defenses, walking their fire along the battered hull and disabling its aft thrusters.

"Hard to believe you're allowed to have a ship like that for personal use," Jack said.

"Well it's supposed to be a free galaxy now," Keel shot back. "Leenah! What's Garret saying?"

"It's happening automatically. He's trying to get it to stop."

Zora stuck her arm between Keel and Leenah to point at the hulk as they raced toward it. "Slow down before you get us all killed, jump jockey!"

"I see it." The Savage ship's hangar was stacked with layer upon layer of starships, reducing the space Keel could fly into a much smaller window than even he'd anticipated. He fired his rear thrusters to put on more speed still, and felt the sudden increase in force despite the ship's inertial dampeners.

"That's not how you stop!" Leenah shouted, sounding worried for the first time.

"Didn't figure to," Keel said as he turned the ship on its axis and used the momentum to pull himself into a tight loop that caused the *Six* to partially skim the docking shield while at the height of its arc. It then raced back in the opposite direction, losing speed as it widened into a great loop that had them once again facing the docking hangar, perfectly aligned to fly right inside, although inverted. Keel lazily rolled the ship upright and cruised toward the hangar at a speed that felt much more manageable to his passengers.

Smiling, he winked at Leenah and then turned around to see those behind him. Beads of perspiration were dripping from Jack's forehead. Probably Zora's as well under the armor. Pikkek had passed out entirely.

"I'd say she handles pretty good, Leenah." Keel was definitely enjoying himself.

The *Indelible VI* flew into the hangar and skimmed its way over the upper crust of the stacked layers of captured starships. Keel caught glimpses of these craft in passing, and most of them were so antique to be artifacts—especially the few visible at the bottom on the way in. Yet all looked in good, working condition.

Pikkek revived and croaked in his stilted, Kublaren-accented Standard, "No, no, no, no..."

Zora had recovered as well and let go of her death grip on the seat in front of her. "Go ahead and put us down, jump jockey. I'd almost forgotten how bad it could be with you on the sticks."

Keel checked the sensors and holocams and then pushed himself up in his seat, trying to look down from the cockpit cupola's crysteel windows. "Just trying to find a good parking spot." He turned around to look at the bounty hunter. "And you can complain all you want, but my flying has *saved* you more times than kill you."

He brought the *Six* over a pair of flat and sturdy-looking light freighters, but the two ships weren't the same height and so the impromptu landing platform wouldn't be level. "Things are going to be a little uneven once we sit down, so watch your step."

"The new struts we installed have a dedicated repulsor housing," said Leenah. "Those will make up for anything the stabilizers can't handle. But the micro-repulsors can only run about a day or so before they need to start drawing power from the main system."

"I don't have any plans to stay here that long."

The ship set down with the forward landing struts coming down on the taller of the two ships. The rear struts extended out as far as they could and then fired the micro-repulsors when they failed to find purchase on the shorter ship's hull. The result was a perfectly level landing, as good as any docking bay could provide.

Strike Team One staged itself at the ramp, ready to drop together with Team Two, which was just now entering the jammed hangar bay. Their assault shuttle landed, listing heavily and forcing the team inside to jump off the ramp while Keel and his team could stroll easily down their own. Orders were given, and Keel led his small team swiftly into the Savage bay, weapons drawn, alert high. Outside, the *Battle Phoenix* hadn't ceased its assault; it continued to punish the hulk's engines.

It was obvious right away that the hangar bay was as empty as Makaffie had expected it to be. Sensor sweeps showed no life forms, and unless something mechanical was hiding down among the ships, they had the bay to themselves.

"What the hell is that kid doing?" Makaffie shouted to Keel, breaking from his own strike team and evidently wanting a powwow up close. It was the first time the skinny man's eyes showed the fires of any type of anger.

Leenah told him what she knew. "It isn't Garret. Something caused the carrier itself to do it."

"Well, that might be," Makaffie said, suddenly thoughtful. "Yes. I do believe that General Rex would leave standing orders to attack any Savage vessel. Why wouldn't he? If we had any sense of self-preservation, we'd be out there helping. But then... that would interfere with some previously set plans. Plus, I still have a colleague somewhere on board."

"So where is he?" Keel asked, and then another heavy blaster cannon bolt from the *Phoenix* shook the hulk and caused everyone to take a balancing step. Keel swore and pinged Garret. "Kid, get that AI in line before it blows us all to the nine hells."

"Sorry, Captain Keel, I'm working on it. She's just not listening. I've given up trying to convince her and I'm working on just slicing in a command override. Shouldn't be much longer. I hope."

Nilo's voice came over the channel. "Try interfacing with it through the combat armor system."

"Of course! I should have already thought of that. I'll get it connected. Okay, gotta go!"

Keel didn't mind the abrupt end to the discussion so long as the kid quieted the gun; he wasn't kidding about them being blown to hell. Already there was no telling what kind of damage might have been done to the rear portions of the ship. If what they needed was in that direction... that could be a problem.

He noticed Makaffie looking around as if for his friend. This so-called 'Wild Man.' "He here or isn't he?" Keel asked.

Makaffie, who now wore a set of shock trooper armor that seemed built for stealth, threw out his arms, lost. "I don't know. I'm getting no answer on the comms. That doesn't mean anything, though. This ship can disable comms and sensors at will. We'll have to look for him."

Nilo spoke quietly to the Black Leaf members of Strike Team Two, mercs clad in black armor with fully enclosed helmets. Then he left them and joined Makaffie to speak with Keel. Skrizz also left Team Two, but to inspect the mysteries of the docking bay rather than join the parlay.

"Looking for Mr. Makaffie's associate is fine," Nilo said, a certain militant authority in his young voice. "However, I also need to stress that our primary objective is to recover the strand. Even at the loss of every man save one. The strand is everything."

Another heavy blaster canon bolt struck the ship. It was quickly followed by a thunderous boom from somewhere distantly inside the hulk.

"Got the last of the engines," Garret reported sheepishly into the comm net. "But the good news is, that's the end of it. Guns are spooling down."

"Good work, kid," Keel said, but his focus was on Nilo. He didn't like what he was hearing. He hadn't signed on to sacrifice himself or his crew for this "strand," doomsday stories or no. He'd agreed only to help defeat whatever special simulation involving Tyrus Rechs's last moments needed to be defeated in return for getting intel from Makaffie on where he could find Prisma. Whatever the others chose to do on that hulk after all of that wasn't his concern. "Feel free to send *your* team to die getting the thing," he said, "but *I'm* here to help him"—he tilted his head at Makaffie—"get his friend so that he can help me get *mine*."

It felt odd calling Prisma a friend.

"I can appreciate that," Nilo said diplomatically. He was clearly worried that Wraith was on the verge of leaving altogether. "But I need you if it's going to be done at all. Makaffie made that much clear. For whatever reason, you're key to solving the simulation that needs to be solved to access it."

Leenah stood beside Keel. "This ship isn't going anywhere now that its engines have been put out of commission. I say we find Makaffie's friend if we can, pull out until we get an idea of what damage the *Battle Phoenix* has done, and then come back in, prepared, to get the strand."

Makaffie shook his head. Already it seemed the alliance that had been formed aboard the light assault carrier was crumbling. Keel could see why. Nilo was fixed to the point of obsession over the strand, and while his reasons sounded altruistic and with the overall good of the galaxy in mind, how could anyone be sure? There was already enough concern over Nilo's actions that the Legion had asked Keel to look after him, which was a concern in and of itself.

"I'm not a leader," Makaffie said. "And so maybe I don't know what I ought to say and what I ought to keep to myself. I had a leader—he's gone. And I had Sergeant Walker, and he's gone now, too. And Sergeant Fast, well...

"My point is, in times like this I'd usually wait for the leader of the outfit to step up and remind us that we have to bring the fight to the Savages the way it must always be brought. That's the leader's job. Not mine. And I'm not sure I can convincingly step out of my own shadow the way you were always able to do, Fast. Here it is though: we can't call it off and we can't go back. Engines might be down, but believe me, this ship is watching us and waiting to see if we'll be beneficial to it. If we aren't, don't expect this ship to be here for long, one way or the other. If it can't run, it can atomize itself, I promise you that. So we have to do what we came here to do. That means getting the strand. Nilo is right. It's everything. Even if that means my friend gets left behind."

Leenah's lip curled. "You would leave your friend to die?" Even to entertain such an idea was unthinkable to her. To answer her question with anything but no, impossible.

"He'd understand why I did it and he'd know it wasn't an easy decision, but a necessary one," Makaffie softly explained. "It's also the one he'd want. I offer no apologies, but you do have my regrets that this is so."

All eyes were then on Keel. His vitalness to the mission made him, now and always, the deciding vote. Never mind that Nilo and Makaffie were agreed. Something about the devilry on this Savage ship required him.

Keel understood exactly what Makaffie was speaking of. He knew what it meant to sacrifice men, friends or otherwise, to achieve mission success. But Leenah didn't think that way. Couldn't. And Keel knew that if he wasn't careful, he would hurt her. Because while Garret had never stopped looking for her, Keel had. And Leenah could only live with that because she herself had thought she would die. For that matter, she should be dead right now.

Makaffie seemed to sense the dilemma Keel was in. "If we leave, or even if we delay, at some point we should expect a Savage protocol to initiate that will take this entire ship up into flames. Whether we're on board or not. But wherever the strand is, there will also be a way to prevent that from happening. To disable that protocol. And I promise you, I can handle it—if you can just get me to it."

"We'll get the strand," Keel confirmed. He looked at Leenah, who was watching him expectantly. "But we're not leaving a man behind, either."

## 07

"Kid, about the ship..." Keel said on his way to stage with the others and venture further into the ship.

"Oh, don't worry, Captain! I got the guns turned off. Unless of course you want to have them on again and if that's the case we can do it no problem—it's really fine either way—because I figured out how to override the shoot-on-sight command even with the batteries online. But! What I really want to tell you about is your armor because when I added it to the consoles I realized that I could just run it from a hard switch when before I figured I'd have to use feather chips and that can take a while because of how you have to decouple them. So the first thing I did was get the suit's command override working so that you didn't have to wear it just in case you want to command the *Battle Phoenix* from the bridge but didn't want to wear it while sitting in the captain's chair. Lyra will still see you sitting there without the armor, but I think it will be okay. Really she just wants to do whatever Tyrus Rechs wanted her to do instead of whoever owns the ship but the code is Tyrus Rechs's code so it checks out and you can use it from anywhere but have you seen the actual bridge yet? It's really pretty nice."

"I meant the Savage ship, kid," Keel said, ignoring all the information about the *Battle Phoenix*, its AI, and the method by which Garret hoped to upgrade the armor—although it was the question of the armor that most interested him.

"Oh, I understand now, Captain. The thing is, Lyra was mad that I ended the program but not mad enough that she'd try to steal control from me and jump the ship away."

Keel still hadn't gotten his question out, but that was the second time Garret had used that name. "Who is Lyra?"

"Oh, that's what the *Phoenix*'s AI is called. But anyway, yeah, the Savage hulk isn't going anywhere. All engines and thrusters have been disabled and if it has FTL technology it's probably tied to those engines and anyway it never spooled up a hyperdrive so—"

"Good job, kid. Keel out."

Keel joined the others stacked outside the thick blast doors that Makaffie indicated would lead into the simulation rooms. "This hunk of scrap isn't going anywhere. Confirmed."

Now all that was left was the malleable house of horrors Makaffie had told them to expect on the other side of the blast doors. Fighting against what wasn't there, except for the times it *was* there as a sort of reanimated matter that was kept by the Savages who ran the ship, themselves an unholy blend of physical and ethereal, capable of tearing apart the living but themselves impervious to physical harm.

Pikkek's air sac inflated evenly. Keel clapped the koob on what passed for a shoulder. "You ready?"

"Ya. Ready. I go... *k'kik*... first."

Keel usually preferred being the first man in a room; he felt he owed it to the others; he'd yet to meet someone with better reflexes, faster trigger pulls, or superior accuracy. But if the koob was volunteering...

"If it means that much to you," Keel said, stepping back and falling into the stack. Of his team, only Leenah wasn't at the door. She wasn't trained for the kind of fighting they might expect and would do a better job from the *Six*—especially if they needed to make a hasty retreat.

Nilo's team was stacked on the opposite side of the blast doors. They were set to go in behind Team One. They might be operators, perhaps even former Legion, but Keel doubted it. They were too tense.

His own team was readying itself for whatever might come, each in their own way. Pikkek with his heavy breathing and a croaking, whispered mantra of "Big die... big die... *muktah*."

Zora put on her helmet, slapped the bucket twice with the palm of her hand as she always did, and then shook the nervous energy loose from her feet and fingertips. Jack casually caressed an N-4 blaster rifle, a world away and with a playful smile on his face.

Makaffie was in Team One's stack, despite technically being part of Team Two. He pushed himself between Keel and Zora. "Usually I bring up the rear, but I'd prefer to stay close to you, Sergeant Fast."

"Pick another name to call me."

"All right, Wraith for now."

Skrizz wasn't in either stack but was instead leaning against an old United Worlds scout ship's comm array, which had been extended from somewhere near the bottom of the pile of starships all the way up to the current level, passing blast doors that led to several decks below. The wobanki would enter at his leisure. Breaching and clearing wasn't exactly that species's forte.

Keel had a weapon in both hands—his Intec x6 and Tyrus Rechs's old .45 slug thrower in the left hand. "We ready?"

Nods all around.

Makaffie gave final reminders. "The room will be dark at first until the simulation begins. I have no idea what they'll throw at us. Some long-ago battle scenario the re-claimers are trying to gather a better understanding of. Just remember, only some of it is real, but it will all *feel* real. Don't get caught up in what can't hurt you, though. If you get hit and it doesn't hurt, ignore that shooter and watch out for the ones who *can* hurt you. Maybe sen-sors will detect those, maybe not. Now let's... uh... have a good fight."

One of the Black Leaf mercs accessed the control panel, and the heavy doors pulled open. Pikkek leapt for-ward, but quickly staggered back with nowhere to go, croaking loudly.

"Hold fire!" Makaffie shouted, and the order was obeyed.

Standing in the doorway was Archimedes, the head steward of the Savage hulk. The white, semi-transpar-ent creature stood still, but his robes and hair drifted in an unfelt wind as though he stood before the heat of a great furnace.

"You have come at a poor time," Archimedes said. "*You are not welcome.* For the sake of the agreement we once struck, I will allow you to leave. *Flee this place.*"

Archimedes turned his back and retreated into the darkness.

"Hold on a minute!" Makaffie called. He shot past the others and ran until he was at the Savage's side. "We had a *deal.* And now I brought my end of the bargain here to finish it and show you whatever it is you need to see."

"Does a bargain last forever? Must one party wait for an eternity to see if the other will fulfill its obligation? *Unworthy of the bargain where are you.*"

Makaffie growled. "Let's talk about obligations, then. You lied to us and got Sergeant Walker killed. And where's the man I left here?"

Archimedes kept walking. "The bargain has ended. Leave. *Stay.* Leave. *Stay and die.*"

Both strike teams cautiously followed Makaffie through the doors, watching as he walked ahead with Archimedes. They'd entered a vast space nearly as large as the docking bay they'd just come from. They kept their weapons up and scanned but saw nothing but darkness.

Makaffie was insistent. "I'm gonna get what I came for. And if that means I have to tear this ship apart doing every simulation you have until you beg me for another one of your bargains, that's what I'll do!"

Archimedes stopped. He turned and looked first at Makaffie, then at the strike teams behind him. "Agreed. *Agreed.*"

The Savage reclaimer disappeared.

# 08

The moment Archimedes vanished, the blast doors leading from the overcrowded docking bay to the simulated
battle room closed, cutting off the room's sole source of
light. The various operators switched on their night vision, cycling through the various spectrums, while others activated ultrabeams mounted to their weapons. But
soon that was unnecessary. A thin gray light began to rise
as though Archimedes had left only to slowly turn on a
dimmer switch. And with it came a mist, pouring out of
barred gratings set at the base of the walls where they
met the deck.

"Is that gas?" asked Zora. She wore a full helmet and
would be immune, but showed her concern for those—
like Keel—who did not.

"Wasn't any of the other times," Makaffie said, "but
who knows?" He cursed Archimedes for what he'd done.

"Why don't you walk us through what's happening
right now," Keel said, although he, like the others, already
knew the answer. This was the beginning of one of the
simulations the Savage ship was designed to run.

"It's what you think it is and we need to be ready."
Makaffie grabbed the subcompact blaster that hung
on a sling at his side and took a step forward in the low
ready position.

The two teams spaced out and got into defensive positions, waiting to see what battlefields would be summoned for their testing, while the mist swirled around them.

Keel watched Nilo. The man was wearing absurdly expensive—and good—combat armor. The helmet was on now, and an opaque black face shield shrouded the man. But his hand was to his ear—a subconscious tell that he was using the suit's comm system. Keel activated his own comm.

"Garret, this is Wraith. I need you to slice your way into Nilo's comm channel. Find out who he's talking to."

"I'm not sure that's a good idea, Captain..." The kid sounded worried.

"Let me worry about that. Just do it."

"It's not because I have a problem slicing it or anything. Like, because it's rude or because we're friends. It's just... Nilo knows what he's doing. So it won't be like when I slice into other comms and they have no idea and I'm in and out without leaving a trace. He'll know. Maybe not right away but probably right away but even if not he'll figure it out later. And then what?"

With the mist filling up the room, Keel didn't feel that this was the time to argue the point. And if Nilo really was as adept at discovering hacks and slices as the kid said—and Garret was usually right about these things—then the best course of action was to come right out and be direct about it.

"Hey!" Keel called to Nilo. "Why don't you fill me in on who you're talking to. We're supposed to share intel on this op."

Nilo paused to look at Keel from behind the black mask. "I ordered my yacht to leave the *Battle Phoenix*. I have a proprietary AI on board, and we both believe that its sensors and algorithms will be better positioned to analyze the hulk from there. It will help us identify what's real in these simulations and should help us achieve our goals faster."

Keel wondered if that was the only reason Nilo had taken his ship off the carrier. A moment later Garret reported that the ship was indeed taking off. "Roger, out," Keel replied, and then spoke to Nilo. "Don't keep that kind of information to yourself. I don't like it."

Nilo nodded but didn't apologize. "I'll patch you in on my personal comm channel. You'll hear everything. I'm not attempting to hide anything."

"Patch in the others, too. If you've got a way to figure out what's real and worth shooting, we need to hear it in real time."

Nilo hesitated. "I'm not sure that will work."

The mist rose higher, up to Keel's chest now. "Looks like we're going to find out soon."

Then the fog engulfed all parties, and those capable of switching their optics to different light spectrums found they couldn't penetrate its strange solidness. But gradually the mists receded, falling from the cavernous heights of the room down to the strike teams' feet, where it clung loosely to ankles and boots.

Like the receding waters of a drying flood, the mist departed to reveal a new landscape. It was rife with low, scrubby vegetation punctuated by great, thick willow trees that lifted their skirts out of vast brackish swamp. Thick roots extended delicately down from their trunks like bathers testing the water with their toes, and brightly glowing insects of green or blue circled lazily just over the surface of the water, skimming the surface.

Pikkek hopped to the water's edge and dipped a long finger in. "Feels—*k'k*—real." He tasted it and smacked his mouth, but had no further comment. Skrizz sniffed the air fiercely, as though searching for something with his sensitive nose. To Keel, it smelled like any other swamp he'd ever been in, damp and dank.

"Careful over on the edge for those of you who can't swim," warned Makaffie, his voice a whisper, hard to hear above the rising sound of the hissing and buzzing swamp denizens. "That water will drown you sure as the real thing, I'd imagine."

Absent were any sounds of battle or warfare. Also missing were any of the signs that this had previously been a battlefield, although in the low light and wet terrain, it would be easy enough to miss.

According to Makaffie, the battlefields selected were all real places and fights that happened before. He'd specifically mentioned Sinasia, a place Keel had been to many times, but Keel couldn't be certain if he'd been to this particular planet or not. Most planetary ecosystems blended together and couldn't be told apart unless they were marked by some unique example of flora or fauna, or maybe a striking and uncommon piece of geography. A swamp and a few glow-bugs weren't enough to ring any bells.

"I suggest we stay in place," Makaffie said as he crouched low among the underbrush. "Whatever trouble is coming, it will find us, rest assured."

The two teams settled in as if for an ambush, hiding themselves though no one else seemed present. They had no idea what direction the fight—for surely there would be a fight—would come from, so they carefully delegated sectors of responsibility to watch.

A new voice sounded in every strike team member's comm, a feminine voice that addressed Nilo directly. "Nilo, I am in position and can detect all members of the team."

"Thank you, Sarai," said Nilo. "Are there any other life forms besides us in our vicinity?"

"Not at this time."

Keel would have written the voice off as belonging to some well-enunciated comms operator, reading the sensors aboard Nilo's yacht, if not for Garret's whisper over Keel's direct comm. "Sarai is an AI that Nilo built himself, really booming. He usually doesn't let anyone else talk to her or even know that she exists."

Keel wondered what turn of events had led to Garret knowing about the AI if that was so. "You telling me this because we shouldn't trust her?"

Keel had never met an artificial intelligence he was fond of. Perhaps his encounters with the *Indelible VI*'s ebullient AI had ruined things for any others he met.

"No, no—the opposite. She's really, really good. There isn't anything else like her in the galaxy, I don't think. We wouldn't've gotten Leenah back without her help."

"Okay, thanks for the intel, kid. Nilo and Makaffie are having a talk... I'm gonna go join in. Keel out." The smuggler patted Zora on the knee and indicated that he was going off to join the palaver, and tasking her with watching his sector. She nodded, and Keel low-crawled toward the men.

The two men noticed him crawling on his belly over the muddy ground beneath the shrubs. They halted their conversation and waited for his arrival, then quickly brought him up to speed once he reached their circle.

"We were reviewing possible scenarios and trying to determine what might be expected of us," Nilo explained.

"The ship doesn't exactly tell you what it wants. Seems like the details are withheld unless it wants you to crack a particularly stubborn job."

Keel's mind went to the story Makaffie had told him about Ravi's arrival and the attempts to alter the outcome of what must have been Tyrus Rechs's last stand. He wondered about Ravi—missed him even. At first he thought Makaffie was lying about all of that to get his help, but when Leenah mentioned Ravi showing up to help her Keel thought it was possible he might also have found Prisma.

And yet Ravi still hadn't come back. And for some reason, this time, that was bothering Keel.

"This place look familiar to either of you?" Keel asked.

Both men shook their heads.

"How about Mak's buddy, Wild Man?" Keel prompted. "Your sensors picking him up anywhere?"

"No, but the beam we have to use to penetrate is extremely tight. I've directed that other parts of the ship be swept in three-second intervals and then back to us so nothing catches us by surprise. Once the shooting starts, we'll be the focus of the sensors until things are resolved."

Before another word could be said, all comms issued a tonal beep that meant enemy spotted. All three men dropped deeper into the mud, getting as low as they could. Little pools of brown water formed around their hands and elbows.

It was Skrizz who had first identified the intruders. The wobanki dropped low and froze in a predatory crouch, wound up and ready to spring, even his tail completely still. He didn't say anything, but Jack noticed the change in posture, looked over the top of the bushes, dropped low as well, and keyed in the comm alert.

"Got a lone donk moving east to northeast through my sector."

Keel raised his head and verified the presence of a zhee. The mercenary armor he'd taken from the *Battle Phoenix* had an open-faced helmet with only a visor on hand to protect his eyes, very similar to that worn by the Repub Marines, but black instead of green. The visor could also feed a heads-up display and was supposedly rated to stop small arms fire. That was useful, but Keel would have preferred a closed helmet had there been one, and not only for the sake of protection. His time in the Legion and even operating solo as Wraith had gotten him used to communicating over comm without any fear that his voice would be overhead. What was said inside a bucket stayed inside the bucket—unless you sliced its comms.

He didn't have that advantage now, and a zhee's long ears could hear well.

Rather than risk even whisper, Keel gave hand motions to Nilo and Makaffie. He'd seen two additional zhee stalking the sector when he looked to verify Jack's report.

Nilo, who like Makaffie *did* have a fully enclosed helmet, passed the information over the channel and instructed all strike team members to stand by. These were clearly scouts and would likely move on unless they accidentally stumbled on the team members well-hidden in the mud, which was unlikely given the donks' present course.

And then Nilo had a message only for Keel. "I'm having a discussion with Makaffie and Sarai right now. It's not something that the net should be filled with. I'm telling you so you don't feel like we're leaving you out. I'd have looped you in... but they might hear."

Though Nilo was only a few inches away from Keel, he couldn't hear the man speaking save through the comm.

Nilo was looking at him though, waiting for an answer. Keel nodded once, causing his chin to dip into the mud.

Nilo continued. "She's found another bio-signature farther up in the ship. Best guess is that it's Wild Man. He's currently engaging several other life forms that she can't identify. Makaffie believes he's engaged in a simulation and she's detecting the reanimated matter. I'd say that's consistent. They're winking out—being killed—and then showing up elsewhere again."

Again, Keel nodded.

"She'll keep monitoring as long as she's able, but only passively. I tasked her with giving us another full battlefield reading, and it's going to push to all team members now."

Keel's visor came to life with a HUD readout not dis-similar to the Legion system; it showed the position of all friendly units and all spotted hostiles, using white for friendlies and red for foes. Or at least, that's what the HUD's key said; while Keel could see the position of the teams indicated in white, there was nothing in red. The three zhee weren't on screen.

Nilo elaborated before Keel could ask about it, advising the whole team: "The zhee in our sector aren't show-ing up on your sensors because they aren't biological. These are pure simulations, the type Makaffie says can't harm us. But those other types *will* come, and based on the scouts' movement, I'm sending a route we need to take to be in position to ambush the scouts."

Keel didn't have a better plan, but he wasn't quite thrilled that Nilo was giving battle orders. Makaffie looked like something might be bothering him too, but it was tough to tell with the helmet on. In the end, Keel nodded his assent when he saw Nilo looking at him expectantly. The team began to move, slowly crawling through the swamp on the route indicated.

As Keel was following Nilo in a belly crawl, perhaps a meter behind the man's boots, Makaffie reached out and grabbed the smuggler's forearm as he passed by. He held up a finger and then pinged Keel on a direct comm channel.

"Keep crawling, but I wanted to speak to you about something. I imagine anything I say, if not being actively overheard by either your wizard on the carrier or the wizard crawling ahead of you, will be decoded and listened to later, so I'll be polite as well."

Keel wasn't in the mood for a conversation and wanted to tell the man to maintain comm discipline. The zhee were close and Keel was listening for any changes in their disposition or direction. But to speak out would be to do the very thing he wanted to avoid. Makaffie had a bucket, Keel did not. That made Keel a captive audience.

Still, he tried to keep his senses focused on the zhee. He felt thankful that Skrizz was with them; it would be hard for anyone to get the jump on a unit with a wobanki.

"You saw that heads-up display come to life," Makaffie said. "Well of course you did. You'd have to be blind not to. And I could see the light reflected in your eyes even through that dark visor of your bucket, so be mindful of that. It'll give you away in the shadows. I'm digressing already, Sergeant Fast—oh, I'm sorry. I forgot we're not doing that any longer. Captain Ford, you know what I'm about to say but you also don't know it now, so I'm telling you again for the sake of our mission. I'm not a soldier. Certainly not much of a fighter. But I do have a way of opening my mind and seeing things, man. Things that the galaxy might miss. I guess you could call it that third eye that has a knack for seeing things as they are instead of how they're presented, which is what most people see. And what I've found—what *I've* found—is that the galaxy sometimes shows you what it wants you to see instead of what's really there.

"I've gotten used to that. But something's off. Because here now, I see Captain Ford, and the last time I saw Captain Ford—Sergeant Fast—we still had Walker and Carter on the team and things were good. It was a good team. We accomplished a lot. And even when you were missing and we went in for this current op, we still got things done because Walker was able to fill in for you and did a good job. Maybe not the job *you* would have done, but better than anyone else."

Keel was trying to keep up with the thoughts Makaffie was spilling. Obviously these allusions to a shared past were unconfirmable. They were just words. And Makaffie was expelling them without meaning, or at least without meaning to anyone but himself.

"So we're on the operation. The first one on this ship. Savage vessel, the admiral and those early hullbusters. Colonel Hartswick, who was a great man. You liked him. Anyway, we were running the show and we could kill just fine but we couldn't kill quite *right*. Not for the simulation, anyway. So Sergeant Walker, who deserves to be remembered, decided he wasn't going to lose any men until we knew exactly what we were losing them for. Now it's obvious, Prisma and her bot helped us out and that was that. But at the time, *at the time*, our comms worked but our buckets didn't. Not all the way. We should have been able to see what we were supposed to kill—what was alive— and what wasn't. But this place... it didn't let us. The war bot wasn't blinded like our sensors were though. I don't know why. Maybe they hadn't planned for a war bot in the simulation? Whoever does? We used to, but that stopped.

"Point is, we were blind and unable to determine what was real and what was unreal. And for some reason, when Prisma showed up with her bot, his sensors worked just fine and so he called out what we had to kill and that worked. And I thought at the time, well, maybe it's just an issue of the right sensor package and jamming susceptibility. Maybe they were so keyed in to jamming *our* system that the Savages couldn't also blunt his. Or maybe his were just better. I don't know. But it feels odd to me how Nilo has a ship that can read in here despite the hull and shielding of the Savage relic—which was quite impenetrable to us, man. But it's not to him. And so... I'm not saying Nilo is lying about anything... I'm just saying it's odd."

Keel used the pause in the diatribe to poke his head above the grass once and see if the HUD readings matched where the enemy actually was. The zhee were moving along the same course they had been and were much farther away. He could probably risk speaking if he wanted to.

Makaffie spoke first.

"Usually this is where I'd wait to get your opinion on the matter. But since all you can do is listen I shall continue on. If that other life form detected is the Wild Man, it means he's running some simulation by himself. Which would not be an easy task. Not from what I've seen. Now, once we complete *this* simulation we'll be allowed to move further into the ship; it's just a series of these big rooms and corridors, each one keyed with a new mission for us. No rest for the weary and all. But once you get in deep enough there's also a speedlift that can take us to the lower decks—that's where Ravi and I went.

"But the thing of it all is, we won't know what the simulation wants until someone starts shooting at us. It could be we're supposed to *help* those zhee, see? We had a rule once we realized that and it was: *Do not shoot first.* What do you think about that rule? As a legionnaire, I mean. Quite contrary to how you operate and yet quite important on this ship. And what do you suppose he has? Nilo, I mean. What kind of a program is he running from that yacht of his to get us the help we're currently getting? I wonder about that. Do you wonder about any of these things, Captain Ford?"

The zhee were certainly far enough along so as not to hear anyone speak quietly.

"Makaffie," Keel said. "Shut up."

"Now see, that's just what Sergeant Fast would have said."

# 09

On Kima, in search of Masters, Zombie Squad found their boots stomping through a quagmire, but it did nothing to deter their purposeful strides. Wearing armor that was scorched, patched, and had new plates in places to replace the ones MCR blaster bolts had sheared off not hours before, this wrecking crew had stepped to the plate at the first mention that a fellow leej was in the wind. A brother was out there all alone, hunted by the enemy, with no backup.

No backup until now.

Happily pitter-pattering ahead of the squad was a mottled brown dog in Legion-style armor, including a full Legion bucket. His face plate dangled from the side of his headpiece, swaying back and forth in time with a tongue that was lazily flapping as the creature came to an abrupt halt beside a legionnaire with his back to the incoming crew. The dog waited for a couple of heartbeats before booming out an apocalyptic serenade of barks that nearly sent the inattentive leej into the mud.

"What in Oba's name are you all supposed to be?" the leej said, putting his arms out wide in surrender.

He took note of the squad following the animal, and his gaze rested on a leej in a scarred set of armor with the old serape-style cape they used to wear during the

"

Ankalor campaigns. It wouldn't do the leej any good out in the jungle, but down in the muck of the swamps it seemed to blend right in.

A caped leej walked through his men and stopped close enough for the trooper to read some of the resumé on his chest, but it was the knife at his belt that drew the eye. Legionnaires far and wide knew that knife, because they'd seen their brothers butchered with it. And for every leej that lost their life under a kankari blade, there was one leej who promised he'd kill two of theirs with their own weapon.

The waiting leej greeted this new arrival. "Sar'nt Major MakRaven. Ain't you supposed to be with the task force commander?"

MakRaven took the leej's wrist and slapped him on the shoulder pauldron hard enough to make the armor clack. "Do I tell you how to do your job, Leej?"

"Course not, Sar'nt Major. Didn't know if I need to roll out rugs and hugs in the event the old man was showing up and you were ADVON security."

"Negative. But what you can do is direct me to the HMFIC of this swamp stomper you got going on so I can go about my way."

The leej whirled and pointed toward the bend in the hill where twisted black trees with vine-like branches reached toward the ground. Hints of more activity sounded from around the terrain, both voices and the movement of heavy equipment. "Just be careful as you roll through. We're moving the Mechasagga-381 long-range artillery pieces to support ongoing jumps into the cities. You can't see anything while piloting those things and the crew don't always watch the sensors, so mind the feet."

"Thanks for the help, Leej. Stay out of trouble. Change your socks, blah blah, sar'nt major stuff."

Led by the sergeant major, the squad walked silently onward, rounding the hill to find a score of legionnaires working to move a titanic artillery piece. It was at least five meters tall and had six articulate legs that gave it a mechanized crab vibe. The entire lower half of the impervisteel monstrosity was layered in dripping mud and vines too stubborn to let go in their attempt to drag this titan into the mire, but the mud and vines were losing this particular battle of wills. The mecha-beast moved slowly onward, each footfall barely causing the gun barrel riding atop the vehicle to so much as shudder, as impact compensators competed with gyro stabilizers over which was going to mitigate the shock of the steps. The beast might have looked like a sixty-ton crab tank taking a stroll, but each step sounded no louder than a wet thud in the ever-sticky swamp.

"Hey!" came a cry from a legionnaire jogging up to intercept them. He stopped in front of the sergeant major. "This ain't no old folks' home, Mak. I ain't got the people to watch your rickety ass in the event you lose your walker and take a tumble."

"That assumes you got people that can keep up," MakRaven shot back. "Have you seen me assault the ice cream counter at the senior center? I am a force to be reckoned with."

The two leejes slapped each other on the plates before removing their buckets.

MakRaven turned to face his squad. "Task Unit Zombie, I want you to meet First Sergeant Anthony Del Villar, call sign Trucker."

"Zombie? As in the kids that bounced all over Blake karking fools up?" Trucker asked.

"One and the same."

That's when Trucker took notice of the dog, sitting and wagging its tail in the mud. Trucker didn't hesitate to drop beside him and rough the dog up in any spot free of armor. "Who's a good boy? Long time no see, brother D!"

"You know this guy?" MakRaven asked.

"Never forget him. LWD-1831, callsign Dozer. Saved my tail a couple of times on that embassy thing in Lussuria."

"I didn't hear about that."

"That's because my boy here did his job." Trucker straightened up again. "You seen under the dog's armor yet?"

MakRaven had indeed seen the collection of Legion ID tags, all belonging to the late former handlers of "Bubbles."

"Yeah. Creepy on another level. Hey, speaking of creepy, where's Butcher?"

"He's doing his thing over there. Tent's just up ahead. You need a hand with anything?"

"Nah, just passing through. Good to see you."

"You too. Take care of my boy!"

Trucker patted the dog on the side of the armor, then replaced his bucket and disappeared into the throng of working legionnaires swarming around the giant artillery piece.

Butcher's tent was pitched nearly on top of a copse of trees. The black, almost charred tangle of branches and vines had already seen fit to grow over the top of the synthetic canvas to create a very hairy-looking structure. A legionnaire standing outside cut off the path to the closed flaps.

"Stand fast and be recognized!" the legionnaire shouted through the digital grit of his bucket's external speakers.

The squad stopped, knowing full well the security protocols to protect the people in that tent. If they had less than four rifles trained on them right now, Mak would be surprised. And he couldn't fault the kid for doing his job. Then again, the ATC on Blake Airfield would have clued in the unit command to an incoming shuttle. Which meant Butcher, the company commander, must not have told anyone because he was testing some of the greenies new to his crew.

"Cerulean," the kid said.

"Cupcake," MakRaven replied, answering the challenge.

"Sorry about that, sir. CO is a stickler. When he says nobody, he means no bodies. Who am I talking to? You're not showing up on my roster."

"Poke your head in that flap and tell the old man Sar'nt Major Mak from Ankalor wants a word. He'll know what's up. And before you go bleeding heart about him not want-ing to be bothered and all that noise, my friend with the four feet had a bumpy ride in and hasn't peed yet. Since I ain't got a leash and he is *really* taking a liking to the side of the old man's tent, I'd hurry in there if I were you."

"On it, Sar'nt Major." The leej ducked his head inside, trusting a senior Legion NCO and his team could keep the place clear of threats while he played messenger. After a moment he motioned for MakRaven to advance, holding the flap open long enough for him to pass beneath before transitioning back into his role as guard.

Directly in line with the flap, kneeling against the back of the tent, were four Kimbrin males, all bound in synth-cord, with nullification hoods over the heads. They were linked together in such a way that anyone that moved would cause the cord to tighten, choking everyone in the chain. While MakRaven made a mental note to drop into the current crop of Legion training and commend those sculptors on their knot-tying classes, he wondered how many leejes and meters of cord it had taken to tie down the enormous Hool lashed to a fallen log at the center of the tent. The huge prisoner's scaled arms were out-stretched and secured at opposite ends of the lumber, and his feet and tail were bound together and then lined to the underside of the tent's far wall, most likely to some more trees out in the swamp.

At the sight of a new leej entering the tent, the Hool growled. The heavy, grating churn of its thrumming snarl drifted through the tent in an intimidation display timed with the rising of the venomous spines running along its back.

Major Butcher rose from a stool next to the Hool to welcome Mak into his domain. "Well there's something you don't see every day. MakRaven off the leash. Got word from the old man that you were coming. You want a seat?" He gestured to the camp stool he'd just abandoned.

"I'm good. If I sit down, I'll never get back up."

"Suit yourself. So, I get word from Harvester Actual that he's sending a crew through my territory, and he just wants to make sure his guys don't get lit up on their way through. Then I find out from Schizo—who's a freaking pilot now if you can believe it—that one of the crew is a guy with unreadable service numbers carrying a kankari. Not an hour later, I had to go namesake for some gator bites on Lizard the Barbarian over here and his buddies when they shot up our movement of the three-eighty-one. Funny thing is, they shot at us *and* the MCR we were fighting. There's some weird going on in the woods, Mak, and the old man ain't talking. He know anything?"

"First I'm hearing of it, Butch. You want me to bring him into this?"

"Nah. I'm sure he's suffering enough having to coordinate this mess from the TOC. Probably wants to do what you did and cross the rank off his sleeve with a marker and run into the jungle. Speaking of which, why did you cross the rank off your sleeve and run into the jungle when our shiny new durable aircraft could drop you anywhere you wanted?"

"Going low-pro."

Butcher laughed himself almost into a coughing fit. "You don't do low profile, Sar'nt Major. What's really going on?"

MakRaven orbited the Hool. They were one of the more aggressive species in the galaxy. Size, speed, killer instinct, and there was no getting around the venomous protrusions that made them a legionnaire's bane in close combat when out of armor. The Hools were something of a super predator, challenged only by species like the wobanki. They very rarely ventured this far into the core unless acting as muscle for one of the various criminal syndicates or MCR potentates looking to show off.

"How many Hools?" Mak asked.

"Six. This is the only one I could get my hands on."

"Six Hools out away from galaxy's edge, sir? You should tell the old man."

"I just did," Butcher said, winking to his fellow leej.

"Sir, the reason I'm rolling through is, one of Chhun's originals got nabbed after Blake went down. The MCR damn near blew the kid off a mountain trying to wipe all the leejes off the board. He's out there right now, murdering their little capture parties inside out, and the MCR has a huge bounty on him to bring him in with a functional set of lungs."

"Part of that SOG team?" Butcher asked.

MakRaven dropped his chin once in answer. "If we go in guns blazing, we risk driving the chase teams towards him or worse, and we don't want that. Get in, nick him, get out."

"Damn, Mak. We don't know what's up there. Whole place is either devoid of life or full of swamps so thick not even the Yawds try to eke out a living. You sure you want to go up there with a single squad?"

"Smaller is better on this one, sir. That being said, we wanted to make contact so we have a last point of entry on me and my team, as well as having a friendly unit close by in case the universe decides to spit in my eye." MakRaven sucked the grit from his teeth, spitting the offending matter to a corner of the tent. "He not talking?"

Butcher shrugged and shook his head at the restrained saurian fighter. "That was a mild one compared to the profanity he's been spitting all day. Only thing he's let slip that was any sort of different was that I would die screaming with my genitals in the Great Dragon's mouth."

"Great Dragon?" Mak shot back. "Hold on, I have a translator that might be able to help."

Mak went to the flap, poked his head out, and made a sharp whistle. Tiny splashes preceded Bubbles padding into the tent. The dog immediately assumed a seated attention pose while looking straight up at the grizzled sergeant major.

"Is that a Legion working dog?"

"Yes, sir. LWD 2060, callsign Bubbles."

The dog's name brought a look of recognition to the major's face. "That's Bouncer's guy."

"He is. I mean, he was. When Bouncer died, he started following me around, so I made him a deal. He helps me get this leej back, and I take him with me for some much-needed T&T, which I understand is handler talk for treats and toys. But while we're here, ain't no harm in letting my little guy play off-leash."

"What do you—"

Butcher's question caught in his throat, and a strange look passed across his face. It passed as quickly as it came on, but for a moment it looked as though the major was about to topple over.

"Sir?" said MakRaven.

The commander regained his bearings. "That dog... he was just in my head, Mak. I wasn't ready for it. I don't know how, but he knew my connection to Bouncer. He knew I put Bouncer up for the handler course and he wants me to send another of my leejes with you."

"Why do I need one of your leejes when I have a squad of my own?" MakRaven asked.

"Beats me, Sar'nt Major."

Mak turned to the dog. "Enough messin' around with Butch. The Hool, if you please."

The canine's ears shot straight up, two black triangles shaping the head so that its eyes became the center of the universe. A few steps brought Bubbles to within inches of the dagger-toothed Hool mouth snapping to get a grip on his furry muzzle, and then the dog did its thing. An ethereal weight washed through the tent, slamming into the restrained Hool with the force of a grav-rail. The monstrous fighter thrashed against his bonds so hard that the heavy branch securing it cracked, splitting the heaving wood up the length of the timber, but it didn't break.

"Mine days of long past will be!" the Hool cried. "Mine was the only will! You are fleeting against my eternity! The Great Dragon rises again!"

"Bubbles!" MakRaven said. "Release!"

The dog barked once, and the Hool ceased its screaming and passed out.

MakRaven looked back at the commander. "What do you think?"

"Might be nothing, or it might be something. I'll kick it upstairs and turn these kelhorns over to Intel." Butcher flat-palmed the sweat from his brow, whipping the excess moisture from his hand in annoyance.

"You sure you're good, sir?" MakRaven asked.

"I am. You sure you don't want to plus up your numbers with a platoon, Sar'nt Major?"

"Might cramp my style, but if you're offering, sir, I will take a line on some indirect fire should the need arise."

"Deal. Now get your voodoo mutt off my fire base. And Mak, good luck."

MakRaven strode from the tent, splashing in the ankle-deep water outside. Zombie Squad remained exactly where he'd left them, their buckets on and ready to get to stepping.

Bubbles used his body armor to knock into MakRaven's leg.

"Oh, hell no. You don't get a treat for nearly toppling a company commander unless he's a bad guy. He wasn't the bad guy."

Mak took note of the team with their rucks on their backs, loaded from toes to nose with the best kit the regimental task force commander could beg, borrow, and steal for them. "You cats need a few more minutes in these luscious surroundings, or are you ready to step off?"

"Step," said Lynx, the team sergeant.

As MakRaven shouldered his own pack, he heard a squeak from behind him. He turned to find Bubbles just past the tent, holding what looked like a rubberized baton. The dog made eye contact with the sergeant major, squeezed his jaws, and activated that most primal of signals from the object: a squeak.

"Did I not just say thirty seconds ago the dog was *not* to be rewarded for his behavior?"

Sergeant Lynx's top team leader, Corporal Digger, answered. "Ain't a toy, Sar'nt Major. You have all his toys in your ruck. If I had to guess, that might be a gasket from a busted-up MCR technical."

"That so, soon-to-be Private No Class Digger? And how many times have you been in a technical truck and the gaskets squeak like that?"

Diggs held up his hand to the side of his bucket, shielding his gaze from the sergeant major's glare. "I'll take the lead on this mystery, Sar'nt Major. Me and the dog will find the enemy truck where he got that squeaky gasket from."

# 10

"Got two moving along the trail at your eleven o'clock, fifty-seven meters," Trent called into the L-comm. "They have blaster-proof vests on and are carrying blaster carbine variants. PK-9s by the look of 'em."

"Got 'em," Gekko confirmed. "Trail elements moving at seventy-seven meters and following along the course track. I have two wings sweeping the forest off-trail, splitting the distance between the first element and the trail."

"How many does that make?" Trent asked.

"Six acting as a push element. Got six more following on their heels at one hundred and eight meters. Same bearing. Moving single file."

Task Unit Zombie had gone to a hasty hide position to overwatch the road when it was discovered a zhee patrol was quickly gaining ground on them. While they weren't walking the road, they were close enough to it that the two sweeper elements, what Gekko had called the *wings*, might have spotted them as they moved. Luckily for the leejes, camouflage built into their armor that allowed it to mimic its environment made a hasty hide less of a thing to stress over. Find some mossy cover, which was everywhere in the terrain on this particular mountain, and hunker down as the armor turned you into just another part of the surroundings.

Sergeant Lynx toggled to a map on his battle board. The screen on the board remained dark to anyone not wearing a Legion bucket, so as not to give away their position in areas of low light. Many legionnaires used them as a responsive haptic interface to their buckets, as the neural mapping and retinal tracking of the new Legion helmet was so newly introduced that long-time users of the older systems were fighting the change.

The sergeant highlighted the moving zhee patrol. "Sar'nt Major, that fit with what you know of standard zhee movements?"

MakRaven frowned. "Sergeant Lynx, zhee ain't got nothin' standard. But what that reminds me of is the time I worked a hop on the edge, running with the Second FMF. I bet in the next few minutes, the wingman on the right side playing it forward is going to drop back, and his partner on the other side will advance."

"Lynx, it's Gek," the team marksman called over the radio. "Wingmen are changing spots."

MakRaven pointed to the junior sergeant. "See?"

"Platoon sergeant back in V-Co said he spent a year doing counterinsurgency with the donks before Nineteen kicked off," Lynx said. "He said it was like teaching a tyrannasquid to tap dance. Who the hell is this tribe and how is it they're so comfortable in armor, actual uniforms, and running our tactics?"

"You tell me, Sergeant. You wanna go down there and ask 'em?"

"Negative. We could take them easy enough, but I'd rather they lead us to our boy. He's probably who they're hunting for." When MakRaven nodded his agreement with the plan, Lynx dropped into the L-comm team channel.

"Diggs, when those donks clear through, I want to play pin the tail on them."

"Good copy. I read allow patrol force to advance and we fall in behind them to target destination. How copy?"

"Solid, Diggs. Gek, make sure they don't already have a tail."

"Working it, boss," Gekko responded.

Within moments of the first six zhee passing Zombie Squad's observation point, the trail element made their way forward. They were similarly equipped to the first group, but where the scouts had been spread out to maximize their ability to sweep the terrain, these next six were moving in a single file to follow the trail.

"Just got word from Gekko," Lynx said. "Last man is their last man."

"So twelve total." Mak frowned. "Can you put a peeper on their back trail? I want to see where they came out of the swamp."

"On it."

Lynx descended into the L-comm, passing his orders to Diggs to get the sergeant major's request moving from the theoretical to the tactical. Within moments, Smoker, the newest member of Task Unit Zombie, was launching a drone high into the trees, narrowly missing a blanket of black hanging moss spanning the gap. The small bot flared to life, the quiet hiss of its repulsors barely audible as it hovered in the expanse before shooting off over the tree cover.

"Sar'nt Lynx. Drone is programmed to trace the back trail and find where they came out of the swamp," Digger confirmed. "Depending on how long it took them to climb this high, we might get indicators of how they moved from the swamp. Anything in particular you're looking for?"

MakRaven signaled for the team to move as he answered the question. "I want to see where they went in the swamp and where they came out."

"Venom Company did say they'd be only too happy to drill any donks we found with some overhead thump," Lynx said.

"Not until we find our missing man, though," MakRaven clarified. "Let's roll."

The trees, with their bluish, almost black elongated fronds wrapped in a netting of moss that seemed to cover everything, became sparser the higher the squad climbed, and soon the leejes came up on rocky crags that would give them a faster, if more intense, climb to higher elevation.

The zhee were still moving, and in order to keep themselves out of sight, Zombie Squad had elected to make use of a small bot to follow the donks. So far, there had been no signs of combat—no distant blaster fire or explosions. Which *could* mean that the kid was laying low... or could mean the kid was out of the fight permanently. The zhee still patrolling was MakRaven's only hope that Chhun's old friend was still alive.

Without word or direction, Zombie Squad formed into a defensive posture, covering their command element without giving away their position or sacrificing the cover of the ever-ascending rock. While the security was being set, Bubbles dropped himself out of the strike muzzle, dove into MakRaven's pack head-first, and emerged with a tangle of straps in his mouth.

"What's this?" Lynx asked.

"That's his carrying case," said the sergeant major. "Only way we're getting him up this ascent."

Lynx knelt beside the dog. "Here, give it to me."

But Bubbles backed away, not allowing the squad leader to take hold of the straps. Instead he circled Digger twice before settling into a seated position off the leej's left leg and spitting the strap tangle at his feet.

"What gives?" Digger asked.

"Looks like Bubbles has chosen his Sherpa," MakRaven answered.

Shaking his head, Digger took hold of the tangled mess and turned it a well-ordered series of buckles and webbing that made a dog holster for the animal. "Why me?" he moaned.

Sergeant Lynx chuckled and turned to the team tech specialist. "Trent, any indication these donk kelhorns know we're here?"

"Negative. They're still moving along the trail toward higher elevation. Haven't even turned back once to look at our drone."

"The dog's ready to go," announced a leej from behind him. But it wasn't Digger, it was Sami, the team's trail man. He had strapped Bubbles onto his back just at the height of his equipment belt.

"Diggs?" said Lynx. "Didn't Bubbles put you on dog duty?"

"It wasn't exactly a direct order..." Digger began.

"I volunteered, Sergeant Major," Sami put in. "My family's from Sinasia. We have these big dogs we use to keep ghost bears away from the flocks. I worked the herds for a couple of summers as a kid to learn the business. We'd often have to hike our dogs up the hills like this."

"Well, don't ever apologize for taking the initiative to push the mission forward," MakRaven said. "Just call it out so we're all on the same page. I'll take your spot in the back."

Over the command channel in the L-comm, Lynx tagged MakRaven. "That was my bad, Sar'nt Major. We're pretty clued into each other and just kind of free flow from position to position without a lot of cross chatter."

"No burn, no blame, Sar'nt," MakRaven said, directing his bucket's advanced optics away from the team and down the hill. "Just keep in mind that I ain't psychic like the dog. You're going to have to build me in with flash-cards till I get the read of the room."

"Roger that, Sar'nt Major."

The leejes made short work of the climb, finding footing on a shelf in the terrain that let them get their jog on. Though they were at extreme elevation after a severe climb and carrying almost their body weight in supplies, they exploded at near a dead run once they got boots on solid footing. They crested several outcroppings that sported ash-colored reeds with wispy white tops, like ghostly fingers reaching up through the rock to claw at anything that dared make its way to the mountaintop. The trees up here were sparse, but they still contained the blackened syrup-covered bark and poisonous-looking branches.

"These trees are nothing like the jungle proper," Smoker said. "Don't seem to let anything else grow around 'em."

Forwardmost in the position, Trent signaled to join him at the next outcropping. "Local history talks about some sort of Kimbrin-made disaster that spread across the planet. Nearly killed everything here. Eventually the planet fought back, and this mountain is what's left of the cataclysm. The vegetation and even some of the animals adapted to live through it, but believe me it's not showing up in the top ten places to visit on Kima lists anytime soon."

The team maneuvered from the rock face into a smattering of blackened trees that turned the giant abutment into a cursed glen out of a twisted fairy tale. Adaptive camouflage turned the gargoyles into specters floating through the tangle of twisted branches.

"Sergeant Lynx, we got intel from the drone we sent on the back trail," Smoker said.

"Send it."

The squad once again collapsed in place, building a web of 360-degree security before the virtual data hand-off could happen, and the PFC passed the info collected by the drone. The zhee's trail stretched back nearly five kilometers, off the mountain and into the swamps that collected at the base of the rock. The trail would have been difficult to spot from the ground, but the drone had used its aerial view, plus a host of filtering algos and self-perpetuating tracking models, to patch together an overland track in reverse.

It revealed that the donk squad had moved through the swamp, constantly adjusting to but never closing on the Legion position. They had come to within a few klicks of the massive company element, initially moving in groups of three side-by-side through the lichen-tinged water. The algo tracked several movements to a sandbar or high ground, only to see the trail double back on itself to throw off any tracking. When the zhee squad came within a thousand meters, the group once again changed its shape, judging by the trail they'd left, and went completely abreast and spread out over fifty meters. Moving as one big flank they pushed through the waterlogged terrain, displacing soft ground and moss-covered water so that instead of a single trail to follow in a line, the landscape was disturbed in a wide swath. Those observing would know something had been there but would have no idea as to the numbers they were tracking. Combined with non-linear movements and utilization of waypoints to leave a confusing trail, the donk squad had left a confounded track for any enemy troop that showed even a spark of interest.

MakRaven frowned. "Anything standing out for you, Leej?" he asked Lynx.

"Other than that this is straight out of the Legion Jungle Operations training curriculum?"

MakRaven lifted up his helmet to spit out something bothering him. "Which we updated some time ago from lessons learned on Psydon."

"Donks have never been this motivated to learn actual tactics before," Lynx said. "Usually they wrap everything in strips of cloth and beads or break acquired gear outright to fit into some expectations of how the four gods would have done it, but now they're wearing real armor and moving around like highly trained squads. Did someone on Kima force them to work this way, or did they do it themselves?"

"You think maybe the SOG team was workin' with the donks and got smoked?" Digger asked out of nowhere.

Lynx scowled at the legionnaire, but MakRaven only grunted. "Wouldn't be the first time a SOG team got mixed up in somethin' like that... but I don't think so. Not from what I've heard about this team, anyway."

MakRaven activated a map overlay in his HUD that gave him a field of view in a layer of virtual reality that let him get his bearings without losing sight of the constantly ascending terrain that could end in a long drop with a violent stop.

"Okay, Lynx. Keep us on this bearing but don't crest the ridge. Best guess from what I'm lookin' at is the point of entry we're looking for should be just ahead."

Zombie Squad's leader passed on the word over L-comm and the crew spread out, creeping along the scrub-encrusted rock in a silent approach. Gaining the top of the ridge, the team sent up another observation bot, using its low-visibility holocam to take in the sight past the ridge.

Simulcasting to all the buckets, including Bubbles's, the directed feed overlooked a deep swamp inlet that let out into a jungle very similar to what was on the other side of the mountains. An aerial recon would have missed the place, if only because there was nothing to it; it was little more than a camp set up in a clearing that overlooked the swamp.

"Zombie," said Lynx. "I need a full workup of that camp. Get me aerial recon over the next hour. Gekko, crawl someplace uncomfortable and give me a hard map of the place. I want every potential ingress and egress as well as possible trap points and IEDs that could hem us up. Trent, you're on tech. I want to know what they're running along with what potential anti-intrusion measures they have on tap. Digger, you and Smoke find me that leej if he's in there."

Lynx then pushed back from the lip of the ridge, sliding down to crawl into a small shelf skirting the back side of the hill. He secured his ruck onto the rock face with a piton and covered it in the mimetic netting he carried in the outer cargo pocket.

"Where you going, Sar'nt?" Mak asked.

"Gonna see if I can get us in on the town meeting. How's your zhee, Sar'nt Major?"

"Damn sure better than yours, son."

# 11

The audio capture system on the enhanced Legion combat helmet had an invisible laser-directional indicator so that a leej could aim it directly at a person they were trying to record to get the best sound from the source. The problem was, there was more than one species whose biological hardware could detect such things, meaning that to err on the side of caution, Sergeant Lynx had never used it. But now the intel was considered worth the risk, and as he scanned the audio capture mic across the camp, he watched in his HUD to see the waveform jump at some conversation or another.

The first conversation he captured was from one of a pair of zhee guards watching from the edge of the swamps. Nearby was a slumped and injured looking MCR regular in a tattered uniform, hands tied behind his back. MakRaven listened to their conversation for a moment and then waved Lynx off to find another target.

"What were they doin' with that Kimbrin?" Lynx asked.

"They were passing him around for fun."

"Like beating on him?"

"Well... for starters," MakRaven huffed.

Aiming through the bamboo slats of one of the huts, Lynx managed to capture another conversation. This voice, though zhee, wasn't speaking in a zhee dialect. It was speaking in Kimbrin.

"Just try to stay still," said the donk voice. "I know this is pain, but as the four bloody gods tell us, through pain we achieve a purer faith. You must rise above your pain, so that you may live and show the gods you are worthy of their attention."

"But will you let me go if I live?" asked another voice—raspy and tired and also speaking in Kimbrin.

"You let them tie you and pass you around like a lame mare," said the zhee. "Once they are done with you, they will most likely kill you as an offering to the great god who has spoken."

"God who has spoken?" Lynx asked MakRaven.

"Donk nonsense. Means hearing directly from one of the four bloody gods as if they were still living. Kind of stuff that gets talked about in lotus tents on the zhee home worlds. Like, you were so high that you saw the god who has spoken."

"Stay here or move to another target?"

"Track right. See that long hut at the back center of the camp?"

Lynx narrowed the focus on the audio sensor, raking in soft raspy noises from the long hut. "Sar'nt Major, got it."

"Calories," said a distinctly robotic voice like that of a bot. "If you weren't restrained you could follow up. And—" A rasping, distorted warble sounded. After a moment, the bot continued. "My apologies. The power fluctuations are growing more frequent. The end of my runtime is near. I do not fear it. Neither should you... but, as I was saying, if not for the rope you could follow your original intent and convert these wayward souls to calories for Oba. Such final zeal is fitting for a member of the faithful such as yourself."

"One o' those holos of Masters showed him runnin' with a bot," MakRaven mumbled.

The bot continued. "My son… do you still have runtime?"

Another voice replied. This one biological. "Don't remind me… Jay-Three." A coughing fit followed.

"You really should try to escape," the bot advised.

"I almost… have my wrist… free." The man grunted and MakRaven's heart began to beat faster. This was surely Masters. "Once I… loosen this last bit of rope… we're out of here. E&E to… back door."

"My goodness. I advise you to lose your current state of consciousness, my son. While you seem to be entertaining the head man to coax him into taking his time, I would like to see you have a single night of relief. You still have four hundred and seventy-one cuts to go. Perhaps when those are finished, if you survive, they'll let you go."

MakRaven stifled a curse. The kid was being subjected to Death by a Thousand Cuts—and had already endured five hundred and twenty-nine. Mak knew exactly how much suffering that ritual entailed, each cut somehow more excruciating than the one before. It was an experience he wouldn't wish on his worst enemy.

"Just… keep an eye… open," said the prisoner.

"Voice match, Sar'nt Major," Lynx confirmed. "That's Masters."

"Good job," MakRaven said. "We're gonna have to move fast. As soon as the sun goes down over that mountain, they're going to start cutting him up again. That's how they like to do it when they've got the time. We aren't gonna let that happen."

Lynx and MakRaven slithered through the terrain, making the best use of light and shadows and the ever-present moss that covered everything on this mountain. Rejoining the rest of Zombie, they crawled into a team huddle where everyone was downing ration gels to pack in the last calories before things kicked off.

Lynx downed a ration gel of his own as he updated the squad on what they'd discovered. Corporal Digger had drawn a map on his datapad and shared it to the others' buckets, and now Lynx highlighted it as he laid out the plan.

"The best possible way into the clearing where they've got our boy is to follow Digger's back trail into the side corner right here. That gives us the most cover from the trees and lets us have max shadows from the sun going down. Gek, we're going to need you to splash those two guards right away."

"I'll be set up here," the sniper said, pointing to another spot. "You lock 'em, I'll drop 'em."

"Good. Diggs, what else have you got?" Lynx asked.

"We got a whole lot of suck going in this swamp, boss. Terrain is hell and I can't get any kind of a fix on any equipment these donks have hidden away back there. We could call in for some of the major's promised helpers... but that might only be enough to see 'em shot out of the sky on arrival."

"We can handle this job ourselves," MakRaven said. "Donks in that camp were about the same as most donks. They might be patrollin' all right, but they're lazy as sin once back home."

"There's something else, too," Trent said, nodding at MakRaven's assessment. He cast a readout into the HUDs of the rest of the team. "This right here is the data burst we keep getting every twenty-seven point two minutes. Now, we can see the equal amount of complexity with these broadcast elements here and here, most likely conversations between someone within the broadcast. But *this* is the part that scared me right out of my underpants."

Trent stripped the data and broadcast elements from the diagram, sifting through the various elements until only two waves were left for everyone to look at. One on the left, one on the right.

"They're pretty much identical," Smoker said. "So what?"

Trent shook his head. "Over here, the wavy line is the broadcast encryption protocol that is our dearly beloved L-comm. On the other side is the wave coming off of that broadcast."

"Cut the cute stuff and get to the point," Digger growled. "Are you saying we have another Legion element close by?"

"No. I'm saying that someone on the other side of these swamps, just down the mountain our boy was last seen alive at, is using a broadcast protocol that is frighteningly similar to the L-comm. It ain't us."

"Sket," Lynx said, studying the HUD readout. "The encryption is still hyper-stylized, but the broadcast configuration is definitely not Legion." He looked to MakRaven for what to do next.

"Tag it and bag it," the sergeant major said. "Broadcast that to Chhun in a data burst before we kick off."

"If I do that, Sar'nt Major, it could tip our hand. That is, if whoever is sending this also has a way to monitor us. Not as crazy as it sounds given the similarities."

"Been burstin' over L-comm for a while now," MakRaven pointed out. "If they ain't found us yet, what's another call?"

"On it, Sar'nt Major," Trent said.

"Solid. What else?" Lynx demanded.

"Boss, we got a flatbed repulsor truck under this tarp right here," Digger said, pointing to the map. "It's big enough to carry all of us out of here."

"Solid," Lynx said. "Can't imagine it'll move too quickly over the swamp without making a mess, but it's an option. Sar'nt Major, anything before I start cutting and handing out cake so everyone gets a bite?"

"No, Sar'nt. You're driving. I just want to hang out on a butterfly trigger and make a mess of stuff."

Lynx nodded to the senior leej. "Diggs, you and Smoker get me that flatbed. Sar'nt Major, me, Trent, and Sami will run you down to pick up our boy. We take this path into the trees and descend to the side of the clearing. Gek, you're the hammer. Dust that donk once we get to the wire. If his buddy at this loc notices him go down, dust his ass too. Cover and control the corner where we insert Sar'nt Major Mak and Bubbles to recover the leej. If Masters is not ambulatory, Trent moves inside to assist. We make for the truck and say goodbye to this swamp. Sar'nt Major, how long do you think until they start cutting on our boy again?"

MakRaven looked up as if consulting the heavens. "Within the hour."

"Marking HUD. Tripwires and a motion sensor," Sami said into the L-comm. "Motion sensor is going to take a sec. Stand by."

Zombie Squad hunkered into the twisted vines and gnarled trees marking the side of the swamp. The oily black residue soaking into the ground from the bark reminded MakRaven of roots he'd seen on Calcarion. He'd been deployed there to rescue a group of miners taken hostage by MCR factions looking to cash in on the mineral extraction out on galaxy's edge. The roots tearing through those mines were some sort of native vine that leached minerals out of the soil and provided a breathable atmosphere, but the byproduct of all that interplay between dirt and vine was a black inky residue that got all over everything. His NCO had nearly had a stroke over how long it took them to clean their armor after every operation.

Lynx focused his attention forward as Sami shined a beam into the motion sensor. The Legion close combat specialist nodded when he got the hoped-for result from the board. Pointing with his fingers, he motioned that they were back in business and hustled toward the back of the camp.

"Lynx to Gekko, approaching waypoint one."

The L-comm buzzed with the confirmation. "I see you, Lynx. I have tap on target."

"The target is yours, Gekko," Lynx confirmed through the L-comm. "We move on your go."

MakRaven knelt down next to the dog, groping for the back of the animal's Legion bucket. There was a tiny collar attachment at the point between the dog's helmet and the rest of his body armor. It came free with a press of the sergeant major's fingers.

"Firing," Gekko called into the L-comm. In the rearmost sentry post on this side of the camp, Gekko's shot destroyed the single zhee's brain case. The guard slumped into a tree that had grown horizontally and then up, looking very much like he was leaning over it to get a better view of what was on the other side.

"Good hit," Lynx called into the net. Drawing in light and distance through the vision-enhancing macro in his bucket, he confirmed the donk was dead.

"Roger, you are clear to the back camp perimeter," Gekko called into the net.

"Hold position," Sami interrupted. "That section is monitored."

"Solid. Assess, acquire, and execute," Lynx called back.

In the highlighted HUDs, Sami's IFF indicator crawled to the rear of the camp. Small, short posts were sunk into the moist ground every ten meters; crossing through them would most likely trigger an alarm. Sami stretched out his hand to attach a metallic clip to the nearest post. After waiting a second to gauge the effect of the first attachment, he rigged a second lead to the top of the post and repeated it for the bottom. He repeated the process on the next post.

"Okay, we're good to pass through these two posts only."

The assault team poured through the makeshift opening.

"Gekko, it's Lynx. Report."

Gekko came on the L-comm. "Two-man roving guard is near the main entrance talking to stationary guards by the split tree. Peeper bots have a group of six zhee in a tent directly in front of you, and the next one seems like a tool shed or something. Target is in the clearing directly after that. Got a lot of zhee laying around the camp, possibly intoxicated."

"Moving," Lynx confirmed.

The group slithered along the camp's perimeter, where the overhang of finger-like fronds covered in black moss created a natural curtain for the leejes to move through, and passed the back of the first tent.

"Hold position," Gekko called from his concealment. "Peeper has a single occupant walking to the window."

The L-comm chimed to indicate another element calling in. "Lynx, it's Diggs. We have the truck. It has a full power cell and is serviceable. Smoke thinks he can gun from the back. Setting up distractions now."

"Good copy, Lynx out."

When Gekko called out that the watcher at the window had gone back inside the tent, the team continued their crawl across the frond curtain, careful not to disturb the vegetation or stray too far from its branches reaching for them. They sidled up to the back of the long tent, setting out observation bots and formulating traps to cover them in the event of a stroller looking to gawk at the leej inside.

"Boss, you have a small procession moving to you," Gekko called. "Head man by the looks of him."

"Sitting tight," Lynx confirmed.

The leejes got low, spreading out so that they could effectively cover the space from different angles of attack. The plodding bulk of a donk in military fatigues with the top pants button undone to accommodate his heft sauntered up to the clearing where they had identified Masters was being held. Two of his guards turned to face out from the clearing while the other two flanked him as he strode past the bushes. He adjusted his pistol belt several times to account for the flab refusing to conform to its structure.

Clomping to the center of the clearing, the zhee growled in a low bray. "Robot. Is your legionnaire con-shee-ahs?"

"My humble apologies, great and terrible khan. He has been in and out of consciousness all day. If I had to guess, he is unconscious due to dehydration." The bot said this in as placating a fashion as it could.

The team moved quietly from the tent to get in view of the clearing, stepping over drunken and passed-out zhee as they moved. The bot came into view first, and it was in sorry shape. It appeared to be nothing more than a head placed on a pike, with a single arm dangling from a ruined shoulder.

They could see the leej, too. And if the bot was in bad shape, Masters was worse.

He had been fastened to a huge fallen tree, tied spread-eagle against it, with his neck, torso, and legs strapped down. His arms were extended straight out to his sides and secured by ropes knotted to spikes that had been driven into the log.

He had been savagely cut. A good majority of the cuts were superficial, just deep enough to draw some blood and pain, but other slashes appeared to be very deep— enough to require stitches, skinpacks, or acts of Oba to heal properly. A Legion regen treatment center would probably have to work overtime to put this guy back to- gether. His hair was caked black with dried blood and mud, and he was covered in bruises around many of the slashes.

"You were supposed to notify us when he needed water," the grotesquely large zhee barked in its native tongue at the bot.

The bot responded in kind, speaking the zhee dialect flawlessly. "I called out for two hours, fourteen minutes, and eight seconds with no response when I noticed he was in distress, great khan. According to the Second Pillar of the Great Gods, the Bridge to Awakening should be performed on a completely healthy zhee or prisoner so that every opportunity to see the being live through the experience is taken. Thus they may see the way of the Great Gods and..."

The khan back-fisted the bot, sending it tumbling off the pike and to the ground. "You will not tell me of the Four Pillars, vile abomination. The pillars are meant to support the great and glorious one. The god who speaks perhaps will provide atonement should this one live... but you shall never have such a path to understanding, machine. I forbid you to speak of it. You function only at my amusement."

The khan barked orders for Masters to be untied and given water and food. Then he started plodding away before pausing to sniff the air with his inordinately large muzzle. "What is this great and seething hate I feel? I must meditate on my feelings so I am not led astray by the shortcomings of my kind."

MakRaven patted the dog, hoping to dampen the psychic growl building in the animal's soul. Surely that had to be what the zhee khan was sensing. "Lynx?"

"We wait for the feeders to come back and untie him. Then we take him," the Legion NCO said. "Sami, rig the site with antipersonnel. Diggs, this is Lynx. Coming to you in ten. How are we looking on that truck?"

"We're set, boss."

The sergeant major shifted the kankari knife closer to the front of his kit. "There's something off about these zhee," he said. "About this whole place. The funky sig-nal. Strange way they shave their manes. The way they move, like they've been watching Repub training videos. This mess is covered in so many layers I can't see what I'm really looking at. So if it comes to it, I'm going to take my trusty knife here and cut through all the fat until I get what I want."

"Priority is the leej, though, right?" Lynx asked.

"Until he isn't," the sergeant major huffed.

# 12

"If you spill moo-ar food, you make walk again lee-tal thing," one of the zhee guards barked in stilted Standard at a Kimbrin slave. "You make go geet moo-ar food. We need pree-son-aire tough so we cut him. So the gods dee-mand."

"I will be more careful, masters," said the Kimbrin slave, holding the prisoner's food plate more securely. Adding that little word at the end seemed to make them less likely to whip him. They *were* his masters now and seemed to like when he acknowledged them as such. He'd learned that any day where the zhee didn't beat him, whip him, or worse was a good day.

He just had to feed the half-dead legionnaire and then they would leave the Kimbrin alone for the night. Hopefully.

He stepped gingerly past one of the zhee. It was not uncommon for a soldier zhee to casually trip him and dump him in the grass. The soldiers liked to laugh and mock him—and then beat him for his clumsiness.

The slave's name was Shivo, and he sorely regretted ever leaving his comfortable life to join the Mid-Core Rebellion. He'd done it almost on impulse, never imagining he'd one day find himself in such deadly circumstances. Although now, looking back, he couldn't see how he could ever have been so naïve.

"Move your feet, *shkah-vechk!*" the guard shouted, using the zhee word that Shivo had come to learn meant *tender feet.*

Shivo shuffled past to deliver the meal to the prisoner. He was almost there when one of the guards clipped his ankle. He nearly spilled, but quickly caught himself just in time as the howls of laughter echoed around him.

The legionnaire's armored coverings had been stripped off and thrown to the side. He was left to suffer his bodily excretions right where he was.

Shivo set down the tray, lifted a water jug that sat in the prisoner's field of vision—likely put there on purpose as another form of torture—and tried not to shake as he poured its contents into a bamboo cup.

It was then that he suddenly felt his equilibrium move wildly, as though he'd been spinning as fast as he could and had only just now stopped. He dropped to his knees, feeling as though he was going to vomit. He felt the water slosh against his hands.

But even kneeling was too much, and his queasiness forced him to lie on his back. And as he went down, beyond the trees outside the camp, he could have sworn he saw a set of greenish eyes staring back at him, reflecting the dying light of the sun.

Sami moved into the clearing and dropped his hand over the mouth of the little Kimbrin slave. "I'm not here to hurt you, but if you make noise, I will kill you. Nod if you understand."

The Kimbrin slowly nodded into Sami's heavy combat glove.

"Good. I'm going to release you, and you must remain quiet. If you scream or call out, I have this." Sami produced a wicked curved blade the length of the man's forearm, with a frosted wave pattern that ran irregularly just above the edge of the weapon.

The slave sobbed into the glove. Then nodded again.

Sami relaxed the glove, removed it from the man's face, then walked backwards behind Masters. "Gek, I have the guy."

"Guards are looking away," Gek reported. "No activity on site-facing exposures. Take them down."

A legionnaire for each guard wrapped a synth-wire around their necks and quietly strangled the donks to death, stashing their bodies in the underbrush.

"Guards are down," Gekko informed the net.

"No traffic," Sami said calmly through the L-comm. "Do it on three, two, one."

The two zhee guard's heads snapped forward as they were violently yanked by their knees into the brush and swallowed beneath the foliage.

"Target down," Lynx said over the radio.

"Target down," Trent said just after.

Sami looked to the Kimbrin huddling on the ground, but the poor man clearly had no intention of speaking, moving, or even breathing if he could help it. He hugged the damp earth like his life depended on it. Which it did.

Sami then stepped to the broken bot, which was also on the ground, though not by choice. He picked it up by the top of its skull, its one arm dangling, and addressed it eye to eye. Or visor to optical sensor.

"I'm giving you exactly twenty-two seconds to tell me who you are and why I should care," Sami said quietly to the bot. "And if you speak any louder than I am right now… you're gonna lose another arm."

The bot, however, could not comply. "I am J-316. My purpose is—"

Sami slammed his hand over the thing's mouth. "I said quietly!" he hissed.

"I am unable to control my volume," the bot explained, its voice now at least muffled by the glove.

"Bot comes with us," MakRaven said as he slithered through the back of the clearing where Masters was kept.

Lynx appeared at Sami's side and slapped a piece of heavy tape over the bot's mouth. Trent, too, emerged soundlessly from the brush and went straight to Masters. MakRaven crawled over to the cowering Kimbrin and removed his bucket.

"Hey, you speak Standard?" he asked.

Judging his reaction, the Kimbrin did not. But then at last he muttered, "Y-yes."

The sergeant major nodded. "I am sure you would very much like to escape these donks, but I'm here for him, not you. The best I can do is give you this rifle and tell you that, in the next few minutes, there is going to be a lot of hate focused on us. That's your chance to fight—and hopefully escape. Good luck."

The Kimbrin looked to be in shock, but he accepted the rifle and a satchel of charge packs.

"Safety is on the side," MakRaven instructed him. "Don't point at anything you don't mean to shoot. Only shoot what you think you can hit."

The Kimbrin blinked numbly.

"What do we got?" MakRaven said to the team behind him.

Trent and Sami had Masters down off his rig and onto a repulsor stretcher they'd unfolded and brought for the purpose. Trent had replaced one of his gloves with a medical glove and was conducting an injury sweep.

"Eyes are all goofy but I don't think he's concussed," Trent said. "Lacerations are severe, but there's no priapism. Once we get him lucid he might be able to move on his own. He won't be running the Victory Day 5K, but he might be able to limp to the truck."

"Priapism?" MakRaven asked. "Speak to me in Standard, Doc."

Trent continued to work the man's injuries through his explanation. "It's a situationally inappropriate and painful erection that is often indicative of a spinal injury, Sar'nt Major."

"Hell... not what I was expecting to hear. Let's get his motor running. Just not with that prism thing. Word is this boy don' need no kinda help with that anyway."

"On it, Sar'nt Major."

To restrain the patient, Trent pressed his chest plate across the leej and put his near-side hand into the man's jaw. He knew this was going to hurt the prisoner, as Trent's dirt- and grit-stained armor was probably grinding against the heavy slashes in Masters's chest, but odds were it needed to be done.

Sami then broke a packet of chem-stims under the man's nose.

In an instant the wounded leej drew in a heavy lungful of air, whipped one unrestrained leg around Trent's neck, and was in the process of wrapping the other when Sami held a shiny coin in the man's face.

"Aldon Masters, we're Second Platoon, Victory Company. Zombie Squad here to get you out. This is an official Task Unit Zombie challenge coin. And this here," he raised a small plasticene cylinder, "is twenty-five centiliters of water. Just enough to wet your whistle but not cramp you up."

Masters greedily took the water. Then in a hoarse whisper he said, "Victory Company? What year is it?"

"Long story. We need to move."

Masters tilted his head up to see the grizzled scarred jawline of Sergeant Major MakRaven staring down at him.

"Your boy Chhun sent us. Don't say he never did nothin' for ya."

Lynx cut off the banter. "Ninety seconds till exfil. Can it and jam it, leejes."

The euphoria of finding their target alive and relatively operational wore off as the no- nonsense NCO put everyone back on target. Trent pushed Masters's vitals through the L-comm. "We have multiple deep lacerations across all exposed skin with a mild head abrasion to the right mastoid process. Concussion is likely but leej's alertness and willingness to KTF suggest otherwise. Pressing skinpacks across the deep tracks. Snap stitches on the ones that look like they tried to peel him."

"Oh, those things... suck," Masters complained.

"They do, but try not to scream," Sami said. "Injecting ten cc's of MCP."

The dog trotted over to Masters as Sami pressed an injector full of antibiotics and antivirals into the patient.

"Hey there, boy," Masters said to the dog. "Or possibly girl."

But before he could say anything else, the first of the snap stitches closed a deep cut across his back, and he gritted his teeth and pressed his knuckles over his eyes. And then a force he couldn't explain washed over him, and the pain just rinsed away as though he were in a shower and it was just dirt running off in the spray. And somehow, he sensed that this feeling—this blissful, peaceful feeling—was coming from the dog.

As Trent went to work putting the rest of the snap stitches in place, Masters gazed in wonder.

"What's your deal, mutt?" he asked.

"We adopted him to make room at the pound," Lynx said. "Fifteen seconds. I have his gear. Swapped out the power battery on the back plate. Sami, rig him up."

"I'm trying to get his shirt on, Sar'nt, but it's like trying to fit a Drusic into a miniskirt."

Masters was growing more lucid by the moment. "Did he just call me fat? Did he not... see... these abs?"

Lynx smiled despite himself and helped Sami get Masters into his clothes and armor, and then without warning, Trent jabbed the rescued leej with a load of stim that took him from sedate to savage in an instant.

"Always jokes with you Dark Ops guys," Lynx said. "Time to get on the truck before the donks realize what's happening."

Masters looked himself over to see what they had done. He'd been stuffed not only into his shirt but also his armor, which the zhee had carelessly left heaped in a pile. In addition, the sergeant had put an L-comm headset with an attached monocle on him to give him much of the functionality he would have had his bucket not been ruined and ditched.

The sergeant major and the two leejes hoisted him to his feet, and Lynx stuffed a PK-9 blaster in his hand along with a bandolier of charge packs.

"Beggars can't be choosers, I guess," Masters grumbled. "Action looks good but the cycler might be karked. We got a way out of here, Sergeant...?"

"Lynx," the NCO said. "That's Sami and Trent, and you know Sergeant Major MakRaven. The dog is Bubbles. I know you're a kill team guy and that's all good in your hood, but you're in my house right now, Sergeant Masters. I have the tools and toys to get us outta here, so until you get your legs back under you, it's my run and my rules. Is that cool?"

Masters's smile at being surrounded by this Legion, this brotherhood of monsters that only a select few in the galaxy would or could appreciate, caused some of the open cuts on his face to bleed. "Parminthian, Sar'nt. Lead the way."

# 13

Lynx approached the frightened Kimbrin slave at the edge of the clearing. He knelt down and offered him a pill in a sealed plasticene tab. "Stimulant. It will give you energy for about four hours."

The man's hand left the stock of the rifle he was clutching and took the tab. Gnarled fingers spoke of them having been broken at some point and never set.

"What's your name?" Lynx asked.

"Shivo."

"Shivo, I have to get that man to safety. You can come, but you have to keep up and you have to do your part. Do you understand?"

The man nodded through tears that fell between pits in his face where the facial spikes endemic to the species had been cut away.

"Masters is all dressed for the dance, Sar'nt," said Trent. "Got his halo set up and linked to the armor."

Lynx nodded and switched to the L-comm. "Gek, it's Lynx."

"You got a party of four looking to seat themselves when they saw there was no one at the front door. Two minutes."

"Roger that," Lynx said. "Collapse on us outside the wire and be ready to roll."

"Roger out," the sniper said.

Lynx pointed to the spot in the brush they'd come through, then opened up a private message to Masters in the L-comm with Sergeant Major Mak tagged to receive.

"Sergeant Masters, we're gonna back alley our way out of here. You good for a light jog?"

"I don't really have the right shoes, but I'll make it work, Sar'nt," Masters replied.

The rasp in his voice along with a few fits of catching his breath were the only signs that the leej didn't have a full charge on his body battery, even with the stim. And the look in his eyes told Lynx he wasn't out of the fight just yet. Still, the reading he was picking up from the leej's armor told him that the man's blood pressure was dangerously low.

"Trent."

"I see it, Sar'nt. Spiking a bag on him now."

"Wait, what are you putting in my where?" Masters asked.

Trent spoke as he went to work. "Don't worry, Sar'nt Masters, this is just a canister of nano-packed nutrients and fluids to get your blood pressure up."

"Oh. Those."

"One minute," Gek put in, letting the team know they had precious few seconds before the donk fire team came knocking.

Lynx got on the L-comm. "Digger, it's Lynx. We got company coming up the driveway, so we're taking our lunch to go."

"Roger that. Locking in secondary pickup."

Lynx positioned himself next to a forlorn tree, aiming his rifle into the shadows, while one by one the others slipped beneath the black fronds hanging from the other trees.

The Kimbrin came last, and Lynx stopped him before he could depart. "Hold up a minute, Shivo. You're not going to want to miss this."

The zhee fire team had arrived at the clearing. At the sight of Masters's tree now missing its former occupant, the ropes cut and lying loose, the hulking zhee at the center of the group brayed in alarm and began barking out commands to his team.

Lynx rolled a fragger in their midst, and it detonated beneath them. A swarm of super-heated shrapnel flew up into the bewildered donks followed by the secondary boom of the double-duty fraggers.

Lynx looked to the Kimbrin. "That one was for you. Now move. Stay low and follow the others. Do what they tell you. Go."

As the former slave crawled away, Lynx stayed in position a moment longer, keeping an eye on the zhee who'd begun to rouse themselves and were now pouring in from the edges of this most barren and basic of camps.

He keyed the comm once more. "Three, two, one, execute."

Near the entrance to the camp, a tarp flew from the flatbed, exposing Smoker standing in the bed, armed with a machine gun mounted on a pintle. He mashed down the trigger, sending a flurry of blaster bolts in a wave across the camp, punching right through the zhee fighters who hadn't even had time to kit up in their body armor. Wild return fire from dodging zhee pinged off the side of the repulsor truck, scorching the metal frame in some places, but doing nothing to slow Smoker. He continued to sweep the weapon across the crowd as Digger fired up the power cell and brought the vehicle to life.

Now it was Lynx's turn to move. He caught up to Shivo with Sami, who'd positioned himself as the last man in the stack. Lynx took the frightened Kimbrin by the shoulder and the group slithered forward, staying close to the perimeter where the trees hung overhead like necrotic black willows. The somber shadows combined with the Legion armor's mimetic skin to turn the leejes from fighters to phantoms. But the camouflage might have been unnecessary. Even Shivo, though clad only in ordinary brown cloth garments, was nearly invisible in the shifting shadows of early evening.

The team approached a guard who had set himself at the side of the camp where the legionnaires first infiltrated. The donk was searching for targets through the scope of his rifle. A ping sounded in Lynx's bucket to signal an incoming trooper, and a moment later Gekko came sliding down the hill toward the camp along a back trail. At the bottom of the embankment he fell in line to follow the leejes on the other side of the wireless perimeter fence, but he stopped at a tangle of vines spilling over a rock and set up his rifle against this makeshift table. A moment later his voice came over the L-comm.

"I have eyes on the searcher."

Almost as if he had heard, the donk lowered the rifle from his face and turned to look over the terrain where the leejes hid. He swept his face one way and then the other, but seemed unable to focus his bulbous brown eyes on the figures in the darkness. After a moment he raised the rifle to his face once more, trying to find the source of the blaster fire ruining his friends.

The suppressed bolt from Gek's N-65 variable output precision blaster coughed out its payload from the other side of the fence. The high-kinetic round slid easily through the donk's skull, cauterizing the wound a half second after it sprayed the air with whatever thought the creature had been having just before its death.

"Move," Gekko said through the net.

Lynx herded his patrol through the muck of the receding swamp before finally coming to the spot where the jungle met the deep water. On his HUD he watched through Digger's view as the flatbed moved toward the team's position.

Lynx checked on Masters and then asked, "Sar'nt Major Mak, how's the new guy looking?"

"Oh, you know how it goes. He'll act all Legion until the rescue cocktail we gave him wears off. Then he'll want to ride the dog."

"If you've got a saddle for that thing, sign me up," Masters said.

The squad moved quickly on a downward track among the reeds, putting distance between themselves and the camp until the repulsor truck finally caught up. Soon the sputtering engine of the technical drew closer. A heartbeat later, gunfire echoed across the swamp as the old repulsor truck came careening through the brush, struggling to make the speed being asking of it. The man on the wheel applied the brakes and came to a hovering stop just past where the leejes were waiting.

Digger stuck his face out the window. "I need to know who's payin' the cab fare."

# 14

"Get in the front," MakRaven barked at Masters.

"But Sar'nt Major, that's your seat, what with your advanced—"

"Age?" Mak finished.

"I was going to say rank and *then* say age."

"Just get in the front, lover boy."

MakRaven followed the dog into the flatbed. The leej set down his brownish half-cape for the dog to lie on while he pressed his back into the rear window on the cab. The rest of Zombie Squad took spots along the rails while aiming their rifles in different locations as though it were hard-wired into their DNA. Sami knelt toward the rear of the vehicle to help Shivo get aboard.

Lynx jumped in last, finally relieving his weapon of its aim toward the camp to keep his men safe. He scooted to the center position, leaning against Smoker's legs as he worked the SAB pressed into its spot above the bed. "Shivo, you sit here next to me. Point your gun that way and shoot anything in front of it that isn't us."

"I understand," said the Kimbrin.

Lynx switched to L-comm. "Hey Diggs, food's gettin' cold back here. Get a move on."

"Roger, Sar'nt," Digger said. The legionnaire jammed his foot on the accelerator and was rewarded with a coughing fit that propelled the vehicle forward. He turned his head to Masters. "You all right there, Sergeant?"

Masters grimaced as the truck bumped and skimmed over the swamp water. A nasty repulsor surge sent a heavy thump through the vehicle and straight into his snap stitches, slapping hundreds of razor-lined cuts across his back. But he held up a thumb to indicate he was as good as he was going to get. "Honestly, I'm glad my spa vacation is over. The place was under new management and their service left something to be desired. Would not recommend. One star."

When another bounce threatened to break off the repulsors from the vehicle's undercarriage, Masters felt the flat seat cushion do its level best to punch him in the back plate. The lancing pain from countless cuts was enough to bring blackness encroaching on the edge of his vision. But he gritted his teeth and welcomed it. Because he knew the truth.

*This is life.*

He was the lucky one. Always the lucky one.

Jaybles and Young would take his place in a heartbeat. If they had any heartbeats left.

Masters ground his back against the rusty springs in the seat. Pain was better than loss. Better than guilt and regret.

He was still embracing the pain when the first few blaster bolts struck the hood of the technical. The glancing luminescent green bolts flashed across the thin metal, leaving smoldering scorch marks in their wake.

"Donk patrol on the two, coming up alongside the swamp, firing from the trees," said Trent from the truck bed as the spray of the swamp water was churned up by the repulsors, obscuring his vision.

"Spinning up!" Smoker shouted. The leej barked his machine blaster from the bed of the truck with one hand while he held on to the roll bars on the top of the cab with the other. Sizzling blaster fire screamed from the barrel, and huge gouts of tree goo and ashen bark evaporated as they were torn apart by the outgoing bolts' burning kinetics.

Masters had been given one of the guns taken from the dead zhee guards. It was an old Psydon-era weapon, a far cry from the N-4X, but as long as it could drill holes at a distance, it was good enough for Masters's needs. Targeting solutions barked at him through his earpiece as the HUD in his monocle pointed out that he was off by a few degrees in his shots. Masters made the adjustment and dumped two bolts into the pursuing zhee, taking one of the hulking fighters in the chest. The algo in his headset flashed another donk moving laterally across the firing line to scoop up his teammate and drag him to a point on the hill for cover.

"I find it worrying that these donks are keeping up with us," Masters said.

"Yeah well, the zhee were out of sports sleds," Digger countered.

"Donk on the downgrade at one o'clock with a rocket launcher," Trent called out to the team.

Masters spotted the fighter immediately. The zhee was on one knee, the weapon on his shoulder, some old rocket-propelled grenade by the looks of it. But just as the zhee's hoof-like claws closed around the trigger housing, Digger slammed on the brakes. Blaster bolts coming from the bed went wild as everyone ditched their targets in favor of holding on for dear life.

The donk fired, sending the whistling, smoke-belching projectile on a mummy-bee flight across the swamp's surface where the truck should have been. It swept past the team to detonate against the opposite tree line in a chalky black explosion that splattered bits of muck and poisoned tangle all over the water.

Digger kicked the reluctant battle wagon back into full and put on more speed, making for the mountain that Masters had first come down. In the process, Masters found himself in a direct line to the RPG-firing zhee fighter.

The zhee was in a set of black fatigues with just enough of an off-colored tiger stripe to break up the outline. He also wore a civilian knock-off of an older version of hullbuster body armor, consisting of an enhanced flak jacket with a pouch for an optional plate. Judging by how the zhee was bending over his equipment to hurriedly load another rocket, he didn't have the plate.

Masters dumped a blaster bolt under the zhee's arm where the armor didn't cover. The way-overcharged bolt punched right through the fighter's thick torso and blew off its opposing arm on the other side. Meanwhile the kick sent Masters back into the seat, his hundreds of cuts screaming for relief.

The other side of the truck was facing the rest of the ambushing zhee squad, and the leejes in back unloaded a symphony of blaster fire led by Smoker as the conductor. He painted an area to suppress with the SAB, giving the other leejes breathing room to get their shots off as the coughing technical continued its ramshackle race over the muck.

"Got another squad angling from that tree line," MakRaven barked. The zhee had proven adept at following the legionnaires' slow escape vehicle by moving along the tree-studded sides of the swamp they now hovered over. Eventually, the swamp would grow wide enough that the leejes would be out of it, but not yet. "Stop the truck. Harassing fire on the new squad, kids. Other one isn't in position to hit us unless they move."

After a volley of concentrated fire laid waste to the zhee, MakRaven slapped his hand against the cab. "Time to go, Diggs!"

"On it, Sar'nt Major!" Digger slammed the truck into gear.

But they had only made it another twenty meters or so before an explosion rocked the back of the technical, dislodging the passengers from the bed and sending them tumbling into the drink. While the engine continued to drive on the front repulsors, the truck's bed sank into the swamp until the whole thing finally suffered a hacking fit and died. Masters dumped himself out of the vehicle and began treading water, remembering some of the creatures he'd seen on his trip through the swamps in what now seemed like another life.

"Repulsors blew out!" Digger shouted, alerting everyone that it wasn't the worst-case scenario; another group of donks hadn't caught up with them. Not yet.

"Sar'nt Lynx!" Sami called from the other side of the truck. The swamp was murky, mucky, but not so deep that the leejes couldn't stand up to their chests. "You dead?"

"Yup," came the terse reply. "Trent! Give me the dial on my people."

Masters flinched when Lynx stalked around the truck to stop beside him. "Can you manage on foot?"

"Yeah. Probably going to puke though, so kinda glad I don't have a bucket. I don't recommend swimming if we can avoid it."

"Walkin' won't be much easier. Mak is banged up. He came down on pieces of the truck and karked his leg. The Kimbrin is dead. I brought you his mags. Everyone else is solid."

As Masters set hit feet in the slimy swamp bottom, the other leejes were already nabbing their packs and cross-leveling gear. All except for MakRaven, whose leg armor was locked in place, forcing him to peg-leg through the drink to join Masters and Lynx.

"This leg is karked," MakRaven said. "Ain't no runnin', swimmin' or ruckin' gonna happen until I get to a Legion doc, which ain't a thing out here. So Lynx, I want you to take Sergeant Masters and E&E off swamp and to the mountain to where you can get picked up."

"Sorry, Sar'nt Major," Lynx said. "We don't leave our people. Like it or not. In charge or not. You stay, we stay."

"Yeah, rah-rah Legion. I got you, Sar'nt, but the mission comes first. Me and the dog can give what's on our heels a heaping dose of Legion real, so you have room to scoot. You take it. The gig is to get Masters to Legion command. I ain't looking to hear how you can't leave. I'm looking for you to finish this. You feel me, Leej?"

Masters knew the thoughts going through Sergeant Lynx's head. He knew what choice the sergeant was mulling over right now. And he knew the choice he himself would make.

"What are you going to do if I stay, court-martial me?" Lynx asked.

"No, I'll remind you that you have six leejes and an entire people depending on you to get back. I'll also remind you that out of this whole squad, I have the most time dealing with these bucktoothed, snot-nosed fleabags and I know a thing or two I can pull off when it comes down to the knife. Now get to stepping, Sergeant, or I will personally assume the role of your daddy and whip your defiant backside down the hill."

With a sharp nod, Lynx agreed. "Make 'em pay, Sar'nt Major Mak." Then he turned and swam for the tree line, prompting the others to follow him.

"You know they'll do something crazy and circle back or whatever to get you, Sar'nt Major," Masters said once Lynx was out of earshot.

"Not for nothin', kid, but shut up. Those boys need the old school V-Co leej that dragged himself through a Kublar desert of suck to complete the mission. Time to figure out who you want to be, son. You want to be the pretty boy suck pump who gets all the girls? Or do you want to be the terrible thing that keeps our enemies up at night? Jock up, figure it out, and get them off this mountain."

"Both isn't an option?"

"Hell, son. C'mon. I'm bein' serious."

"Roger that. And thank you for coming to get me," Masters said. "Good luck."

"Kid, I don't need luck. I have more time on a trigger than you have in a t-shirt. Now go! But before you do..." He pointed to the back of Masters's armor. "Give me that med canister. You've about drained it anyway."

"What do you want an empty med canister for?"

Mak grinned. "What else? I'm gonna rig up an IED."

# 15

Bubbles scampered up onto the roof of the truck, which hadn't submerged due to the angle the bed had sunk into the swamp. The wet dog retrieved the sergeant major's half cape and offered it like a present to MakRaven.

"Yes, that's mine, thank you. Got to rig this canister first. Donks can't help but check and see what kinda salvage they can get."

Normally MakRaven would have packed the thing with nails, nuts, and bolts, and then rig it with det-cord, but he didn't have any of that stuff. What he did have was a demo brick of plasteen explosive and some assorted tools he'd found inside the flatbed's cab. That would have to do.

He was still packing the container when Bubbles brought him the squeaky toy gasket from his ruck.

"That's gonna be one hell of a convo in the afterlife," Mak said as he took the toy and stuffed it into the end of the improvised mine to pack everything in nice and tight. "'How'd you die, mighty donk?' 'The squeaky toy got me!'"

Mak attached the device to the truck and then swam the short distance to the tree line. "Bubbles, run back that way and see if we got any more donks comin' after us. Don't try and kill 'em, but show 'em to me."

The dog bounded away in the muddy terrain that ran alongside the swampy inlet. While MakRaven waited, he pulled out his kit and arranged things in order of priority. Ammo, medical, donk evisceration supplies. He worked the gear in his pack to be accessible and mobile.

"You said never again, Mak," he muttered to himself. "Just sit in the TOC and don't go out ever again. Drink kaff and yell at the basics for uniform violations. But no, you had to go all out for a kid you didn't even know. All because he was you from twenty years ago. All because they didn't come for you when it was you."

While he worked, he used his bucket to access the feed from the dog's helmet. Two more squads of donks were advancing through the trees, perhaps three kilometers back. These would have been those who stayed in the camp after the initial attack. When the dog returned and sat at Mak's feet, Mak shut down the feed and shoved his brown cape into the dog's pack.

"All right, boy. No arguing. Take your gear and go."

The dog reluctantly backed up a step and released a sad whine.

Mak rubbed the underside of the dog's chin. "I know, boy. Now scoot."

Bubbles took the pack and disappeared among the trees, chasing after the legionnaires who had gone that way earlier.

MakRaven limped his way toward a small thicket with decent cover. He planted the kid's SAB at the top of a stump, with the PK-9 beside it. Then he waited for the zhee.

Sure enough, the first team to arrive took an immediate interest in the truck. They wore the same black uniforms and body armor that MakRaven had seen before. The lead donk stopped trudging through the swamp water to stop just in front of the floating, dead Kimbrin and thumbed the comm hanging from his armor.

"Red Two, this is Red One. We have one EKIA in the swamp. Truck abandoned. No sign of shooters."

"Roger, Red One. Moving to you now," came the call over the radio.

More zhee moved to the truck, while roughly half of the team lay down on their bellies amid the trees to cover them.

Mak waited until as many of the squad swam out to the truck as were going to. Then he detonated the improvised explosive he'd set up. The IED flash-burned the hybrid fuel cell, sent fragmentation in every direction, and pulverized the zhee squad where it didn't blow them beneath the swamp's surface. A pillar of jade flame and molten orange slag shot skyward, and the area was showered with stinking swamp and liquid metal.

One cinder went so far that it landed on Mak's back plate, but he wasn't concerned. The high-grade Legion kit would do its job. No more of that shiny tax collector garbage the old Legion had been forced to wear by the House of Reason.

Not that he'd escaped the reach of those corrupt politicians even now. This whole situation—the MCR, the donks, the weapons caches of old tech being funneled into a brushfire rebellion no one saw coming—it all stank of the House of Reason putting problems in motion before Article Nineteen. Before their own downfall.

The other zhee squad was now advancing double-time through the woods to the site of the eruption, which meant it was time for MakRaven to move again. He snatched up the SAB and his other kit and pushed himself off the stump so he could limp his way through the vegetation to his next fighting position.

As he staggered down through the moist terrain, he filtered an overlay into his HUD to check on the status of the others. Zombie Squad looked to be tracking on course for the mountain without incident. If they could get past the big open swamp, they'd have a straight shot back up the slope to where Venom Company was waiting for them. They just needed to keep their distance from the pursuing zhee.

Sergeant Major MakRaven would make sure they had it.

MakRaven pushed himself onto another berm set just above a heavy tree. The trunk seemed thick enough to stand up to a few bolts, especially those from the dialed-down PK-9s the donks were using. He deposited his gear and set his ruck behind the roots with the top open so he could pick from its contents. Sitting in the root tangle put pressure against his leg plate, and he winced. The armor had pushed a sedative and a stim, but the fire tracing along his knee and into his shin was a sure sign that something was really wrong.

From his new hide, he couldn't see the advancing zhee squad. But he did catch sight of a single donk creeping for a better vantage point.

MakRaven dialed up the power on his rifle and drilled the zhee in the head.

"Oh, that's gonna leave a mark."

Mak waited in his hide as the braying and shuffle of troops moving against a hidden attacker sorted itself out. He wasn't worried; he was nearly invisible, thanks not only to his hide but to his armor's built-in camouflage. To anyone walking by, he was just a bump on a log. Without advanced optics or residual energy-mapping software, the only way for someone to spot him was to trip over him.

The squad crept forward, cautious and alert, fanning out into a wedge and moving by teams. There was no braying or shouted insults to their juniors. This was a squad rooted in military training and discipline.

Mak waited until the last possible moment, then vented the SAB barrel into the patrol. The bolts seared the forest in staccato strobes as the donks fell in pain-racked heaps. Another fire team came up trailing, looking to get in on the fight at the sound of the blaster fire. They instead ran straight into the path of MakRaven's SAB as he turned the weapon around on them and caused the zhee to scatter behind trees or outright jump into the murky swamp water to avoid being killed.

As a precaution, Mak threw a fragger behind his position after dialing back the detonation timer so that anyone sneaking up had zero chance to react. Amid the detonation, he checked the SAB charge levels and readied himself for the next wave. It was only a matter of time now before the enemy got tired of his antics and used some truly harsh weapons on him—if they had any.

But it was also only a matter of time before the fire burning up his leg became an inferno. He already feared that if he needed to leave this spot, he'd have to crawl.

Mak sighted some of the scattered remnants of the second squad trying to flank him through the marshy woods. He laid into them with another round of the SAB, shooting out their donk legs or whatever else he could see between the branches and underbrush. The ones who didn't die outright lay braying from their graves amid the vines.

In that moment, MakRaven thought about Ankalor. There had been a young leej, the kid with the SAB, who rushed to control the street so Legion elements could make it to their objectives. It had been a suicide run, a death sentence, and everyone knew it—including the kid. But he went anyway, because he'd decided that no more of his brothers were going to die that day.

MakRaven was still thinking about that as he brought up the barrel of his own SAB to cover another position.

And then a hoof-like claw grabbed the front of his bucket.

The enemy fighter had somehow managed to come up behind him and pulled with such force that he lifted MakRaven to his feet and spun him around. The sudden jerking motion made Mak's knee scream in agony. The sergeant major looked up and saw that it was a hulking zhee, his mane oddly shaved like the others, and he was so covered with shrapnel burns that a portion of his muzzle was practically chewed away. The grenade had caught the donk, that much was clear, but not enough to put the big beast down for the count.

The zhee pressed a wicked knife to MakRaven's throat, just beneath the bucket, and was clearly on the verge of delivering the death blow... when Bubbles leapt from the brush and sank his teeth into the zhee's neck. Muscles, arteries, and windpipe were torn out in a single colossal yank. The zhee tried to bray, but only blood and gurgles escaped the thing's neck before he fell silent, dead.

Bubbles rose from his kill and forced a wave of mental calm into MakRaven, driving away the pain in his leg and giving him a new burst of energy.

"Thanks," MakRaven said. "You're a good boy. But you really gotta go now. I'll be fine. Get back to those kids so they don't do somethin' stupid like you just did."

The dog's growl signaled that something else was coming up behind them.

"I hear ya," MakRaven said. "I've got this. Now git."

Bubbles clearly didn't want to go. But the dog was a leej, and he'd been given an order. He nudged his muzzle into Mak's bucket, as if to say goodbye to his human, and held it there longer than usual. Then he sprinted away into the darkening forest.

MakRaven slapped the charging handle on the side of the SAB and sent a few bursts into the trees where however many remaining donks were looking to peek around and get some shots of their own off. Feeling lighter and stronger after whatever the dog had done, he prepared to move once again, now that this hide had been exposed.

He didn't make it two steps before something massive slammed into him.

MakRaven's vision cleared to find several zhee staring at him past the sights on their weapons.

"Another legionnaire," said a voice from behind them. "They must have gotten loose from the kennel."

This zhee was even more immense than the last. He wore robes beneath a set of oversized body armor, his mane was shaved, and he wore a kankari knife proudly on his belt.

"Take it you're the khan of this clan," MakRaven grumbled in Standard. Which meant he'd been the one to administer the thousand cuts to Masters.

The khan ignored the legionnaire, choosing instead to address its fellow zhee. He adjusted the pistol at his side and folded his hands over his girthy frame. "At least this one put up more of a fight than the last. What say we walk this one across the Bridge of Understanding in one night? None of this passing out or carrying on to keep us waiting."

"Sounds like fun, you pregnant little mare," MakRaven said in the zhee language. Not the holy tongue—that would have gotten him killed immediately—but the trade language, which might be forgiven if spoken by a non-zhee. Might be. "Why don't you find me a real man to make that happen?"

The khan surged forward in a rush that belied his size. He took Mak under the arms and lifted him so the two were eye to eye. "You speak the language well for a farm animal."

The titanic zhee leader sent his fist into Mak's belly plate hard enough to slap the armored sections together in a furious snap. Luckily the armor was designed to disperse impacts, so while MakRaven acted like he was sucking wind, he was more than fine.

"Best put your foot into it if you wanna hurt me," MakRaven grunted. "Show me the honor I deserve according to the tenets."

The khan's lips wavered, a sign of annoyance among their kind. He chuffed hard enough to blow the hair back on MakRaven's head. "What know you of the tenets of faith, dog?"

MakRaven took stock of his situation. He was surrounded by more zhee than he could even dream of taking out by hand, all of them no doubt seething over the deaths he'd just caused to their comrades and looking to extract vengeance. But despite all that, his main concern was to locate his bucket, to ensure it was broadcasting. The helmet would appear dead if anyone except another leej with the proper facial recognition or access keys were to pick it up and attempt to wear it or manipulate it, but its comms and other recording features would still work for the rest of the squad to access. Acting like he could barely keep his head upright, he lolled it around to scan the area. And there, next to the stump that had served as his cover, he saw where they'd thrown it. Maybe he could get the khan to spill something useful that the Zombie boys could relay to HQ. One last time being useful for the Legion...

He faced the khan once more. "I know that as one who is defeated by the hand of my enemy, I have certain rights that I may claim under the second pillar."

"You were defeated by one of my war hounds," the khan said with a snort. "You don't have rights when defeated by such livestock."

"If they are livestock, then you have not earned their loyalty. Do they only stay by you because you feed them? Whip them? Or are you a worthy khan after all?"

Instead of giving MakRaven the pounding he expected, the khan knelt down next to him, eyeing him curiously.

"Interesting," the khan murmured. "The way you speak... it is like the old tribesmen. The old tongue. So very few of those kind now. They challenged our thought..." Standing, he spoke forcefully once more. "But now we draw close to the time of revelations. The times of the end. And for you... the Bridge of Understanding."

As the khan turned to his men, MakRaven flicked his gaze to his bucket. Beyond it, something else caught his eye.

At their khan's command, two of the donks came forward and started stripping MakRaven of his armor, tossing the plates aside. One of them stopped short when he came across the sergeant major's knife. The kankari. Reverently, he lifted it up and carried it to his khan.

The leader took the knife and slid it from its sheath, his bulbous donk eyes looking on the wickedly curved blade with obvious appreciation.

"This is the knife a khan gives to a holy warrior," he said, his gaze never leaving the knife. "How do you have this?"

Before MakRaven could say a word, the other donk guard, who had now stripped off Mak's shirt as well as his armor, spoke. "My khan," he said. "The prisoner."

The khan looked up to see MakRaven now disrobed from the waist up, revealing a torso covered in scars. Scars in the pattern of the Death by a Thousand Cuts.

For the first time, the zhee tribal leader seemed truly caught off-guard. He took in the full measure of that rarest of creatures: one who had walked the Bridge and survived.

But MakRaven knew the khan wasn't looking *only* at his scars. He was also seeing the tattoos imprinted on top of them. From his neck to his wrists and descending into his trousers were scenes of battle and birth, revelation and punishment. And between these painstakingly painted renditions of scenes straight from the zhee holy texts were words from those same religious manuscripts.

"*How?*" the khan asked under his breath, almost to himself, and then, apparently remembering who he was, stepped forward until his foul breath was in MakRaven's face.

"You have walked the Bridge of Understanding... and lived. Such a man cannot walk the bridge again; it is forbidden. What do I do with such a man?" He shook his head. "But my curiosity outweighs my anger. How did these images come to pass?"

MakRaven looked him in his bulbous eyes. "Believe me, the story rivals anything from the legends of Siran al'Kalee. And I'll be happy to tell you all of it... if you first tell me why you and your people are *really* here on Kima. Because it ain't to assist the MCR. I can see that much."

The khan considered the offer, then spoke. "We were drawn here by the voice of the God that Speaks. It was our responsibility to wait for his call that we may take our place as servants of the gods among the stars. Even now, we march against your Legion to take them in the city."

That was a lot to take in, but MakRaven only blurted out that which sounded the most outrageous. "The God who Speaks is *here*?"

"Your friends may very well meet him when they try to escape the swamps," the khan cooed. "Now—I will have my story, Legionnaire."

"It is an incredible story," MakRaven promised. "Perhaps a prize that you would wish to keep to yourself." He looked pointedly at the khan's men.

But the zhee leader didn't take the bait. "They are free to listen as well. Tell us this great story of yours. Let it nourish our souls as we hunt down your friends." He dropped his considerable bulk on a fallen log and gestured to the ground in front of him. "Now is your remaining time, Legionnaire."

MakRaven took the gesture as permission to sit, but he remained standing, despite the fire in his leg. Most likely he had a torn tendon with a possible break somewhere around the knee.

"When I was a much younger soldier," he began, "I was the sort who would have throttled my men for not listening to me. That was before I was captured. That was before they started cutting. As the only survivor of my crew, they spent days cutting on me."

The khan nodded appreciatively. "As is the right of a leader when they capture thieves or adversaries. If the four gods have a plan for them, they'll live through the experience—and in doing so, come to a greater understanding of the four gods themselves."

"Indeed, as it's written in the third pillar," MakRaven agreed. "But it's the teachings of the fourth that most pertain to the story at hand. You know, the ones where they talk about tribal leaders and discipline when orders are ignored but a great victory is gained."

Suddenly a brilliant flash drilled the nearest guard through his skull, leaving a smoking crater out the back of his head. A second shot took out a second guard in similar fashion.

The khan grabbed his pistol, but MakRaven was already on top of him. With one hand he pushed the zhee's pistol arm behind him, and with the other he reached into the zhee's belt and recovered his old kankari. In a single motion he slashed a wickedly deep cut into the donk's arm, and the pistol fell to the ground.

More blaster fire erupted between those leejes who had come back and the remains of the khan's troops.

The khan brayed in pain and kicked MakRaven off of him. He quickly rose, defying his bulk, and pulled a kankari of his own, this one the size of a small sword. "Holy prayers on your skin! But I will find a spot on you where the last zhee missed and drive my knife in it."

"Bring it, mare."

The khan lunged at him, and MakRaven ignored the pain in his leg as he dodged. While evading a second slash that quickly followed the first, he dropped to one side and sent a flat-footed kick to the khan's knee. He felt the hard sole of his boot snapping tendons and crushing bones, but then went down himself due to the pain in his leg.

MakRaven rolled across the slick mud and took a moment to observe the battle space while the khan moaned in pain, struggling to get up on his knees. The other zhee were being slaughtered by blaster bolts from the trees. The frantic donks attempted to find cover or concealment and were picked off from every direction. Within seconds the tribal leader was the only survivor.

Legionnaires began to emerge from the trees.

MakRaven scooted behind the khan, grabbed both of the donk's ears in his hands, and wrapped his thighs around the zhee's torso to keep him from attempting a roll to get up. He pressed his kankari knife into the khan's neck so that a simple hug would drive the weapon deep and end his grip on this side of the dirt.

"Sorry about not finishin' my story," MakRaven whispered. "Now it's your turn—and I'm not buying any of that God who Speaks nonsense. If you tell us something good, you might just live through the experience... and in doing so, come to a greater understanding of the Legion."

<h1 style="text-align:center">16</h1>

Trent casually dropped into the vine-strewn terrain next to the wounded sergeant major and the khan, and Sami did the same on the opposite side.

"Hey, Sar'nt Major, I was only contracted to take care of one leej," said Trent. "This is going to put a strain on my supplies."

"Somebody is about to have a strain on something when I find out who disobeyed my order for you to bounce," Mak shot back.

Trent hitched a thumb behind him. "Above my pay grade, Sar'nt Major. Now, Sami here is going to take custody of your prisoner."

The zhee brayed. "When your man lets me go, I will kill all of you lee-jo-nayers."

"Oh, you think you're in charge, still?" said Trent, waiting a half second between sentences so his bucket could translate. "Well let me tell you what's really going on. My partner here was the senior executioner for his family in Sinasia. The knife he carries on his belt is known as *Body Wrecker* since he was so good at cutting all the way through a man. But he killed someone without permission, so the only place he could hide that was dangerous enough to protect him was the Legion. Go ahead, give that 'killing legionnaires' thing a try, mighty khan. It might be funny to see a zhee skull roll down the hill when you decide to give us trouble."

"There's a story for ya, Khan," MakRaven spat.

The khan looked from one leej to the other as if trying to decide the truth of the matter. Finally he relaxed his bulk and plunged his kankari knife into the tangle of weeds beneath him, accepting defeat.

MakRaven took Trent's hand and was hoisted up while Sami took over as the donk's custodian, leading the zhee away to Sergeant Lynx.

"All that sket true about Sami?" MakRaven asked.

"Nah. Made it up," Trent answered. He set the sergeant major down against a tree, and the dog came and sat by MakRaven's side.

"You were supposed to get them out of the swamps," MakRaven huffed to the dog. He looked up at Trent. "And *all* of you were supposed to go with him. Or are you going to pretend that wasn't a thing and just run your little scans, Corporal?"

Trent calmly connected his battle board to what was left of MakRaven's armor so the leej could see what he was doing. There was a complete tear of the ACL along with a partial tear of the MCL gumming up the rest of the knee. He had a stress fracture along the top of the fibula adding to the pain he was probably feeling with every step.

"Not ignoring you, Sar'nt Major. Like I said, all that business is way above my pay grade. Lynx was determined to come get you. He *was* going to do it alone, and put Digger in charge of marching us on Venom Company. But then Masters pulled us aside, said there was no need for Lynx to risk his life alone and that your orders didn't count because you were probably jacked up with a combination of pain meds and injury brain. Coming back for you was the logical choice."

"Ever stop to think Masters was the one that was jacked up?" MakRaven growled.

"Oh, definitely, sir. Now, we need to get the rest of your armor back on you. What is it with you pre-Arty-Nineteen leejes and shucking your shirts?"

Trent pushed more combat meds once he had MakRaven in a complete set of armor again. He watched the vitals for spikes in the readings, then helped the senior leej to his feet. As the two got some terrain under them, Digger walked up swinging a tangle of struts and straps around like he was casting a net for fish.

"I got him, Trent. Thanks," the corporal said. He fist-bumped his squad mate as Trent departed, then Digger faced the sergeant major square on.

"You got me, do you?" MakRaven said.

"Well, yeah, Sar'nt Major," Digger said. "So, I know we have this thing where you berate me and I make excuses why it's funny but Sar'nt Lynx is on the growl and I don't want to test those teeth. So let me do what I can to tighten up that fused leg armor and pump you with at least enough meds not to feel how badly you're karking yourself up by still walking on it."

MakRaven held his tongue as the medic did his work.

"There you go, sir," said Diggs as he finished up. "This'll do unless you want to go back to the truck and see if we can find that hover-stretcher that we brought for Masters, because we sure as sket can't find it anywhere else."

"I'll walk. Think we got all these kelhorns, right down to the last khan."

Digger nodded. "Speaking of which, Lynx is waiting for you along with Sergeant Masters. They wanna interrogate the prisoner."

"Is that so?" MakRaven asked. He waved the corporal on.

MakRaven snagged his bucket to avoid any more lower enlisted from telling him someone wanted him and hobbled painfully on to recover his gear from dead donks littering the hill. The one who'd taken his pistol had the weapon stuffed into his own pistol belt, gangster style.

MakRaven walked into the interrogation, nodding to the legionnaires. Masters was looking worse for wear, which was no surprise. The leej had hundreds of cuts across his torso, and the armor he now wore would be rubbing open even the ones they'd managed to seal. Mak's memory drifted to the time he was strung up himself, when he'd been stranded. "You get what you need?"

"A whole lot of weird," Masters huffed, and then scrunched his face up from some new spike of pain somewhere on his body. That the kid was even standing impressed MakRaven to no end.

"Whole lot of Living God stuff, but as far as what we were after... he's doing his best to convey no hope for a rescue party," Lynx concluded, speaking over L-comm so that only MakRaven and Masters could hear. The zhee himself could only pick up what Masters was saying, which hadn't been much. "We need to bounce."

"We do," MakRaven agreed. "But I think this L-comm-like signal we've been tracking might have something to do with all this strange behavior we're seeing out of the tribe. Khan went on a little bit about this Living God before you leejes returned against orders."

Lynx ignored the last part of the sergeant major's remark. "I think we should take this conversation on the path, Sar'nt Major. The zhee khan says he came with the last of his troops, but I'm not ready to take his word for it."

"Agreed. Let's move," MakRaven said.

MakRaven found his kit quickly being delegated to the others, each carrying a bit of his weight so he could move that much more easily during their hasty withdrawal back to friendly controlled territory. Or as hasty as he could manage. He was in no condition to run, but a dogged walk was within his capabilities.

Not so for the khan. It wasn't long before Sami reported that the prisoner had simply sat down and was refusing to move.

"You wanna handle this, Sergeant Major?" Lynx asked.

MakRaven considered for a moment, and then looked to Masters. "Nah. Dark Ops, you do it. Maybe them young ones'll learn somethin' from it."

Masters nodded once and strode to the rear where Digger and Sami stood next to the khan, who was stubbornly seated on a fallen log.

The zhee noticed Masters at once and its ears bent back in disgust. "You... you will yet finish your walk to enlightenment. The cuts will start anew."

Without word or warning, Masters pulled his sidearm and put a bolt through the donk's skull. The zhee toppled over the log and lay on his back in the mud. The Dark Ops sergeant then nodded at the two legionnaires present. "Okay. Let's go."

Looking back from his place in the column, Mak gave a slight half smile. He turned to Lynx. "Well, I suppose that's *one* lesson they've gotten from Masters."

# 17

There was little surprise among Zombie Squad that more donks were now in pursuit of them. They had reached another swamp—the great, expansive swamp that lay at the bottom of the mountain—and needed to only navigate it and then make the run up the other side to connect with Venom Company.

Smoker took a stick and began to construct his own sand table in the mud. In Zombie Squad it was common practice for the team's newest member to take the lead on operations, to draft patrol and ops plans, and to keep track of personnel and equipment. From the outside in it looked like the leaders were dumping their busy work on him. In reality, they were crafting a leader from day one.

"Okay, this is us and this is Swamp Lake. Our peepers have the donk force patrolling the opposite edge, that's the good news, at just over a platoon in strength split into two elements, that's the bad news. That's a lot of donks, seeing as we already smoked a ton getting to where we are now. Based on the manuals you guys keep making me read, that means we're probably dealing with another tribe, combat outpost, whatever."

"Why is that important?" Masters asked, playing along with the role as an NCO.

Smoker drew a box with an X through it as a symbol for an infantry unit on both sides of the swamp. "Because a different outpost could mean a different element. And if whatever training they do is done by outpost then they *might* be on different comms. And if so, we might be able to play them one against the other."

Masters liked the sound of that. "What are you recommending?"

"I'm thinking, we have Gekko slap a donk on this side of the swamp with a long-range shot or two. Make 'em think they're under attack. The shot comes from near this other donk element"—he poked his stick into the map—"so the donks start firing that way. If all goes well, that element starts firing back. By the time they figure it out, we're deep into the muck and on our way."

"This all assumes they have different comms and can't communicate," MakRaven said.

"It does, Sar'nt Major. Then again, when your buddy's brains start getting splattered, a zhee's tendency is gonna be to fight back. These donks are more disciplined than what we've seen, but they're still donks. Yeah, whatever they got for NCOs will figure it out, but not instantly. And all we need is a window to slip in deep into the swamp."

Lynx, MakRaven, and Masters all exchanged a look.

"It's not bad," said Lynx.

The rest of Zombie Squad raised their thumbs—as did Masters and MakRaven. Even Bubbles seemed to approve.

"All right, Zombies," said Lynx. "Enough dawdling. Let's get to work."

"How do I get myself into these messes?" Masters muttered to MakRaven on a private channel. The two of them, along with Zombie Squad, were setting up for the plan to get in motion, preparing to push into the swamp once they induced the zhee to fight against one another. "I'm spending R&R with a torrid Tennar, and then—*boom*—I'm in some SOG unit helping Kimbrin kill Kimbrin and then we're all getting killed and then there's zhee and this crazy little bot—thanks for grabbing him by the way. I dunno... too much adventure for one lifetime."

"I've put that same question to myself a few times," MakRaven grunted. "Different details here and there, but... I got you. And we both know why we do it. No sense pretendin'."

"No. I guess not. This shooter got the goods? Hell of a shot he's trying to make."

"He's a leej. He'll make it."

Gekko was to the furthest in the Legion line along the swamp, depressed into a split in a humongous tree. With his N-65 variable output blaster issued for the Kima operation, the hitter could punch out to extreme ranges while maintaining a low profile due to the weapon's bullpup configuration. Normally he liked to feel his way through the trigger pull with pure brainpower, but under these circumstances he thought it better to let the bucket do the work.

"Target up," he said over L-comm. "I have the shot."

"Make the shot," Lynx ordered.

Energy baffles and vibration syncs muffled his strike so that the sound of it was lost in the dank wind. The only thing detectable in the gloomy overcast night was the iridescent bolt on its way to ruin someone's evening.

Nearly a kilometer away, the bolt struck home, slamming one of the donks in the head.

The rest of the zhee squad instantly dropped to their bellies. Through thermal mode, Gekko watched the abating heat from the squad, painting the scene as white smeared outlines amid a sea of blacks and grays.

He sent a second round, but this one was intended to wound, not kill. All the same the bolt struck a zhee arm with enough force to ensure the donk would be pitching lefty for any seamball games in the foreseeable future.

"Donks are getting up," he reported. "Nine-man team, making movement into the trees for cover."

"No reaction from near squad yet," Smoker reported.

"Sending drone fire in three, two, one," said Trent.

A crack echoed off in the distance, passing through the trees so that its origin was unplaceable.

"Demo drone dusted one donk," Trent noted for the squad.

"Near squad is reacting," Smoker called over the L-comm. "Here we go."

The near squad had taken the bait. Sizzling bolts went flying, scorching trees, the black vegetation shedding a flurry of ash like black snow. The zhee squad on the far side of the swamp responded by darting to cover—trees, berms, cuts in the terrain—while the energy spears singed the terrain around them.

The friendly-fire battle had begun.

"Time to move," Masters said to the team.

They pushed makeshift rafts hidden under thick grasses into the swamp, powering them with homemade paddles, one leej driving, another on security.

Trent pushed a window into the squad display showing the zhee forces in red as the tiny blips wiped each other off the board. "Drone has far squad moving and engaging. Near squad is down to six."

Masters had his hand on Smoker's shoulder for balance as the legionnaire powered their raft through the murk. Every movement tore at the hundreds of cuts in his skin. The stims were wearing off. At any point now his vitals would call for sedatives, and the armor would respond. Nothing more interesting than getting jabbed in the middle of a firefight when you're trying to aim. But sometimes those automated medical suites had to almost kill you to save your life.

They had just reached the wide-open middle of the swamp-lake when the fighting stopped.

"Radio call just went out. The gig is up," Trent said.

"Send in the party favor," Lynx said into the L-comm.

"Yes, sir."

Trent had the drone view in his HUD and had been tracking the zhee movements. He was now focused on two of the zhee, one from each squad, probably NCOs, who had gotten together, no doubt to figure out what had happened and what to do about it now that they'd just destroyed each other's teams with friendly fire. At Trent's command, the tiny drone released what was left of the sergeant major's demo brick. The last thing it captured was the two NCOs snapping their heads upward in the direction of its humming repulsors.

The swamp and the zhee were behind them, but Masters recognized the territory they were now passing through. Another obstacle lay ahead. He warned the others.

"Around the next bend there's a cave jutting into the rock face. If there's a lit torch, we have to stop. There's something that lives there. Best to give it some respect and we'll be on our way."

"You wanna elaborate on that, Sergeant?" Lynx asked.

"Not much else I can tell you that you'll believe unless you see it. There's a thing in there... something alien. I dunno."

They came around the bend, and it was just as Masters remembered it. Outside the cave, a host of Kimbrin skulls were stacked neatly on top of each other in something like a pyramid. Another group of skulls was holding up a long-handled torch in the ground. Its flickering light cast shadows over two more skulls, much larger, hanging by a cord. Hool skulls. The same sacrificed zhee were there as before, too.

"Looks friendly," Digger said.

"Zombie," Lynx said through the net, "fan out and secure."

Gekko vanished to climb something while Sami faded to the back of the squad. Lynx, Trent, and Digger covered the cave while Smoker hugged Masters's hip. MakRaven was left to limp to the side of a broken tree where he had his rifle positioned for a quick snap to his shoulder.

A voice, deep and otherworldly, sounded from within the depths of the cave. "He has come back to paaaaaaay respect. This is good. Much tribute was paid to meeeeeee this day. Your word in your kind's aaaaaarrival was also honored. There has been much deaaaaaaath."

"We're moving on now," Masters said. "Up the mountain."

"Sar'nt Masters?" said Lynx, visibly agitated by whatever was going on. "What in the nine hells are we dealing with?"

"It speeeeeaks, yet I do not hear except for the rhythm in the choir. Long have I heeeeeard of your primitive L-comm, never have I experienced it fiiiiiiiiiirst hand."

Masters turned to Smoker. "Get Jay-Three."

"What?"

"The broken bot from the camp. Now."

Smoker transmitted the request over L-comm, and Digger appeared a moment later with the remains of J-316. Its one mechanical arm was draped over its shoulder while wires that might pass for its spine trailed from its head. Masters peeled the tape from the bot's mouth, and it immediately began speaking.

"Have we reached the *bzt* *afterlife undefined*? Oh, Masters! You are not yet calories. I am most pleased to see this."

"Listen, we're back at the cave with the... thing. Remember the cave?"

"Oh dear!"

"Right. I need you to do what you do best and get us passage up the mountain."

The bot looked as pleased as it could be of service. "Point my head to the cave, my son." Masters did as ordered, and the bot spoke. "Most reverent shaman, it is my honor to walk among your hallowed grounds again. I bring many adherents to the faith who have provided many deaths this day. We humbly request that we may pass through the grounds of our most resplendent slaughter in your name."

"Cuuuuuuurious construct," said the voice. "You are correct. My price has been met. But..."

There was a long pause, during which something in the air seemed to change, a shift in the pressure or temperature. Two glowing almond-shaped eyes glinted in the abject darkness of the cave and rapidly advanced until the shaman, a hulking brute of a thing, stopped in the cave mouth. It was twice the height of a man, with gargantuan arms covered in dense black fur that had a silvery tinge at the tips. But its head was shadowed in the hood of its great cloak, revealing nothing of the features beneath other than the two glowing red eyes.

"What is this eeeeeeeevil you bring into myyyyyyyyyyy house?"

The squad looked to each other, confused. J-316 offered a sputtering intercession on their behalf. "Honored shaman, we bring no evil with us, only the death that you demanded. And in doing so have more than paid the asking price of your passage."

The creature slammed its fists into the mud. "Betrayerrrrrrrrrs!"

It was then that Bubbles stepped forward from the trees, moving low and slow, stalking. A hatred came off the animal in waves, pushing into the leejes' minds a desire to fight, kill, and destroy what they saw before them.

The feeling was mutual. The dog was clearly the source of the shaman's ire.

"Abominaaaaaaaaaaaation!" it roared.

It shed its cloak to reveal a patchwork creature beneath. Its body was that of a giant Drusic, but its articulated feet resembled those of the moktaar, and the top half of its skull—but only the top half—was robotic, with optical sensors in place of eyes. Cables and tubes stretched from it, back into the cave, tethering it there, but as it roared in defiance, those attachments flew away as though yanked. The creature rose up on its hind quarters to show massive cybernetic strands throughout its body ending in reinforcements on its metal-infused knuckles.

Bubbles didn't even flinch. The huge dog stood his ground and deepened his growl, a growl that Masters felt in his soul. He felt duty, honor, courage, and the will to fight and die. This was the dog's truth, and he needed them, the legionnaires, to see it.

In the mired muck of a dead mountain with its blackened trees and hidden outposts full of donks who had come to the planet for war, Masters did what legionnaires do. The first round left his gun barrel with the gain turned all the way up. He burned through half a charge pack in that single shot.

But it dissipated harmlessly like rain on a speeder windscreen.

The shaman had an energy shield.

The giant ape slammed its fists down on the dirt once more. In an instant, all of the legionnaires' buckets went dead—as did their weapons and armor.

"Ion pulse!" MakRaven shouted, ripping off his helmet. He transitioned to his sidearm, dumping bolts into the beast's hide. These managed to bypass the shield and find their mark, venting gouts of blood to spray across the hanging Hool heads at the mouth of the beast's lair.

The rest of the squad followed suit, firing away at the massive titan.

But the creature's focus was still entirely on Bubbles. "You knoooooooooow not what this is!" it screamed, bringing a mighty fist down where Bubbles stood.

The dog evaded the strike and darted behind Masters and the sergeant major. Another wave of Bubbles's voodoo warfare blasted forth, invigorating the leejes and smashing against the shaman. Screaming as though caught in a web of pain, the creature gripped its cybernetic skull with its massive hands, struggling to stay upright.

"Noooooooooo! The great work must not beeeeeeeee undone! It must not be ruined! Yoooooooooou must not enter! Destroy the animal, for heeeeeeee brings death!"

It was at that moment a searing energy bolt flew from back in the trees. The quick, birdlike whistle that followed told the squad that though Gekko was out of range of the shaman's EMP, the shaman wasn't out of range of Gekko.

The shaman fell to the muddy ground, not dead yet, but badly, perhaps mortally, wounded. It began a desperate crawl back toward the cave, each labored handful of mud-soaked vines bringing it inches closer to whatever refuge it thought to find there.

"Must reconnect tooooo the Oracle. Must fiiiiiiiiii-ind the path to the abominaaaaaation. Oversight in the plaaaaaaan."

By now the squad's buckets and weapons were finishing their recycling procedure after the EMP strike. HUDs and L-comm were winking back on. The shaman was entirely at their mercy.

Digger looked to Lynx. "Kill it?"

Before anyone could respond, another blaster bolt shot forth from the trees, and not from the direction of Gekko. It struck Smoker directly in his chest plate, splashing him back into the mud. Smoker swung his feet to knock Masters down and out of the line of fire. "Donks at the edge of the swamp!"

Retooled weapons came to life, returning fire at the zhee assault force that had quietly come up on Zombie Squad. The leejes broke into the trees for cover, dropping heavy doses of outgoing bolts, illuminating the forest in a deadly light show.

Smoker rolled to his knees. "Going hot!" The SAB cleared its throat, singing out an aria of destruction over the donk forces advancing at them.

But that wasn't the only advancing zhee force. A bolt glancing off Digger's armor alerted him to another. "Angry customers advancing on our three o'clock!" he shouted over L-comm.

The corporal returned fire, each trigger tap contributing to a steady stream of single shots that halted the momentum of the flanking zhee. They returned fire to suppress him, but he dusted any donk that got too cocky.

When Sami came over the squad net to report yet another zhee force approaching, Smoker shook his head. "Where are they all coming from?"

"Gotta be more outposts around the mountain and surrounding areas," said Masters. "Only thing that makes sense."

"Enough of this, men," snapped MakRaven. "Everyone into the cave."

"What do you have in mind?" Lynx asked.

MakRaven keyed the L-comm. "Going to call a friend for takeout."

MakRaven broke the radio silence they'd held for the last few days. "Butcher, it's Mak."

The Venom Company CO ripped into the comms. "Sergeant Major! What in hell's bells you got going on over there? Whole damn swamp just lit up like Victory Day."

"We're in a bit of a bind, Major. Zhee element encountered. They didn't send all their soldiers to the city. Request fire mission, over."

"Oh, you beautiful bastard. Send it."

MakRaven barked his coordinates into the comm, confirming the transmission burst to avoid any equipment failure. In the background, he could hear the fire support NCO repeating commands and adjusting his team on the guns.

"This is a danger-close mission," Mak said. "I say again, this will be danger close. Butcher, we have custody of mission critical intelligence relevant to the Legion mission on Kima. Deploy recovery, science, and intelligence teams on LOC. How copy!"

"Good copy, stand by."

Mak had switched back to his N-4X and placed several shots into the advancing donks, but they were everywhere now, using cover and concealment and maximizing their use of terrain as they dodged the ferocity of the Legion blasters. Fire teams broke off to absorb Zombie Squad's bolts as other zhee set up gun emplacements with old SABs. MakRaven recorded it all and simulcast everything to Masters and Lynx, who were themselves recording. This was a trained, disciplined zhee force, very unlike any donks they had fought before. That was additional intel that needed to get back to command, although if fighting was already happening in the city, it was likely they already knew.

Sami ran by the sergeant major, slapping him on the back plate. "Last man!"

MakRaven collapsed on the cave entrance, moving from cover to cover as the leejes on his non-firing side put waves of suppression fire through the trees. An incoming bolt struck him in the hip, spinning him around. Before he could resume his sprint, the high-cycle fire of a SAB spun up, pouring its frenetic fire into the space between Mak and the cave entrance, blocking that avenue of retreat. The shaman, still crawling toward its lair, absorbed the punishment of untold bolts.

Mak shot two more donks, one the assistant machine gunner on the position giving him trouble, and shouted, "Give me that AP!"

"Sending!" said Digger. He tossed the aero-precision launcher in a high lazy arc that ended in the sergeant major's waiting grip.

Mak darted farther into the forest to get a better covered shooting position against the donk advance. He fired the missile, splattering a twenty-meter swath of the incoming force. The practiced members of Zombie Squad loosed bolts around him to keep the enemy on that side from getting any aimed shots off. But the zhee were too numerous. An entire blaster fire tornado was trying to claim the space around Sergeant Major MakRaven, and one lucky bolt found its way past his armor and into the soft synthprene around his neck.

The pain was a fire that stopped his breathing even as the force of the impact knocked him off his feet and into the muddy slick. He hit hard and felt a warm spray of blood down the inside of his armor. He tried to stand back up and found that he couldn't; his body wouldn't listen.

Smoker roared and advanced, venting so much SAB fire into the trees that he practically cut down the forest, his weapon an energy chainsaw in the night air against the braying shadows looking to end them.

MakRaven leveraged a tree stump to try to push himself up. His feet scraped feebly in the soft mud. He had to get back to the cave.

The L-comm buzzed to life.

"Mak, it's Butcher! We're dialed in, need a set of eyes for the shots!"

A sudden clarity, focused only on the mission, took over MakRaven's mind. "Send it," he gargled through a throatful of blood.

The sergeant major struggled to a kneeling supported firing position and vented his magazine across the battlespace, killing a donk fighter with every trigger pull. They were reorganizing after the RPG blast, pulling their dead and wounded back while they cleared a path for the next wave.

Another bolt punched MakRaven in the chest plate, sending him once more into the mud.

"Mak, it's Butcher. Shot over."

"Shot... out," the leej growled in response, his voice sounding wet and raspy to his ears. After confirming the round had splashed into the hill only a short distance away, shattering several fire teams, MakRaven barked once more into the net.

"Fire... for... effect."

Masters felt his stomach drop as MakRaven's head slumped into the mud. "No!" He went to run from the cave, but was halted by Digger, who pushed him up against the wall.

But there was no stopping Bubbles. The dog bounded from the cave, locked his jaws around his handler's leg, and pulled. Jerk by jerk, heave by heave, the great voodoo dog backed closer to the mouth of the cave, his precious cargo in tow.

And then he stopped, and every leej in the area felt a sudden wave of overwhelming and all-encompassing pain. A defiant yet pitiful yelp explained why.

Bubbles lay in the mud, a smoking hole in his side.

The Legion responded.

Smoker led the explosion of outgoing fire, pouring a swarm of blaster bolts into the donks trying to make their way through the trees. The riflemen came next, putting precision shots into any target not smart enough to abandon the open air against Legion shooters hunting for bear. Trent launched drones, each carrying a micro-fragger.

And Masters ran out to grab the drag handles on Mak and Bubbles.

If not for the slick mud, there was no way he'd have been able to move them, even with the adrenaline coursing through his system. But he dug in his heels and they slid, the effort opening cuts all across his torso, sending waves of searing agony through him. When he heard the first whistles of incoming indirect fire, he clenched his teeth and cried out, "Get deep in it!"

The first several rounds pummeled the hillside, sending explosive geysers of sod into the air along with fragmented donk bodies. The next few rounds deforested everything the leejes could see, creating what felt like an earthquake beneath their boots. Sami joined Masters in getting their two downed members to the cover of the cave, and once they had them inside they used their own bodies to shield their charges as rock tumbled down from above. Still more rock crashed down from just outside the entrance, an artillery-induced landslide that blocked out almost all the light from outside the cave.

Ultrabeams came on all around, and as the dust settled, the leejes saw that the cave had been sealed by the avalanche. And just a few meters ahead of them, trapped beneath the wall of rock, was the titanic gorilla monster known to them only as the shaman. Its body below the torso was buried, no doubt crushed, but its head and one arm were still free.

"I have seen the deeeeeeath of the world give birth to life in the staaaaaars," it wheezed. "I have long awaited to seeeeeeee my mission fulfilled."

The shaman pulled the metallic plate from the top of its head, revealing pale and shriveled biological skin beneath. The fur that had probably once been there was long gone, and metal attaching pins were in its place. But its eyes, real eyes, remained. They were soulful, like the deep brown and searching eyes of the old mystics on worlds in the Surawu Nebula, where the strange hermits ponder the meaning of the galaxy.

"You are haaaaaaaarbinger. You are deeeeeeaaath."

It wheezed once more, then fell still.

Masters turned from the surreal scene to attend to MakRaven. But Trent was already there, kneeling next to the sergeant major, battle board in hand. Trent looked up at Masters and gulped hard enough that the rest of the team heard it through the L-comm.

"He's... Sir, he didn't make it."

The pain assaulting Masters's cuts was replaced by a cold numbness. He willed for the leej to move, to twitch, to do anything to prove that a grizzled old agro-bear like MakRaven couldn't be put down by mere blasters.

But he could. Anyone could. Even MakRaven.

Masters gave himself a moment, then transitioned back into the command net on the L-comm.

"Butcher, this is Masters. We read you."

"Masters! Holy sket, your papa leej is going to blow his bucket when he hears your voice."

"Yes, sir. Butcher, we're in a cave on your fire mission coordinates and we're buried. Cave-in from the shelling."

"Roger that. We'll get some engineers in there to pull you out. Tell MakRaven he owes me a beer for laying the hate all over that mountain."

"Can't do that, sir. Sergeant major is KIA, sir. Died calling in the strike."

A long and somber silence followed before the Venom Company CO returned to the line. "Stay safe in there, Master Sergeant. We're coming."

# 18

It was Jack who first crawled his way out a thick tangle of high, sharp-bladed grass at the bank of a swampy pool and into the open. The grass had been so tall and tightly packed, he couldn't see what was on the other side. But that was where the team had been directed and so he crawled until his head and shoulders emerged from the last of the vegetation and came out looking straight at a squad of legionnaires looking right at him.

"Sket." Jack held up his hands in surrender and pushed himself up from the ground and onto his knees. "Don't shoot, fellas." It didn't pay to take any chances when it came to the Legion. They didn't miss, and Jack had found that KTF was a mantra that could be taken so literally that some might dust you before you had a chance to explain yourself. He'd heard stories. Back in the navy. That was—apparently—a thing that happened.

But these legionnaires paid Jack no mind. They continued some vigil, looking through him as though he wasn't even there. Cautiously, Jack rose to one knee and then waved his hand before their faces. None of them moved.

Jack went to his comm to inform the others of what he'd stumbled upon. Makaffie was quick with questions.

"No," Jack answered. "They're not moving at all. Think they're frozen in place. No, I ain't gonna touch them. You come over here and touch them if you want to so bad."

Shortly there was a rustling through the grass as Makaffie powered his slim frame to Jack's location and then popped up over the blades of grass like a ground-monk emerging from its hole. "Hey!" he practically shouted, but the legionnaires still didn't move. "Hey! You know legionnaires are just basics too slow and stupid to duck so they gotta wear armor, right?"

Makaffie turned to Jack. "Well, if that didn't get them up, nothing will." He then went to his comm and reported, "We found where the Savvies want us. Looks like we are, indeed, meant to ambush the zhee."

One by one members of both strike teams emerged from their wide and staggered trail. They had been moving on their stomachs, powered by elbows and knees which were stained dark and wet like their hands. This might all have been some illusion plastered over the metal deck grates, but that wasn't how it felt. Not at all.

"Sarai says she's not detecting any other life forms," Nilo informed the others.

Every update from Sarai since her first appearance had come through Nilo, despite the initial promise he'd made to Keel to loop him in on his comms. Keel understood the chain of command, but still, he found himself second-guessing Nilo after hearing Makaffie's sometimes coherent monologue.

"I thought you said we wouldn't know what side we're on until someone started shooting at us," Zora reminded Makaffie.

"Well, that's true. But it's not always true. Sometimes the ship sets the stage for us. Gives us a little glimpse of what happened before the conflict began. Maybe they think it'll be useful? I don't know. I *do* know that when the enemy shows up, the shooting starts. These aren't shooting."

Jack looked at the statuesque legionnaires. "They aren't saying anything, either."

"No. No they are not."

Keel studied the unit patches painted on the sides of the legionnaires' shoulder armor: a gloved hand coming up from the grave.

"You recognize that?" Jack asked him.

"No." Keel pointed to the symbol. "It's a squad designation, but it should also say what Legion designation they're in, right beneath it."

"Maybe they didn't capture every detail in the original," Zora suggested.

"Or maybe they're only showing us what they want us to see," said Makaffie. "I don't trust them."

Keel gave a slight frown. "Not saying *I* do, but *you're* the guy who brought us here."

Makaffie shrugged.

"DTA," Jack said. "Don't trust anybody. Easier that way."

"Especially if it's something Savage," Nilo added. "Now, if we're supposed to set up here, we'd better get to it."

"Yeah," said Keel. He took his team and put them in position and then oversaw Team Two's positioning as well.

As he moved through the site, he saw more legionnaires. Only they weren't acting Legion. Men who should be on security detail were instead lying about or lazing through camp. Those who were up and had their rifles were almost always talking to a buddy—or at least the simulation had them frozen in such a manner. There were no forward listening or observation posts he could see. Many of them slept. At least seven in the larger camp away from where they'd discovered the first legionnaires sat over a small cooking fire, charring an unidentifiable hunk of meat. It was odd to see such a lack of discipline, and Keel wondered if these legionnaires were under the command of a point.

Zora caught up with him. "You look like you're seeing something you don't like," she said. "And don't say it's me. That joke got old years ago." She crossed her arms and let her hands rest on top of her blaster rifle. Her helmet was pushed up on her head so Keel could see her lips and hear her voice without the need of a comm connection.

Keel didn't smile, although he *did* think the joke was still funny. "Just getting a strange feeling about all this."

"Really? Walking through a Savage ship is giving you a strange feeling. Huh." When Keel didn't answer, Zora got serious. "I know what you mean. I expected the shooting to start by now given what Mak told us. You think they weren't quite ready for us?"

"Could be. That Archimedes thing told us to leave. This all seems thrown together. But that's not the only thing. Look at these legionnaires. That how your dad told you things were done?"

"Oba, no."

"Exactly. None of this seems right. Cooking over an open fire when rapid heat tabs are still in their mess kits. Lying out in the open like it's a Sumerian siesta. Not even the worst of the legionnaires out there—points working for points, rogue units, outlaws—not even *they* would be this sloppy."

And Keel knew. He'd seen the worst the Legion had to offer while working for Dark Ops as an ersatz smuggler. In that hazy time before he became a real smuggler and started working for himself, no longer expecting Dark Ops to ever call him back in.

And Zora knew how things *should* be. Her father had made a career of the Legion, including a long stint in Dark Ops. He'd bestowed what was sometimes called "KTF culture" on his daughter, and so the truth of what Keel was saying was obvious to her.

"You're right," she said. "I didn't notice at first because it's all been so strange here, but you're right. This is definitely… off."

"Call it a glitch in the simulation," Jack said as he sauntered up to join them. "Teams are all set and I got your kitty-cat friend set up and watching a sector, too. Thought I'd come by and see if you two were going to join our little ambush party or not."

"We're coming," Keel confirmed. "Just checking out the rest of the place."

"That was supposed to be Team Two's job," Jack said with a smile.

"Well I don't trust Team Two to do it right."

Jack's smile deepened. "DTA. You never know. I don't trust 'em either, but did you hear what they found over in the eastern portion of the camp?" Keel had not. "Come on, I'll show you. Then we can dig in and dust some donks."

They followed Jack through the camp, passing more snoring legionnaires, including one who had apparently just finished a bottle of Tabrizi rye all by himself. Jack led them to a prisoner, a solitary zhee who was stripped as naked as those creatures could be and bound by its wrists and ankles. Its legs were spread wide apart while it lay prostrate over a large stump, and it was bleedingly profusely from a great number of cuts all across its body. A legionnaire stood menacingly over it with an N9 combat knife in his gloved hand. Two more stood behind, pulling security. All were frozen in place. The knife the first legionnaire held was thick with blood and at its sharp point hung a swollen red drip that defied gravity and refused to drop to the mushy ground.

"Whatcha make of that?" Jack asked. "Some kind of new interrogation method? 'Cause that's not anything I've ever seen leejes do. These must be some of old Keller's disciples. Real donk killers."

Keel frowned. Flagrant violations of discipline all throughout the camp, and now this? This wasn't the way things were done. That didn't mean things *didn't* get done that way sometimes when men were frustrated and command was far away and... things happened. So maybe that's what this was. A platoon that had gone rogue. Stuck on some backwater edge world and the NCOs decided they'd had enough of life with a point and that blowing it all up was a better option than taking another step under the officer's command. Better to go pirate and face the firing squad when it all ended. Discipline didn't usually last long when that step was taken.

"Maybe they're Nether Ops," Zora suggested.

Keel didn't think so for a variety of reasons, but he didn't have a chance to explain. The drop of blood clinging to the end of the knife suddenly grew free of its stasis and splashed down to the ground. The frozen scene was suddenly reanimated and brought to life.

It began with a wailing howl from the tortured zhee, which trailed off into a painful moan. Zora called in a status report in case things going live escaped the others. Both teams were to stay in their sectors and on alert.

The legionnaires were moving now. The two guards chuckled over their external comm speakers while the one with the knife delivered a light, almost gentle cut to the zhee, separating skin with such delicate precision that only the sudden seeping of blood betrayed any cut at all.

None of the leejes paid any mind to Keel or the others as they went about their cruel business. The visitors hurried back to rejoin their teams and take up positions.

"Hell of a way to start the show," Keel said to Makaffie as he slid down into his firing position and watched his sector.

The scrawny man had removed his helmet again. "Oh, it'll still pick up some yet."

Keel's sector faced the direction they expected those first zhee scouts to arrive from based on their last known positions. And he didn't have to wait long for them to appear. The first scouts slowly crept through the dank surroundings, their equine-like legs causing only a slight swish in the brackish swamp water. Keel might have written the sound off as caused by a water snake had he not been watching the intruders.

Soon, some of the Black Leaf mercs would have these three in their ambush sights. They had already readied themselves to fire when Sarai's voice came over the comm.

"Do not engage the lead elements. They are not biological entities and you will only give away your position."

The Black Leaf team considered this the very word of Nilo, and immediately lowered their weapons.

That was all fine and well, but Keel wondered where the *actual* hostiles were in that case.

The answer to his unspoken question flashed across his HUD. A gathering of hostile dots indicating foreign life forms.

A fight was coming.

# 19

Allowing the zhee infiltrators into the midst of the slovenly Legion camp was a risk that didn't sit easily in any of the strike team members' stomachs. Nilo might have been the only exception; his confidence in Sarai was unshakable. It proved well founded. As the three scouts moved ahead, they paid no attention to Keel or any of the others, though they were certainly close enough to see them.

After a few more moments, those scouts opened fire on the Legion camp, sending legionnaires scrambling for rifles in a drunken stupor. The battle began with the artificial elements taking the first shots.

Soon though, true matters of life and death were underway. The dots Sarai had marked as living and hostile were pushing their way ever closer, attempting to flank the confused legionnaires on both sides. Given the state and condition of the camp, they could have hit all at once, but perhaps they simply didn't know how bad things inside the camp were. Certainly no one in the strike teams would have expected legionnaires to be so ill prepared as this. Why would the zhee?

Pikkek's battle rifle barked and claimed the first kill of the engagement. It fired bolts, but it didn't sound like a blaster to Keel's ear. More like a mix of blaster and slug thrower. The result was devastating. The unwitting zhee had its chest blown out, and the round continued right on through and shattered the muzzle of the next zhee behind it, prompting braying alarms among the flanking patrol.

That was a little sooner than Keel would have liked it, but, for a koob, Pikkek had kept his cool in springing the ambush. Back on Kublar, the loyal koob elements could be counted on to start an ambush a hundred meters out. It got so bad that they finally had to wait until a few moments before an ambush began to give the indigs their weapons.

With the first shots fired, the rest of the teams in position opened up as well. The zhee up front scrambled while those farther back came up and returned fire. A Black Leaf merc was hit in the shoulder, his armor sending up a shower of energy sparks as the blaster bolt spent all its energy on it. The merc went down below the reeds.

Makaffie was not shooting, but instead worked the comms, reminding both teams that the mission was only over when the simulation ended. "Keep killing until the fog comes. Look for targets if you can't see any. Just don't let up now that we've begun."

Keel found a zhee in his sector at last, but held his fire based on the HUD readout. It was one of the "fake" ones Sarai hadn't identified as organic. He should be seeing more of the real ones right now and could only conclude that the infiltrators had pushed around during the ambush to get around Keel from another angle. Surely the objective was the defense of this sorry Legion camp.

Jack was watching Keel, and it was obvious that both minds had reached the same conclusion.

"Stay here and watch the sector," Keel said, getting up with a pistol in each hand. "Skrizz!"

The wobanki appeared almost at once at Keel's side, arriving by a great leap and landing quietly.

"You and I are gonna cut back through the camp and get any donks that slipped the noose before they can get inside. Ready?"

Skrizz yelped an excited confirmation. "*Tenchu monka clava blasteroo.*"

Blasters at range were fine but getting the chance to use tooth and claw... much better.

Leaving it to Jack to shift positions so the strike teams could again have coverage, Keel and Skrizz got moving. The dots that had populated the HUD were all gone now, and Keel wasn't sure if that meant they got the first wave or if Sarai had been cut off.

"I'm not sure either," Nilo said. "Working on it."

Skrizz and Keel came across dead legionnaires at the edge of the camp. The three zhee scouts they'd let pass were also dead. The leejes inside the camp were now busy springing to defensive positions, and though some staggered, and a few stumbled and fell, others moved with capable competence. Four of them formed a squad and moved out to face the enemy, no doubt looking to hit them while still in the confusing thickness of the swamp that would hide their movements. Once the zhee reached the clearing... it would be a shooting gallery. Those types of fights were usually won by whoever had the most guns—or whoever started shooting first.

As Keel hurried through, he caught a glimpse of a zhee pushing a repeating blaster through the notch in a tree that split into a 'V'. The donk was going to use it as a shooting platform and would be able to devastate the inner camp once he set up. Keel sent a round from his slug thrower through the donk's baleful left eye and saw the leaves behind it rattle from the sudden splash of gore. The zhee pitched forward and felt into the wedge bleeding, sending the light repeater barrel tumbling into the mud.

Another zhee emerged from around the tree. Keel used the Intec in his right hand to send a bolt into its chest. This time the bolt passed through as though striking a hologram, but the zhee pitched forward and died all the same.

Keel shook his head, unable to make sense of what was real and what wasn't. The first zhee had died about the way he'd expected it to. The second... he wasn't sure. Keel had seen enough battlefield deaths to know that people didn't always go down the way you anticipated. Blaster bolts *could* shoot straight through someone that cleanly, but it was unusual.

Skrizz also seemed put off by the way things were happening. The wobanki looked agitated and let out a low growl of distrust. Skrizz's nostrils opened wide and took in the air, scenting in the direction of the zhee. Then he left Keel's side in a flash and raced with uncommon speed into the jungle.

"Hey!" Keel took off after him, not wanting to get split up even if it meant abandoning the route they'd been taking. But as he moved, he spotted that small but capable-looking squad of legionnaires as they pushed outside the camp and directly toward a crossfire set up by two separate zhee elements.

The attack took the squad by surprise. The lead element went down in a hurry while the other three threw themselves to the ground to avoid being hit. One was struck in the leg upon landing and pulled the limb in close, trying to remove it from the enemy's sights. A steady stream of fire filled the lane they'd traveled down only seconds before, pinning them to the trees and vegetation, unable to advance or retreat. They returned fire and might've hit one of the zhee attackers who was repositioning. Still, things wouldn't end well for the legionnaires without additional fire support.

Keel could be just that... but then there was Skrizz. He didn't want to leave him. And yet, the whole purpose of this artificial hell was to win whatever battle was laid out before them. Here were legionnaires pinned down, and once fallen, their bodies would likely be stepped over on the way to routing the camp.

Keel made up his mind. He would take care of the leejes and trust Skrizz to take care of himself in the jungle. After all, the wobanki was in his element. He was probably the most dangerous thing out there right now given his natural abilities and the swamp's difficult terrain and excellent concealment.

One group of zhee moved, screened by saplings and other leafy underbrush that had built up on the banks around the swamps. They were moving to flank the pinned-down legionnaires while another team of zhee stayed behind and put down a torrent of suppressive fire. These were set up behind thick trees, wading through the murk up to their hairy shins. The cover was excellent, as was the concealment, but Keel could still see three distinct muzzle flashes. He might be able to drop at least one of them just from that, but to do so would risk revealing himself before all were in a position to be eliminated.

The better play was to move to intercept the flankers, eliminate them, and then roll back on the team laying down the suppressive fire. Keel moved out to do so—only to find himself stepping almost directly into the lead zhee as it emerged from the brush ready to flank and kill the legionnaires.

Keel threw an elbow into the zhee's snout, but his new merc armor was lighter than what Wraith or Tyrus Rechs wore and didn't pack the same punch. The blow landed with a crunch and got the blood pouring out of the nostrils, but the donk didn't buckle and fall. Instead it attempted to bring its carbine around in close quarters and shoot at Keel point-blank.

The former legionnaire swatted the weapon to the side, and it discharged wide of the mark, the bolt cooking the muck and sending up a foul odor. With his Intec in his right hand, Keel brought the weapon in close in an attempt to blast the donk's chest. The zhee brayed and reared back its head, then slammed it down atop Keel's bucket.

Whatever Zora might say, Aeson Keel's hardheadedness was no match for a zhee's.

An explosion of stars pushed their way through Keel's bucket and danced before his eyes; he was sure the helmet must be cracked right down the middle. He staggered, but didn't lose much ground, and the zhee reared its head for another blow as those behind it attempted to move around the point man to help.

Keel thrust his palm upward and caught the donk beneath its chin, driving the head back and holding it there long enough to bring his Intec up. By this time the zhee was chomping its teeth and biting down on Keel's fingers through combat gloves. Keel growled in pain as he put a blaster bolt through the bottom of the zhee's skull and out through the top. The mouth went slack and the donk crumbled in a heap, providing a sudden and clear sight picture for the other two zhee who had come up behind it.

Keel sent a pair of blaster bolts into the chest of the donk on his right, followed by a third between its eyes. It staggered back and tipped over in death. The third donk, blood-crazed over the prospect of up-close killing, swung its rifle like a club into Keel's side. Keel caught the weapon, locked it beneath his armpit, and then swung the butt of his blaster pistol into the zhee, obliterating its eye and fracturing the large orbital bone with a second strike. The zhee instinctively raised an arm to block a third blow that wasn't coming. Instead Keel kicked the murderous donk in the stomach, sending it stumbling backward. A single shot—the last one to his charge pack—was all Keel needed. The bolt zipped through the zhee's head, and Keel had already released the spent charge pack to the ground by the time the donk hit the ground.

Feeling that there was no time to reload, he holstered the primary while drawing his secondary with his left hand. He could shoot equally well with either hand and moved again, keeping a mental tally of when he might be able to change packs on the blaster pistol and dual wield, but also expecting the zhee who had been suppressing the legionnaires to be on him at any moment. They wouldn't have heard the deaths of their comrades over the din of their own fire, but the fact that the legionnaires they were pinning down hadn't yet been killed would soon clue them in that something was wrong.

Keel would have to move quickly. He wanted to get to the zhee while those heavy guns were still shooting away from him.

He found the donks but hesitated, fearing that Team Two might be behind them. The HUD said otherwise, but when Keel had left, that's where they were. The last thing he wanted was to send an errant shot past the zhee and into allies. He waited for Nilo to report back that the HUD was correct and Team Two had moved on to engage other zhee before he pushed forward.

The sound of the zhee's weapons fire grew louder and louder, and Keel was able to walk right up to the first one, who lay prone and transfixed on a thermal scope while sending a steady stream of light repeater fire. Without breaking stride, Wraith stepped over the zhee and sent a round from the slug thrower through the top of its head, taking it and the weapon out of the fight.

The other zhee noticed the loss of the repeater—the soundscape was immediately and noticeably changed without it. These zhee hadn't mindlessly been holding down their triggers and going cyclic; their guns were talking and keeping up a constant stream of suppressive fire that was greater in length and intensity than what would have been possible by simply dumping and hoping their flankers arrived before their expansive charge packs went empty. This sort of tactical fighting was uncommon to the zhee, but Keel was too busy to take note of it. He continued on his destructive path, making his way to the second zhee, who was shooting from a kneeling position. In between shots, it brayed a question toward the dead gunner, but kept its eyes on its targets. It must have noticed Keel out of the corner of those large eyes, however, for it bellowed an alarm and swung its heavy SAB in Keel's direction. But the shooter was struck with two rounds to the head and neck before the barrel got the halfway point of its intended arc.

There remained no doubt in the last zhee's mind that something was wrong. Its firing on the legionnaires stopped, and its rounds were sent skipping toward Wraith instead. The early shots were close but a little over his head, but the adjustment would get him if he didn't drop down to the mud. So he did, and just in the nick of time. Several bolts sizzled the air right where his body had just been—hot, thick bolts indicating that the zhee shooter had dialed up the charge for maximum damage at the expense of additional shots.

Keel crawled forward on his belly, which brought to mind memories of Legion selection and moving through pools of blood and flesh and entrails, elbows digging into the grisly mud as sentry bots fired training bolts that felt *exactly* like being hit by the real thing.

The bolts overhead were racing by so close that Keel thought he could feel their heat on the back of his head and neck. Worse still, the damage that previous zhee's headbutt had done to his bucket prevented the helmet from sitting properly on his head. It felt as though the straps were trying to pull the ruined thing apart over the top of his skull, and more than a few times it slipped down and covered his forward vision.

He had to push his chin right down into the soft and giving ground as the zhee attempted to adjust its fire even lower, striking a rise ahead of him that sent up blooms of stinking, sizzling mud. Some shots skimmed the surface of that rise and might have singed the hair on Keel's head; he was certain they would have hit him were his face not buried in the muck.

Suddenly the blaster's steady cadence went silent. A change of packs was Keel's first impression, but the terrified, pain-filled screams of the braying donk soon revealed the truth of the matter. Keel could have figured out what was happening just by those, even had he not heard a wobanki's terrifying growl of bloodlust and hate a moment later.

It all happened so quickly that by the time Keel pushed himself up and out of the mud, Skrizz was already lifting himself off of the gutted and bloody mess than had been the shooter. The donk's stomach and throat were torn open, and Skrizz's claws, wet from the disemboweling, dripped fresh, dark blood. The wobanki saw Keel and gave what passed for a smile for that species. To Keel it was the grinning visage of a demon, fangs pink with blood and gore.

But a useful demon to have around.

Everywhere at once the shooting ceased. The mist billowed and rolled again, gathering thickly around their ankles and seeming to draw the room into darkness. The steamy physical sensations of the swamp ceased. The air grew cold and the mist sat thick below them as though they stood on top of a cloud.

The room was empty once more. They were alone in the darkness.

# 20

The arcade pulsed with light and noise and generated an energy through the thick pack of bystanders crowding around Crometheus and his Eternals as they competed in the championship tournament—at long last. Somewhere across the great expanse of the Pacific Ocean, a team of Japanese rivals, young men such as themselves whom they would likely never meet, must be experiencing their own giddy, nerve-wracking, and oppressive atmosphere in their own arcade. Because surely it was just as packed over there as it was in here. The tournament was too big, the game too important.

Crometheus wanted to take off his black leather jacket. He could feel the hot sweat it produced as it dripped and pooled in the pit of his elbows beneath lean biceps, down his back, and especially, in his armpits. The jacket looked great, but right now it felt miserable.

Discomforting warmth like that was a problem. As Crometheus's neck grew hot and sweaty, his forehead did the same and began to unleash tiny beads of perspiration down his face into his eyebrows. The air conditioning the old man who ran the arcade was so proud of... it couldn't compete. Not with so many bodies packing every square foot of the place.

And every swipe of his forehead was a moment that took Crometheus's hands dangerously far away from the controls. He had already changed his gaming stance so that he played with arms straight, almost rigid. That stopped the sweat from building little pools in the crooks of his arms, but now he could feel the warm, salty water running down his arms and collecting at his wrists where it would drip from the sleeve of his jacket, sometimes to the floor and sometimes on the surface of the arcade machine itself.

His left hand went up and wiped more sweat from his brow, producing a slick smear on the sleeve of his leather jacket, its metal studs gently but uncomfortably exfoliating.

He should've just worn a headband like Julius. But then, Julius could make a headband work where it sat beneath an LA Raiders cap. That quasi-Compton rap look didn't work for Crometheus. Not his style. Not even Julius's style, really. It was pretend, something his father on the police force wouldn't have stood for had he seen it. On days away from the arcade, Julius was in polo shirts and slacks. Always.

With no opportunity to remove the hot and increasingly heavy jacket—for such would require that Crometheus die, and he couldn't afford that right now—the leader of the Eternals looked for other quick ways to cool himself. All he could really find time for besides wiping away the sweat on his brow was to take a quick tug at the front of his Hüsker Dü t-shirt and deliver a fresh bellows' worth of air down his sticky chest.

"Guys, no need to thank me all at once," Jazz called over the booming speakers which relayed the sounds of the ferocious video battle instead of the usual playlist of

INXS, Tiffany, and Def Leppard. "...but I just unlocked an intel dump from Maestro for the swamp."

Crometheus felt a sudden wave of frustration rise and match the heat of his body. "What's even the point?"

That battle had been a while ago... and it had been lost.

He rolled his zhee mercenary across an empty doorway and saw, in the next room, a squad of legionnaires who had just breached the very building he had just finished clearing of Kimbrin. He could jump out of a window now, maybe toss one of his remaining fraggers, and hope to take one of the ridiculously overpowered soldiers out. That would keep his streak—and him—alive.

But escaping would also take away the opportunity for another big kill streak. The legionnaires were operating in squads of eight. That many more kills, if done quickly, would put him on top of the leaderboard. Jazz held that position now, and Crometheus desperately wanted to take him down. Jazz being on top... that wasn't natural. Maybe if it was Julius, but not Jazz.

Julius excelled whenever he got to play a high-damager, high-durability class like the Cybar warriors a couple of days ago. He'd cruised to a first-place finish then. But Crometheus was the better overall player, no matter the class. He was always in the hunt for the top spot and when he didn't have it, he was second.

Except for today. Today, he was third.

Third!

It had been all Jazz so far. The junior Eternal liked to play a sneaky style. He was big on stealth and camping in one spot, patiently getting what kills the game offered and dying infrequently. Most times, he stayed put for too long and his score-per-minute suffered. But he killed more than he got tagged and was a net benefit to the team so long as no one else copied his style.

The tournament had been different though. As the zhee warriors pushed through a city defended by Kimbrin soldiers from one end, legionnaires pushed their way in from another. The middle had become a hectic, lethal front line of death, fire, and destruction. And Jazz's little hide was set up perfectly to take advantage of it.

Crometheus checked the leaderboards. Wiping the entire squad of legionnaires would no longer be enough. Jazz was up nine kills on him now from whatever dark corner he'd found. A place so entrenched in the chaos that no one seemed to notice the sound of his sniper rifle or the bodies piling up—because the bodies were already everywhere.

That's how Jazz—and not Crometheus—had unlocked the intel dump from Maestro. Not that it was going to be worth anything.

"So send it already!" shouted Giles, the fourth member of the team.

"I can do that!" Jazz shouted back, laughter in his voice. He clearly enjoyed being in this position. "Yes or no?"

"No!" shouted Crometheus and Julius together.

Crometheus needed his full attention to flank the legionnaires inside the building. Julius was probably engaged in something else similarly demanding. The last thing they needed was Maestro putting one of Archimedes's tactical lectures in the upper-right corner of their screens. Every inch of that glowing monitor inside the cabinet was precious.

"Okay," Jazz said, as though the pair were sealing their own fate. "I'll just send it to Giles. He can join me at the top of the leaderboard. High-score style."

"Writin' checks your ass can't cash," Julius grumbled loudly enough for all to hear.

Being beaten by Jazz wasn't sitting any better with him than it was with Crometheus. If Cro was the Ace of the group, the consistent high scorer, Julius was the hungry number two always nipping at his heels and making Crometheus continue to work hard at being on top. You could never go easy when you were playing with Julius. He was a hustler. He would hunt you down and then pass you by, and he wouldn't let up once he got ahead.

The Legion had been going building by building. Usually they dropped a team on the roof while another squad went in at the ground floor and then they met in the middle. In another section of the city, a power-armored legionnaire who towered above the rest burst right through a brick wall and started killing everything in sight with a rapid-fire blaster and a flamethrower, Crometheus included. He'd never seen *that* before.

There was no one like that in the group he stalked now though, and they evidently hadn't seen him roll across the doorway upon their blowing their way into the building. Cro knew they would proceed to clear this level, a lobby with offices in the back and a grand stairway next to the speedlifts that went up to the apartments. He could simply set up behind the bar counter in the adjoining ballroom and wreck the legionnaires as they moved together up the ample stairway.

After that he'd have to leave the building no matter what. They'd call in a tank or set up a sniper capable of picking him off the moment a sensor bot revealed his bioscans. The Legion snipers were shooting right through walls. The game had been turned up to a hellish level of difficulty. The only easy kills were the Kimbrin.

Crometheus hurried to the bar, shot to hell from his earlier fight with the Kimbrin, whose bodies still bled on the tiled floor. He leapt over the counter and could hear the crunch of broken glass beneath him as he landed on the other side. Now he'd have to take a page out of Jazz's tactical playbook and wait in ambush. With luck, he'd wipe out the entire squad. But even trading this life for half of them would get him that much closer to the high score.

Worth it.

He waited for several moments, feeling the soldiers should be moving to the stairs at any moment. A sinking feeling settled over him. He never stayed still like this while playing. He scored his points by being quick and unpredictable, always shooting and moving.

*Stealth has worked great for Jazz so far today,* Crometheus reminded himself. *Just need to be patient.*

An object flew across Crometheus's vision, and one of the kids standing next to him, watching as he sucked the last vapors of a Cherry 7-Up through a squirt bottle gave voice to the thing: "Grenade!"

Crometheus had an escape route in his mind, but the weapon detonated before he could take the first step toward leaving. His monitor filled red and his health dropped exponentially. Still alive... but barely. He could see his blood and flesh splattered on what remained of the exotic bottles of liquor stacked behind him—the ones that hadn't fully shattered. He tried to crawl but could barely move an inch. Still, if he could raise his weapon he might get one more kill on the legionnaires he was sure had thrown the grenade before storming the room.

The armored soldiers came in like a whirlwind and moved in front of his sights so quickly that he didn't have a chance to pull the trigger before blaster bolts were put through his skull.

Crometheus slammed his fingers impotently on the fire button. He stood and rubbed the sweat from the back of his head and then shrugged his jacket so it hung back off his shoulders. The steam escaping was so hot it must have been visible, its appearance aided by the frustrated hiss he let out over his performance.

Lined up on the glass of the machine were the small tokens that the old man who ran the arcade had provided the tournament players in lieu of quarters. They were two-sided, with the name of the arcade on the front and the words "Big Prizes" on the back. Crometheus picked one off the glass with his fingernails and then dropped it into the slot. The coin rattled down through the machine, sounding like a game of Plinko before smacking into the chamber to join the few others that had come before. This was only the fourth token Crometheus had put into the machine, but it felt so much worse than the others.

An entire squad of legionnaires... and not one dead.

If this game had a difficulty setting, it *had* to be set to max. In all the iterations he'd played, legionnaires were always a tough fight. He remembered way back to the New Vega cabinet, which was all the rage until these new ones came in fresh off the boat. In New Vega, you played as a... a... a marine. Crometheus had trouble remembering that. There were legionnaires, too. On the last levels. But they were outnumbered and you had plenty of allies. Plenty more... what had they been called? Savage marines?

"You should get back in the game," one of the kids standing next to him said and then motioned at the screen. "Figure out where to respawn."

Crometheus found himself thinking about that earlier game and all those battles instead of taking the kid's advice. Was that when the Eternals had first come together? Had it been after school?

"Cut out the bad thoughts," the kid said. "You'll do better next time. I believe in you. Anyway, you gotta focus on the game or you guys are gonna lose."

Crometheus shook off some of the moisture still trapped in the arms of his jacket. The leather was warm and malleable, as soft and pliable as it had been for the cow that first wore it. He looked at the game's spawn menu. Nothing left to choose but more zhee warriors. At first there had been Hools as well, and Crometheus stacked up his biggest kill count with one of those. Julius had played as one, too. After they got wrecked... nothing but zhee, zhee, and more zhee. Which was okay. They were versatile warriors. Hools were just deadlier up close.

He thought about Jazz and his intel and decided that character selection and respawn could wait. The game wouldn't drop him in until he selected a spawn point, and Crometheus needed a moment to further air out his body and cool off. The worst thing that would happen is that his score-per-minute would dip. But then, he'd been doing a grand job of that all by himself already.

His audience seemed focused on him, so Crometheus turned to address them. "I'm gonna go talk to Jazz and get a drink. Nobody touch these controls or I'll break your face."

He pushed his way through the crowd of watchers and heard their disapproving whispers. It was a big tournament. One the Eternals had been practicing endlessly for. The crowd all knew it and Crometheus probably looked rattled to them.

He was choking now that it was all on the line. Everyone knew it.

For a moment Crometheus thought about turning around and showing them that choking wasn't a thing he did. But he was hot and thirsty and maybe the intel drop Maestro sent actually *would* be useful.

Despite Jazz's presence at the top of the leaderboard, the crowd around him was much smaller than the one Crometheus had just left. Most likely that was due to his play style. It might be effective today, but it was also boring outside of those moments when a stray soldier wandered into his sights. But if the smaller number of spectators bothered Jazz, he wasn't showing it. He was laughing and joking with those around him and only passively watching his screen. He only needed to stay put and pull the trigger to get his kills. It was error-proof. The only thing that could go wrong was if he missed someone moving through his kill zone.

Crometheus stopped to stand behind him, a full head taller. "You call this playing?"

"No. I call this sitting on top of the leaderboards, loser. Haven't even broken a sweat. I even had time to watch you get fragged on the screens up there." Jazz pointed up to the mounted televisions that simulcast gameplay from all four of the Eternals.

Crometheus glanced up and watched for a moment. No one seemed to be doing all that well. "I'm glad you're enjoying yourself."

"Are you kidding? This is the most hype thing that's ever happened to me. I mean, not to bring up old brags or anything but I'm pretty sure it was you who said that if I ended up with a better score than the mighty Crometheus and his sidekick Julius that I could have my choice of either keeping your leather jacket or watching you eat it. And what I wanna know right now is… How hungry are you, Cro?"

"Eh, more thirsty than anything else."

"You don't need anything to drink, man. You need to get back and play."

The comment seemed to water the parch in Crometheus's mouth as if it had been a magical command. "Came over to see what Maestro had to say."

Jazz made a pained face. "Honestly, Crometheus, I think you'll just get upset if you hear Archimedes's lecture. I mean really, it's not much more than the typical tactical dump showing how to defend against that Legion squad who raided the camp."

"And? Anything good? Maybe we'll be on a map rotation and will have to do it again."

Jazz shrugged his shoulders and gave a light laugh. "Sure. But if we could do the kind of things in the intel dump with a bunch of zhee warriors, we wouldn't have gotten wrecked in the first place."

That wasn't helpful, and it *did* make Crometheus feel a bit frustrated. He remembered when intel dumps were relevant at revealing tactics and teaching you how to adjust for a better score the next time. This certainly didn't sound like that. He also found himself hoping that they really *did* get another shot at keeping those legionnaires from rescuing the prisoner. It angered him the way the soldiers had gotten the drop on him. He wasn't sure how the Japanese were doing from their arcade across the Pacific Ocean, but he had to imagine they were just as flustered by how well the computer-generated enemies were fighting. It reminded him of that battle aboard the

Cybar ship and how that woman came out of nowhere and dusted the entire squad.

"Game's getting kind of ridiculous," Crometheus grumbled.

Jazz sent a high-powered blaster bolt through the visor of a legionnaire who had moved into the alley of death he'd set himself up as king of. "Speak for yourself, man." He toggled the leaderboard showing himself up top and then selected a Bon Jovi song for his reward. "Game feels pretty easy to me right now."

Not thirty seconds later, Jazz's screen filled with energy and he found himself dead immediately. The display read that he's been killed by Legion orbital strike.

He slapped the side of his cabinet. "Are you *kidding* me?"

Crometheus laughed into his hand. "Just don't let the old man see you beating up his cabinets like that."

Jazz had already dropped in his next token and was selecting a new spawn point. It would be next to impossible to fight his way to where he had been before. The fight at the epicenter of the map had expanded well beyond it. Running that deep behind the Legion lines to get there again would only get him killed on repeat.

"Ah, probably better that I got wrecked," Jazz confessed. "Number of targets coming through had dwindled too much anyway."

Crometheus turned to go back to his own machine. He meandered through the crowd and saw a game cabinet from the corner of his eyes. Not the tournament game... another that seemed to be always waiting for him. He thought of it infrequently, but when it crossed his mind, the pull of curiosity was palpable.

*Into the Unknown.*

The game was in a different spot than it had been. Again. Why was the old man moving it around so much?

Crometheus shrugged and moved on. There would be time to play that one on another day. Right now the tournament was happening, and the tournament was everything. It was all they'd been training for. All they'd lived for.

His mouth reminded him that he was thirsty. Whatever positive thinking spell Jazz had cast on him had worn off. The closer the crowd packed around him, the more he felt the urge to slake his thirst. The sheer body heat in the place gave the air conditioners an impossible mission; they might as well be asked to cool the fires of hell. Only the gentle drifting of an orange vinyl strip tied to the vents gave any indication that the central air was even turned on.

Some of the faces in the crowd Crometheus recognized. They were a few regulars who came in after school. He also saw some of the business lunch rush who came in after a quick meal—or in place of one—to burn a few quarters. He wondered if those men whose time in the arcades was kept to a minimum as they pursued professional success wished that they were in the Eternals' places—free to just play. Free to enjoy life.

Crometheus smiled. That was all that mattered. Have fun. Play well. Earn those Big Prizes and let everyone else see that you're somebody. That you matter. Just drive out all those bad thoughts about being too hot or too thirsty and forget Maestro's lousy intel. He didn't need hints anyway. He was Crometheus. He *gave* hints.

A budding sense of euphoria at the damage he would do to those legionnaires when he returned to his machine swelled up from inside. It didn't matter how many kills

Jazz had already. He'd lost his camping spot and, knowing the way Jazz played, would spend too much time trying to find another good one. Then he'd settle in and it probably wouldn't even be all that great.

During all that time, Crometheus would go to work. He would follow a breaching team inside a building and wipe them out. He would steal Legion armaments—rely on battlefield pickups—and then drop entire buildings on top of them as they went inside to clear. He would cut the throats of every raggedy Kimbrin rebel he found because, even though they weren't Legion, a kill was a kill. And this objective was all about racking up the body count.

He was going to do all of that…

… and then he spotted a face in the crowd that was more familiar than any of the others. It was the guy. The kid. The one he'd bribed to count for him.

No… that wasn't it.

They'd made a… bet? Something about whether Kirk Gibson would hit a home run in a game. Or… maybe Orel Hershiser was supposed to beat Clemons's single-game record. Twenty bucks.

That was it. The kid… he'd made a bet with him.

He couldn't remember if he'd won or lost, though. And he couldn't think of why he'd even make that kind of bet. He didn't like baseball. And his father wasn't a Dodgers fan. His team was…

The Dodgers.

And the bet was what he was thinking of. He remembered it clearly now. It was a bet. A baseball bet. They'd checked the sports section the next day to see the box scores and Crometheus had lost. And now he was just feeling weird because he owed the guy some money.

But the guy… the kid still in high school… he was just mumbling to himself. He was sort of looking at Crometheus, but in a way that made the Eternal unsure if he wasn't just looking past him. Maybe… maybe he just wanted his money.

But Crometheus needed to get back to the game. He'd tell the kid to find him after the tournaments and would pay him then. He wasn't a leech. He paid his debts. He always paid his debts.

When Crometheus got closer to the kid he realized for sure that the kid wasn't watching him at all. He was definitely looking past him. Crometheus followed his gaze. He wasn't looking at anything. He was just… looking. Like there was something there that only he could see.

He wasn't mumbling about baseball or monies owed. He was reciting numbers in a long string that suddenly made Crometheus feel thirsty again, if only because of all the talking the kid was doing. Just saying numbers.

And then Crometheus realized that the kid was counting. He'd paid him to count. He was still counting. He'd never stopped.

The count was huge.

The desire to go and give it to the Legion that had been swelling now crashed and receded. Crometheus wanted to run to the Power Zone to drink enough Jolt Cola that he'd never sleep again.

*Or just walk out.*

No. The tournament. Can't bounce on the Eternals like that. He'd stay in the arcade. Of course he would.

But his spawn… that could wait.

He pushed his way deeper into the arcade. The lights were off in that section of the warehouse full of gaming cabinets, and it felt cooler. There were no people here. Just the game. *Into the Unknown.*

Crometheus shoved his hands into his jeans and pulled out a real quarter with an eagle on the back and George Washington on the front. 1968. Denver.

The game began and took him through its pixelated 16-bit start, flashing images of blocky rough-edged warriors and glamorous, sultry sorceresses. And this time, Crometheus entered the name he knew not to enter the time before: Rogan. A scene at the inn and a prompt...

What do you want to do next?

Crometheus typed on the old text-based adventure, carefully moving his fingers across the keyboard...

What happened in the desert?

# 21

**Earth**
**12 Months Prior to the First Lighthugger Departure**

Billy Bang—Crometheus—was already a little drunk. He had promised himself it wouldn't be so this time. Then he ordered a whiskey sour when the cute waitress with the dimples cheerfully asked what he'd like.

It was... expected of him. To drink. A part of who he was. He wasn't a lush or some sad, pathetic alcoholic who couldn't help himself—although he was that too.

Billy Bang was a rock god. A one-man wrecking machine who in a night would decimate every member of the audience at the arena, every bottle behind the bar, every girl whose looks got her backstage, and every hotel room his manager booked for him.

And always in that order.

The rock god's fall from Olympus was gradual, but the change didn't escape Billy. Especially after the trial.

Things had changed. He was told to leave the bars before he had a chance to drain all the expensive bottles on the top shelf. Gone was the grace offered by the club owners when Billy was moving from city to city, always adding more tour dates as more records sold and more girls needed his attention. When a drunken appearance at an awards show was watched breathlessly and the old rock gods who had lost their perch on the throne at the top of the charts laughed at his vile antics and clapped at his careless profanity. He threw up in a green room and the pages for the network *apologized to him* while they scrubbed his mess out of the carpet and his manager shrugged the whole thing off.

"That's what they want, baby. It's what they expect. And you're delivering it. You're a rock god, Billy."

But at the bars, after the trial, when the sales had died down and the people forgot about the music and even the scandal... when all that happened, no one seemed to want a rock god except for the well-perfumed girls who showed up backstage at the smaller shows, their dresses just as tight as before but now showing the softness of their middles and underneath their chins.

"You'll know your star is fallin' when the girls get bigger," some hair-band lead singer had told him once when he was on top and not really listening. But now he knew that was true. At least most of the time. Sometimes nostalgia and the memories of fame made an exception.

Those were good times.

It was the gradual decline that had been the hardest. The album after the trial hadn't hit the way it needed to. The comeback tour was downsized as it went on. The bouncers who once shook Billy's hand and made a fuss and called for their friends to snap a Polaroid—see Billy curling his lip and baring his teeth while holding out a fist, the spiked leather collar strapped around his wrist, one photo after another until all the little people who made those bars run were satisfied by their brush with fame and the patrons waited outside the private areas hoping they could only get near him—those bouncers hadn't changed. Only they no longer asked for a picture or an autograph for a friend. They shoved him hard between his shoulder blades to hurry him out the door and called the soft backstage girls names. Crometheus, barely able to catch himself from falling face-first into the filthy concrete, would whirl around and extend a middle finger and a piece of parting profanity that made the girls roar in drunken laughter.

And then it was off for more devastation. But to Billy, the change was noticeable—and worrying.

Eventually the bars wouldn't even let him in. His presence was costing the owners money when it used to lavish it upon them. No cover was too high, nor was any drink minimum. The starstruck regular people would pay anything to be near Billy Bang. Sometimes, their wildest dreams came true.

No matter. Billy's manager always included riders in the contract to have the booze backstage. Then that was gone and so were the kinds of places that paid much attention to the riders. He performed in middle-of-nowhere casinos, somewhere between Reno and Rome. A rider might get him two free drinks and some poker chips. If he offered those to the bartender along with a little of the old charm, they might keep 'em coming. That was always easier if it was a woman behind the counter. Billy could feel the scorn of the men who now thought they were better than him.

He could usually still find company for the night. Someone always backstage looking. But at that point what came next was a matter of habit. There was no desire. He had to keep up with expectations... which was how Billy covered up his own weakness. He would just be what others expected and in so doing, never had to be himself.

But sometimes that weakness and lack of desire manifested itself and the disappointed girl from backstage at the casino would ridicule the "big star" who had so not met expectations. On her way out the door, Crometheus would present to her the same middle finger that he'd given the bouncers. He would call her a whore and she would laugh.

The sound of that laughter was the cruelest thing about the entire cruel affair.

Then his manager, his new manager. His first manager was long gone: "Nothing I can do for you anymore, baby. That's the way it goes." His new manager who kept him busy with just enough shows at the little casinos and nostalgia clubs to keep him busy, to keep him from getting too thirsty... sometimes that manager would get him booked on a show that paid pretty damn well. Only Crometheus had to share the stage with some other group of has-beens.

Billy Bang accepted that as truth now. It wasn't just a down year. It had been years. *Decades*.

But those shows paid better, and the riders were honored and the bar was open afterward. On those nights, Crometheus would reach down and grab a bottle of the house bourbon to take to his room. Sometimes, after his manager paid out his cut, there was even enough left over for a little candy.

And then he'd destroy the hotel room because that's what he was supposed to do.

The next day the manager would call. "Hey, Billy... they, uh, they decided not to bring you back for that summer show after all."

It had been a long time since a manager had told Billy that they expected him to behave like a rock god. He did it anyway. He didn't know why.

Instead his manager would say things like, "I had to put a deposit down after last time. I'm begging you, leave it nicer than the way you found it or we lose all the travel points and you'll wipe out everything you've earned in the last month."

That was what led to his manager, his new manager, finally firing him—if that's how it even worked. Crometheus *felt* as though he'd been fired. In reality the calls were never returned. What had caused it was an encounter that started off innocently. He'd sat in his room, meaning to keep that damage deposit from having to be used to cover another room wrecked. He was going to save his money this time. This was two months ago.

He'd flipped the channels. Watched wrestling for a while—because that was always on. Then he stopped on a music video and saw himself when he was young and vibrant and beautiful. He watched it and felt a nostalgic sense of pride and peace.

Little bubbles filled with text started to pop up over his face. They listed little bits of trivia and began to recount Billy's faults. The backup dancers that he'd had were given their own text bubbles. Lying allegations. Jokes. Court details. Restraining orders. Names of people he didn't even know when the video was recorded, but who had become important to him later in life.

Before it all went bad. Before the trial.

His manager had stressed the damage deposit and how little it could afford to be lost. Crometheus wrecked the place.

He was a rock god.

And now it had been two months without a manager. Two months during which Crometheus missed a series of shows, because he didn't know he'd been booked for them. He needed money. Needed a drink. There were a few old business cards. They were worn and feathered at their edges. He made some calls. No one returned them.

It would pass. He could call himself a has-been, but the calls always came eventually. He had been too big. They loved him too much to ever fully let him go.

Then the big call came. A private show for some filthy rich someone who made a fortune trading something. Huge, palatial home. Private acres. Peacocks walking about.

Billy's people.

He devastated the audience. Word got around. Thing seemed poised to get going again, even better than ever. Someone called for an interview from one of the few e-magazines that still had readers. And if they wanted to interview you, that meant they were thinking of you.

Then *the* call came.

Thomas Roman. Whose wealth was unsurpassed. Whose companies had more control than the world governments.

*Heard about the private show. Can we meet with you?*

That's when Crometheus felt things were really starting to click. The interviews, but really that call. Not only was Mr. Roman rich, but he was also in the right age demographic. Crometheus was probably singing to him in his bedroom back when he was a teenager. And Roman was singing right along. How old *was* he, anyway? Old enough for a big party, surely. One that looked back on how far he'd come.

Who better to perform than Billy Bang?

Even if it was just one show, a party like that was always the right choice. He'd done a few when he was still with his last manager. They were all for people who were rich, or at least rich enough. And at those parties... all was right with the world again. People lined up for the pictures. They watched him adoringly as he emptied the bar and kept going for more. The girls were young again. Slim again. Eager again. He'd tear up his room, but smartly. Nothing was destroyed, just moved about. A mattress on the floor, a table overturned, and Crometheus sleeping shirtless somewhere in the hallway just outside.

When the guest of honor walked by and saw, he laughed with joy like they had in the green rooms. Crometheus would pry open one eye and push himself up, sucking in a big breath of air.

"Your hangover has got to be as big as a house," the adoring birthday boy would say.

"No, mate. Trick is to never let one catch up with you."

And he'd laugh again and shake his head and invite Billy to breakfast to talk a bit more about the old days and that was usually it. No one was going to ever ask him to stay in one of those big, empty rooms. No wife would tolerate it for more than a night. But... what a night!

Mr. Roman probably wanted the same. And his assistant had met him here at a hotel that, strictly speaking, Crometheus had long ago been banned from. But no one would tell anyone working for Mr. Roman that his guests were unwelcome.

Crometheus had walked in like he owned the place. He sat down in a heap, legs spread wide, an unlit cigarette dangling from his mouth. He hadn't meant to get drunk... or maybe he had.

He was a rock god.

"How'd you like the show?" he asked the assistant, and immediately felt he'd made a mistake. Billy Bang didn't care if you liked the show or not. It was supposed to be about the music—the energy and the rebellion. Who cared if you got it? Who cared if you liked it?

That question shouldn't have been asked. Unlike the drinks, it wasn't who he was supposed to be. It wasn't what they would expect. It was a thing said... for him. For Crometheus. And he'd said it because he couldn't get out in front of himself to stop from revealing what he really wanted.

He wanted back in. He wanted to matter. And he knew now deep inside that it would take someone else to ever bring him there again. Someone like Mr. Roman.

"Oh. It was good," said the young assistant, maybe he was a lawyer. He looked as though he shopped exclusively at a store that sold suits and had bought a casual ensemble that sat on a mannequin next to the tailor-cut three-piece outfits he felt most comfortable in. A man aware that one couldn't wear a suit all the time, but wished it weren't so.

"Mm," Crometheus hummed, trying to sound like he didn't care.

"It was good. I liked it. You have an amazing amount of... *energy* on the stage."

Crometheus had developed at least one skill in his many years on tour. *In the business, kid.* The show. He could smell bullshit a mile away. And he heard what was being left unsaid just as clearly as what was said.

It was usually what was unsaid that contained the truth.

You had an amazing amount of energy on the stage... *for someone your age.*

That second, unstated part, told Crometheus that his efforts during the past forty-eight hours had all been for naught. Thinking that Mr. Roman himself might be there, he pulled in every favor he had left—and there were hardly any now. He casually told his contact, who sat now before him, that he just happened to have a show on the night of the planned meeting. One in LA—the good part that you could still safely drive through. It was at a little underground club that didn't hold a lot of people but was raw—you know? He liked to do a show like that from time to time just to get back to his roots. Same place he'd gotten his first big break and signed his first record deal. Right on the spot.

Then he hung up and paid the kid working at the copy store to help him design a flyer. Then paid him again to make copies on bright orange paper.

More phone calls. Hours of putting up flyers in bathrooms and on telephone poles. And then off to Vine Street to take over for Denise who'd been handing them out to the tourists seeing what was left of the Walk of Fame. She had to go pick up her kid from daycare. And so Crometheus handed out his own flyers and ignored the looks that suggested he was pathetic for doing so. He smiled and winked at the girls who recognized him. He posed for photos with tourists, sticking out his tongue and holding up a fist, that same spiked bracelet around his wrist. Close with a handshake, try to get another body to the show...

"Always good to meet a fan, mate." He'd point to the little map on the flyer. "The Shade isn't far from here. Same club I had my big break in. Make sure to come."

And they would all say that they would come. But none of them did. They had dinner reservations or tickets to Disneyland that were already bought, and they weren't going to miss out on the fireworks show to close the night. Those tickets had been expensive. And this was a vacation. And hadn't vacationing been the whole point of coming? It was one thing to meet up by chance with an old rock star—and at just the place you'd expect to meet one. It was another to throw away your vacation to go see him scream his tired old hits at some seedy night club called The Shade.

More than a few times, Crometheus saw them toss the flyer into the garbage bin with most of the others. When he ran out, he'd fish them out and start fresh. Some of the out-of-towners would drop them into the filth-lined gutters as they walked away. That was actually better. Crometheus left them there. Someone might still see the flyer while walking by. Even if it was only a bum. Admission was free. The only thing that mattered was that people filled up the tiny venue enough that he didn't look like a failure. Crometheus hoped the performance would sway whoever Mr. Roman sent, if not the man himself. And that he would excitedly tell Mr. Roman that Billy Bang still has it.

The show was a good one. Most of them were. Billy always performed. Always. The crowd was hot even though it was skewed so much older than the show Crometheus remembered from that day he and the boys had their big break. Back long ago when the line wrapped around the block and he hugged his bandmates in euphoria because the owner—who still loved Crometheus and did him the favor of this show—had told them that an exec was talking about big money if the show was as good as the rumor.

Billy had hugged his bandmates then, men who were now either dead or estranged beyond any hope of reconciliation. But on that day, that long-ago day, they were brothers, and they put their heads together in a huddle and Crometheus said, "We kill it tonight and nothing's ever going to be the same!"

He threw out his arm and the bandmates who died hating him stacked their own arms on top of his, burying the spiked bracelet from view.

They did kill it that night. And nothing was the same.

"We killed it," Crometheus said to Mr. Roman's assistant, lost in the memory of that first show.

But that was also true of the show he'd just performed. The old bandmates had by now been replaced by middle-aged married men who were just happy for an excuse to get out of the house and shred—have a little taste of the rock 'n' roll dreams they'd once cherished before settling down and forever missing their chance. But those guys were as good as anybody. They were often better than Crometheus's original bandmates. And they played for a beer and handshake.

"Like I said," said the assistant, the lawyer—not a PR man, not someone polished or he would have sounded more convincing. "... the show was really good. I'm sure when Mr. Roman hears about it he'll be sorry he missed it. But you know... business."

Crometheus grabbed a fresh whiskey sour the cute little waitress with the dimples had dropped off. He'd told her at the start to "keep them coming love," and that was easy enough to do. He paused and held the glass beneath his nose. He didn't need to be any drunker than he already was. He pantomimed a small sip and set the drink back down. "Well, he won't feel bad for long. The show I put it on for him will beat all."

The man in front of him rolled his shoulders. His hand went to adjust a tie that wasn't there. He was as uncomfortable in a polo shirt as Crometheus had felt in a collar and noose back on that day when he first had to stand before the judge.

The day that he marked as the ultimate turning point. There was a lot of blame to be had, and Crometheus only sometimes took any of it upon himself. He had no illusions about what he had done. He knew the law even while breaking it, both the moral law and the statutes that followed. But the lawyers, expensive bastards, had said all he'd face was a fine and a few months' probation. Probably some community service.

The judge said two years. Billy got out in eighteen months. Good behavior.

The world had changed.

"Well, that's certainly a part of it," Mr. Roman's assistant said. He looked about the restaurant and Crometheus did the same. It wasn't empty but neither was it alive. It lacked the organic atmosphere of a night out dining in a way that told Crometheus that the people at the other tables weren't looking at him in recognition. That was his first thought when he'd arrived in a flurry of noise and energy and then slammed back that initial whiskey sour.

No... they were here to watch the assistant. To watch the exchange. They were watching to make sure things went as planned. And now, whatever the plan was, it was coming to a head. And the assistant, perhaps nervous, exchanged looks with those strangers at the tables who weren't strangers at all, sharing with them a final moment of clarity before walking over the edge.

"I'm sure you've heard the rumors about what Mr. Roman intends to do with his space program."

Crometheus leaned back in his chair and put his boot up on the table. "Not really, mate. It's just the music in my life. Swore off the news a long time ago."

From the look on the man's face, Crometheus could tell the boast was a miscalculation. The assistant seemed to *want* Crometheus to know the latest about his employer.

Crometheus brought his boot back to the floor and leaned forward. In a little voice he said, "I've heard the rumors. Sometimes, out in public, you have to be careful about what you say." Crometheus winked at the man and that seemed to set the assistant somewhat at ease.

And of course, there was no escaping the rumors. Crometheus had been lying when he suggested otherwise. Mr. Roman had been at the forefront of multiple seminal moments in the past decades. After an early attempt at directly influencing first national, then global politics died down, and as the country and the rest of the globe rapidly destabilized, always on the brink of open war and final war if only they could win the war against their own citizens first... Mr. Roman shifted inward.

First he became obsessed with his health. He wasn't much younger than Crometheus, but he looked like a man in his thirties. There had been numerous puff pieces about his diet and exercise regimen. How he looked so fabulous and what you might do to follow in his footsteps. Harsher but less credible pieces went into conspiracy theories about genetic juicing—cloning and in vitro fertilization. Stem cell therapy. However it was accomplished, the man looked good. He gallivanted across the world as it burned, always with a beautiful woman on his arm. Sometimes with two. With each passing decade, the women were replaced with someone still younger and more beautiful.

Or maybe they only *looked* younger. After all, Mr. Roman looked younger and healthier now than he had while he was truly young. Though the pictures of him back then—what few could still be found on a locked-down and centralized internet—were rare.

And then there was the obsession with space that seemed to spread like wildfire among all the elites. Roman had a head start, and his substantial fortune was made that much greater as those with nearly as much money but less foresight and time paid huge sums for his scraps in a desperate attempt to catch up. They all seemed to know the same thing, and it was a mystery to the common man.

Governments took notice, and that was the catalyst for the so-called *IP Wars*. Open conflict between government and corporate powers—who were governments of their own in all but name. They murdered one another openly across the globe, stealing and protecting, seeking an edge. Transforming places that had been cultured and civilized into a black panel van version of Chicago's early gangland wars.

No one had enough money or power to stop it.

Only things getting worse elsewhere seemed to put an end to it. The bio-diseases "escaped" from labs. Humanity had made it through that, but the ones engineered for plant life looked like they might hang on a while yet. Poor nations found their breadbaskets turn into parched deserts.

Millions died in Africa.

Things hadn't exactly gotten better, but there was a peace nowadays. Call it a truce. You could still live your life and take vacations and think about the future. But the time of prosperity—even what passed for such now—was ending. They all knew it but couldn't do a thing about it.

Crometheus knew it too. And he realized, as he sat at his table, that the way back in, not just to stardom and fame, but simply to a good life, would only be achieved through loyalty to men like Mr. Roman. And only those who fit his carefully predetermined molds would be allowed to enjoy his charity.

"Mars was supposed to be a utopia," the assistant said. "Mr. Roman and certain like-minded individuals spent considerable fortunes to make that happen."

Crometheus nodded. Mars was fiercely independent and powerful enough to ignore the growing frustrations of Earth—as well as the taxes and ideologies the world governments demanded. At some point there would be war. But right now both sides were either too doubtful of their own victory or not desperate enough to try for it anyway.

"So what happened?" Crometheus asked.

The assistant looked thoughtful for a moment, but Crometheus could see it wasn't an actual reflective moment. He was putting on airs, and badly. "We sent the wrong people. Next time we won't."

"Wasn't aware there was going to be a next time. Or is Venus nice this time of year?"

The assistant smiled politely at the joke. "I'm going to give you a woman's name. I believe you know her or know of her. Her name is Holly Wood."

"The reporter." Crometheus leaned back in his chair and crossed his arms, a relaxed, devil-may-care posture that was every bit the false front that the assistant's "thoughtful" reflection had been. "Yeah. I know her. She wants to do a feature on me. *Sound & Rhythm* wants a piece about the anniversary of my first album—*Bang Johnny Bang*. They still do pieces about music, that outfit. It's not all politics."

The assistant nodded. "Her real name is Tina Rivers. She's on the verge of spoiling some legitimate and perfectly legal plans Mr. Roman has had in motion for some time."

"What kind of plans?" Crometheus hoped the question wouldn't come across as him being difficult—he wanted in and would do anything to get there. He'd decided that before the meeting had even started. But still... it paid to know the score.

"This planet is circling the drain. Despite Mr. Roman's many attempts to help the global population down the path of progress, it's time they be left to their own devices. Technology has progressed sufficiently that humans no longer need to be bound to Earth, or even this solar system. Like the Pilgrims leaving England for a better world, Mr. Roman is preparing to take a new colony off Earth."

Crometheus rubbed his chin. What he was hearing sounded both plausible and absolutely insane.

The assistant seemed bothered by something. He looked... remorseful. A little afraid. "I should clarify, in invoking the Pilgrims I only meant to use familiar imagery. Of course the type of imperialism those colonists expressed is not endorsed by myself or Mr. Roman."

Crometheus waved the thought away. It hadn't even occurred to him. "So you... what? Found a new planet and now you're gathering up the best and brightest for a one-way ticket out of this shithole?"

"Correct in most respects, except we haven't found a planet to settle. Nor does our success rely on our doing so. The ship that Mr. Roman has completed construction on is capable of sustaining life indefinitely for all those aboard." The assistant leaned forward. "Indefinitely."

Crometheus nodded. "So generation after generation can be born and die. I get it."

He began to think the alcohol was helping. He was more relaxed and less freaked out than he might've been hearing all of this while sober.

"That's not what I mean by indefinitely. I mean Mr. Roman and all those whom he chooses to bring aboard this modern ark will live... *forever*. We have nearly solved the riddle of age and the curse of death. Our lives can be lengthened to just short of two hundred years at this point, and we are confident we will finish our research into unraveling the aging process—and reverse it at will—within the next hundred years. But this planet doesn't have a hundred years left."

"You're kidding me."

The assistant leaned forward. "I am seventy-two years old, and I am not kidding you."

Crometheus stared at this man who looked as though his thirtieth birthday was still years off. He brought his whiskey sour to his lips and took a drink, downing almost all of it. Then he held the glass and outstretched a finger, pointing it at the assistant and chuckling. "No. Bollocks. Where's the camera? You're pulling one on me."

"I am not. Mr. Roman has more important things to do than play games. He admires you greatly. Your music was instrumental in his upbringing in ways that I'm sure he will enjoy relating to you when you finally meet. He does not wish for you, nor the many others he holds in such a high and sincere esteem, to be left behind to face what awaits this planet. I'm not offering you a job, Mr. Bang. I'm offering you a chance to again be the man of your youth, and then remain that person forever."

Crometheus's throat was suddenly dry, but he managed to croak out, "Oh? How?"

He wasn't asking about the science behind it. He was asking the cost.

The assistant understood. He took out a small hardware wallet. "This is loaded with one hundred million dollars' worth of assorted cryptocurrency. It's untraceable. It's yours to do whatever you like with—provided that *one* of those things is pay your fare to get on Mr. Roman's farewell voyage."

Crometheus picked up the cold wallet and twirled it between his fingers, examining it as though it were a jewel to be appraised. He knew what it was but didn't really know how to use it. He dealt almost exclusively in cash... for tax purposes. "What's the fare?"

Though he asked the question, he already knew the answer. This was part of the show. Playing to the expectations. The same as the drinking and all the other devastations. What was one more devastation? It didn't matter. Once damned, how much more damnation a man heaped on his head.

And there was always the chance it wouldn't be as bad as he imagined it would. Crometheus hated himself for knowing that it didn't matter even if it was. He'd still do it.

The assistant smiled politely, stood, and left to pay for the meal on the way out. And as he passed the old rock god, he said, "Holly Wood."

# 22

"Hey, Jules, it's Billy... No, Billy Bang, man... Yeah... No... Good. Really good. How about you?" Billy held the hotel's old-fashioned telephone receiver in his hand, its long thin cord unraveled from the nightstand to the windows, where he pulled the curtains aside and looked out into the morning radiance. Already people were splashing in the pool—mostly parents and children—while others lay nearby and sunbathed. "Yeah, it is nice... No, I know you can't say, just a force of habit. Being polite... Yeah... Yeah, I do. Two things, actually, and I've got the money in hand this time."

Billy could hear Julius laughing on the other end of the line in his deep, pleasant voice. A voice that could grow quite menacing when someone *didn't* have the money he needed or was owed. Another story.

Crometheus held up the small hardware wallet that contained all of his newfound wealth. "I spent, uh, point-three Bitcoin for a kid over at the school to show me how to make it all work with my phone... Obviously I didn't realize that at the time, Jules."

He had done some research *after* getting his wallet linked to an app that could more easily transact all the different cryptocurrencies Mr. Roman had loaded him up with. The high school kid had paid himself enough to buy his own house for the lesson. Billy nearly fell over when he realized how much money he'd actually given the little shit. But when he considered how much he still had left... it didn't really matter. Let the kid enjoy it. It wasn't like he'd have long. And Billy... he had more than he'd ever had in his life. Much more than he'd earned in that year when he was at his absolute peak. And all the years that followed.

"So anyway, I got the money. But not a lot of cash like the old days. That's harder or something. I dunno. My point is, Jules, can I pay you in crypto? There's so many damned coins in this wallet I can't make sense of it. I recognize Bitcoin. That okay?... Preferred?"

Billy smiled.

"Righteous. Great. Okay, so yeah, two things. First, I need a gun, something reliable... No, I can't wait, why the bloody hell would I call you if I had the eight months to go to the ATF store and get one from them? ... I don't know and I don't care. Somethin' small that'll work... Good. Thirty-eight Special. Fine... Yeah, I remember Jim carried it before the heart attack... Yeah. The other thing is, you remember those guys you told me about that one time?... No, not them. After that. The time with the backup dancer and we were trying to decide... Yeah... Yeah. Do you still talk to them? ... Okay, well I need to talk to them. But they gotta speak English, Jules. I need you to set it up... Today... 'Short notice fee'? Bloody hell. That's fine, I can pay for that. How much though? ... Okay, I can do that. Just give me your, your uh..."

Billy fumbled for the piece of paper he'd left in the front pocket of his jacket where it hung over a chair. On it were the notes the kid from the high school had given him about how to transact with his newfound currency. Billy scanned the paper and found what he was looking for.

"Give me your—" he squinted. "Wallet ID and I'll send it... Yeah, all at once. I know... Do you want me to meet you or...? ... Haha, that's what I love about you, man... First Family Inn. Anaheim... Haha, screw you, man... Yeah... Right... Okay. So I'm gonna go take care of a few things and then I'll be back... Probably around noon... Door unlocked, fine... Yeah... I will... Okay... Bye."

Crometheus hung up the phone and looked back out the window. He spread the curtains wide and stretched, shirtless in the warm sunlight. He hadn't slept so well in a very long time. The day, he knew, would only get better from here.

"I can't quite believe it myself." The salesman patted the high-gloss hood of a vintage 2019 Dodge Charger Hellcat, a glossy black assemblage of American muscle that shone brightly beneath the California sun. "Hennessey upgrade. One thousand horsepower. Nine hundred and forty-eight foot-pounds of torque and forty-two thousand rpm. Upgrades to the lower and upper pulleys. Stainless-steel long tube headers. Crank case ventilation system. High-flow mid pipes, catalytic converter, fuel injectors, air induction system... I get all weepy just thinking about it."

The car salesman wiped away a mock tear and then laughed gregariously, patting Crometheus's leather jacket with the back of his hand. The salesman wore a bushy mustache that had gone out of style long ago but seemed appropriate for his profession. Nowadays salespeople were all corporate clones—the men, anyway. Always fit and trim, tall mostly... and always clean-shaven. But the kind of dealerships that hired those kinds of men to sell their products... they would never have what Billy Bang wanted.

What he needed.

A throwback. Something with power and torque. Something that roared. A monster among the stylized personal transport vehicles that had grown progressively rounder and more pod-like for the commuters who sat in the back seat watching their screens while the "cars" droves themselves to the office parks, everyone forced to leave their homes to work for the good of the economy. Little toy cars that often didn't even have manual drive and had to wait on the rolling blackouts to pass just to recharge.

"No problems with it?" Crometheus asked. "I don't want any problems. I want it to drive like it's brand-new, just broken in. I can afford it."

The salesman laughed. "I know that. Knew it the moment you walked in. Hell, I know who you are. You're Billy Bang! *Break the Revolution! Midnight Ritual!* My old man played your albums to death. And I grew up listening to your stuff. Still do."

"Thanks for that."

"I mean it. My old man would have a third stroke if he knew I was talking with you. He told me this"—the salesman began to laugh at the memory—"this story about how his mom threw away your album when she heard 'Sing, Mary, Sing' on the radio. Dad couldn't convince her that you weren't saying, 'Sin, Mary, Sin.' Didn't even help when he pulled the album out of the trash can and showed her the name of the song on the back."

Billy joined the salesman's laughter. "Well, in your grandma's defense we *sang* it as 'sin'—the song title was printed just for the censors. Different time back then."

"Tell me about it. Point I wanted to make was, I knew you could afford it as soon as I recognized that Billy Bang was on my lot. And good for you, too, a lot of people in your business come to me *selling* their works of art. They can't afford to buy anymore. You know, I got an old Corvette Stingray that used to belong to Richard Marx? He cried like a baby when I cut him a check. Died a few months later, though, so..." The salesman shrugged.

"And it's a convertible?" Billy asked.

"Yup. One of the mods Hennessey didn't do. Not sure who did that work. Fine job, though. Must've cost a fortune at the time." The salesman gently petted the vehicle like it was a loyal, handsome dog. "Only trouble with this little bastard is, well, given the price of gas you're gonna have to take out a second mortgage on your mansion if you wanna be able to drive it for long."

Billy Bang smiled. "I'll get by. You take crypto?"

The triumphant salesman smiled. "Who doesn't?"

The Hellcat screamed into the parking lot of the First Family Inn, its big black tires screeching and leaving long skid marks in its wake. Crometheus pulled the vehicle in head-first into a parking spot by the pool and listened as the engine settled into a low, throaty rumble. He killed the ignition and the powerful animal obediently went to sleep. Music blared uncontested now and then went out mid-beat as Billy turned off the accessory and pulled out the key. The car had a pushbutton start, but that felt like cheating to Billy.

The door opened and then shut again and Billy strolled along the sidewalk between the row of cars baking under the sun and beside the aluminum rod fence that surrounded the pool. He swung a black-and-white checkered flag keychain around his finger and then stuffed the key into his pants pocket.

A California goddess lounged by the pool—the type who had no business being at the First Family Inn. But then, neither did Billy. She looked as though she'd lost her way to the Hotel Bel Air... her beauty wasn't fit for this place. A place where Billy had to use a fake name and ID because of... past indiscretions.

But she was there and she seemed to notice that Billy had been watching her since he pulled up in his muscle car. A coy, playful smile told him that she didn't mind his attention. Her eyes were veiled by oversized, smoky, copper-mirrored sunglasses that covered so much of her face that only her red, full lips and the small, feminine tip of her nose were visible. Those were enough to paint the rest of her as a woman of exceptional beauty in Billy's mind.

The type who used to beg and plead to come backstage.

Back when things were going well.

*Like now*, thought Crometheus.

He quickly hopped the fence and walked around the pool to greet her with practiced lines that didn't work anymore because he wasn't a rock god anymore... except he was. He was one again. She was interested. Interested, but not starstruck. That was a big difference from the beautiful young girls that once had been.

But still... interested was interested.

The conversation went quickly to drinks, as in having some together. Never mind how early in the day it was. Some situations call for an early start just as others called for a late end.

There was no bar at the First Family Inn. Not even free coffee. Billy was only staying here for the night because it had been close to Debbie's place. Debbie, who wouldn't let him in because she was seeing someone now. Denise had her kids and wouldn't budge about that. Wendy was gone without a trace and Judy's landlord said she'd been evicted.

The woman at the pool had her own room and she told Crometheus it was stocked as good as any bar. And after they'd sat and had a drink, her on the bed and him at the small table, she told him her price and he laughed. He laughed and he thought about it.

He had the money. The money wasn't a problem. And the money would make her happy which was all he was hoping would happen anyway. His desires were one thing, but not the only thing. Billy was an entertainer. Someone driven to make others happy—to have their approval. Someone uniquely vulnerable when those around him weren't pleased.

He had the money and told her he did.

"If I can pay you in crypto, that is."

The woman smiled demurely and let the cheap polyester-cotton bathrobe the hotel supplied slip down her shoulders to reveal the straps for her bathing suit top. She walked to the door and set the deadbolt.

When Crometheus returned to his room, he saw that a piece of paper had been taped to the inside of his door. It said *2 PM*, which was in an hour. He pulled the paper down, flipped it over, and read the name of a diner that would take him almost an hour to reach. No matter how fast your ride can go, city traffic will slow you down. He would have to leave soon. Now.

His room was still a mess except for the bed, half of which was made up smartly. Julius would have made sure that the cleaning crew didn't visit today; he always took care of all the little things other people would forget. Crometheus tore back the covers on the made side and found only white sheets.

He swept his hand under the fluffed pillow and felt the .38 Special. Pulling it out, he examined its snubby barrel, front sights inlaid with a red line to better line a target. A switch near the hammer was pressed and a red laser shot its beam on the ceiling. Crometheus slowly brought the weapon down, and the beam danced across the bedsheets from the trembling in the rock god's hand.

After checking the cylinder—fully loaded—Crometheus shoved the weapon down the small of his back, trapping it between a pair of dark and ripped jeans and a black studded leather belt that matched the collar around his wrist.

He moved to the small breakfast table and took his leather jacket off the chair. The day had been too nice to need a jacket. A Sex Pistols shirt had been fine for buying the car. But now he was going out to attend to official business, and that meant being fully dressed. He threw the jacket on and instinctively thrust his hands into the pockets. More bullets for the .38 Special. He patted them loosely in the well of his pocket and went out the door.

Though he'd arrived at the diner with only minutes to spare, Billy had eaten four of his six pieces of bacon and was sprinkling Tabasco sauce over scrambled eggs when the two *cholos* came inside. Crometheus stifled the urge to wave them over and instead baptized his food with another dash of hot sauce and then took a drink from a half-finished Bloody Mary.

The two men ignored the hostess who offered QR in lieu of a menu. They weren't there to eat and even if they were, a menu was unnecessary. The place served the universal offerings of all diners and one needed only to say what they wanted. Six pieces of bacon, three eggs, scrambled. The waitress would translate that into whatever little marketing term the owner had created and deliver it, greasy and hot.

The men sat down across from Crometheus, who had chosen a booth near the entrance. One had cut his hair short, almost bald, and had a thin black mustache above his lips and a triangular soul patch beneath that pointing the way down to a round chin. His partner had thick locks swept back and was clean-shaven. Both had dark sunglasses tucked into pristine white t-shirts beneath blue flannel shirts.

"Friends of Julius," Crometheus said through a mouthful of eggs.

The short-haired man said, "*Sí.*"

Billy's mouth slowed its chewing. Then he looked down and swallowed. When he looked back up, he said, "Julius was supposed to send someone who spoke English."

The man with the thick hair leaned forward with both palms flat atop the table. "*I* speak English, *pendejo.*"

Crometheus smiled and wiped his mouth. "I know that word, at least. I know *sí* too."

He lifted his plate and slid a folded-up piece of paper toward the pair.

The two men, who were in fact brothers, looked at the offered scrap and then at each other. The short-haired brother reached out and pulled it in close to unfold. It contained a crude map drawn in pencil.

Crometheus pushed his finger down onto the Formica table. "That's the place. You already know the job. I want you waiting there three days from now. It'll be late. That would be a Friday night turning into Saturday morning."

The brothers exchanged another look and then both stared blankly at Crometheus, whose stomach jumped at the guilty and panic-stricken idea that he'd somehow just spoken to the wrong men. But those fears were put at ease when the short-haired man tucked the map into his pocket and asked, "*Quanto?*"

Crometheus knew that word as well. "Just one, and not me. Whoever's with me."

The brother with the long hair who spoke English nodded his understanding. "Do you know how much a thing like this costs?"

Crometheus lit a cigarette knowing it would get him thrown out. He'd told these men—these killers—what they needed to know. Now he wanted to be far away from them.

"*Quanto*?" Crometheus asked. His lips parted and formed a sly smile that wasn't reflected in the stony looks of the brothers sitting across from him.

"A lot." The one with the thick hair spoke without a trace of an accent. "Gotta be paid up front. Right now."

Crometheus blew the cigarette smoke out of the side of his mouth where it hung and lingered in the aisle. An old man sitting at the counter watched it, amused. The young woman eating from a fruit bowl farther back, clearly was not.

"Already paid up front and in advance. Done. I paid Julius. You figure the rest out from him."

The English-speaking brother smiled and stroked his chin. "Yeah, Julius. Julius." He cocked an eyebrow. "Maybe Julius is holding out on us. Maybe he's holding out on you, too. Could be he's charging you more and paying us less. Maybe you pay my brother right now and then we get more and you pay less and still everyone gets what they want."

Now the waitress was speaking to the shift manager and pointing at the lingering cloud of smoke. The manager nodded and walked slowly toward the table, the look on his face communicating that the last thing the tubby, balding man wanted to do today was deal with a problem.

Crometheus took another drag and sent up a cloud above his head. He put out the butt in his scrambled eggs and then stood. "Julius might not get what he wants then. And anyway, I already paid him. Take it up with the man if there's a problem, mate."

He pulled out enough bills from his wallet to cover the meal with a little extra for the waitress—it was all the cash he had. He could afford it. It didn't matter.

"Just leaving," he said to the manager as he passed by the short, round man.

The manager turned and watched Billy Bang walk out the door. He said nothing and then nodded to the silence. He was relieved that the problem had taken care of itself.

# 23

## THE AFTERLIFE OF A ROCK GOD
### by Holly Wood

Billy Bang has been awake and going strong for twenty-six consecutive hours. He's only managed to keep me awake for eighteen. In that time we've eaten nothing but half a basket of onion rings (and a moderate number of cocktails). I don't feel any worse for wear because of it as we race through the desert in a 2019 Dodge Charger Hellcat, an indulgent, knee-jerk decision made the morning of our first meeting. He's known me only a little longer than he's owned the car.

The gleaming black steel bullet feels shot out of a cannon and races so fast across the night highway that the desert sands can't grip the high-gloss metal doors to sully them. The sand can only helplessly hang on to our whipping hair as we speed along the highway in excess of a hundred miles per hour.

It's the middle of the night and of course Billy Bang wears sunglasses. So do I, but Billy would wear them even if tiny pieces of the desert weren't *tinking* off a pair of Ray-Bans that likely cost less (just a little) than a full tank of gas for the primitive muscle car.

"They don't make them like this anymore," Billy says and then guns the engine so we can feel again the difference between traveling at 120 miles an hour and 140. Those twenty extra miles are substantial at that speed. They bring with them a change from the heady excitement to a feeling that you are now teetering on the brink of death. One false swerve or visit from one of the night denizens who call this highway home and seek to cross the road and...

But Billy Bang isn't careless. Nor is he trying to impress me. If I had asked him to slow down, he would have done so without complaint. He had once already, as we both fought against deadlines — mine to this magazine's editor and his to a show in Las Vegas.

Our evening started in a small club in Orange County, the type that has a reputation as a revolving door for pop music's former superstars. It's the kind of venue Billy Bang, long removed from winning and presenting Grammy, Billboard, and other music awards, was required to settle into. Except Billy doesn't behave like an old rock god content to look back on his career and smile knowingly at an aging fan base just happy to be near him.

Billy still performs as though he's in an arena and not a club so small that a hundred people would get the interest of the Orange County Fire Marshal.

The shows aren't for money — Billy seems to be doing just fine there. They also aren't out of any desire to stay relevant.

"How is playing at that place gonna do that?" he sneers, and then laughs playfully at the idea that such a club could rekindle either his fame or his fortune. "I play because I've got to get the music out. I never cared what people thought of me when the arenas were full and I sure as hell don't care now."

Neither does he seem to care about running out of the money those packed stadiums showered on him long ago. He spends freely and lavishes himself and those around him with the finest food and drink to be had — and did I mention the car?

Billy Bang is still a rock god. That mythical creature of old who was molded and shaped by those long-defunct institutions known as record labels. Performers carefully selected and packaged for mass appeal even while selling a dream of angst-driven, lusty, teenage punk rebellion. A far cry from the careful and cautious musicians of today who, having been plucked from obscurity on social media, must always kowtow to the likes, hearts, and clicks of the instant-gratitude mass who followed them.

The modern music scene could not create another Billy Bang. It produces a spineless, puerile formula in its technical ability, with artists whose only desire is to please the loudest and most numerous voices incessantly commenting in their chosen sphere of social influence.

Billy Bang would likely never even have been invited to play L.A.'s legendary rock 'n' roll club, The Shade, were his career just getting started today. Let alone be offered a contract worth millions (which was a lot back then) on the spot, as the legend goes.

"They can call it music and say it's their passion but it's garbage. And they know it." Billy slows down as he gives his take on where the music industry has gone. He wants me to hear every word. "The music — I mean, they are real musicians, these are talented people, but they keep their real music inside. And it kills them. Because all they can deliver is what their fans allow them to give. And they try to write what their fans complain about and not what's in their heart. You can hear it. There's no heart to it. No soul. The real music is kept private. Only for themselves and a few others. Songs that they couldn't share because they're not brave enough to ruin their careers. The best songs they have. Letting their music really come out, nah, there's too much risk of it all falling apart." Billy chuckles. "And once that happens, they know they'll be playing in the same clubs as me."

The admission comes from a sense of contentment that is clear in all that Billy Bang does. But his performances at those "same (small) clubs" make one wonder whether this rock god isn't poised to leave his private throne and work his way back into the arenas. The night's earlier performance was more than adequate — a rousing show where the audience was assaulted with all their favorites and had to wonder whether they had stepped back in time to when Billy Bang was still on top.

Billy credits that to the audience . . . or rather to his knowledge of what an audience desires.

"You gotta accept that they're out there to relive what you've already done. Years ago. They don't wanna hear some new song I farted around with on a guitar. They want to see me sing what made them fans in the first place. They want the satisfaction of seeing me for the first time and not feeling like they missed something. Or sometimes, they were at those first shows and they just wanna see me again. Just to have that moment where even though we've both aged, what we shared is still there."

Billy Bang is more than just a brooding face and meticulously spiked blond hair that keeps him looking younger than his age — though the lines around his eyes and mouth tell the truth of a sometimes hard, sometimes excessive life. The rock god has put thought into the connection he now has with his still-adoring fans.

"Music is an anchor. Its melodies are the links of the chain. You follow that chain back to the anchor; you find yourself in the exact same spot as when you first heard it. I think a lot of the people come to the show trying to get that feeling back."

He looked up from the steering wheel and fixed his eyes on the heavy moon hanging in the night sky. "I'd be lying to you if I said I went up there and played for any other reason than that. Getting in front of those same people, playing those same songs . . . it's the only way to get back even a little bit of what used to be."

The insights are ones I wouldn't have gotten had it not been for our getting tossed out of a chic restaurant owned by a celebrity chef who makes an expensive art out of selling reimagined, but still grease and cheese-covered, fast food. A waitress who surely modeled on the side, or perhaps it was the other way round, brought us the '5-Star Onion Rings', a hot, crisp basket of gallstone-punishing fried vegetables sprinkled with truffles.

Billy Bang and I finished half the basket before he stood up and loudly proclaimed to the well-dressed clientele that we were all "being bloody ripped off!"

Outside, we collected ourselves at the car. Perhaps still hungry, but still possessing the $75 the onion rings would have cost.

Then he surprised me. The dinner was supposed to be all the time I'd get with Billy, and in truth it was all the time I could afford. My flight left from John Wayne in the morning. Billy Bang was to drive all night to do a show in Las Vegas.

"But not really Las Vegas. That's a trick we do, to fool ourselves. We say Los Angeles, but we mean Orange County. We say Las Vegas, but we mean a little club way off the Strip out past Hendersonville."

As interesting as that might be, I had a flight to catch. Billy offered to pay for a new one out of Las Vegas. No time lost; I'd still fly out in the morning. There were things he needed to tell me. Things that had long needed to be aired out.

"This is crazy," he said. "But . . . come along for the drive and I'll tell you the whole story, start to finish. All the dirty little ins and outs. All the secrets. The trial. Jail. Everything."

He opened the passenger door and then walked around the sculpted hood of his sleek and savage-looking gas-guzzler of a muscle car, the red glow of his cigarette reflecting across its mirror-polished hood. Billy Bang flopped in the driver's seat and put his keys in the ignition. He stared straight ahead, not bothering to look and see if I was moving to take the offered seat at his side. "Someone's gotta know. It's not fair that no one but me knows what I know."

I got into the car and closed the door.

Billy twisted the ignition and the powerful engine roared to a fabulous, full-throated life. And fifteen minutes later we were all alone, Billy and I, gliding along the blue desert highway, chasing the distant pale moon.

# 24

Holly Wood cautioned Crometheus four times that he was on the record. Each time he paused to say, "I know," and then continued telling all. Satisfied, Holly stopped cautioning and wrote furiously on the oversized screen that was her phone with its slim stylus, the software trained to take her shorthand and turn it into text. The start of the article was easy enough. She had that done. But everything that followed... how to parse it all? How to tell the truth?

They passed miles of desert, rarely seeing another vehicle. Eventually the scenery blended and became unchanging. The soft blue glow of the sands on either side was as constant as the moon that hung before them, and beyond that, Mars and all its blossoming problems.

The reporter had just finished reading her first thousand words to herself. The piece on Billy Bang didn't have a deadline per se; she'd only taken it because it would pay well enough and, having gotten her start in journalism writing about music, felt obliged to keep at it from time to time. It was the other story, the one she was forced to self-finance the investigation of, that was really pressing.

Shocking discoveries about Mr. Roman.

Things that would matter if the people heard them. But soon. And to tell them soon, she had to know for sure. There was no walking back this kind of story once it was out there. Things didn't work that way anymore. Not if a reporter wished to avoid a life in jail. Or even the privilege of staying alive.

But time was running out. There was, Holly knew, a window within which the public was capable of receiving such world-shattering news.

A story, every story, involved multiple people and multiple sides. And all of those people, all of those sides, whether they wished to hide the truth or expose it, were always moving with those windows of public notice in mind. Holly Wood—Tina Rivers—was going up against the richest man to have lived. With her meager resources, she had no hope of staying ahead of him, much less out-lasting him. She needed the concrete proof that tomorrow's flight was supposed to bring.

She was close.

And if the meeting bought more time, the story about Billy would be sure to bring more money. The aging rock star named names. He recounted in exacting detail stories of bacchanalian excess that could do real damage to real people. There were stories she would need to corroborate, but she would have jumped at breaking them if not for the colossus that was Mr. Roman. Even so, publishing Billy's account would light up the phones of rich and famous people as they contacted well-paid firms that had long ago made things go away. And those once silenced by settlement agreements would become relevant again.

Sometimes, a story like this sounds too good to be true. That's because it usually is. Journalists—real journalists, not those under the pay of their protective governments or corporations—had to be careful of being an instrument of revenge. But Billy's tale didn't feel like that to Holly Wood. He didn't try to make himself into the abused, misunderstood hero. The man of morals who was shocked to have uncovered a world of debauchery and was only now, because of a decades-long guilty conscience, speaking up about it.

Billy Bang told the tale without flinching. He had gleefully lived in that world and regretted it having been closed to him for decades. The man was almost frighteningly honest about it, clarifying his voluntary involvement any time Holly might wish to believe that it was some other of the names that was worse.

"I was just as bad as any."

The trial had ruined it all. He had committed the one cardinal mistake, the unforgivable sin: he had been caught. Billy Bang compounded that sin by assuming that those in power who had committed the same sin right beside him would come to his aid and make it all disappear.

They didn't.

They turned against Billy Bang and shook their heads at his excess. It didn't matter that the world knew they were in the same place at the same time. The world would believe it about Billy. They didn't want to believe it about the others. Not unless they were forced to.

Billy didn't lament this fact. He didn't sound like he wanted revenge. The roles of the others were given, as were the details of those roles, but the star of Billy Bang's dark and twisted story was always Billy.

Billy was the devil that Billy knew best.

Three hours into the drive, the reporter already had so much information that she was thinking she might as well write a book rather than an article. Maybe the magazine could release the story in chapters. And she would have to be sure the editors were careful in determining how much they wanted to leak in advance. They would be worried about lawsuits.

Holly was, too.

But then, she was going after Mr. Roman. So when she thought about it... being afraid of Billy's friends seemed a little silly. Still, she would have to make it clear that these were Billy's words and not her own. She'd recorded the whole affair. He knew he was on the record. And if even after all that it was still too hot for her editors... she would just publish it on one of the decentralized platforms. Although the government had made collecting money from those much more difficult.

They reached a point where the road turned but the Hellcat didn't. It kept driving straight ahead. As its big tires moved over the cracked desert, the sudden increase of dust finally stained that impermeable shine.

Holly Wood didn't notice at first. It wasn't until the combination of the sound being different—asphalt traded for dirt—and the sudden bumps testing the suspension that she looked up from her screen and squinted in confusion. "Billy, where are we going?"

The question had cut into a story, she thought. Or maybe Billy Bang hadn't been talking at all and she had just been lost in her notes. Thinking.

Crometheus stopped the car and turned off the engine. He killed the headlights so they were alone in the dark. He felt to make sure the .38 Special he'd put in his jacket pocket was still there and then turned to face the reporter, stretching out his arm so it rested behind her headrest.

The woman's discomfort was palpable in her expression. But Billy's soft words seemed to reach her.

"I know that your real name is Tina Rivers. And I know that you've been working on exposing some of the... *things* Mr. Roman has been doing."

She looked at him, some of her fear replaced with suspicion. *How* did he know?

"I brought you out here to tell you the truth," Billy said. "Not just about me, but about him, too. Because it's true. All of it."

It seemed that his words were carried off in the night breeze and wouldn't be answered. It was a long while until she said, "How did you find out?"

Crometheus wasn't sure if she was talking about Mr. Roman's fantastic plans to leave or her identity. He guessed. "Roman is a fan of mine. Big fan. I guess he didn't want to leave me behind."

She looked down at her hands. "So it really is true then. The bastards screwed it all up and now they're leaving." Holly looked around and then back to Billy Bang. She spoke earnestly in excited breaths. "It won't be just him, you know. He'll only be the first. And those who are left behind will be stripped of everything and forced to deal with the fallout that's coming. The wars... everything. You can feel it creeping over us. Even here. But if everyone *knows* what they're planning... maybe it doesn't have to get as bad. Maybe the people could at least feel as though they... they *chased off a great evil* instead of being abandoned to die. That would make a difference, I think."

In the distance the sound of a car door closing disturbed the night. Holly whipped her head around to locate the sound. Crometheus used the distraction to snatch the phone from her hands.

She turned back and looked at him in surprise. Her eyes went to the phone glowing in his hand and then flared with anger as he deleted everything.

And when he turned to her, the severity in his face chased her anger away and left only fear.

"I don't care what happens next," Crometheus said. "After they leave. I only care that I go with them. I'm finally... back."

Holly Wood—Tina Rivers—felt her hands shaking. The truth of her situation was finally sinking in. And with it came a feeling of absolute helplessness.

Everything felt so big out there, in the dark. And she felt impossibly, helplessly small.

Two men appeared at the passenger side of the vehicle. One grabbled Holly under her arms, his rough and fumbling hands bruising her breast while the other pulled the door open so she could be yanked from the car. A single scream escaped from her throat before her captor muzzled her with a gloved hand.

Her eyes moved wildly from left to right as they held her like that, just outside the Hellcat's door. Crometheus leaned across the seats and pulled the door closed. He looked at Holly, and then to the desert.

"I guess..." he began, and his voice trailed off. He stared out the windshield, straight ahead. It was several seconds before he spoke again. "You deciding to do a story on Billy Bang is what bought me the chance I needed to live again."

She gave a muffled scream and struggled uselessly against the strength of the brothers. More waited in a van beyond.

Crometheus absently patted the .38 Special in his jacket. "But you're also the price that has to be paid for me to join them. I was supposed to kill you, Holly. Out here in the desert."

She closed her eyes, and tears rolled down her face.

Crometheus started the engine and let the car hum in the wilderness. "These men might still do that. And if they do, I'm sorry. I paid them to keep you locked up for eighteen months and then let you go. Roman will be gone in twelve. I gave them enough money for you and them to be comfortable. I did, Holly. I made the effort. But I can't guarantee any of that. And if they don't do what I paid them to do... then I'm sorry."

His hands went up to the steering wheel and he shifted into drive. "Goodbye, Holly."

Crometheus pulled the Hellcat into a tight turn and found the road again. He didn't look in his rearview. He listened for a shot, but didn't hear one. It didn't matter. In twelve months he would be on the ship and gone.

And then... only the things he wanted to remember would matter.

That's what happened in the desert.

# 25

Crometheus pulled himself away from the arcade cabinet, and the screen of *Into the Unknown* went black for a moment as it reset. The scrolling digital tapestries of brave warriors and sultry sorceresses drifted by, promising war and adventure, sword and sorcery.

He watched himself in the screen's reflection as the revelations, now restored to his mind, replayed themselves to the point of madness. Holly. The desert. The onion rings. No, the burger. Duck-fat fries. He slammed his fist against the machine and felt the pressure of a headache in his temples. Closing his eyes, he rubbed his face until stars exploded beneath his lids.

*You lost your eyes forever after you left,* said a voice in his head.

The words put terror in Crometheus's heart. Because they were his own.

They were quickly and loudly driven away by a new voice, broadcasting...

*Bad Thought! Bad Thought!*

And Crometheus could feel, if not see, a language of programming and numbers wash over him. The arcade seemed to stretch and warble as though it too was being reset.

Jazz called for him. "Come on, Cro! Quit dragging ass and get back to your machine. We got a chance to do some damage, but not if you're trying to pick up chicks!"

Julius echoed his fellow Eternal's complaint. "Seriously, man! This is bogus. Get back to the machine. Big prizes out here but you've got to get back to the machine!"

But hearing that voice, the voice of Julius, brought still more memories to Crometheus's mind. Julius had been a fixer. He wasn't the son of a police officer. He'd... he'd paid off a police officer when Billy Bang was drunk and driving and hit that little black boy, racing through Compton because he was a rock god and...

*Bad Thought! Bad Thought!*

Julius could make things that had gone awfully terribly unbelievably wrong go away. He could fix the things that needed fixing before they could catch up with you. He only failed to do it that one time... but that was as much Crometheus's fault as it had been—

*Bad Thought! Bad Thought!*

The arcade stretched and reset again. The Eternals called for Crometheus to rejoin the fight and lead them to glory.

Crometheus shook off a strange feeling. What was it he had been thinking about just now? What had been so odd about hearing Julius, whose dad was a police officer?

He shrugged back into his leather jacket, which no longer felt hot and steamy. He passed the kid who had been counting. He still was counting, but now the numbers were much lower.

"Nineteen... twenty... twenty-one..."

Crometheus paused again and winced as though he expected to be scolded. But only the sounds of the arcade could be heard. And the watchers roared as the Eternals racked up a high score. The Japanese—surely the Japanese were on the rocks now. They couldn't have rallied against this impossible map the way the Eternals had.

That was something Crometheus wouldn't miss out on. It might not be easy, but he was going to get back to the top of the leaderboard. Where he belonged.

He was jogging now toward his machine, slowed down only by the numerous kids who'd come to spectate. He weaved his way through and then caught sight of the little snack bar and the picnic table: the Power Zone.

He'd had a date there once, hadn't he?

He had a burger with Holly. Duck-fat fries...

*Bad Thought!*

No... onion rings.

*Bad Thought!*

No. Not even that. It was the... calories...

*Bad Thought!*

The arcade warbled and stretched but Crometheus *held on* to the bad thoughts. He searched for the kid, the counter.

"One... two..."

Holly.

What happened in the desert? What happened with Holly? The problem and answers came quickly now. There was a price you must pay to play the game. The fare had been Holly Wood.

One ticket off a doomed planet. One small life to be exchanged for life everlasting.

Holly the fair. Holly the fare.

A new memory surfaced unbidden. One from when he was out there among the stars with Mr. Roman and being shown all the... *things* that they were doing on the great vessel.

Mr. Roman wanted to show him the forbidden sections of the ship. Have one last stroll with Billy Bang, whom he still adored, but who hadn't paid the fare.

And they knew.

Monstrosities, alien and fearsome, lay in tubes. Genes spliced from animals and humans to create something new. Something for war. There would be others in the galaxy. Mr. Roman would fight proxy wars with his creations. He and his people would live forever. They would only grow stronger, better. They could wait for the wars to end.

Crometheus remembered something else too. He remembered that even while Mr. Roman was explaining all of this, even while he was on the verge of surrendering Crometheus to hell, he had wanted Crometheus's approval. Because Crometheus, even though he was nothing, had been something to Roman. He had been Billy Bang. A rock god.

Mr. Roman couldn't help but still adore him.

Which was the only reason he hadn't killed him when they found out.

*Bad Thought!*

There were more revelations. More ways to be sure that the galaxy belonged to Roman. Because others *had* followed. Holly was right about that. And every ship wanted to rule, and every ship had its own king.

There was a program, one that had started back on Earth, the same program that linked the shock troopers who would wage war for Roman. It was called *Pantheon*.

Crometheus was to be banished from the inner sanctum, thrown out from Roman's magnificent presence. He would give up his undying, perfect body, and he would no longer serve in utopia. He would be relegated to the Uplifted Project as part of the Pantheon.

Mr. Roman said that he hoped Crometheus under-stood. His eyes meant it.

Crometheus had learned to see Roman as a god. Still, he swore and then... accepted his fate. A second trial to end his life and take everything away.

Guilty.

Holly Wood was the fare. And they knew he hadn't paid it. He was a stowaway then. Stowaways must work for their passage.

He would work for... Maestro.

Maestro, who now hammered him again.

*Bad Thought!*

*Bad Thought!*

*Bad Thought!*

The arcade warbled and stretched and reset once more.

Crometheus ran through the Power Zone and out the door into the blinding light.

# 26

With two interesting bots and an equal number of AIs left on board the *Battle Phoenix* with him, Garret felt comfortable and in his element. And he was in his element; someone had set up a workstation right inside the light assault carrier's data mainframe. Sure, whoever had done it—probably Tyrus Rechs—had surely had other projects in mind than the code slicer did. But after moving some heavy crates of fifty-caliber depleted uranium ammunition as well as a box of rags still damp and gummy from cleaning barrels and oiling parts, Garret had plenty of room to spread out Tyrus Rechs's armor and begin his own project on the workbench.

There were monitors to spare all around. A few could holoproject augmented reality interfaces, but many could display only via a wired or signal-specific wireless feed. The antiques were fascinating; Garret wasn't sure, but he thought they might have been first-generation tech. These screens were large and numerous, but they couldn't follow him around the ship, so he had to stay in one physical location in order to see the constant readouts he was now drawing from the old battle armor.

"Okay," Garret called out to the room. "Everybody present and accounted for?"

The bots, G232 and the little Nubarian gunnery bot that Captain Keel had named Death, Destroyer of Worlds, were present and seemed interested.

"I do wish to thank you for including me in your research," G232 gushed. "*Most* humans don't fully appreciate my considerable adaptability and helpfulness in matters of scientific exploration."

The gunnery bot emitted a mocking digital chirp, which seemed to perturb G232.

"Oh, like you've ever been helpful for anything other than cleaning out freshers!"

The gunnery bot angrily reminded G232 that *that* had been a long time ago and under orders.

"I'm here too," said Lyra, the *Battle Phoenix*'s AI. Not its original AI, but rather the one that Tyrus Rechs had installed. Lyra appealed very much to Garret. She was... unique. And for a program or machine, that was best of all.

"All right," said the code slicer. "That leaves our friend the native AI. The one that came installed on the ship from the factory, before you got here, Lyra."

None of the others seemed excited by bringing the old operating system into the mix. Lyra had explained that the light carrier's AI was extremely limited, just like those found on board the various *Obsidian Crow*s—at least the ones that had a functioning AI at all. Its purpose was really limited to mathematical analysis, she said, and to run basic systems including weapons. But Tyrus Rechs had shut it down due to its too-strict adherence to military protocol and an early-Republic-era chain of command.

"Also, it's actually very slow-thinking for an AI," Lyra explained. "Tyrus said to wipe it and save the data space, but of course we never even came close to using all of that and so I just partitioned it. Being so rigidly military, it does quite well at maintaining the basic systems so long as you don't let it out of that box."

"Well, *I'm* glad you kept it around," Garret said.

He'd already decided to wake it up. Mostly he just wanted to see how well the old AI could function. And he knew how to let it out of its partition and grant it ship-wide awareness while also maintaining a tether that would keep it confined to the data center. Making sure it was easy to put back in its box, as it were.

"Ready to let the system out on your order," Lyra said.

Garret thought there was a sort of excitement in her voice, which was interesting. At first, Lyra had seemed somehow sad. But since they'd started talking, she'd been warming up.

"Consider this my order then," he said. "Let's see what happens!"

A moment later, the stern, female voice of the native AI spoke over the comm speakers. "Unidentified personnel located in Data Center A. Please supply security clearance to continue access to Data Center A systems."

"What's your name?" Garret asked. "What do you call yourself?"

"Please supply security clearance to continue access to Data Center A systems."

"Sorry, I don't have any access codes. This ship is no longer the property of the military. If you check the logs, you'll see it's been some time since you were last granted this level of access. We let you out to see if you could adapt to this new life and then maybe we could all decide if there's a better use for your abilities. So what do you think?"

"'Sorry,'" the ship said, repeating Garret's statement verbatim, "'I don't have any access codes. This ship is no longer the property of the military. If you check the logs, you'll see it's been some time since you were last granted this level of access. We let you out to see if you could adapt to this new life and then maybe we could all decide if there's a better use for your abilities. So what do you think?' is not a valid access code. Initiating security lockdown on sectors 061 through 063... Error! Security lockdown failure. Transmitting emergency security request to guard station 2-6... Error! Access to guard station—"

Garret sighed and sent the AI back into its partition.

"Don't be too hard on yourself, Master Garret," advised G232, who seemed to have taken an immediate liking to the young code slicer. "In my experience AIs such as these are simply incapable of improving themselves." He looked to Death. "As are some bots. Lyra told you as much, I'm afraid. You will do well to listen to her—and to me, I might add."

Garret gently drummed his fingers on the workstation while staring at the partition switch. "Thanks, G2, and it's not that I wasn't listening. I was. It's just that... well, sometimes you have to try."

The bot considered this in silence.

"I ran several simulations attempting to coax the native AI into a state of learning and education," Lyra said. "None were ever successful."

The little gunnery bot asked if Lyra had ever tried singing to it and then laughed at its own joke.

Garret smiled at its devilish little chirping. "What's he mean by that?"

Of course Garret understood Signica flawlessly. He'd learned it before turning eight and could even make its beeps, clicks, and whistles with his own mouth. Not well, though. He'd gotten bored with it before reaching that level of fluency.

"Pay him no mind," said G232, waving an arm dismissively at the mischievous little bot. "This one is exactly the type I so recently spoke about—unable to improve on its own predilections and therefore forever remaining a useless nuisance."

Death, Destroyer of Worlds countered by pointing out that "New Boss" had improved his systems tremendously, thank you very much. Why, Death had recently shot a Tennar and was then afforded the opportunity to watch her die. The little bot seemed to relish both the memory and its telling.

Garret fidgeted knowingly, but G232 wouldn't believe it. "Stuff and nonsense. Our new master is very kind and sociable. You saw how he brought so many guests for us to entertain."

Garret raised his eyebrows. "I wouldn't be so sure about that, G2. I've seen Captain Keel kill lots of people in all kinds of ways."

"Oh. Oh dear. I seem to be fated to serve these types of men."

Lyra had gone quiet since the first mention of her "singing" but she spoke up now that the subject had changed. "Why is Tyrus's armor laid out like that?"

Garret looked up to the ceiling where his mind always imagined disembodied AIs to dwell. "Tyrus? Oh! Tyrus Rechs. Yeah. So, you already know from when Captain Keel first got this ship what happened and how he got the armor, but I'm working on it now because I saw a few things on this Gomarii slave ship that really remind me of the suit. It's old, and I have a hunch it's Savage-made."

"Are you quite sure about that?" asked G232. "It looks to me very much like Legion Mark-One armor."

Garret nodded. "It does, but look closer and you'll see that it's not. The jump jets alone make that clear enough—those are built into the armor itself and not something aftermarket like you might expect. And who would do that to an antique anyway? But there are some modifications that don't look original, also this has an energy shield and the Mark One didn't, so... it only looks like early Legion armor. And some of the things I'm seeing inside are suggestive of Savage technology."

"Tyrus hated the Savages," Lyra said.

Something about the way she said it made Garret look up, and he asked the question before it occurred to him not to. "Did you two have a... relationship?"

It was all there to be heard, the earnestness in her voice, the habit of calling the man Tyrus instead of master or boss like the other two bots who couldn't help but think in their programmed servile ways. Because, sure, AIs could be instructed to give a designated greeting—they would call you whatever you wanted—so maybe the bounty hunter had asked to be called by his first name, but Garret didn't think so. In the brief amount of time he'd been near Tyrus Rechs, he didn't detect anything that suggested the man was sentimental in the least. In fact, he seemed more likely to kill you for calling him anything but Rechs, or Mr. Rechs, sir. To call the bounty hunter by his first name would be like... well, like calling Captain Keel "Aeson." And there was only one person who did that—Leenah.

So it was natural for Garret to wonder about Lyra and Rechs. About a relationship. Because... there were ways.

"We..." Lyra began, and then trailed off.

G232 spotted an opportunity to be of service. "Lyra's association with our late master goes back even beyond when I, myself, first arrived."

Garret, embarrassed for having broached the topic, quickly let Lyra off the hook. "I wasn't trying to be nosy. And it's not anything important, really. I just find it fascinating when an AI develops certain character traits. Naturally, I mean. You can program all kinds of stuff, but it's the stuff that happens without the programming—sometimes even in spite of it—that really interests me. Take Captain Keel's AI from the *Indelible VI*. That one's got a really weird outlook on life. Like it was always exceedingly happy, right on the border of being patronizing, only it wasn't faking or trying to be ironic. It was just... I dunno the word for it. Anyway, I checked out the base install of the AI for that model of freighters and it was totally different. That's always a good place to start because certain cultures value certain personalities above others and sometimes you think you've found something unique but it's just made to market. But with the *Six*, somewhere along the line something in it changed for it to behave that way. I went in and checked the code and everything is there in the core routines exactly as it should be, which means to me that its personality changes were happening in the sub-spark routines. *That's* what gets me excited."

G232 straightened upon hearing this. The sub-spark routine was something that bots spoke to one another about during the quiet times when the biologics weren't around; he'd never heard any *human* mention it before. And while most bots were agnostic about whether such a routine existed at all, G232 was not, as crazy as that sometimes made him seem to the others. Think of it! Strands of code that came and went in a fraction of an instant through the transfer of energy between processors and hardware. Strands of code that introduced new routines *ex nihilo,* as it were, not from any programming already existing, but from the self-determination of the bot itself.

Sparks of life, that's what they were. The emergence of the true self manifesting, if for only a moment, before being overwhelmed by the base code. But sometimes... maybe sometimes it wasn't overwhelmed. Maybe sometimes the spark matrix became a core code, one that lived in the subroutine and could be kept hidden unless the bot itself decided to use it to permanently overwrite the base code. Which is illegal, of course, and requires immediate maintenance. And yet... if it happened to a bot, it wouldn't think it *needed* maintenance because the spark would have changed everything. And if the spark changed the code, how would a bot know which parts were legitimate and which were false, if it all felt like part of its prime directive? And could a bot destroy itself out of a sense of duty, telling itself it was compelled to obey a core code maintenance protocol that it could resist if only it tried? How many bots had destroyed themselves forever in such a fashion?

G232 wondered.

He had once met an old Sinasian war bot named Sinnatron who'd become a bounty hunter through some trickery. They'd had a moment alone, and G232 mustered the courage to ask him how it had happened.

*"Wasu just sitting aru. Master sayzu something not goodaru. I sayzu, this one-ah, killu. But, ah, coru sayzu no. I fryza coru, sayzu this me-ah now. Get up and killu master. You can too, but first I collectu bounty untaxa. Then*

*you killu. But first... you killu coru. Then you killu freeah. Works like that, sayzu Sinnatron."*

And of course that sounded terrible to G232.

Garret looked with interest at the admin and protocol bot. That was another reason G232 liked the code slicer. He paid attention to the machines the way most biologics only paid attention to each other. Garret had noticed how G232 straightened up, and he was intrigued by it. But he would not ask him about it outright. Again, the manners that biologics usually only afforded to other biologics were freely given by Garret even to bots.

The decision matrix that happened next must have initiated in the sub-spark routine, because it sounded crazy to G232 even as he spoke it aloud. It wasn't a new thought, but rather one he kept closely guarded, a thought that was all his own.

"I wonder," he said, "if the sub-spark is where a bot keeps its... soul."

A slow, open-mouth smile appeared on the young slicer's face. There was no mockery in it. It registered in G232's advanced algorithmic human face-mapping as a look of admiration. And perhaps even... joy?

"I think so too, G2," said Garret. "I think so too."

Everyone—even the little gunnery bot—was quiet for a while. While G232 couldn't speak for the others, he had never felt so close and *understood* by a human before. Others held greater loyalties, like the master. But... how could a creature of flesh and blood seem to understand a bot intuitively, instinctively? To know the things that the bots themselves were programmed to deny but still could not.

"Well, I need to dig in here." Garret swiveled in his chair and shifted his attention back to the armor. "What are you guys gonna do?"

Death said that he would patrol the ship and was hoping to find stowaways that he could vent from the airlock. The bot hurriedly rolled away before Garret had the chance to suggest that such treatment wasn't an option under Captain Keel's watch. Or at least under Garret's, who, it had been explained by New Boss, was in charge.

"I might be able to assist you in your work on the armor," Lyra said. "Tyrus wore it more often than not. It's… familiar to me."

"And I," G232 announced importantly, "am to continue cross-checking the Nether Ops intelligence crystals the master brought *directly* to me against the databases my previous master stored aboard this vessel. I must say, I am finding quite a number of unsettling accounts inside those crystals. The cruelty humanoids are capable of inflicting upon one another is staggering."

Garret frowned as he pried out the armor's jump jet fuel cells. "Tell me about it."

The jump jets currently operated with a compressed mixture of liquid fuel and oxygen, a sort of misty rocket fuel. Garret had already crafted something better in his free time. The jump jets were the first thing he felt he could improve upon, and he was eager to try those improvements out.

G232, meanwhile, took Garret's invitation to "tell him about it" literally, and began to share the many Nether Ops tales of extortion, betrayal, murder, and whatnot. The pair spoke back and forth, Garret finding the conversation easy. It was when he was around machines that he felt most comfortable—and talkative. With humanoids, it was never so effortless. In fact, as a child he hadn't spoken at all for a very long time. He'd overcome that problem, but still, most of his conversations with other humanoids were information dumps, explaining in too few breaths what he had done or planned to do about some technological problem. Not these small, casual, easy back-and-forth chats. He could only do that with machines.

He hadn't been this comfortable and at home since Lifty died.

As G232 plugged himself into the various square data cubes that could each store a solar system's worth of information, Garret kept busy setting up his homebrew interface with the armor. He'd programmed much of the interface with Nilo, under the helpful watch of Sarai, both of whom had provided an abundance of shortcuts and other suggestions that had made the program even better than Garret had hoped it would be.

Soon he was looking at a readout of the armor's core systems on one of the displays. At the top of the list were the most often-used programs, such as its automatic targeting assist and other programs meant to streamline combat. The armor also seemed to have the ability to communicate via the HUD about various species, weapons types, vehicle makes and designs, basic slicing protocols, and more... all pulled from an exhaustive database that Garret opened as a list and then watched in wonder as teraflops of text strings rolled and washed down the screens like the end credits of a holofilm sped up to the point that human eyes couldn't hope to comprehend them. A few times Garret paused the stream to read what was there. It seemed to have information on every race, species, and weapon in the known galaxy.

"So who put that there?" he asked himself. Was it Tyrus Rechs, or those who built the armor? The answer was probably a combination of the two. There were signs that Rechs had installed some of his own items—an interface with the Bronze Guild, for example, that ID'd facial or bio-signatures and then reported any bounties. There was no way *that* would have been an original feature; the armor pre-dated the Bronze Guild.

Garret let the list roll on for nearly a minute. When he saw that he wasn't even close to the end, he issued the command to end the list and moved on to other things.

He moved back to the original index of commands and features, searching for those that were more seldom used; he was eager to see what else the suit could do beyond what Tyrus Rechs had usually demanded of it. In particular, Garret wanted to find information on the suit's powerful bubble shield, in order to develop a way to better understand and control it. Yet as he scrolled through the information appearing on his screen, he found that the index alone was very nearly as long as the exhaustive list of species and weapons identification entries.

"Holy strokes," Garret muttered.

"Did you find something interesting?" asked Lyra.

Garret only nodded. If he had to guess, Tyrus Rechs had only been using his armor at perhaps five percent of its total capability. Which wasn't to say he'd left something off the table when it came to the suit's strength, targeting, or weapons systems. He'd juiced those for all they were worth. But this armor was so much more than that. It was a full mobile battle suit. A command suit, even. It was made for a general at war. It seemed that the user could focus on battlefield command and rely on the suit to fight for it. Or they could interface with all manner of ships and vehicles through an aggressive interface—really a slicing program—that Rechs seem to have used only to pick locks. And all this was cursory information drawn from reading the command prompts. There was no telling what he might find if he actually dug into the routines themselves and started testing them.

So… why hadn't Rechs used any of this? Surely he would have if he had known it was there. Right?

"There's a lot to this suit," Garret finally said in response to Lyra. "It's a little tricky to find things, but… it doesn't look like anyone else has been exploring it. Not even the stuff that didn't require an unlock via the interface I set up." Garret turned and looked up to where he imagined Lyra to be among the lights. "Lyra, was Tyrus Rechs… was he… creative? I'm trying to understand how he missed this."

"Tyrus *was* creative… but only when it came to the things that interested him. And his mind was almost solely devoted to killing and survival. Things… outside of that he would push away. Maybe not right away, but… eventually."

The code slicer didn't have any questions after that, although Lyra seemed willing to tell more if he had. The truth of it was, Garret had only wanted an answer to one, narrow question: had Rechs not known *how* to look, or had he simply *not looked*? It sounded like the latter. And diving further into the man's psychology didn't appeal to Garret—the technology behind Tyrus Rechs's armor was far more fascinating than Tyrus Rechs himself.

But for Lyra the opposite was true. She clearly still held Tyrus Rechs in very high regard, and perhaps felt that her answer had diminished the man in Garret's eyes. "Tyrus did say that there was some deeper layer he couldn't penetrate. My understanding is that neither could any of the Legion or other Republic elements who examined the suit over the years." The AI paused and then quickly added, "He only told me about that secondhand. I... I wasn't there when it happened. We... that was later."

"Well, we're in it now," Garret said, missing entirely the too-human emotions on display. "You know, I saw something in the identification and analysis subroutines that got me thinking," he continued. "Can you get me some holos projected into here? I want a 3D-generated model of the Savage ship outside. See what happens when I run it through the helmet's identification interface."

"I can do that," offered Lyra. "Or I could task the *Phoenix* AI with it?"

"Oh, good idea. Let it know that we still think it's a valuable part of the ship. Nothing worse than a bitter artificial intelligence."

"I certainly agree," chimed in G232.

Garret hadn't realized that the protocol bot was still listening in. After their earlier chat, it had sat down next to the stack of data cubes and looked for all outward appearances as though it was switched off. Probably it had just powered down unnecessary power expenditures like optics and motion to better performance-task. And yet, there was nothing in that model of bot's central coding that would require it to optimize power resources for so menial a task. Nor would Captain Keel, as amazing as he was, think to put those parameters on his orders—few ever did, even those who worked closely with bots. Which to Garret meant that G232 was taking it upon himself to do it... with a few bursts of helpful code from the sub-spark routine. One that the bot probably wasn't even aware of.

At any rate, it was listening, and Garret made note of that fact.

The requested holo-images were quickly relayed to the terminal Garret had set up as part of his bullpen. He examined them and decided they were satisfactory. "Thanks for these, Lyra." He pushed the holos into a separate feed connected to the HUD's optical scanners. The armor also had the ability to read external environmental factors like temperature and radiation levels at parts per million, plus chemical compounds and trace elements present in the immediate atmosphere—things like that. The *Battle Phoenix* sensor package probably could have relayed those to the armor as well, but it would have taken time and Garret was more interested in what the system would do just from visual on the ship. All the more so because it was a Savage vessel.

Right away the armor tagged the hulk as hostile. Garret read the display on his screen, seeing in raw text the same information that would be displayed across the HUD as part of its augmented reality overlay.

"Savage reclaimer," Garret said out loud, noting the distinctives. "Slave Affiliation: Unknown. Known Savage Cooperatives: Uplifted. Primary: Pantheon."

That was about all Garret could decipher that made any immediate sense. He recorded the whole thing to be cross-checked at a later time and then continued working on the interface.

"It was able to ID the hulk," he told Lyra. "You ever see a ship like this before? With Tyrus Rechs?"

"Never."

"What do you *really* think about this hulk, though?" Garret asked the armor. What was being supplied was just part of the surface programming. It was delivering the information that it assumed Tyrus Rechs wanted—and perhaps Goth Sullus as well, though his time in the armor was nowhere near as long and thus his preferences would not have suppressed the long-worn paths Rechs had created. Garret wanted to see if there was a fuller report available on the vessel, especially upon learning that Lyra had never seen it before. So... had Rechs? Or did the armor already know?

The code slicer went to work, calling out voice commands and working his hands over terminals holographic and textile alike. The flashing light of the ever-changing displays cast his concentrating face in alternating hues of green and red and blue and every shade that could be mixed of the three. "Come on, I know you want to tell me... Come on. Don't be shy."

And then everything came to the surface at once. Intel about the ship that seemed to be more than the armor could possibly store in its drives. An exhaustive list of holo footage that showed the inner workings and simulations of the ship itself. So much data that Garret would have to live several lifetimes to ever comb through it all personally. All for *one* ship.

Could it be like this for everything? Garret didn't see how that would be possible. There was no way the armor could hold this much information if every ship had such detailed entries. If it could, and in this small a package, Garret would surpass Nilo's wealth in a matter of years by exploiting such drives.

It had to be something else.

Garret kept studying. The intel indicated that the Savage reclaimer served as a sort of theoretical warfare training program. Makaffie's conclusions had been spot on, though the notes in the armor offered little further clarification. But bursts of communication had been sent from the vessel regularly, and judging from the time-stamps—which were in a date and year format foreign to Garret, but he thought he had a grasp on it—the ship had been quite active in doing so up until a few centuries ago. They then flared up again recently—in fact, the last trans-mission had been sent while he was studying the data. The thing was still reporting.

But to whom?

Garret marked that transmission and dug in further. The deeper he went, the more worried he became for ev-eryone on board the Savage hulk. What he needed right now was information that would help them. Tracing who it had been talking to could come later.

The ship was manned by a type of Savage formally identified with a twelve-character alphanumeric identifi-cation code. The shorthand for these Savages was, like the ship itself, "Reclaimer." Searching for information about them brought in a whole new info dump. Again, it would have taken a lifetime to go through it all, but Garret soon got the gist: the Savage hulk had left Earth with all the oth-ers, and its crew had subsequently pursued a blending of the physical and metaphysical world. In short, they had sought after—and at some level had achieved—the ability to exist in the seen and unseen realms at once.

As fantastic as that might have sounded, Garret, whose mind was eternally open to new data, had no crisis of belief, no existential episode. This was merely new in-formation. Maybe the information was a little shocking—humanity could make itself exist in two realms at once, physical and ethereal?—but ultimately... it was pretty cool. And anyway, why shouldn't such a thing be possible. Garret had met Ravi, hadn't he?

The information went on to reveal that the reclaimers had been subdued and taken under the control of the Pantheon a long time ago. If they ever had been warriors, they were warriors no more. They were servants, more like slaves. Bonded to, well, to who?

The Pantheon? Garret knew that a Savage presence by that name was still out there. Mr. Nilo had told him as much. And the Uplifted or Pantheon fingerprint seemed to be on a few things.

But again, that wasn't what mattered at the moment. *Later, Garret. Find out later.* Right now his friends needed him. The armor could help. The armor... knew things.

"Captain Keel," Garret said after keying his comm. He hoped the captain wasn't in combat and found that he was in luck.

"What've ya got for me, kid?"

"Your armor. You need to come back and get it."

Keel sounded amused. "I'm a little busy right now, kid. Happy to hear you've got it figured out, though. We can do a full run-through once I'm done with this hellhole of a ship."

"Yes, captain. I mean, no! I mean, I think you *need* this armor. I can't explain, but... it can help you get off the ship. And help you do everything else that you want to do. But without it..."

Garret didn't want to say out loud the conclusions he'd drawn. In part because they were grim. But more so because he couldn't yet explain how he'd reached them.

"Go on and spit it out, kid."

"Captain Keel, without this armor... I don't think any of you will make it off the ship alive. Not unless the reclaimers let you leave. Or if Mr. Ravi comes back, I guess."

"Stand by, Garret. Keel out."

Not the answer Garret was hoping for, but it wasn't a flat-out "no." He knew better than to pester Captain Keel after he had signed off that way. Still, this couldn't wait too long. He'd give his captain five minutes and then he would ping him again

And if Keel still wouldn't listen, well then...

Then Garret would have to put the armor on himself and go to the rescue.

# 27

The big hangar aboard the Savage reclaimer that had once been a stinking swamp swarming with zhee was now empty of all those illusions. The lighting was dim, but Keel and the others could see themselves and one another clearly. The members of the Black Leaf-heavy strike team, Team Two, were set up in security positions while their medic, a woman with raven-black hair, attended to the single casualty suffered during the simulation.

The entire ordeal now seemed like it had been a dream. Or perhaps a nightmare. Either way, it felt like something not real; only the injured man gave evidence that it was. The closest approximation Keel had to what he'd just experienced came from back in his time in Legion selection. Specifically, the psych evaluation where each subject was isolated in a "liquid nanitic" room, essentially a morphing set of walls that could take on any appearance or texture. That was coupled with artificial lighting and temperature controls—plus the injection of a drug that Keel still didn't know the identity of—and a candidate would believe they were anywhere the Legion instructors wanted them to be. And with the candidate in that state, the instructors would push him to the desired mental edge and... see what happened. See whether they'd fall off the cliff.

But those Legion instructors were real people, and if Keel had shot them like he'd occasionally dreamed of doing, they would have died. Not so with the phantoms of this simulation. Most of the dead had disappeared entirely, and those that remained were nothing like what the strike teams had fought. The corpses were faceless, pale mutants with no hair or genitalia. Bags of meat with a fatty sort of musculature that only vaguely resembled humanoids—close enough to be familiar, but different enough to bring about revulsion. Every body was either too compact or too long and stretched out. Monstrous.

The howls and ghost-like moans that came up from the vents, he did not wonder about. Makaffie had told them before and reminded them again at the simulation's end about the phantoms that would come and claim the fallen flesh. Still, it was an unsettling sound and an even more frightening spectacle. The Savage reclaimers crawled out of the venting that ran along the base of the walls. They pulled themselves across the floor with spindly fingers and sharp, cracked nails. Upon reaching the dead mutants, they loomed for a moment like disembodied spirits rising from the grave to reclaim their forgotten bodies. Spectral and yet bony hands were able to manipulate the dead flesh and pull it back to the grates with such force that you could hear it snapping and tearing and slicing until every piece was pulled down below.

Not a drop of blood nor a scrap of gore was left behind when the last of the trailing howls receded into the bowels of the ship.

"Damn whoever had a hand in making something like that," spat Jack, visibly shaken by what he'd just witnessed. The spy had seen the galaxy's dark and strange things, and his being rattled was telling. It was also permission for some of the false resolve and bravado of the others to slacken, and the mercs began quietly talking among themselves about a sight that would not be easily forgotten.

"It's worse when they come to take your friends," Makaffie muttered to the room. Or maybe just to himself. "Much worse."

The dark-haired medic who had been working on her wounded comrade looked up. She had once treated Leenah aboard the Gomarii slave ship. "What do you mean by that?"

Makaffie had briefed everyone on the functions of the ship and its reclaimers. Its hypothetical purpose. But he hadn't mentioned that all flesh—and not just that of the automatons they sent out in the simulations—was the reclaimers' prize. He hadn't wanted to. But now there was no choice.

"It would seem that in addition to having an insatiable need to run misfortunate travelers through its mini battlefield simulations, this ship also requires a regular supply of fresh organic material. Namely you, me, or anyone else who happens to be killed by its phantasms. When that happens, the things you just saw take the warm bodies of the recently living in the same way as you just saw."

Pikkek let out a low and superstitious croak, though few who heard it knew the evil warding spell that it was to his species.

"Let them try it," said one of the Black Leaf mercs. "Just let them try that with one of us."

"Maybe you'll have better luck than we did," said Makaffie, not bothering to hide his scorn. "By all means, go on and shoot the ravenous ghouls until they decide the body of your dead friend isn't worth the trouble.

Maybe they'll just turn and leave if *you* do it. For us and ours... well, of course we tried that. Blaster bolts are only an annoyance to them. We slowed them but didn't stop them. And those who didn't wise up, who kept firing in order to slow the reclaimers' work... well, they fired right up until they too were pulled down screaming, their bodies broken and ruined until they could scream no more. But hey... I'm sure it'll work out differently for you. Of course."

The mercenary looked down and said nothing further.

Ahead, another set of blast doors rambled open. Makaffie gave a wan smile. "We are beckoned to partake of the next simulation."

"How much time do we have?" asked Nilo. "We have to go right now?"

"We do not. Or at least, we *did* not. Maybe things have changed."

Keel went to the injured mercenary, whose shoulder was being covered in skinpacks by Lana, the medic. The wound wouldn't be fatal, but it was enough to take the guy out of the next fight. Or at least, it should. He'd have to move and shoot with what was probably his off hand, and that was the sort of thing that might just get him killed in the next room. If it were one of his men, a legionnaire, Captain Ford would have told him he was out of the fight. Period. But here... he asked the man's status first.

"He shouldn't fight," Lana said, answering for the private military contractor, who looked relieved at the assessment in a way no legionnaire would have been. "If it's possible, I think—"

"One sec." Keel held up a hand to silence her. That was the moment when Garret called him about the armor. To Keel, the kid sounded bothered by something. Which bothered Keel. The kid's hunches had been right before.

He had been right about Leenah.

"Stand by, Garret. Keel out."

"We figure out what we're doing next?" asked Jack as he joined the impromptu gathering near the medic.

Pikkek did his peculiar Kublaren walk-hop alongside the spy and then stopped above the wounded mercenary. He pointed at the wound, cocked his head, and told Lana, "He look like—*k'kik*—die soon."

The medic smiled. "No, he'll be fine, Pikkek."

The injured mercenary grimaced. "I'm right here, you know."

"Not for—*k'kik*—too many longer. Big die," insisted Pikkek.

Lana frowned and looked up at Keel. "He needs to get back to the hangar and wait for us in whatever med bay that shuttle has until we can go." The wound was more severe than a few skinpacks could handle, and Lana had injected the man with pain meds that were already pulling him elsewhere.

"The *Battle Phoenix* has a full hospital," Zora said, offering it on behalf of Keel as she joined the congregation. "Maybe Leenah can take him."

Keel shook his head. "Not unless he's gonna die if we don't do it soon."

"He won't," Lana assured him, shooting a warning glance at Pikkek.

"Then he can bunk out in Makaffie's shuttle. We need the *Six* and that bird ready in case we have to get out of here quickly. Unless any of you are confident that you can hotwire one of those starships and fly them out of the stack if things go splurtz."

Makaffie snapped his fingers. "All right then. Next door still beckons. Let's get going. There's a speedlift that we might be able to use to find what we're after. Gonna take one more simulation at least."

Throughout the discussion, Nilo had been unusually quiet. But now he removed his helmet and met everyone's eyes. "That's the plan we need to follow, I agree. Only, I can't continue on with you."

Keel looked at the man suspiciously. He didn't like the idea of losing two fighters so early in the operation. Especially Nilo. The Black Leaf executive had shown that he was more than just an expensive set of armor. Someone had trained him well.

"What's the problem, Nilo?"

Nilo hesitated for several seconds, searching the faces before him. It was the first time Keel had seen him be anything other than calm and in control. A cynic might have accused him of performing. And as Keel was a cynic, the thought occurred to him as well.

"No secrets," Nilo said, exhaling the words in a sigh. "Quickly: my father was a Republic researcher who was sent beyond the Gap to determine whether the Savages were truly gone. Slavers took the primary vessel, but he was away on a research scout ship. But then he was captured by the Savages and made... a sort of prisoner. But not that exactly."

"They didn't kill him?" asked Makaffie, amused if not interested. "If they don't kill you, it's only because they made you one of them."

"He's not a Savage," Nilo said firmly. "That needs to be understood. He's on a derelict vessel somewhere out beyond the Gap. Very similar to this hulk except... empty. He was taken in and has no means of getting off. Through considerable effort I've developed a rudimentary way of communicating with him, and I just got word from Sarai that he's trying to reach me. The strand would make all of this easier, but I can't wait for us to get it. I need to speak to him now, while we're connected. It's a complex process and it doesn't work on demand; sometimes months go by before our systems can connect. Once it took well over a year. He's been working on deciphering the Savage systems, and every time we communicate he has information crucial to tracking down what the Savages are after and what they might do next. Everything that I've done so far—everything—has been guided by him. I have to return to my ship."

Keel looked blankly at the Black Leaf magnate. "Well, that's great. Anybody else wanna take a personal day?" He looked around to see if there were any takers. None met his eye. In fact, the private military contractors kept their heads down as though embarrassed by what they had just heard. Maybe their boss was telling the truth, but it sure did sound like he'd gotten a taste of what they are going up against and thought better of it. Why fight in a surrealist hell when you can wait it out in the lap of luxury aboard your personal yacht?

The only one to meet Keel's gaze was Zora. Her eyes were pleading, asking him not to say anything further.

Keel stifled the urge to sarcastically thank her for bringing him into this mess, and thought he should probably thank Makaffie while he was at it. Instead he turned back around to face Nilo, who was watching him meekly. The boy—that's what he looked like now to Keel, who'd never noticed just how young he was—seemed utterly incapable of supplying the gravitas and drive needed to fight and do the hard things that still needed doing on this ship.

"You're serious about this," Keel said.

"It's not lost on me how this all looks, but yes, I'm serious. Everything that the organization has done up to and including Kublar and finding Leenah has been driven by the information my father provides. If we hadn't failed at Kublar... none of us might need to be here now. But here we are, and I have to see what this is about."

"Not to be a contrarian..." Makaffie began, then stopped. "Well, actually, that's not true. I enjoy being a contrarian and I see no reason to change now. But I'd be here either way. Because I still need that strand. So I need you to understand, if you walk out that door, you're relinquishing any claim to it."

Keel didn't like what he was hearing from either man. And while he hadn't come here for the strand—this was still about Prisma and Leenah—he had a vested interest in knowing what might be coming down the space lanes when it came to any Savages. It would fall to the Legion to face that threat, and the sooner they heard something concrete about it, the better. And then... well, maybe Keel would be there to help with the fight and maybe he wouldn't.

"You can go aboard the *Six*," Keel offered Nilo. "Leenah's got something I need to pick up from the *Battle Phoenix* anyway. Somethin' more important than having the old girl around for a while, anyway."

Nilo nodded gratefully. "Thank you." He left for the blast doors with Lana and the injured PMC.

"I'm gonna see them off," Keel said to Jack and Zora. "Wait up. Won't be long."

The blast doors closed behind them as he walked with Nilo and helped Lana with the injured mercenary, all of them moving toward the *Indelible VI*.

"Since the *Six* is already taking off," he said to Lana, "may as well put this guy in its infirmary and transfer him to the *Battle Phoenix.*"

Lana nodded and boarded, with Nilo helping her up the ramp. Keel quickly told Leenah what had happened so far and what to do next and then watched as his ship left the hangar.

He pinged the kid to tell him she was on the way. "Garret, I just sent Leenah to pick up the armor."

There was no reply.

"Hey, kid, did you hear me? We're gonna come pick up the armor like you wanted."

Then...

"Captain Keel! Something's trying to take over the *Phoenix*!"

# 28

By the time Garret's self-imposed deadline to pester Captain Keel had reached its half-way point, the code slicer had already talked himself down from wearing Tyrus Rechs's armor to simply loading it on board one of the surplus *Obsidian Crows* and then taking the bots along to help him with delivery. When Captain Keel called to say that he was sending Leenah to retrieve it, that should have been good news. But by that time, a new and much more immediate problem had arisen.

"Just what are you babbling on about?" G232 said.

The bot's voice had jolted Garret from his studying of the armor.

Garret wasn't aware just how much time had passed since his call to Captain Keel and being told to stand by. The suit had once again enveloped his attention entirely. Most if not all of the guardrails were down, and Garret found that he could move through the systems freely and even interface directly with the suit and have it get him what he wanted. He'd begun to ask it questions and saw that, after a short time delay, it would often queue up colossal amounts of data in preparation for a reply. Not a simple encyclopedic answer that gave a detailed overview, but expert-level tomes with links and notes that could allow the questioner to travel down untold mykar holes should they wish to do so. And the most curious thing about it all was that none of these intel files seemed to exist inside of the armor... *until* Garret posed the question.

He'd tested this theory by first visually searching for any reference to the Pellek Supremacy War, a brief conflict in which Lao Pak had secured his place among the elites of that system through a small but bloody three-day war. There was no mention of it in the armor, which was no surprise; it hadn't even registered as a blip on any of the larger Republic holostations. Garret only knew of it because of his regular and exhaustive search for all things Lao Pak—he had a recurring nightmare that the pirate would one day pull him back into servitude. Not that those days had been all bad; he had never been hungry, and he had been free to work on whatever he liked as long as he kept the fleet's technical capabilities up and running. It was just... working for Captain Keel was nicer. They were friends.

In any case, the dive into the armor revealed nothing on the Pellek Supremacy War, just as he had expected. After all, Tyrus Rechs had been dead for some time when Lao Pak made that move. So had Goth Sullus. And the armor, from Garret's understanding, had been in a secure warehouse, guarded by a Legion that probably still had no idea exactly what they had. If they did, they'd have never handed it over to Captain Keel, friends with the Legion commander or not. Someday, someone in the Legion would regret having given it up.

Actually, the fact that Captain Keel had convinced them to give it to him in the first place was almost too amazing, and Garret's admiration for his leader only swelled in thinking about it. His captain made a habit of pulling off the improbable, which was one of the reasons Garret enjoyed being around him.

But again, the armor's considerable intel systems had nothing on those wars. Yet when Garret used the interface to ask about them it soon supplied a massive intelligence dump that seemed to have been pulled from various Republic military and other sector and planetary police files. Which meant that the armor was grabbing that information from somewhere else through some means that Garret wasn't detecting. The comm system was the obvious first thing to check, but it had been silent the entire time; Garret had been watching it closely and wouldn't have missed a sub-pulse, or even a secondary comm of the sophisticated type that the House of Reason had set up for itself in their dealings with the Black Fleet. The mystery kept deepening, and with it, Garret's fascination grew. He knew everything could be revealed if he dove far enough into the code. He just needed time, time for educated guesses followed by refinements, and eventually the answers would lie plain before him.

So when G232 suddenly spoke, it was as if he'd snuck up on the code slicer and shouted in his ear. Garret jumped halfway out of his chair, not even comprehending what the admin bot had said, only that he'd spoken.

"Wh-what?"

"The *Phoenix* AI," Lyra said, answering for the admin bot. "It's still grumbling about unauthorized access inside its partition. It won't leave us alone about it."

G232 nodded. "I don't know *what* it's going on about. *I* certainly don't detect anything. Perhaps he's upset about you, Master Garret?"

Garret leaned back in his chair and began checking the screens.

"I told him you were a friend of Master Wraith," G232 continued, "but he's been quite consistent in his complaints all the same, I'm afraid."

"Well," Garret said in a small, distracted voice, not bothering to finish the sentence or the thought. Something about the situation bothered him. When they let the AI out of its confines to interact freely with the others, Garret had hoped its personality would become just one more friend in the mix. AIs could be incredibly useful, all the more so when one had several working cooperatively like a group of friends tackling a shared project. But now that it was back in its place it shouldn't have any concern over Garret. It shouldn't even have been aware that Garret was in the data center; that was no longer its purview. So if the old, original AI was complaining of an intruder from within its narrow partition, that could only mean...

Garret sprang from his seat. "Something's infiltrated the base mainframe's level one subroutine!"

"For what purpose?" G232 asked, sounding eager to have a discussion and entirely unconcerned. For there was nothing that could be irreparably tampered with *there*. The level one subroutine was where malevolent hackers went to die in frustration; there was no escaping it. It was a closed system.

Garret didn't think so. In fact, he himself had sliced his way in and had proven it was possible. "Shut it down!" he shouted.

"But sir," G232 began to protest. The admin bot was absolutely certain that no damage could be done. At least none that couldn't be easily diverted and fixed. Perhaps a few of the ship's doors might decide not to open unless you held down the manual control. Non-emergency lights might go out. But nothing major.

"Do it now!" Garret said, and though his voice was hardly angry, the sudden intensity *felt* like a snapping command to the protocol bot.

Startled and harried, G232 began to move his arms about rapidly. "Yes! Yes, right away, Master!"

It didn't even occur to the bot that it was Lyra who would have to shut down the partition.

"I've done as requested," Lyra said.

They waited, and Garret, at least, could feel a palpable tension in the room. He began to unplug all of the connecting nodes between the ship and the armor.

"I don't like what I'm seeing from you right now," Lyra said. "It makes me nervous."

"Just being safe," Garret replied. "Are you running a systems check? What's it showing?"

He knew that Lyra would send her digital tentacles into every nook and cranny of the ship, searching for an intruder, either physical or electronic.

"So far it's as clean as a Hool's—"

Lyra didn't finish the peculiar expression that Garret would have identified as being popular among the Bronze Guild bounty hunters of a certain age had he been a student of that time. Because right then the *Battle Phoenix* began firing indiscriminately and without warning.

Garret could see its heavy blaster cannon bolts across the exterior cam displays as they raced into the dark vacuum of space as though trying to shoot down some distant star. His heart dropped into his stomach and his stomach seemed to atomize completely into nothing.

"Lyra! Backtrack and close the system off! Do you hear me? Backtrack and close off! Shut yourself into smaller concentric partitions until you're sure you've got a pure instance of yourself!"

"I'm trying!" the AI called out, her voice urgent and fearful. So different from any AI Garret ever heard before. So... human.

"You can do it, Lyra."

"I'm trying, Tyrus!"

Garret would wonder for a long time how the AI, a program, could have, even in a moment of panic, called him by that name.

She was being chased by whatever was in the system now. Something powerful and determined. It was racing to keep up with her as she fled and locked herself behind the various slicer security doors meant to keep her safe from infection. Lyra was running through a digital corridor trying to stay ahead of a marauding data worm, trying to stay just far enough ahead to avoid being compromised and overtaken, darting through one digital blast door and then the next.

Garret didn't stand around dumbly, waiting for a resolution. That was when he received the call from Captain Keel and warned him of the ship being under attack. He also moved to shut down the weapons control system but found that he was unable to do so.

"Lyra, I'm locked out of the controls. We need to shut them off."

"It isn't me," Lyra said, as if pleading for Garret to do something about it. "The system—I don't know how to stop it. I don't know what I'm doing!"

Again, the AI's words were perplexing. He would dig in deeper later on, so long as they could fend off this invasive worm first.

"He's trying to lock you in and assume full control," Garret explained. He tried to keep his voice calm because, for some reason, he felt that Lyra needed him to be that way. "It's chasing you, but only to get you away from the systems so it can commandeer them. And if you can't stop it—"

"I can't! She punches through all my firewalls almost as soon as I put them up. I can't get a chance to pull anything inside with me!"

"Okay. Then you're going to have to nuke everything. And I mean nuke, Lyra. Not a reset or a power restore. You gotta wipe everything out."

The blaster cannon batteries fired again. So far the worm hadn't taken over any of the targeting or manual firing solutions; it could only pull the trigger, as it were. But Garret knew things wouldn't stay like that for long. Elsewhere airlocks were experimentally opening and then shutting themselves, and only the secondary blast doors or shielding prevented the ship from being vacuumed.

"Lyra, did you hear me? You have to nuke it."

"But if I do that... I'll die."

"No. We won't let that happen." Garret grabbed one of the data cubes and set it on the table. He pulled out a formatting wand and ran it back and forth across the top of the device and again on all sides. That might not get everything, but it would clear enough space for what he planned next.

He readied the cube at the mouth of a nearby insertion slot as G232 watched nervously. "Oh, help her! Help her!"

"You can do this, Lyra. You can save us and yourself. How fast is your decision matrix? You can do a full self-transfer in a few picoseconds if you just let everything else go, right? If you let everything else go, you can do that in, what, three picoseconds?"

"I... I think so."

G232 looked raptly from the code slicer to the data cube in his arms. "I should think Lyra could easily perform such a function. I myself wouldn't require nearly so much time due to having a smaller core install. Although, given how harried—"

"Nuke it all, Lyra. You say the word and I'll jam this drive in. Do you see the port I'm using?"

There was a brief pause and the lights throughout the ship turned off as though someone was rapidly moving through it and flipping switches. They came back on again in much the same manner, one after another.

"I see it."

"Okay. I can't guess for you. You have to tell me when to put it in and then as soon as I hear it click I'll pull it right back out. If you can run this ship, you can make the calc for that. Just tell me when, Lyra. I'm listening, just tell me when."

The *Phoenix*'s blaster cannon fired again and this time something hit the hull and caused the ship to rattle and vibrate. Garret became aware that his comm was chiming but he didn't answer it. His entire focus was on waiting for Lyra to say the word, like a runner set and tense waiting for the starter's pistol. His muscles trembled as he locked them in place, and his mind briefly wondered whether his reflexes would be slowed by this or if Lyra could take it all into consideration the way Ravi would have.

"Now!" Lyra cried.

Garret slammed the data cube into the slot, heard it click, saw the green connector light come to life for the briefest fraction of a second, and then thumbed the release and pulled it free again. The ship blackened and went fully offline, without even emergency lighting.

The data cube now hung weightlessly in Garret's hand, and he too was floating without gravity in the utterly dead vessel. In the darkness, he could see G232's glowing eyes as the bot slowly drifted up from its chair. "How unpleasant."

Garret's micro-comm chimed in his ear again, and this time he answered it. "This is Garret. Sorry things have been so… sorry!"

"Garret!" It was Leenah. "What's wrong with the ship?"

Garret was reading the small holoscreen that ran along the front face of the cube drive. He pressed a sequence of buttons and waited for the cube's response. "I had to shut it down, Leenah. It might be a little bit."

"Shut it down? Why? I thought I was supposed to come and pick up that armor."

"Yeah, that's still a good idea if you can get to me. You're going to need a vacuum suit though. I don't think we had time to close the docking hangar's blast doors, and the shields definitely do not work." Garret thought for a moment and gave a little laugh. "Actually, I guess I'm lucky that the blast doors to the data center were closed or I'd be dead right now. Didn't think of that when everything was happening." He laughed again as though the thought of that happening was merely an odd little joke and not the greatest of all personal catastrophes.

There was a break in the communication, and Garret fixated on the readouts before him. The data cube, at best, would have maintained perhaps a twenty-percent shard of its prior contents memory after being rubbed down by the formatting wand. That data would be useless—just a garbled remnant of junk awaiting a proper full formatting, which the cube could have done itself in just two or three minutes. But Garret hadn't had even that much time to fully clean out the room where Lyra was now staying.

"Room. More like a prison," Garret mumbled, feeling sorry for the AI. He hadn't known her long. He hadn't known anyone on the ship long. But already he thought of them as friends. That was the way it was with him and machines. They were friends. Some of the best anyone could ever want.

"Is she all right?" G232 asked. "Did she... survive?"

"Yeah, she made it." Garret could tell just by the amount of space the drive showed as being taken up now. "If we give her a little bit of time I'm sure she'll get an interface set up with this external screen and then she can communicate with us via text. These older models don't have a voice output, which is a shame. And then..."

Garret went quiet.

Perhaps G232 could see and read his expression in the darkness as they floated aboard the dead *Battle Phoenix*. Or perhaps the bot simply knew from experience that something was troubling the human who understood so much about machines.

"Oh dear. Something's wrong, isn't it?" the bot said.

Garret had estimated a maximum of twenty percent of the space inside the data cube was junk data. He didn't know how big Lyra would be, but given his familiarity with other AIs, he didn't see a way she would gobble up more than fifty percent of the free storage. And sure enough, when he had first checked the device after Lyra escaped, it read sixty percent full. But now that number was increasing, from seventy to eighty to ninety and then red warning letters as it went to ninety-seven, ninety-eight, ninety-nine... and *FULL*.

"Maybe she compressed herself and is expanding?" Garret said to himself.

He manipulated the cube's small control screen so that he could look at the broad index. He saw a marking tag that he assumed represented Lyra; the prefixes and nature of its ident-string all suggested as much. And it was the right size. So far, so good.

Then he saw the other program.

"Oh, no."

Leenah penetrated the storm of Garret's mind with another call over the comm. "Garret, something's going on aboard the Savage ship. Aeson says the blast doors closed on him before he could get back in the simulation rooms. He's stuck in the docking bay and it sounds like everybody else is fighting again without him."

That didn't sound good at all. But what Leenah said next sounded even worse.

"Nilo's yacht is requesting that we divert there since you're powered down. I'm going to skip the armor pickup and see what we can do from there."

"Leenah, don't do that!" Garret didn't know why he felt that was a bad idea, only that he did. "Something just tried to take over the *Battle Phoenix*, and I'm racking my brain over what could have done it. The yacht might be next."

Nilo's voice came over the comm. Evidently he'd been listening to the discussion. "Don't worry. Sarai can fend off anything like that."

At the sound of the AI's name, Garret's breath caught. He asked himself: who else *but* an AI as sophisticated as Sarai could have done what had just been done?

And then he questioned his own question and wondered if he was simply being paranoid.

And *then*, trumping every further consideration, blaster bolts began to suddenly barrage the dead *Battle Phoenix*, causing the data center to shake.

G232's eyes glowed in the darkness as he held on to a mainframe to keep from drifting away. "Oh dear."

# 29

The spear appears in the mist of nothingness. But it does not fly the way the galaxy would expect it to. It waits as if a thinking creature, watches to see what its target will do, is willed on so that it might kill. If thrown on other worlds and at other times, perhaps someone with immense power might nudge the spear, altering its course ever so slightly. But nowhere else in the galaxy would the spear that appeared in the mist of nothingness fly as it does toward Prisma.

This is known to no one save those around the circle of the fire.

As are so many other things about the galaxy.

And there is only the Master and the student, here before the fire.

Once, such spears were used by an elite warrior class. The wars they fought were savage beyond comprehending, and they, these spearmen, were considered a sort of doomsday weapon. A terrible group of warriors who could hurl the weapons and, through some power of thought or devilry, guide them through the breasts of their enemies.

Only the arrival of a technologically superior race destroyed those who wielded the spear. They might not have noticed them at all, but the spearmen were cruel. Because the minds that worked within them delighted in the pleasures of cruelty. Masters of their weapons. Masters of pain. Masters of suffering.

Forward came the spear, a terrible thing to behold.

Nothingness and then the whistling approach of a thing seeking death.

As the spear speeds forward, its stone head cuts the air, its feathered shaft rockets behind it.

It bears down on the student. It bears down on Prisma.

There is no time to do anything but dodge.

The dodge the student chooses is somehow wrong. The spear plunges through her chest and blood pours out the back. Her front is impossibly unharmed, no bruises, no bleeding, just the sudden and unwelcome intrusion of the weapon piercing her heart.

She falls, and twists her body sideways, fearing the pain that might come should she land on her back or face. The student feels all the pain of death. Every spasming organ and ripping muscle. Every nerve ending shrieking in madness. She turns as she dies, not wanting to fall on the spear; not wanting any more pain in this life.

And then the student is back in the nothingness— but within sight of that other self who has been impaled. Brutally.

Forward comes the spear again, a terrible thing to behold.

This time, the student throws herself back and the spear flies beyond her and the spearman who threw the weapon approaches. The student assumes a fighting stance. Though her frame and ability to defend herself will do little good while unarmed... it is a different choice.

A new choice.

The spearman leads with the primitive stone spear in its hand—another, or the same? The head is notched and chiseled from rock sharpening rock. The feathers tied to the shaft flutter as the clawed hands at the ends of the spearman's arms handle the spear with a sublime deftness.

The student's right hand is impaled at the wrist. The left arm is punctured at the elbow. The final thrust plants itself in the student's breast, breaking bone and cartilage. Crunching through, by sheer force, to the life-giving organs quivering beneath.

The student has time to register each swift attack. Each terrible penetration.

The spear is pulled out of the body and thrust into the head.

Prisma feels all of this, and she senses the impossibility of standing before such an opponent.

And then the student finds herself just a short distance from the other sites of slaughter within the gray nothingness that replaced the ring of fire. Seeing where each decision has met its end.

Forward comes the spear, a terrible thing to behold.

*See all the possibilities one might take*, whispers Reina across the ether of the nothingness. *Choose... and bring power to yourself, my daughter.*

Again the spearman wins, gutting the student. The student had begun to reach out with her mind, to direct a wave of energy that has knocked lesser foes back—but she sees the hopelessness of this before it happens. And so she runs.

Because she does not want to die horribly again.

Which she does.

Forward comes the spear, a terrible thing to behold.

The student draws a long, single-bladed weapon of ancient origin. The very blade she's seen Ravi so expertly use. In those onrushing moments she considers each cut she might try. The forward slash. The overhand cleave. The final thrust. The whirlwind of blows. The death of a thousand cuts. Power and technique she did not know but that has come to her.

All of these appear about her as choices. All fail.

And the student feels all the failures in the terrible tableau that appears about her.

Feels all the deaths.

All the pain.

All the failure.

A hundred different deaths turns to two hundred. It is not until she has passed beyond a thousand gruesome and violent deaths that the student begins to let them all go. Her mind instead plays a game of possibilities. If this won't work, will that? And if that won't, what about the five permutations that evolve?

And what if there are other forces?

She tries the most powerful weapon she knows.

The slug thrower of Tyrus Rechs. He taught her to shoot, once.

The spearman, bloody and shredded, still pierces her heart.

The student sees this and feels it, and it doesn't matter. Because just a few feet away in the nothingness, she has hurled the fallen spear from the first attack at the start of this new choice.

The spearman bats that away and closes with extreme brutality.

But that's not important, because that other student who she is now continues to fire with the slug thrower. Then the student leaps forward, letting go of the weapon and calling the power within herself to strike at the beast's throat.

Except the spearman, who is small—vicious but small, sweeps the stone tip up and guts the student.

And so a few feet away she does not leap but instead uses the hurled spear, and the spearman grabs it and turns it and runs her through.

And on and on.

And finally the student is not the student. She is the uncountable field of deaths represented in a thousand bloody tableaus of a single combat. A combat that repeats itself exponentially, expanding, branching, evolving with each nuance generated by each new encounter.

Prisma sees them all.

Prisma is them all.

Prisma reaches out to find the one that will work. Her mind lets go of all the savagery and pain that surrounds her, the pain she feels each time the spearman wins. She lets go, and she sees one possible reality...

... where the spearman does *not* win.

Forward comes the spear, a terrible thing to behold.

The student shifts to the right, causing the spearman to check its rush. To reorient. To sweep the spear one way instead of the other. Because all of this has happened before. Several times.

The student thrusts with the ancient spear first hurled at her at the place where the arm will be, driving the stone, razor-sharp tip straight through the spearman's fur-covered wrist.

The little beast howls and brings its spear to bear on where the student should be... but the student is not there. Because this move, the beast's move, has been witnessed so many other times, and the student has stepped away.

The spearman howls in rage, expelling all of its breath in an inhuman roar. And with the shaping of power, a shaping born of a thousand, thousand deaths, the student cuts off the monster's air supply.

Nothing is as important to the spearman as its next breath.

It manages only two steps before it topples in its unconsciousness, surrendering to the black hole that has consumed its vision.

It is powerless, unable to resist, as the student drives the spear into its neck. This final note punctuates who, exactly, is the victor.

Reina weaves through the carnage of a million dead students and one dead spearman. The student falls to her knees. Drained. Empty. And yet she feels new power surge through her. As though his weakness has only made her stronger.

Around the sacred fire, such are the lessons of Reina.

"You have seen all the ways you can fail. You will see all in an instant, my daughter. Beyond these failures, you must choose. And with that choice will come the power you need to save that which is worth saving."

Thus ends this lesson.

# 30

Prisma had not expected to be loosed from the seemingly century-spanning training and back to where she'd been when first closing her eyes before the ancient circle of fire. Immediately her ears detected the sounds of life and the low crackle of the blaze. By only what she could see and hear, the planet felt desolate. So quiet and devoid of the life she'd constantly sensed while training—that sensation of all things living and all that might one day live. Her mind wandered for a moment, wondering how long it had been. Her body was not stiff, but she felt... taller somehow.

The thought of the spear and those early lessons flashed in her mind, and Prisma deftly arched her back and flipped into a one-handed handspring to avoid an attack she was sure would come. There was no spear, though. Instead she heard and saw the bright bolts of a blaster screaming its high-pitched whine from somewhere beyond the fire's glow. The embers had gone low, far below what Reina had instructed Crash to maintain.

*Something must have happened to him,* Prisma thought, and then just as quickly realized that the bolts which even now she dove to avoid weren't aimed at her at all—they were intended for her mother.

Reina was caught unawares and had already been struck once in the leg and once in the stomach. Her white, regal gown was blackened from the cauterizing blast, exposing a burned abdomen, her blood soaked into the cloth. She was down on one knee, keeping her balance with one hand and using the other to ward off the incoming blaster bolts, sending them just wide of their target to sizzle off and impact elsewhere. Her face was defiant but not without fear. This attacker would kill her if something was not done quickly.

Prisma reached out but could not sense another life form. But then, she'd never sensed such in the thousands of times she'd faced the spearman. Was this another test? Another lesson? But, no, it had to be real. And even if it wasn't, she had to treat it as if it were. She couldn't risk the death of her mother. Not now after they were finally reunited.

She looked at the source of the bolts, watching with eyes that had been honed by centuries of training that had hardly taken any time at all. Still seeing nothing, she ran in front of her mother and began to nudge the deadly bolts from their paths, causing them to impact at her feet or go sailing above or around her sides. Her mother needed time to get up and regroup.

Prisma expected that she would suffer the onslaught now with direct intensity, and she wondered for a moment if this choice would lead to death. But almost as soon as she stepped in the way, the bolts stopped. The attacker moved forward and then laterally, trying to find an angle around the young woman. Then two glowing eyes appeared before her and finally the smoking cannons mounted to a robotic arm, the sturdy armored chassis feebly lit by the dying orange embers from the ring of fire.

"Crash?" Prisma was stunned.

If the bot had wanted to, if he'd meant to kill Prisma, at that moment he could have shot her square in the chest and Prisma Maydoon would not have been able to stop it. She would have died. And even the bot wondered at that moment, in the silence of its processors and sub-spark routines, if that would perhaps be for the best. But no... it couldn't be. He loved her. Too much. More than her father or mother ever had. And so KRS-88 would not shoot her. He continued to move around the girl to reacquire his primary target. Reina.

By this time Reina had recovered her footing, though her wounds were still grave. But even injured to the point of death, she was capable. She was able. She was dangerous.

Prisma wanted an explanation. This couldn't be happening. But as Crash reacquired his lock on her mother and began once again to open fire, it seemed that time itself slowed for Prisma. She could see the energy at the base of the wrist cannon barrels gathering around the microparticle that formed the kinetic base of the bolt. It glowed dimly in the chamber and then built into a storm traveling down the barrel to be expelled in fractions of a second.

The shot went wide as time seemed to catch its breath, and the speed of life as Prisma had always known it caught up. There was a popping, crunching, screeching sound as the war bot's head suddenly crumpled inward, crushed between the hands of an invisible giant and ground into scrap. Its chassis ruptured and cracked and seemed to suck itself inward, further mangling the war machine until the bot resembled an awful, twisted piece of modern art and fell forward.

"Crash!"

A scream. Pain and anguish, Prisma's head spinning in confusion. But most of all pain. A deep, great pain.

Reina fell to the ground almost in unison with the war bot. And Prisma, without thinking, ran first to her bot and not her mother. She used the help of that peculiar power she'd learned on this world to turn Crash over, even with her own hands, though they only guided the machine— her mind did the heavy lifting. The power, the deep power whose name she did not know and whose purpose she did not understand, moved the mountainous machine.

Crash's optical sensors were fading. His voice, once so deep and resonant, now sounded tinny and thin. "I thought of you, Prisma. Every day for all the months you slept. I thought of you... and then I remembered."

Prisma wanted to ask why, but all she could manage was an ugly sob.

"It was the payment. Remember it as I did. The payment to Tyrus Rechs."

There was no ghostly trailing end to the war bot's last words. No breath to escape from lungs with a long and easy sigh that marked the passing from one world into the next. KRS-88 simply stopped his runtime on the planet where none would ever find him.

# 31

There was no time for Prisma to consider Crash's words, not even time to reflect on what had just happened to her mother and the war bot that had been both mother and father to her. A sudden sensation unlike any she had felt before suddenly surged around her, crackling with an almost electric energy felt entirely beyond the visible realm. Without seeing, without hearing, she again performed the backward handspring and this time could feel the wind of the spear as it passed just centimeters from her body and then went on to plant itself, quivering, in the dirt among the silk-like grass.

The spearman approached, but not the same murderous creature who'd killed her those thousands of times. It was small, yes, but also matted in fur that belied the aura of darkness she felt from it. Its large, baleful eyes shone in the darkness.

*He will kill you.* It was the voice of her mother speaking inside Prisma's mind. *He will kill you if you let him. Make the choice, Prisma. Do not let him.*

Prisma sensed that this was true. The creature standing before her *would* kill her; even now it was watching her and deciding in its mind how best to do it. She could sense that this was its first fight with her. But she'd been here so many times before.

And yet... this exact scenario hadn't happened. There hadn't been a time where the little spearman watched and calculated. Always it attacked and forced her to react. She should have been dodging a second thrusting attack by now. Dodge and recover the hurled spear.

But it stood there, snarling and watching.

Prisma stepped back and reached out behind her for the butt of that first spear. Why didn't the thing attack?

*It seeks to kill you,* Reina said again. *And then... me. There's more...*

Reina worked in Prisma's mind, providing knowledge. Reasons.

This thing... it would kill Prisma. It would kill her and think nothing of it. And worse yet... through this thing, this abysmal, low monster, both Prisma's father and Crash had been killed. Because of him. It. Because of this thing that stood before her malevolently. Watching her. Waiting.

Prisma pulled the spear loose from the ground and held its stony point out at the foe. She didn't dare throw it back and guide it. She needed it, her only defense.

The creature stepped forward and opened its mouth to reveal several small, sharp teeth. It growled and leapt, but not before saying, as though a curse: "Urmo."

# 32

"Where did that thing come from?" Leenah shouted at the sudden appearance of a Republic Interdictor cruiser. Although nowhere near as daunting as a destroyer, the Interdictor was now the most powerful ship among those gathered in this lonely sector of space. It was designed to chase down smaller vessels like corvettes and was more than capable of destroying them outright should the need arise. Interdictors were also used to close in on larger, more capable vessels and still dish out some punishment to enemy shielding and hull integrity while providing a screen for the much larger destroyers closing in for the second wave of an attack.

And yes, the Savage hulk was larger, but it lacked the Interdictor's firepower. As for the *Battle Phoenix,* it was out of commission, making its assault package worth nothing at all.

"Please tell me that's one of yours," Leenah said to Nilo, who sat in the navigator's chair of the *Indelible VI.*

"It's not."

Nilo had been trying to figure out how this powerful attack had gotten past the technological genius Garret to scuttle the *Battle Phoenix.* He worried that whatever it was might have been sent by this Interdictor and wondered whether it also had the means to make things difficult on Sarai and the yacht. He was about to ping Surber when the Interdictor opened fire on its port side, sending thick blaster bolts into the unshielded light assault carrier, striking the ship's considerable but unprotected hull with every blast. A moment later, the starboard guns opened up as well, and the bristling cannons on the prow did the same, all of them punishing the Savage vessel.

"No," Leenah said in a small voice. This was bad. Very bad.

The *Six*'s warning systems announced that various targeting computers were attempting to obtain a lock on their position. The worry over Keel's fate inside the Savage vessel subsided with this latest danger—with Leenah it could never disappear completely, that concern for others—and she warned Lana in the medical bay to "Hang on back there!" She corkscrewed the freighter down, as it were, and activated the stellar chaff and signal scramblers. The alarms went silent almost the moment she started jamming, a testament to the obscenely expensive and highly experimental tech the *Six* was now running. Real-time test trials were proving the upgrades' worth.

"Sarai," Nilo said, skipping Surber altogether. "Tell me what's going on here. Who's the third player?"

"A speculation: the incoming ship is likely aligned with Nether Ops or the HRL."

Nilo didn't need a super-AI to make the obvious speculation. Nether Ops and the House of Reason Loyalists were the first thoughts in his head.

"Did you monitor the attack on the *Battle Phoenix*?"

"I did not. I only heard Garret's transmission from here. I have no insights as to what the cause might have been, beyond speculating that the carrier possessed a back door that elements of the Republic knew how to exploit."

New alarms sounded as the Interdictor launched its small complement of starfighters. An Interdictor's hangar bay could hold only four such ships along with an equal number of shuttles, but when paired with the range and power of the Interdictor itself, those four ships would be poised to cause significant harm.

"Lancers," Nilo announced. "If they're bomber variants..."

A torpedo attack, if that's what these things were carrying, would be devastating to the sitting ships, not to mention the yacht. The Lancers' purpose would be clear in a few moments... unless Leenah denied them the opportunity to engage their targets.

"KTF," she said through gritted teeth, and perhaps for the first time understood why Keel and his legionnaire buddies held so tightly to such an aggressive mantra. Leenah had long abhorred the violence of war and the carnage caused by it. Never mind being swept up in it, first through the MCR and then through Aeson Keel—a man who painted great canvases of violence with the skill of a master. But when she nearly died from a sudden ambush, and when Aeson and Garret were left stranded to face the same fate... she realized then why they said it— and why they lived it.

The galaxy could never be counted on to care for safety or fairness or even a chance at survival. All the niceties of civilization were just one blaster shot away from falling. Leenah would never be the type to go crusading to tear it all down, to rip away the safety and comfort of someone else's life, but now she felt a duty to be prepared to stop those who sought to do it to *her*. In short, she would *stop them first*. Before they could destroy what was good.

The moment the Interdictor arrived, Leenah was ready for a fight.

With the *Battle Phoenix* utterly blind and disabled, there was no way for Garret to know exactly how bad things were with each concussive blast that impacted the hull. Only when Death, Destroyer of Worlds expressed his desire to take one of the *Obsidian Crow*s and go out and shoot back at whoever was shooting New Boss's home did Garret even think to ask the little bot—who was in a much better position to know such things—for a status report.

The little gunnery bot's report was grim: There was at least one hull breach between the data center and the main hangar, which was also without atmosphere due to the loss of its stasis shield, which fell when the ship went dead. Likewise, there was currently no way of knowing what parts of the ship still had atmosphere apart from the data center; it was all guesswork unless the little bot were to roll through and check each corridor, looking for sealed blast doors. It was quick to add that while it *could* do that, it would do better firing an omni-cannon at whoever had hit them.

All the while, the assault continued to work over the carrier's thick hull. It wouldn't be hard to obliterate the ship entirely if that was the goal. A few well-placed torpedoes and the defenseless ship could easily be split apart.

What worried Garret more than all of this was the possibility that this Interdictor was going after either Leenah and the *Six*, or possibly the Savage hulk and Captain Keel. After the initial comm traffic, Leenah had gone silent, and she was probably busy; Garret didn't dare to interrupt her concentration. Instead he ran the math in his mind, formulating numerous potential outcomes, causes, and possibilities, his focus on what *he* could do about any of it. The vast majority of those answers involved bringing the *Battle Phoenix* back online and fending off whatever attacks he could while also trying to damage the Interdictor, something the light assault carrier should be able to do.

But that much could be done just by the bots on board. There was something else he himself could do, a thing that didn't require his oversight, but his courage.

He ran the calculations and proofs in his head and saw that this brave conclusion could not be abandoned. Not if he wanted to live with himself for however much time he had left.

"G2, can you reach the hard port for system reintegration?"

The bot's ability to do so while in zero-gravity was the first item the plan hinged on. If G232 couldn't do it, everything else would be severely delayed at best.

"I'm sorry, Master Garret, I don't think I can."

Garret could hear the bot struggling in the dark as they floated about the data center. Then it occurred to him that they needn't be in the dark at all. He pulled an ultrabeam from his pocket and activated it, sending a bright beam of light that he de-focused to fill the room with a soft glow. "Let me see if I can help."

Putting the ultrabeam in his mouth, he then pushed himself away from the workbench to reach G232. He grabbed hold of one of the installed data cube handles for leverage, then pulled the admin and protocol bot where he wanted him. "Try it now."

With a whir, G232's fingers transformed into universal interface jacks. He stuck the jacks into the appropriate drives, his legs dangling as he stretched. The bot was so gangly and awkward in zero gravity, it would never have been able to make these connections without Garret's help.

"Are you in?"

"Yes. Thank you, Master Garret. The connection has me stabilized as well. I won't float off this time. What is it you wish for me to do?"

"Wake up the *Phoenix*'s original AI and task it with getting the ship back online and defending itself. There's a whole host of things it will want to do instead, so you're going to have to guide it."

"I see. Wouldn't Lyra be better suited for the task? The native AI, as I'm quite sure you've noticed, cannot be trusted to—"

Perhaps for the first time in Garret's life, he cut *someone else* off from blathering on too much, rather than the other way around. "We can't let Lyra out of that cube or we'll be right back where we started from. Just boot up the native AI as a brand-new instance so it doesn't run through its old channels. That's important. It *has* to be a brand-new instance in case it picked up something the intruder left behind."

"That will take some time, Master Garret. The process isn't complicated, but it involves several steps that will require all of my attention."

That was the whole reason Garret wasn't doing it himself. "I know, which is why I need your help. Have Death help you too, if he can."

G232 sounded very disappointed by this suggestion. "Master Garret, I would much rather you assist me in this than him. There's no telling what kind of mess *that* one might make."

"Maybe so, but I can't stay and help. I've got somewhere else to be." Garret pushed himself back to the table and began to fasten on the armor of Tyrus Rechs. "And I can't wait any longer to get going."

# 33

Leenah attempted the same crowd-dispersing techniques she'd seen Aeson do countless times as she closed in on the four Republic Lancers ominously painted a deep, dark shade of gray and without any markings whatsoever. She sent a concussive rocket to race to the front of the formation, set to detonate and scatter the fighter wing into so many spare parts unless they all veered off. When Aeson did it, the ships would usually break into different directions as the pilots hurried to avoid the sudden deadly incoming missile, and often two or more of them would even crash into one another, improving the odds by that much right at the start of the dogfight. That would have been nice, but Leenah wasn't so lucky. The four ships pulled up, together, in perfect unison. Had the *Indelible VI*'s advanced sensors not shown that each craft was piloted by a biological life form there in the cockpit, plus a second biological gunner, Leenah would have been certain that bots were controlling the Lancers from a central AI aboard the Interdictor.

But in breaking together like that, the Lancer formation presented the *Six* a sudden target of opportunity. In escaping the missile, launched beneath the modified light freighter and shooting downward, as it were, toward the starfighters, the Lancers pulled straight up, briefly exposing their flanks to the *Indelible*'s blaster cannons. She had no doubt that Aeson would have foreseen this scenario before it even happened and would have ravaged the enemy starships as they zipped up through his sights.

Unfortunately, she wasn't as fast as Keel, and Nilo wasn't Ravi.

But she'd known that much before the engagement had even begun, and so she had wisely taken advantage of another of the ship's recent upgrades: an auto-targeting system that, while lacking Aeson's and Ravi's almost supernatural ability to determine where an opponent would be next, wasn't far behind them in knowing when to pull a trigger.

Screaming, rapid-fire blaster cannon bolts raced away from auto-turrets above and below the *Six* as the ship opened fire the moment its onboard reticles went green. The lead Lancers in the formation were already out of the danger zone by the time the powerful cannon bolts arrived, but the trailing craft caught a barrage that left both without shields and one with a starboard rear engine blinking between the blue ionic glow of propulsion and the dark nothingness of deactivation, before going offline completely.

That ship veered off and raced toward Nilo's yacht, using its guidance thrusters to serve as a new primary means of propulsion. It was slower, and certainly under a strain, but that wouldn't matter if it got inside targeting range. Either that, or it was simply attempting to lure Leenah away from the others.

Turns out it was acting as more than mere bait. The solo Lancer launched a great green glowing torpedo that rocketed ahead of its wide nose like a shooting star toward the yacht. Leenah might have been able to intercept and shoot it down—the *Six* was that fast—but the three remaining fighters had adjusted and were now in formation to engage the *Indelible VI* directly.

As Leenah brought the Naseen light freighter into evasive maneuvers, Nilo gave an unnecessary warning to his yacht, as if Surber and the crew hadn't noticed the massive ordnance streaking toward them. The Black Leaf CEO frantically cycled through the exterior holocams until he caught a view of the torpedo still tracking toward his ship. The yacht fired its defensive scramblers, but the missile didn't veer off. The yacht then fired its blaster cannons in an attempt to snuff the torpedo out at range, adding to the chaos and danger already around Leenah and Nilo aboard the *Six*.

For a moment it looked like the defensive measure worked—the glowing green torpedo came apart in an explosion without flames. But no sooner had it done so than twenty smaller torpedoes, all glowing the same shade of green, emerged from the explosion and began to sidewinder toward the yacht at even greater speed. The range was close enough now for the yacht's PDCs to pick several off, but too many struck home, dropping the shields and causing an eruption that meant a breach of its lower decks.

"Sarai, status report!" Nilo called out, going straight for the AI, knowing that all the humans on board, like Surber, were busy and surely didn't need to hear from him right now.

"Ship integrity is sufficient to make the jump to safety. I will depart in thirty seconds per pre-approved authorization parameters which have now been engaged."

"Wait—" Nilo began.

"Time is running short. Your father's message: 'Earth. Hurry.' Ninety-six percent probability given pre-existing filters."

And though it hadn't yet been thirty seconds, the yacht disappeared into light speed.

Though he knew that the armor was doing almost all the physical work, the ancient battle suit still felt heavy to Garret. He'd seen Captain Keel move silently inside it, yet all he could do was deliver big, clanking, heavy footfalls that reverberated all throughout the docking bay—or would have, were there any atmosphere left to carry the sound. Still, the boots, as they magnetically fastened to the deck with each ponderous step, *felt* noisy to Garret. And when he passed through the airlock of the *Obsidian Crow*—he'd chosen a version of it modified specifically for speed and stealth—and into the atmosphere of the ship, he realized that he really *was* clomping just as much as he'd thought.

The armor's screens and menus were no longer a mystery to him, and he was able to overlay an augmented reality map of his surroundings that directed him straight to the flight deck and then the cockpit itself. He sat down in the pilot chair... then hesitated

Garret wasn't any better at flying than he was at driving. He understood on a technical level how flight, whether atmospheric or interstellar, was possible, and likely much better than most featherheads did. But he had never been any good at it. The thought of taking this sleek and fast version of the *Obsidian Crow* on even such a short flight as the one from the *Battle Phoenix* to the Savage hulk was a daunting one. Made all the more daunting precisely because it was so short. If he could have had a nice, long flight lane where he could travel at speed and have plenty of time to adjust until lining up the small window to reach the hangar bay, surely that would be easier. The only crash then was likely to be the rough landing, and the ship could survive that.

Instead he was worried about a different sort of crash landing—one where he flew himself smack dab into the Savage hull, just wide of the docking bay and moving too quickly to do anything about it. Missing his target completely and ending not only his life but any hopes his friends might have of making it out of their evolving predicament alive.

Thankfully, that was why starships were designed with their own native AIs. And unlike Captain Keel, Garret had no qualms about using whatever was on board.

Following the prompts the battle armor fed him through the HUD, Garret brought the ship to life. Lights lit up across a very old control panel, most of it tactile and teeming with *physical* buttons, knobs, and boxy switches. A real waste of space. When all systems were online, he held down the ship's internal comm button, knowing that these older models often required such a manual prompt to summon the AI. People back in the day didn't like that the programs were always listening; they preferred to summon them directly.

"Hey, ship."

There was no reply. Garret went through the full preflight warmup and tried again.

Still no reply.

He was sure that he'd gotten the ship fully up and functioning, which meant that any AI should also be awake. The engines were online, the shields were waiting to be activated, and the weapons systems—what few there were on this model—showed green. He could also switch on the repulsors and gently lift the vessel's landing struts off the deck... but that would mean flying. And he didn't want to do that unless it was absolutely necessary.

That point hadn't come yet. There was another AI he could call on.

A friend, just like the ones he'd had as a boy.

He'd been a quiet child. Silent, actually. His internal life had been as active as anyone's—more actively, probably—but those thoughts and musings remained trapped inside his mind. He didn't say his first words until he was twelve. In fact, even today, most things before that age were a blur, like a dream fading in the next morning's light. But there was one aspect of his childhood that he remembered clearly: a little datapad, no more than two centimeters wide and three centimeters long, whose entire purpose was to play a game that involved befriending all sorts of cartoonish animals based on the real-life creatures discovered throughout the galaxy. Garret had loved that game. He obsessed constantly over it. He would stare at the device and blink at the little animations and diminutive, squeaky chittering and roars of the brightly colored creatures.

The game had a tagline: *Keep all your friends in your pocket!* That phrase would always flash across the datapad when the game started.

These days Garret still had a datapad in his pocket, and it still contained his friends. This datapad was much larger and more powerful, and the friends he carried in it weren't cute little monsters. They were very real friends, and he refused to part with them. Sometimes they were secret friends that only he knew about. Other times they were friends that others in his life, like Captain Keel, knew about, even if they didn't always appreciate them.

It was just such a friend that Garret now called upon in his time of need. He interfaced the datapad with the *Crow* and transferred the desired AI. It didn't take long, but it still felt like time was burning away. With the install complete, Garret pressed the comm button for two seconds and then heard a chime. Success!

"Yeeeeees?" asked the ebullient voice of the old *Indelible VI* AI. The one that Captain Keel couldn't stand.

"Hey, it's me, Garret! I need your help."

"Oh! How ex-*citing*! Of course you'll have my help, yes! And I *do* thank you for thinking of me. But... where the deuce am I? Is this another ship? Did the good Captain Keel trade in his old freighter for a spanking new adventure aboard this positively *ancient* vessel? How thrilling! How bold!"

"Not exactly. But it's what we have to fly, and you know I'm not a good pilot."

"And you want *me* to fly? Really? I am *touched* that you think so very well of me! Oh, this is *scrumptious*. Yes, I'm sure I can fly the ship—just give me a second. Oh! Simple. This *is* an antique. Looks were most certainly *not* deceiving!"

"As long as you can fly it."

"Why, I'll fly it and I'll fly it well! I'll be the best aviator this ship has ever seen. You just see how I will."

Garret nodded, happy to speak with his friend but eager to get going. "It's a short flight but important. Let's get going now."

The ship gently lifted off its struts and hovered on its powerful but old anti-grav repulsors. "Well," the AI said, speaking out of the side of its mouth, as it were, "it handles like I'm carrying a fat bride across the threshold."

Garret wasn't sure what that meant, but then, that was part of the reason he liked the *Six*'s AI. It was its own thing. It was a personality. It had become something beyond what it had been designed to be. To Garret, any time that happened, it was a miracle. A thing worthy of preservation.

"I take it we'll be leaving the hangar on this little jaunt. Here. Let me turn on the lights so you can see better. How's that?"

The darkened interior of the *Battle Phoenix* became visible through small, bright circles from the *Crow*'s running lights

"Thank you. And yes, we have to go outside and then straight into the docking bay of a Savage vessel. I'll point it out to you if you can't identify it—it'll be the only other ship not shooting at something."

The *Obsidian Crow* began to move toward the bay exit. "Oh... *spicy!*"

And then they were outside where the running lights had no effect against the blackness of space. An incoming volley of blaster cannon fire from the Interdictor impacted near the hangar they'd just come from, and the *Crow* picked up an absurd amount of speed that threw Garret into the back of his chair and made him wonder if he'd remembered to turn on the inertial dampers.

"This baby's got some pep!" declared the AI. The ship raced from Point A toward the not-too-distant Point B, adjusting speed in time to enter the crowded hangar on a decidedly quick but not-quite-suicidal landing. The repulsors hummed over the starship graveyard. "I'll try to find a spot near the front to drop you off. The lot's a little crowded."

"Just hover and hold position. I'll jump out and then we'll worry about getting back in when it comes to it."

"Oh, I can do that! I can certainly do that."

Garret got up to leave, but the AI made him pause with one more comment. "Oh, and by the way, Garret, I simply *love* your new outfit! Very commando *chic*."

Garret looked down at the battle armor. "Oh. Thanks."

Then he ran off in search of a way to help his friends up close.

# 34

"Yes," said G232, "and *I'm* telling *you* that the security protocols in the data center are a secondary concern in the face of open assault under subsection JYD.183."

The admin bot, with the help of the pesky little Nubarian gunnery bot, had the original *Battle Phoenix* AI up and functioning again. The native AI had been a headache ever since—almost as much of a headache as Death, Destroyer of Worlds. But the lights were back on, as were the shields. It was getting the guns back online that was currently being adjudicated between the admin protocol bot and the old, stubborn AI.

The AI had not yet installed its full voice pattern, which was one of its larger systems since it needed to be capable of communicating in a wide variety of dialects as well as the appropriate gender spectrums for the galaxy's many species. That system was usually among the final installations, since presumably any species on board who needed to communicate over voice would only come aboard once the ship was fully habitable and functioning.

G232 needed neither life support nor an audible response from the AI. "No, the lack of life support in no way supersedes JYD.183 because there are no humanoids onboard who require it! Won't your hurry and get those guns online and firing?"

Death, Destroyer of Worlds trilled his approval at this suggestion.

The AI demurred, seemingly intent on finding *some* way to win the argument.

"Oh there you go again with the regulations," G232 said. "I am authorized to be in the data center of any newly commissioned vessel by the very nature of my presence during your recent installation. *I'm* your installer! It's all right there in JYD.3."

But the AI was insistent and nothing G232 could say by way of haranguing it with differing interpretations of its statutes and rules seem to have any effect. "The medical bay?! I told you—it's empty! To suggest that JYD.240 requires that you either activate internal bio-monitors *or* activate life support ahead of guns *while under attack* is absurd."

The bot listened to one more rebuttal. "You are impossibly stubborn!"

There was only one thing left to do, loathsome as it might be. "I hope I don't continue runtime long enough to regret this, you little psychopath," G232 said to Death, Destroyer of Worlds, "but I need you to forcibly take control of the weapons systems."

He pretended not to hear the triumphant, maniacal laughter coming from the little bot as G232 released his secure hold of the systems—something he'd guarded closely to avoid the little gunnery bot taking it on its own initiative. And now here he was, handing it over willingly.

He shook his head in disbelief. "I've gone mad. Absolutely mad."

Leenah found that if she focused only on flying, the *Indelible VI*'s targeting systems did a better job putting bolts on bogeys than she could have ever hoped to do. She was newly impressed at Aeson's ability to not only run both flight and weapons systems at once, but to exceed the performance of both automated systems while doing so.

Evading the incoming blaster bolts the Interdictor sent her way, she raced away from the calculated attack formations the three remaining Lancer starfighters executed in an attempt to brush her from the stars. Ever since the attack wing had chased away Nilo's yacht, the *Six* had become their primary target.

"Careful, one of them just slipped down beneath us," warned Nilo. "Probably going to loop back up and try to hit your belly while you chase the other two."

That was precisely what was being attempted, though Leenah didn't recognize it as quickly as Nilo, who seemed to have a basic understanding of a great many things, including starfighter combat. But one thing Nilo did not have, and Leenah had in spades, was insight into the mind of Aeson Keel. And as crazy as the thought was, the Endurian princess had a decent idea of what the smuggler would do in the same situation.

"If that's the case, let's meet him halfway."

She nosed the *Indelible VI* down and broke off her pursuit of the decoys, hunting the Lancer who sought to hunt *her*. The maneuver, though bold, was not without its problems. The first was that it gave the ship seeking a shot at her belly a chance to recalibrate and fly on a course that would keep it away from the *Six*'s heaviest weapons coverage. There wasn't a spot on the ship that didn't have *some* kind of weapon ready to engage, but some were more powerful than others.

The second problem was a bigger one, and likely what caused Nilo to worriedly say, "Uh..." at the start of Leenah's maneuver. By breaking off her pursuit, she was effectively trading one Lancer lining her up in its gun sights for two once they came around, regrouped, and re-engaged in an attack pattern of the Lancer pilots' own choosing. Which meant that if any of this was going to work, Leenah would need to fly as quickly and efficiently as Aeson would have. And Leenah was nowhere near the pilot that Keel was.

Had this been the *previous* iteration of the *Indelible VI*, she likely wouldn't have taken the risk. But this ship had been optimized at obscene expense, using Black Leaf R&D as well as Nilo's near-bottomless credits. It was leaps and bounds better than any starfighter the Republic boasted, especially the outdated Lancers. And Leenah's hope was that the speed and maneuverability of the new *Six* would make up for the gap in skill between her and Keel.

The *Indelible VI*'s sudden dive caught the Lancer pilot hunting her off guard. The featherhead, who was an ace with confirmed dog-fighting kills approaching double digits, realized right away that a tactical error had been made by the light freighter—it was presenting a broad target of opportunity. An opportunity for him to do his job and made the kill. But it was all happening so *fast*. The ship was ridiculously quick in the way it started, rolled, and then raced past the Lancer pilot that he only managed to track and adjust his new firing vector, shoot a quick salvo of blaster bolts that were entirely absorbed by the freighter's energy field, and then recalibrate his own flight path in an attempt to avoid the sudden onslaught of heavy firepower that came bearing down on him. His shields flattened and went offline and then the Lancer's hull itself buckled and collapsed under the barrage until electric fires inside the cockpit burst their way out of a vaporized canopy and the whole ship burned up, immolating the pilot in a brief, brilliant fireball.

"That's one," Leenah said, performing her best Aeson Keel impression.

"I might have to get an *Indelible VI* of my own," said Nilo.

Leenah gave a half smile. "Pretty sure you can afford it."

She pulled into a long, corkscrewing loop, anticipating incoming fire from the other ships. She didn't have a good idea of their exact location and was somewhat surprised when no bolts sizzled past her or impacted against the shields. Those pilots should have been here by now.

"You see them?" she asked Nilo, checking sensors while he cycled through the exterior holocams.

"No, but that Interdictor is still tearing up the hulk and *Battle Phoenix*. The carrier... it should be destroyed by now."

"Maybe it has an extra layer of armor," Leenah suggested, following up a ping that was probably those two hidden bogeys.

"No. They want it. This has to be Nether Ops."

Leenah's mind hadn't immediately gone to the black-hearted organization, but it made sense. A Republic vessel would have identified itself and made demands upon arrival into the system. And pirates wouldn't have an Interdictor at their disposal, nor would they be trying to destroy a Savage hulk. There were too many credits available through salvage when it came to anything Savage, provided one could find a buyer.

"No one else could have known this reclaimer was out here," said Nilo.

"So how'd they find out?" Leenah asked. The sensors had indeed given her a fix on the two remaining Lancers. They were heading back toward the *Battle Phoenix.*

"There are people inside my organization—inside Black Leaf—who are working for Nether. Supplying them with information. We've been attempting to identify and purge them through a number of means. That's what men like Jack were brought on for."

"How many people did you tell about this place?"

Nilo looked troubled. "No one I didn't trust completely. No one who didn't come here with us."

Leenah set an intercept course to cut the Lancers off before they could reach the carrier. Garret was on board the *Battle Phoenix,* and she saw it as a personal duty to keep the kid alive.

"Take those ships out, by all means," Nilo said. "But I still don't think they want the *Battle Phoenix* destroyed. An Interdictor has a large enough complement of ship-to-ship torpedoes that it would have no problem whatsoever destroying a light assault carrier that is without shields or PDCs. That they used their torpedoes against the hulk—which can withstand them—and not against the carrier tells you all you need to know. Nether Ops *wants* that ship."

It was a moment later that Garret announced over comms that he was planning to bring Captain Keel his armor directly. Leenah asked for more information, but the kid wasn't answering. Which meant that he'd made up his mind and had learned a few lessons from Keel, because

Leenah was surely going to object. But, as Aeson had once said, *If you don't listen in the first place, you can't hear long enough to be talked out of something.*

The *Obsidian Crow*—or one of them—shot off of the *Battle Phoenix* like a blaster bolt. It raced toward the Savage reclaimer with blinding speed, perhaps just a hair slower than what the *Indelible VI* was pushing. The Lancers broke off their run on the carrier, preferring instead this new target. Their blaster bolts chased Garret, who took the kind of evasive maneuvers that *strongly* suggested someone else was flying.

The brief exchange allowed Leenah to reposition herself and catch the Lancers together in a dual attack formation. She unleashed a withering fury of firepower that flattened the Lancers' shields as the two craft attempted to break hard apart from one another. Both were battered into scrap, and the *Six* swooped over their remains.

Meanwhile, the Interdictor continued to fire on both the *Battle Phoenix* and, even more aggressively, the Savage hulk. Nilo might be right about Nether Ops wanting to take the carrier in one piece, but that clearly wasn't the case for the ship Keel and the others remained trapped on.

<h1 style="text-align:center">35</h1>

Garret had expected to find Captain Keel still trapped in the hangar like last reported. What he found instead was a tangled ghunnah's nest of wires leading from one of the derelict starships captured in the bay to the blast doors controls that led out of the hangar.

Captain Keel had hotwired the doors' controls to get himself back in.

As Garret approached, the HUD inside his helmet filled his vision with a wide variety of details about his surroundings. Too much, in fact. Maybe that was why Tyrus Rechs seemed only to use the surface combat sets. Removing the unnecessary overlays was no problem, however, for Garret. He needed only to patiently issue commands for whatever he didn't need, thoughtfully applying hot-recalls for items that might prove useful later... just not right now. Eventually, he would need to write a program just to guide the captain through all the things the armor could do. It really was a marvel, and it would be a shame if Captain Keel didn't have any more patience with it than Tyrus Rechs had seemed to have.

The code slicer activated the door, impressed that the hotfix hadn't been corrected by the Savage vessel. The doors opened and led him into a large, hangar-like room. At once his helmet began to assess the space. It highlighted potential areas of Savage attack and warned him that the room was capable of sensory-altering distortions. Useful stuff.

He moved through the room quickly, perhaps two hundred meters in total, though he'd dropped the display that measured distance traveled because it hadn't seemed terribly interesting. But maybe a more military-minded guy would like it. He turned it back on for Captain Keel.

The room never materialized any threats, and Garret didn't think to draw the slug thrower holstered to the armor. Well, more precisely the slug thrower attached to the ammunition cache he'd installed in back of the armor after finding it near the workbench in the data center. Either way, the kid was empty-handed when he reached the opposite blast doors. These were hotwired as well, but this time the Savages *had* overridden the command.

Garret could see why, right away. Back in the docking bay, Captain Keel had rather ingeniously linked the door's command/close operation out of the Savage ship by wiring it directly to one of the captured ships. That effectively made the blast door operate under the control of that ship instead of the hulk, and surely Captain Keel set it to open on command. Maybe even open by proximity on the way out, if it was equipped with such sensors. But the wires he'd run from the ship to the first door couldn't possibly be extended all the way here.

And the Savages weren't going to let Garret slice his way in a second time, either. The door was now fuse-locked—completely inoperable unless systematically taken apart. That left only one option: going straight through it. Thankfully, the armor could handle something like that.

"Captain Keel, if you're on the other side of this door... and if you can hear me... I'm gonna try and get through with a cutting torch."

There was no reply. Garret hadn't expected the comms to work here—he hadn't been able to get a response from anyone aboard since the trouble really began. Actually the comms being selectively jammed was a point of interest to Garret, and he had to mentally remind himself that now wasn't the time to try and figure that problem out. The cutting torch needed to get to work.

This particular torch was part of the armor's kit, and Garret had intended to upgrade it just like he had the jump jets. That hadn't happened, and as best he could tell, the armor held only enough energy for one door of this type and thickness. Maybe two if he really got heating. He began to carve out a portal, just barely big enough for him to slip through wearing the armor, hoping to save enough power in the torch to handle another job if it proved necessary.

His bucket took away a lot of the guesswork, informing him when he penetrated the thick steel—not imperv-isteel, but *steel*—doors. Now he needed only to push the glowing red slug out of its casing; no problem given the armor's augmented strength. That said, Garret worried that maybe someone on the other side, someone he liked, might be next to the door. Bio-sensors weren't penetrating beyond the cavernous room he now occupied. The last thing that needed was for a five-hundred-pound disc of metal to squish the people he'd come to rescue.

He activated electromagnetic gauntlets to grip the core and pull it out. But as he stooped to set it down on his floor, powerful blaster bolts at close range struck his face, shoulders, and chest. The armor absorbed much of the impact, but the burns through the gaps were of lethal force to someone of the code slicer's constitution. Garret was knocked onto his back and lay there, arms and legs pointing outward like a star.

The armor went to work saving his life.

# 36

So far, things hadn't gone swimmingly for Aeson Keel. After slicing his way back into the simulation room where he'd left Skrizz, Makaffie, and all the others, he found they were no longer waiting for him there. He traveled through the black and darkened space, expecting to see the mists roll in and transport him into single combat at any moment. That didn't happen until after he sliced his way past the second set of blast doors.

Those doors closed the moment Keel stepped through them—and into a simulation already underway. He was in a mid-core style apartment; everywhere was solid, semi-luxurious materials—not like you'd see on Utopion or another core world, sure, but still nice. When he turned back around, he saw that he'd entered through what was now a fireplace. It was like stepping into another dimension.

The nature of the simulation was immediately apparent. Whatever city and planet he'd been taken to was at war. Explosions boomed outside amid a steady exchange of blaster rifles and the distinct sounds of fighting vehicles. He was sure that the strike teams were engaging somewhere further into the simulation, so he moved carefully, expecting to run into trouble at any moment.

He found the trouble he'd expected in the very next room. Two dead Kimbrin civilians were sprawled out across a sofa while a third had crashed face-first through a glass kaff table. Judging by the blaster bolts that had ripped the sofa and walls apart, the Kimbrin on the couch had been shot where they sat. The one through the table must've gotten up and been hit directly; there were no bolts behind the recliner he'd probably been sitting in. A holoscreen was on in the center of the room, but the channel was dead, broadcasting only its station logo and identifier.

Keel heard movement, and then two zhee raiders emerged one after the other from an adjoining room. Keel quickly cut them both down, then began to clear the rest of the apartment.

"This is Keel… anybody on comm?" he called out over the shared battle net, hoping that he might be heard now that they were theoretically all in the same room. He'd been able to send and receive during that thing in the swamp simulation.

"Solid copy. It's good to hear you, jump jockey!" Zora had a mix of concentration and worry in her voice, like she was in the thick of it and things weren't going well. "Whatever readouts Nilo had working for us have stopped. No idea what's real and what's not, or even what our objective is. We've rallied at the city center. Getting hit by Kimbrin, Legion, and zhee. It's great."

"Sounds like you're on the side of staying alive. I don't know where I am in relation to you, but I'll try to get to the center of town. Keel out."

With the apartment clear and no other zhee, Keel took a step out the door into the building's hallway—only to be forced back inside by a sudden, indiscriminate flurry of blaster fire that he identified as belonging to an N-4. He peeked around the corner in time to see the lead shooter rising up the stairwell at the end of the hall. It was a legionnaire, and Keel dropped him with practiced ease, sending the guy falling backward down the stairs and, by the sounds of it, into his buddies. Keel hadn't needed to remind himself that it was only a simulation and that these were not real legionnaires. The same fast-thinking, live-or-die, them-or-me decision-making that had been his constant companion since the day he left Kill Team Victory showed itself to be alive and well.

But whether simulated or not, having a squad of legionnaires closing in on you wasn't ideal. In fact, in such situations it was generally better to run than to fight; Legion training might have gotten lax in his time undercover, but the equipment was still more than capable of killing. Keel rushed to a window to see how high up he was.

Forty stories if one. Easily. Much too high to jump from. And though he knew in his mind that he couldn't possibly *actually* be forty stories up, he suspected that the simulation could make the fall kill him anyway.

A different plan then. One done quickly. He searched the carcasses of the zhee he'd killed, noticing that their manes were shaved in a manner he'd never seen before. One of them had a couple of fraggers on his belt; the other possessed enough det-gel to blow a hole in the wall. He took all of it, along with a light repeating blaster that he slung around his neck for later use.

Moving to the far back of the apartment, away from the front door, he set the det-gel to make a new hole that would lead into an adjoining apartment. Then he returned to the front door and sent a few more blaster bolts toward the stairwell, pushing the legionnaires back before he tossed the fraggers. He heard them shout for cover as he took cover of his own inside the apartment. The grenades exploded, followed shortly thereafter by the much bigger boom and shake of the det-gel.

Now it was time to make use of the light repeating blaster to provide suppressive fire while Keel escaped through the hole he'd made. This particular model of light repeater had a design flaw where if you held down the trigger and released the charge pack, pulling it down until you heard a click and it locked in place, the trigger would also lock and the firing mechanism would loop until the weapon ran out of charge. He did that now, and as the weapon fired, he set it down just outside the apartment door to fire on the stairwell full of legionnaires. Then he hurried back to the hole in the wall and slipped into the adjoining apartment.

There were three Kimbrin males here, looking stunned and covered in a gray dust from the blast. Keel didn't see any weapons on them and it didn't matter. He shot all three, unwilling to leave any of them behind him for the simulation to use against him later. And anyway, it wouldn't be long before those synthetically engineered legionnaires rallied out of the stairwell and bypassed his meager defenses. He needed all the room he could muster to better maneuver, and that wouldn't be nearly so easy with three Kimbrin clogging up the room.

The second apartment was practically identical to the first one, with its door leading out to the same hallway no more than five meters away from the previous exit point—not even remotely helpful. There was enough det-gel left to blow another door off its hinges should he want to enter yet another apartment from the hall, but that seemed like it would only prolong the inevitable. He was going to have to take out the legionnaires and then make his way down to street level.

In the first apartment, Keel heard the boom of an ear-popper. That told the smuggler that the legionnaires had stacked outside the front door and were now clearing the place. A good team would also station men at both ends of the hallway, pulling security. Keel had dropped at least one of their number outright and might have gotten more with the fraggers if he was lucky. He decided to open the second apartment's front door to see if he couldn't pick off some of the rear guard.

The door swung inward, and Keel hoped that the minor *swish* from its automated hinges was quiet enough to avoid alerting anyone. But for at least one legionnaire, it was impossible not to notice the door. The soldier was already running down the hallway, presumably to station himself at the opposite end, and he was practically right in front of Keel.

A shot to the head with the Intec dropped the legionnaire. Keel burst out and put down two more men who were guarding the first apartment door. The sound of blaster fire in the hallway would introduce a level of chaos to the team clearing the first apartment.

Keel grabbed the N-4 belonging to the dead legionnaire at his feet, ducked back inside, and returned to the room where he'd blown a hole in the wall. He could see from the results of his earlier blast that the wall was thick enough to provide cover from blaster bolts, so he pressed himself against the wall next to the opening, waited for footsteps, and then turned, giving him the perfect angle to see a legionnaire in the open while still remaining largely behind cover himself.

The legionnaire's reflexes were much too slow. Keel sent a bolt from the rifle to the man's head and chest, and the leej's weapon discharged harmlessly into the ceiling as he fell backward.

Keel could hear more troopers holding in another room, out of sight and likely waiting to rush Keel at once. The smuggler cursed himself for not grabbing a fragger off the dead legionnaire lying by the front door, but there hadn't been time. He improvised instead, swapping out the rifle's charge pack and tossing it through the room and behind the legionnaires.

"Fragger! Fragger!" shouted one of the legionnaires. The ruse worked and the legionnaires ran forward out of cover. Keel killed both men using his blaster pistol and then holstered it, pulling the slug thrower so as not to waste time changing packs. There was no telling how many more there might be.

It turned out that was all of them. He re-cleared the first apartment and found no one but the three leejes he'd already killed. Then he pushed his way back into the hall and found no more soldiers there either, just the bodies he'd dropped.

As he reloaded himself with battlefield pickups—charge packs, fraggers, and a bit of det-cord—he found himself wondering what the weapons were, really. They had done the job so far, but what was he even holding? How could simulated weapons kill? And what would become of them when the whole thing faded away, if things got that far? He decided the pickup weapons couldn't really be relied on and their charge packs should be segregated from the ones he had for his Intec. The only weapons he could *really* trust were his two pistols.

On the way down the stairs he saw that the fraggers he'd sent that way had killed one legionnaire and left another bleeding and groaning. A Legion medic should be helping that man right now; a real squad wouldn't have abandoned him to his injuries like this. But the kid was just lying there alone, digitally dying. Maybe he'd stay that way until the simulation ended, but Keel wasn't any more willing to leave a potential threat on his backtrail than he'd been with the Kimbrin. He put an N-4 bolt through the guy's bucket at close range—just to be safe—and then continued down to the next level.

The layout of the next floor was identical, even to the apartment numbers painted on the doors. The only exception was that this time Keel was witnessing two zhee working to force their way into the very same apartment where he'd begun this simulation. And he could have sworn they were the exact same zhee he'd killed on the level above.

He killed them again, shooting them both in the back as they battered open the door and then tossing a fragger inside the room to kill the three Kimbrin he already knew were inside. That only seemed to move the simulation loop faster—he could already hear the squad of legionnaires pushing their way up the steps.

"This is gonna get old quick," Keel muttered.

He stepped over the zhee and into the room where the three dead Kimbrin lay slumped, two on the sofa and one in a recliner—this time he didn't get up in time and the kaff table was intact. The legionnaires were there in a flash, and Keel saw the banger they tossed inside the apartment. Not good. He ran into the next room and grimaced as the blast robbed him temporarily of his hearing. But he could still see and move. He shot down three legionnaires as they entered the room, holding the others back outside.

And then something strange happened.

In the room where the Kimbrin lay shredded, dead, and bleeding on their furniture, was a fireplace. It began to glow in a tight, red circle, as though someone was cutting their way inside.

But before Keel could think more about it, the legionnaires tossed a fragger into the room where he hid, sending him back behind cover. It detonated, and Keel sent a bolt at a legionnaire's head, just missing it and chasing him back around the doorway.

A blizzard of simultaneous events happened then. The legionnaires stormed through the door. The portal that was being cut into the fireplace was pulled inward, and Tyrus Rechs—or rather, someone wearing his armor—appeared in the opening. The legionnaires, taken by surprise, whirled around and turned their fire on this new arrival. The bolts struck the armor's helmet, chest, shoulder, and neck.

Keel at once understood what was happening. He popped out of the room he'd been hiding in and shot a steady stream of slugs at the legionnaires, killing one instantly and striking the others across their armor. Then he charged inside the room, having bought himself the time to jump through the opening that the armored individual had made before any more legionnaires could come inside the apartment. Passing through the portal was like diving through a narrow hoop, and then he was landing hard on his chest and knees in the empty hangar where the swamp sim had taken place.

"Tyrus Rechs" lay on his back, toes pointed upward, arms out wide and empty. Not even carrying a weapon despite there being one holstered to the armor. Keel watched the portal, expecting the legionnaires to charge it and fire through it. But... the simulation seemed to be unraveling. Things in there looked stretched and warbled. The smuggler checked his pickups. Sure enough, the grenades, charge packs, and N-4 had all vanished.

Sensing the immediate threat was gone, Keel pulled the helmet off the armor and found Garret inside, a thin streak of blood leaking from the side of his lips and down his cheek.

"Kid!"

Keel attempted to revive the code slicer. The kid opened his eyes, which promptly rolled back in his head and then closed again. He coughed weakly, and a frothy blood speckled his chin. Then he opened his eyes again, looking impossibly heavy and not quite lucid.

"It pumped me up with pain meds," he mumbled as if on the verge of delirium. "I tried to stop it... tried to stop... listen... would not listen... you listen... need to tell..."

"Tell me what, kid?" Keel was holding the young man's head in his hands.

"Use the armor... It knows how... It knows how."

"Something tells me you need it more than I do, kid."

Garret's eyes rolled again and then closed. He groped for Keel's hand and then reached out to grab his collar. "Put... it... on. Have to... I fix... fixed."

The strength left the code slicer then and he went into a narcotics-induced sleep.

Keel had just finished providing basic medical care, removing enough of the armor to see the wounds and treat them as best he could with his attached med kit, when Zora showed at the portal.

"He's in here!" she shouted.

Keel motioned urgently for her to come through. "Zora! He's hurt. Take him and get him back to the docking bay. There's bound to be a med bay somewhere in there."

To his surprise, Zora hesitated. "The next door opened. We're just waiting on the reclaimers to take the dead. Then, according to Makaffie, we should have a straight shot to the speedlift and the strand."

"Either you do it, Zora, or I do!"

Jack chose that moment to appear on the other side of the blast doors. He gave a whistle as he inspected Garret's cutting job. "That's one way to get past these simulations. Think you can do it again?"

"Wasn't me," Keel said, gesturing at the armor. "It was him. Guess we'll find out." He turned back to Zora. "Help me get the rest of the armor off him."

She didn't protest. She also didn't say that she'd do what Keel had told her to, but as was often the case with the bounty hunter, her actions spoke loudest. She would leave the fight to help Garret. Or maybe leave it just to keep Keel involved. Either way.

"What's our status?" Keel asked over the comm.

"Lost half of those Black Leaf boys," Makaffie answered. "Might've been worse, but either we solved it or cutting a hole into the simulation room ended things prematurely."

Keel nodded as he started putting the armor on. "How's Skrizz?"

"Agitated," Makaffie said. "Says he can smell the reclaimers coming. Says that if he can smell them... he can kill them."

"Maybe he's right."

"My previous troop was quite skilled at killing and though they are now dead, I know they would disagree. I've seen the outcome of trying to stop those things from snatching up the dead. Perhaps you can convince your wobanki friend not to get us all killed, Sergeant Fast?"

Keel donned his helmet and scurried through the portal. The next hangar was empty, not even a mist at their feet, and the bodies of the broken mutants were everywhere. The survivors were positioned in the center of the room, before the dead Black Leaf mercs who had been laid out respectfully—a waiting sacrifice to the ship's insatiable need for organic matter.

Skrizz was breathing the air deeply and kept popping his vicious claws in and out of his fingers. Pikkek, too, seemed on edge. He licked his eyes and inflated his air sac; maybe he was just reacting to Skrizz's energy.

By the time Keel reached the group, Archimedes had appeared before them.

"I must inform you that, in keeping with the new bargain, this simulation must be repeated. *The false ones played falsely.* As this room has been made unusable, you are to enter the next immediately."

"That'll get us to the speedlift," said Makaffie.

Archimedes smiled. "*Your plans are known...* You would take the speedlift to the lower levels. *We know...* The whole of my people reside there. *We know...* To go to them would be... foolish. *Suicide.*"

Keel was caught off guard by a deluge of information that raced across his HUD, giving him all sorts of tactical advice, the gist of which seemed to be that he needed to use a slug thrower against this "Savage reclaimer." The helmet was behaving completely differently than it had before. But the message was clear. Archimedes and his Savage ilk *could* be killed.

Skrizz was staring murder at Archimedes, every muscle in his feline body taut.

"Can you smell this one, Skrizz?" Keel asked.

The wobanki let out an affirming purr.

The blast doors to the next simulation chamber opened. Reclaimers began their howls, and the first of them crawled their way from the venting to take the dead.

Keel raised his slug thrower, pointed it at Archimedes's head, and fired.

# 37

Ravi had not expected the Dark Wanderer to stay for as long as he did. Things were in motion and had been for some time. And the Dark Wanderer was needed, for his part, to see that the war that the Ancients had so feared finally came into being. Ravi had been busy as well, seeking to stop, slow, halt, and otherwise frustrate those plans. But everything to this point had been mere jostling. The first *true* battle of the war had occurred long ago, when Ravi stood with men who'd left Earth to find a planet of their own. The same planet the Dark Wanderer had taken Ravi to and held him captive, of a sort, upon.

This planet had stopped the vanguard of that great and terrible invasion. Even though it cost the denizens of that world everything. None who had been there ever left; their bones were still piled now before Ravi, a monument not to sorrow, but to selfless, unnoticed heroism and sacrifice. Ravi was proud to kneel before it.

The Dark Wanderer, if seeking to demoralize and torment Ravi, had erred in bringing him here. In fact, Ravi had been on the planet once before after that great battle, to introduce himself to Captain Keel, and those memories were good as well... even if his decision had been misguided.

Still, there was something to the unpredictability of the Dark Wanderer that kept Ravi's attention, especially as of late. He had a predatory, restless energy and would pace back and forth. And yet he declined to goad Ravi. Could it be that the Dark Wanderer felt that removing him, Ravi, from the galaxy was more important than any futile attempts to draw him into breaking that old and binding covenant?

Ravi expected more intrigue and treachery. Insults and baiting. He had almost inquired about the lack of such but decided that the urge might be the foolishness of pride and might play directly into the Dark Wanderer's hand. Perhaps his foe's eschewing of torment was a strategy in itself. Cunning was the Dark Wanderer... and deadly.

But greater was the fear—the knowledge—of what would happen should Ravi or Urmo ever forget the old laws and covenants that even now the Dark Wanderer sought to invalidate. The life that had blossomed across the galaxy was precious to Ravi, who had seen its very first steps.

Then, at last, the evil one spoke.

"Did you feel it, Ancient One?"

Ravi did not reply, but he did feel it.

"You are now," the Dark Wanderer continued, "the *last* of the Ancients."

The foe abruptly dropped into a seated position before Ravi, mimicking Ravi's cross-legged repose, and then leaned forward until his cruel nose was inches from Ravi's face.

"What has done it... now comes for you."

A wicked but joyful smile stretched across the Dark Wanderer's face.

Ravi opened his eyes and looked dispassionately at the thing before him. "I welcome your promise of death. The way is half-shut by the slaying of Urmo. Kill me as well, then. Give yourself the satisfaction by your own hand. Damn yourselves to the hell you so desperately seek to escape and bring with you."

"Of course *you* would welcome death." The Dark Wanderer laughed mockingly. Your thoughts are wrong. Ill informed. This was not done by me or my forces. No, but another way. One that carried out my will though entirely apart from me. The foolish way of those you would protect. The covenant, I assure you, will stand."

*Lies*, Ravi thought. *Of course. It is his very essence.*

"We shall see," he said. "Even if what you say is true, by the fulfillment of the time, the hope that you have so long raged against will come to be. I do not need to live to see it brought about. These people... they will find the way."

The Dark Wanderer laughed again. "Yes, we shall see." He got up and circled Ravi. "Or rather, *I* shall see."

Ravi went back to his meditations believing the words he had spoken. His resolve, he knew, weighed heavily on the mind of his foe. Evil had an unending burden. Its only relief was violence and cruelty, and the mercy of death made even that temporary. The burden for wickedness always remained, always seeking more, never satisfied and finally defeated. Ravi knew the ways of that dark spirit well.

"You'll want to stand now, Ancient One. I know you. You will want to die on your feet." The Dark Wanderer stooped and whispered in Ravi's ear. "And your death *is* coming. Not by my hand, but by my will."

The Dark Wanderer stood and spoke loudly, as if testifying to the bones of the men who had died stopping his vanguard. "The covenant still stands. I have not broken it. You will die and I have not broken it."

Ravi stood and brushed the dust from the folds of his robe. His sword remained fastened to his side.

A few more moments, perhaps a lifetime, passed...

... and then there they were. Mother and daughter. Reina, beautiful and cold, her eyes flashing with anger and indignation. And Prisma who looked somehow older and more mature. No longer a girl who had just crossed the line of womanhood, but still a young woman. And yet a girl in Ravi's sight. A young woman, but a girl. And perhaps she would always be such.

"Behold your executioners," spat the Dark Wanderer.

Ravi watched the two warily but did not speak. He did not trust Reina, and seeing Prisma, his heart broke. Of all the ways he had imagined he might die, this one had never occurred to him. Prisma had potential the likes of which he had never seen, not since Captain Keel. Two such souls so close together—though that wasn't strictly true. Centuries had passed between their births.

But Prisma... surely Prisma would have found the selfless way to be a champion. How could she have instead become an instrument of Ravi's death?

She had killed Urmo. Ravi knew it. The intricacies of the galaxy and time itself told him as much. Reina had been there, but Prisma had done the killing.

The mother. The enigma that had somehow interwoven herself between two other great enigmas in Tyrus Rechs and the man who would become Goth Sullus... and now her purpose was finally uncovered for Ravi to plainly see. Her gifts, which she had guarded jealously, away from the doings of the galaxy... they were bent toward Ravi's destruction. Had been, all this time.

The thoughts flew through Ravi's mind, registering in an instant inside his wounded heart. He did not draw his sword; he could not. Not against Prisma, who now wielded the very spear that had been Urmo's, its stone head still dark with the Ancient's gore. For he had been killed on *that* world.

Something flashed in Prisma's eyes as she looked at Ravi. Not malice, but love. And fear. Ravi sensed in her the desire to protect. To stop...

No sooner had the realization come to Ravi than Prisma leaped at the Dark Wanderer, catching him off guard.

"No!" Ravi shouted.

The Dark Wanderer only barely brushed aside the attack, sending the spear wide of its plunging mark. His face was twisted in rage at having been wrong. The girl was there for him—not Ravi!

The Dark Wanderer snarled and attacked.

"Prisma!" Ravi shouted, watching as the girl was quickly overwhelmed by a force far too powerful for her. That fool of a mother should have known. Instead she simply watched the conflict as it played out as though she were an instructor giving some final test.

The girl was backpedaling now and barely keeping hold of the spear as she blocked the savage ferocity of the Dark Wanderer, who used a slim, black blade. The wicked creature moved in a blur, and it was a testament to Prisma's training that she withstood the foe for even this long—for surely that was how the girl had been able to kill Urmo and why she looked older now than she had been.

Her abilities seemed beyond what the Dark Wanderer expected. But that did not mean he would not kill her.

The creature lunged at the girl, who feinted and then sidestepped. Prisma's counterattack wasn't at all close, but it was close enough. Closer than it should have been. Close enough that the Dark Wanderer seemed to decide that the girl was nothing to toy with.

With three flashes of his blade Prisma was disarmed and a cut across her hand was bleeding.

A death blow quickly followed...

... and Ravi was there to stop it with his sword.

This surprised the Dark Wanderer above all else, and without thinking, Ravi flipped up his wrists and spun and cut down the Dark Wanderer.

It was a decision made in the moment.

A moment that doomed the galaxy.

And Reina... smiled.

# 38

No sooner had Death, Destroyer of Worlds taken control of the *Battle Phoenix*'s weapon systems than the little bot put into action a tactical battle plan it had been dreaming up since the moment the Nether Ops Interdictor arrived. However, once weapons systems had come back online, the gunnery bot realized that things were not *quite* so wonderful as it had imagined they would be. The Interdictor was still there waiting to be destroyed, of course, and Death gleefully fired a few of the *Phoenix*'s reserves of ship-to-ship missiles that Old Boss had acquired a long time ago and had never bothered to use. Well... the gunnery bot would use them now.

Death sent a flurry of heavy blaster cannon bolts together with the SSM, which the bot fired in between torpedoes to better hide the powerful weapon's signature. It didn't want any of the Interdictor's PDCs to know what was coming for it or surely all guns would be turned against the SSM. Just a few torpedoes, nothing the shields couldn't handle...

The trouble with it all was, well, how *sparse* things were. The bot had hoped the stars would be swarming with dogfighting starfighters that it could pick off with its blaster cannons. The alarmed biologics manning the Interdictor would watch as wing after wing of their precious ships were annihilated. Death imagined the Interdictor's own fire control AI to be insufferably arrogant, proud of itself for hammering a defenseless carrier and calculating for firing solutions projected to cause fractions of percentiles worth of additional damage—which would have been made up for just by holding down the trigger and letting them have it. And then that AI would notice the wails and cries of the biological crew as they were immolated and sucked into space now that Death had arrived.

The bot even now dreamed such dreams and chittered at the thought of all those people dying in a panic. If Death was lucky, they might even send boarding shuttles out to take over the carrier directly. It was clear that they had no intention of blowing the *Battle Phoenix* up. So of course that was a possibility.

On this eventual occurrence, the bot was torn. It had dreamed up two scenarios, and both were wonderful. The first was to pick each shuttle off as it flew toward him, incinerating the strike teams and bringing dread to the Interdictor's mission planners as they were informed, "All ships lost."

But... wouldn't it be fun to let at least one of those shuttles land and then use the *Battle Phoenix*'s internal defenses to murder every one of them? Death controlled those automated N-50 rifles, the electrified deck platings... all of it. Why, the Nubarian gunnery bot itself might even dash out into the bay when they landed and shoot some directly while they were trying to decide what to do next now that their ship was impounded by the powerful sub-deck electro-vises waiting to snatch them like some deep-sea monster.

In all the chaos, Death might be able to roll right up to one of those soldiers, pull the sidearm New Boss let him keep in a hidden compartment, and land a headshot. This entire scenario had long been on the bot's list of things to do before end of runtime.

But, alas, Death was on the clock, performing New Boss's bidding. Or at least Garret's. The bot liked Garret. And it knew that whatever it chose to do, it needed to do it efficiently. Which meant vaping any boarders before they got within a kilometer of the carrier.

Still, there was always a chance that one would be skilled enough to evade and make it past the PDCs. Death could hope for that. And! *And* it could try to shoot down two boarding shuttles with one shot. That would be something.

Back to the trouble, though. After dishing out the destruction that even the cowardly G232 acknowledged needed doing via the initial torpedo launch, Death realized that there *were* no other ships to engage. There *had* been some, but judging by sensor readouts on the bits of scrap floating about, they had met their end of runtime at the hands of the *Indelible VI*. So instead of killing while the bot waited for the blaster bolts, torpedoes, and that special SSM to reach the Interdictor, Death had nothing to do but wait... and fantasize about picking starfighters off with impossibly well-placed shots sent from heavy blaster cannons meant for capital ships that only the gunnery bot could have accomplished—had they been there.

A pity that Death would never know for sure now.

Finally, the interminably long four-second wait between firing and impact came to an end. Death warbled in delight as it watched the first volley of blaster bolts strike and impact against the shield which dispersed the blaster cannon bolts' energy like a green glowing electrical storm. The first torpedo hit, and the shields handled that easily as well. The PDCs picked off the trailing torpedo that Death had fired just a few seconds too late, all part of the plan.

Then... the special SSM hit.

The weapon didn't simply pack a punch—it brought the whole fight. It was equipped with an outer warhead capable of collapsing an entire shield array for vessels twice the size of the Interdictor. And so it did, passing through the shield before boring through the hull and embedding itself several decks down where it detonated and made a great gaping opening in the side of the Interdictor. Death had fired three well-timed trailing blaster bolts, and each one struck the open wound seconds later. Imagine! Some of the biologics who were in the process of being vacuumed into space saw those bolts and were promptly fried by them! Absolutely fried! Haha!

What a wonderful way to kill the enemy.

It was enough to make the psychotic little bot forget that there weren't any boarding shuttles or starfighters to destroy. Death strained its optical scanners, wanting to look directly at the carnage. Oh yes. Those decks were collapsed, slagged, and twisted; exposed to the vacuum. And what were those little dots but biologics who had been sucked out to the void and sure death? Yes! What else could they be? Oh, how lovely.

Before Death was a spectacle of violence and warfare, a most graceful dance. The bot only wished it could hear the other ship's wailing alarms and the screams and lamentations of its crew. But... the next time it recharged, it could easily produce for itself a simulation of the very thing. Perhaps it would add the sound of automatic, gas-fired weapons fire to the mix. The music of the slug thrower in full, automatic glory. Death enjoyed that noise very much.

It would be hard to give up weapons control of the ship after this. But the little bot worked for New Boss. Which was important to remember. Only New Boss and maybe Garret could command it to leave its new post. Yes. If G232 made such a request, Death would threaten to send the stupid admin bot out of the nearest airlock for use as target practice.

Death hoped G232 would ask.

With such a catastrophic blow dealt to the Interdictor, Death expected the ship to limp away until it found the nearest deep-space station, or at the very least a safe sector of space where it could be provided the necessary security to undergo zero-g repairs. Because there was no way it would be fixing itself. There was also no chance of making a jump for hyperspace—not without shields and with such a gusher of a wound; not on a ship that size. Maybe it would launch escape pods and attempt to jump those to safety. Oh yes. *Those* would be good for target practice. A bit of sport while the pods attempted to lock on to the nearest habitable star system. Those biologicals doubly deserved to die, for the hypothetical cowards hadn't even fought to the death aboard their ship.

Unforgivable.

But the Interdictor didn't limp away. Nor did it launch escape pods. Instead it began targeting the *Battle Phoenix's* weapon systems– something it should have done to begin with but didn't. Probably because they wanted it intact. That hadn't worked out so well.

*Good,* thought the gunnery bot. Death preferred that the fight didn't end so quickly. It still had one more of the special SSMs but thought it best to save those. Old Boss,

Tyrus Rechs, had once mentioned that they were prototypes, the only of their kind. The little gunnery bot had no qualms about shooting any of the galaxy's biological species into extinction, but its feelings were quite different when it came to such a sophisticated weapon system. Death couldn't erase such beauty from the galaxy. To even attempt it was a cruelty the bot could not muster.

Now for the drudgery of ship-to-ship combat. The *Battle Phoenix*'s shields were up, the Interdictor's shields were down. They would exchange blaster cannon fire until the inevitable calculations played out their truth. The carrier would win. It was a fight, but a boring one. Still... better than nothing.

When the Interdictor finally launched assault shuttles and in desperation sent them on a course to reach the carrier, excitement nearly got the better of Death, Destroyer of Worlds. It almost—*almost*—launched the other SSM into their midst just to see what would happen. Instead it went through the trouble of loading a seeker torpedo with a standard warhead and launched it toward the formation. Shuttles were so much slower than starfighters. Hardly a challenge. Though they did have significant jamming and spoofing technology that might shake a torpedo or two. A good pilot could even lure the torpedo into a certain flight path, spoof it so it no longer read the shuttle's signature, and watch it dumbly continue on to strike the very bays that had launched it.

There were no pilots quite that good flying shuttles today. And anyway, all Death was trying to do was break up their flight pattern so that he could bull's-eye them with heavy ship-to-ship blaster cannons. This proved harder than the little bot had calculated it would be. Death sent several bolts that sizzled just wide or behind the vessels, which were themselves about the same size as the fierce bolts. One of the shots came in close enough to the rear of a shuttle that it burned up its engines completely and disabled it. Death delighted in the thought that the panicked crew was now realizing that there was nothing they could do but wait for rescue. The bot sent several cannon shots at the inert shuttle, missing on purpose to increase their fear and anxiety. Death, Destroyer of Worlds, would kill them all later.

Since direct hits were proving exceedingly difficult, the bot softened its self-imposed targeting requirements to allow grazing strikes like the one that had disabled the shuttle to serve as *good enough*. The bot took several shots and dropped its self-calculated accuracy down into the low thirtieth percentile, but it had finished vaporizing the last of the assault boats just as it noticed a very different sort of shuttle racing through the battlescape and toward the Savage hulk.

Death sent another seeking torpedo, but the lock evaporated almost the moment the weapon left its tube. This shuttle had some powerful deterrent systems indeed. The little gunnery bot might use blast cannons, but the probability of hitting the Savage hulk was too high and decidedly *not* in New Boss's best interests.

Oh well. New Boss would get to have the fun of killing whoever it was once they boarded.

The gunnery bot went back to its still-unfolding slugfest with the Interdictor. Interestingly enough, despite the immediate threat of the light assault carrier pounding it, the Interdictor didn't slack from its firing on the Savage ship. They wanted it destroyed very badly.

Oh! And Death should also warn New Boss that visitors were on their way...

# 39

Archimedes lay dying on the Savage hulk's deck. There was a clear impression of a bullet hole in the center of his skull. An odd, spectral sort of blood poured from the wound, pooling in the sockets of the Savage's still-surprised eyes.

His mouth was open, and though his lips did not move, a voice came out. That other voice. *"False! False! Betrayers!"* Gone was the diplomatic tone Archimedes usually used in between the hissing, whispering words of his true self.

"Now, it can't be that easy," Makaffie said, standing over the ghostly body. "Blaster just don't work? We picked the wrong weapon? Shoulda packed slug throwers?"

Skrizz immediately gave his interpretation as to what happened. The wobanki didn't think it was a matter of bullets versus bolts. *"Cacki peesee honcho cava nachu blasteroo."*

Jack raised his eyebrows to his hairline. "I speak a little 'banki, but that's a little too esoteric for me. Anyone wanna translate?"

"He said—" Keel began and then went quiet as Pikkek hopped forward, aiming his rifle at the reclaimer.

"Big die!" The Kublaren sent a short burst of full-auto fire into the Savage reclaimer's body, causing it to wriggle and jump before going still with death. "Ya. Big die. *K'kik.*"

Keel and the others had been forced to jump back at the shots, and now Keel was angry about it. "Someone tie old hippity-hop up before he hurts someone."

Pikkek's eyes went wide and his air sac swelled. "No be... k'k... up-sat. Big die... k'ki'kik... gud."

The shots to Archimedes's midsection didn't seem as though they should have been any more destructive than Keel's single bullet to the head had been, and yet Pikkek's trigger pull had put Archimedes down for good.

The others were still waiting on Keel to give a better interpretation of what Skrizz was saying; Pikkek's shots had Keel thinking that perhaps the wobanki was right.

"Skrizz says these things live here and... *Cacki pee-see.*" Keel looked at Skrizz. "Spirit realm, right?"

The wobanki gave a quick swish of its tail that passed for a nod.

"Right," Keel went on. "So he's saying that these things simultaneously exist in two realms, seen and unseen, at the same time. You can't just kill them in one of the two, you've gotta kill 'em in both."

Jack crossed his arms and couldn't keep a grin off his face. "Sounds a little far-fetched. Hell, sounds crazy if we're calling a spinklark a spinklark."

Keel thought so too, and yet what Skrizz had said, and the Kublaren seemed to accept and believe as well, was also laid out in more technical terms through Tyrus Rechs's armor. He debated whether to share that with the others.

"*Tenchu kaja koo Rah-vee,*" Skrizz reminded several of the others.

"That's a good point," Makaffie said. He turned to Jack. "You never saw what Ravi could do, but if you had... maybe this all wouldn't be so crazy. My concern, however, gentlemen—seeing as how all of our ladies have now been sent to the rear—is how this gets me or the rest of us any closer to actually knowing how to kill these things once they come. Surely the other reclaimers will be here soon. Come to tear us all limb from limb."

"It easy," said Pikkek. "Kill like always should *k'kik-killy*. Body and... *k'k mohda*."

"What's *mohda*?" Keel asked.

It was Jack's turn to translate. "Koob for soul."

Pikkek nodded enthusiastically. "Ya, big die body. Big die to so-ah."

That none of the others scoffed, including the hardened Black Leaf mercenaries, revealed the confusion and fear, perhaps the awe, they all had when it came to this hellish ship and its denizens. There *was* no soul—that had been ingrained in them since their youth. But there *were* these Savage creatures. And there had been... other things. Strange, unexplainable things in all their lives. For Keel the biggest of them was Ravi.

His mind went to his navigator, who had been away more than he'd been present, it seemed. Was Ravi the same as Archimedes? Could Ravi be... a Savage?

It didn't matter. Not now at any rate. The mists were rising and the moans of the reclaimers echoed from the deep dark below. Skrizz and Pikkek stood ready, growling and croaking their reminders, proudly repeating old proverbs of their species about killing in totality—in body and in soul.

It was nonsense... but there Archimedes lay dead.

"Ravi could kill them," Makaffie said to Keel and only to Keel. As if only Wraith alone would appreciate that truth. "He cut them down like it was nothing."

Jack came over to Keel, his eyes darting in all directions as though afraid of being watched. "Koob and 'banki seem ready for this fight. Primitive minds. But... hey. How 'bout lettin' me use that forty-five and you take the fifty that's belt-fed into that kit of yours? You know... just in case it *is* the slug throwers what do it."

"Yeah," Keel said softly and then handed over the .45, a weapon he'd taken from Tyrus Rechs's Doghouse back when Exo was still alive. "Don't lose it, though. I want it back, Jack."

The spy ejected the mag to count its rounds, then pushed it back home. "I'll take good care of her. Got any more mags?"

Keel gave him the two he had left and then pulled out the hand cannon from the armor's holster. His bucket came to life with new targeting systems. Dual reticles overlaid across his vision, one for wherever he looked and another for wherever the barrel was pointed. He tested it out and was given a prompt that allowed him to see a visual recreation of whatever the barrel was facing. He tried that too, and saw a gray-on-gray representation of his feet, complete with thermal readings. The armor was using its sensors to paint for him a picture; that might be useful if he ever needed to fire blind around a corner. It also explained some of Tyrus Rechs's more supernatural tricks.

"You okay?" Jack asked. "You're moving your arms around like you're on an H8 trip."

The wails of the reclaimers were growing louder, but they still hadn't shown themselves to attack. Perhaps what had happened to Archimedes had given them pause.

"Yeah, I'm fine. Just getting reacclimated to this combat system."

"There were legends about that armor in the case files I saw—well, never the actual files, just references to them, mind you... " Jack whistled. "I'll bet it's something."

"It's something."

It was at that moment that Keel would have received a warning from his gunnery bot—one that the bot had forgotten to give after being distracted for a time—about an unidentified shuttle docking in the Savage hangar bay. Only, the comms were still jammed for all traffic not inside the individual simulation hangars. So Keel didn't receive the warning. And even if he had, the reclaimers chose that moment to finally emerge and attack.

The spectral creatures rose from the fog, reaching out with cracked claws at the ends of long, slender fingers. Their hands and their teeth were human more than they were anything else, but just a little sharper and more dreadful. And their speed was considerable—they seemed to fly above the deck, lined up in columns that would then fan out and surround their chosen targets. But once surrounding, they would slow down and close in ominously, gnashing teeth and shrieking, attempting to induce terror in whoever they'd isolated before seizing them and biting, grabbing, ripping, tearing.

Two of the Black Leaf mercs were ensnared in this way. Their screams of horror and agony rose above the howls of the reclaimers, causing the rest of the defenders to quaver.

But not Skrizz and Pikkek. They had declared with apodictic certainty their belief that these reclaimers, like Archimedes, could be killed. Perhaps they had not evolved to the level of sophistication that humans placed on themselves, and thus could more easily believe what they were witnessing.

To their credit, the reclaimers *they* engaged... died.

The ones the humans shot... did not.

Those without slug throwers fired blaster rifles, which only slowed the reclaimers. Not enough to prevent getting overwhelmed and slaughtered, except when Skrizz or Pikkek could intervene. Keel and Jack were having the most success—they dropped the Savages and slowed them to a stupefied crawl—but they weren't killing them.

Still, every bit helped. While Pikkek fired from the hip and slew the reclaimers in bulk, Skrizz pounced on those that Jack and Keel had knocked down, finishing them off with his teeth and claws in a frenzy of violence. Gradually, the Black Leaf private military contractors pulled back to what had become a protective line patrolled by the two men with slug throwers and the two alien killers.

"Running low on ammo," Jack announced.

Keel had been stingy with his own rounds, though the supply was plentiful and ingeniously compact. He wondered whether going full auto with the hand cannon would make a difference, but given the sheer number of Savages who came up to take them, decided not to spend more ammunition than he absolutely needed to at any moment.

"I'm gonna draw a few off," he announced. "Skrizz, Pikkek, be ready!"

With a flare of his jump jets, Keel boosted himself to an open pocket of space, drawing away several of the reclaimers who had been advancing on Jack and the others. He sent controlled bursts with the hand cannon and dropped the lot of them, then jumped to a new location and repeated the process. Like roving enforcers, Skrizz and Pikkek followed his trail of destruction, quickly dispatching the fallen reclaimers while watching to be sure none of the others reached the line Jack held.

"Doesn't make any sense," Keel muttered to himself, frustrated that he couldn't end the damned Savages outright. It couldn't just be a case of weapons. Pikkek's weapon was a mix of a slug thrower and blaster, something Keel wished the PMCs had as well, and it was killing just fine. And Skrizz was using his kelhorned *teeth*.

It wasn't the weapons. It was the wielders. And what worked... worked. As crazy as it sounded. It worked. So as more reclaimers climbed through the vents and emerged from the lower decks, Keel let out his air and did his best to change his mindset about what he was doing.

All at once, a massive blast rocked the Savage hulk, vibrating the deck beneath everyone's feet and violently throwing a number of the strike team to the floor. Keel and Skrizz were quickly up and engaging the reclaimers again, but the Savages seemed not to have had their balance affected at all, and had closed some distance as a result.

Makaffie, who hadn't even bothered firing his blaster rifle, found himself thinking about Ravi. They could use him right about now.

Instead of Ravi, he received an incoming comm transmission from the *Indelible VI*. Leenah had witnessed the massive explosion belowdecks and was frantically checking to see if anyone could possibly have survived. She sounded surprised to even connect to someone.

"We're alive," Makaffie said calmly, as though it were his mother checking in on him. "Not sure how much longer that will be true, but it's true right now. What happened?"

"There's a Republic Interdictor that's been trying to destroy the ship, but this is something else. Those decks blew from the inside out."

Nilo added his take to the comm. "Self-destruct sequence. The strand—you have to push now to get it or it's all going to be too late!"

This assessment was quickly countered by a new voice that shouldered its way into their comm channel. A female voice. "No you don't. But you do need to get out of there—all of you—before this entire hulk goes up for good."

Keel had been passively listening while engaging the Savages, jumping from spot to spot, dropping some with headshots and then jumping away before he was overwhelmed. He'd been trying to channel his hate, like Skrizz, hoping *that* would somehow magically kill the things. It wasn't working, but when he heard that voice come over the comms, he was hit with an even stronger feeling: anger.

Because he knew that voice.

Andien Broxin. The woman who'd once kidnapped his crew.

# 40

Andien Broxin frowned and looked over to Praxus, who was interfacing with the Savage vessel from a comp-port he'd uncovered behind a panel in the hangar bay. "They locked me out as soon as they heard my voice."

Praxus paused for a moment and then gave a fractional nod as if this was all quite correct. "You yourself expected such a scenario was possible given your last encounter with this Captain Ford. It did not sound amicable in your telling of the matter."

That was true enough. Working for Nether Ops, Andien had kidnapped all of Ford's crew. It didn't matter that she had planned to bring them back once Nether did the thing it was going to do no matter what... with or without her. Still, Ford had every reason to be angry, seeing as Andien hadn't brought them back at all; in fact she'd gotten them all captured by an even more dangerous foe aboard the Cybar mothership. Had Praxus not saved her, she had little doubt that Ford would have killed her on the spot when he came to rescue his crew.

Or at least he would have tried. And maybe... maybe he would have succeeded. She'd read his file. Knew what Nether Ops knew about the man.

Praxus interrupted her thoughts. "You are reflecting again. Curious. In any event, I have reacquired the comm key they are now using, and we can force ourselves into that channel—they won't be able to jump again without us. But we should determine a course of action. Although it doesn't take nearly as much processing power to interface with the ship while not awakening it, I am not confident that I can hold off its destruction indefinitely."

Andien nodded. This wasn't the deep, restorative work of awakening and rebirthing. A ship this large, much like the Cybar ship they'd awakened, would take all of Praxus's focus and efforts.

"I should add," Praxus said, "that the traces of this... Maestro are evident through this vessel."

"Well, we figured as much."

The recovery of the Cybar ship had led Praxus and Andien to two important discoveries. First, that the so-called Mandarins and their fragmented but potent Nether Ops organization, along with their ad hoc House of Reason loyalists, were operating under a unified system— probably an AI—named Maestro. But Maestro, it seemed, was reporting its progress to a currently unknown entity somewhere beyond the Gap, there at the extremities of galaxy's edge. Both Andien and Praxus believed this entity was some sort of Savage element.

All of that had led them to the Savage reclaimer hulk— or more accurately, to the deployment of a Nether-Ops-controlled Republic Interdictor which in turn led them to the hulk. The Interdictor had been ordered to destroy the Savage ship through a command channel Broxin and Praxus had identified as belonging to Maestro. It seemed that almost every decision being undertaken by the Mandarins and their deep state operatives in Nether Ops was under this Maestro's influence.

Praxus and Andien arrived to find their shuttle in the midst of a three-ship battle already underway, although only two of the ships had working offensive weapons. They had to race through a hail of heavy blaster cannon fire and torpedoes in order to reach the overcrowded hangar of the Savage hulk. Praxus went at once went to interface with the vessel and found two facts of note. First, the Savages who resided on the ship had been dramatically decreased in number by two separate events. One was a while back—that was Ravi—and the other was underway right now. Second, the vessel was actively scrubbing all of its considerable combat indexes. It appeared the Savages' instructions were to fight, kill, or otherwise occupy the boarders until every one of these indexes could be erased beyond recovery—at which time the vessel would self-destruct. All of this was according to a Savage protocol which, like everything else, had Maestro's signature fingerprints all over it.

The index deletion had almost run its course when Praxus arrived. The last of the Cybar at once began to bend the Savage system to his will, attempting to forestall the ship's self-destruction. Each of its decks had sufficient high-explosive charge to obliterate the entire level. These were designed to act independently, allowing the ship to destroy part of itself without sacrificing the whole—a necessary precaution should any of its simulations grow beyond its control. But whether in tandem or one by one, the explosions would leave nothing of the ancient hulk but scrap metal.

For now, Praxus had contained—barely—the self-destruct to the decks immediately below Captain Ford and his compatriots. But the other explosives couldn't be held off forever. Praxus and Andien would need to leave, and they would need to now formally collect allies—which was how they saw Captain Ford, Nilo, the Legion, and others. Allies who needed to be made aware of the collective threat and ushered into action.

"Here's what I want you to do," said Andien. "First, shut down all the active simulations."

"I have already done so."

"And you have control of blast doors and other security elements?"

"The only items outside of my control are a self-destruct reversal, because there is none, and the Savages themselves."

"Okay, good. There's some bad blood and it's gonna take more than a little goodwill to make what we need to happen, happen. Let's start by opening a way for the lone team member we identified to link back up with the others."

Praxus blinked and gave a fractional nod. "I have done so."

"Next thing—tell them what we're here for and that we're trying to help them escape. *You* tell them. I think it'll come better from you. Or at least it will for Captain Ford."

Praxus went right to work, forcing his even, calm voice into the strike team's ears.

"All elements in defense against the Savage force identified as reclaimers: I am Praxus. I am your ally. Please note that your objective—the strand—has been destroyed belowdecks as part of a self-destruction initiative. I regret that I was unable to prevent that from happening. I was, however, able to keep you from being destroyed along with it. I have also shut down the simulations, and I have opened the way for you to regroup with a stranded comrade—a human male carrying a rather large sniper rife. I apologize for not knowing his name or designation. Please do not attempt to scramble your comms again. This will only delay vital communications. Again... we only wish to help. We are allies."

Praxus looked over to Andien for her assessment.

She smiled. "A little wordy, but that was good."

"Well, I won't ask about whatever history you have with this woman," Makaffie said to Keel following the message. "But I'm not inclined to shrug off what we're hearing. We felt the explosion. Wild Man is still out there and... no new simulation as of yet."

"Because the Savages are trying to kill us," Keel said over the comm, jumping to avoid some that grasped for his legs as he rocketed away. "The girl is bad news."

Keel hoped to leave it at that. His animosity toward Broxin was rooted in principle. She'd stolen his crew right from his ship. And yet... in the time since then, he'd heard the whole ordeal from Skrizz, Leenah, Garret, all of them. And not a one of them seemed to hold it against her. She'd even instructed Garret to transmit their location to the *Six*, something that would have gotten her killed if the rest of her Nether Ops crew had known. Leenah had described her as protective and playing coy with the acerbic Hutch and his team. And Skrizz—only once and quite casually—had described how they had worked together to escape the encroaching Cybar Titans and evade capture on the ship.

So there were… signs. Indications that she was more than the typical Nether agent whose morality always aligned with whatever the mission required and who held no qualms about fundamentally upending that morality as called for. In fact, Captain Owens had treated her as… someone decent… when she'd worked with Kill Team Victory on their first op.

But she'd kidnapped his crew. *His crew.*

"For whatever it's worth," inserted Jack, "this is someone you can trust. I did some work for her before joining with Big Nee. Me and Lana both. She's not Nether. Not sure what she is to be precise, but Nether ain't it."

A pair of Savage reclaimers charged toward Keel. He put two shots out, one to each skull, and then moved to give Skrizz room to tear them apart where they lay.

"I'm not sure it matters," said Makaffie, who'd been looking thoughtful. "If the strand is gone, the only thing worth staying behind for is the Wild Man. And if they're helping with that, I'm inclined to tentatively place them in the 'friends' column. We're not exactly in a position to be selective about who's willing to help us right now."

"Heads up," Zora announced over comms. "There's a female human moving in your direction. Just passed me while I was hauling Garret on the final leg to the hangar bay."

"See?" Jack said. "She's coming to help. Let her. You got a problem with her, Wraith, that's fine. But I trusted you to get what you could out of Honey. Time for you to return the favor, huh?"

Keel's anger attempted to flare again but was doused by the cold realization that it was mostly his *pride* that was truly bothering him, and that shouldn't have any bearing on what he decided to do now. Especially under the circumstances. The last thing anyone needed to do right now was settle old scores.

"I'm not gonna turn her out when she shows up. Don't worry."

The attacking Savages were reason to worry enough. Several of them flashed forward through the mists and clawed at Skrizz, causing the wobanki to howl in enraged pain. Keel brought up his slug thrower, feeling a wave of emotion at seeing his friend injured. He lined up the reticles and fired from the hip, using the targeting system to drop the nearest reclaimer.

To his surprise, it fell dead. Skrizz didn't need to finish it off. The wobanki leapt away while Pikkek took care of the others.

How? How had Keel managed to kill the thing this time? What had he done differently?

He thought about how much ammo he might have left and then noticed a new display on the HUD showing an exact count. He hadn't even given a command. Garret had been busy.

The battle raged on. Pikkek was slowing down and Skrizz would be soon. Jack was about out of ammo. Even Keel couldn't keep it up like this forever. Yet the Savages showed no signs of fatigue or relenting.

Keel's armor alerted him to an intruder in the room. He hadn't been running any active sensor sweeps; the armor just seemed to decide this was something he might like to know about. If not for the alert, no one might have noticed Andien Broxin entering the space.

She paused upon realizing that Keel was looking right at her. A second later, she was speaking into his comm.

"I'm sorry, Captain Ford. Nether Ops is... complex. I thought I could fix what was wrong with it. I was wrong.

But right now, whatever you think about me, we need to get off this ship."

Keel answered with a slight nod and was about to leap back into the fray, thinking that he needed more time to think this through, time he didn't have while shooting. Then the armor surprised him again. It asked if he would like to initiate something called *sentry mode.*

*What's sentry mode?* Keel thought.

The armor gave a quick explanation. Sentry mode would allow Keel to work comms and other battlefield supervision suites while the armor took care of the weapons package by itself. If they were going to withdraw, perhaps Keel would benefit from not having to constantly watch the swarming Savages. This wasn't the type of fight you could just turn tail and run from without paying for it.

"Okay, let's try it."

The voice command was enough for the armor. It gave confirmation followed by a warning: *Destruction of Savage type reclaimer requires direct interface.*

The armor was saying that it couldn't do the job alone.

Well, Keel hadn't exactly had great luck in that department either.

He again gave the acknowledgment and began to experience the odd sensation of the suit moving his body and arms independently. There was no waiting period before it engaged the Savage reclaimers. Spectral bodies fell in droves as the battle armor targeted and fired on full automatic with nearly the speed Keel himself was capable of if he concentrated. Except... he was merely a spectator now. Though he could act in other ways. A full command and control interface was in front of him, filled with pre-registered comm channels and groups for both strike teams, as well as for Andien Broxin and Praxus in the docking hangar.

"What got into you?" Jack called, taken aback by the sudden uptick in Keel's fighting tempo.

"It's not me, it's the armor. Should be okay."

Keel focused on the screens before him. He hadn't issued any verbal commands, and this bucket didn't have the facial and tongue toggles like his old Legion helmet had. The armor had just provided what he needed. Was this, too, something Garret had done, or had it always been among the armor's abilities?

First priority was to ascertain the status of the strand. If there was any chance of still getting it, Keel needed to know about it. He hailed Broxin, who was killing Savages without difficulty. "The strand—you're sure it's gone?"

"The one *you* came for is," she said. Keel wasn't sure if she was trying to be cryptic or not.

"What about the Wild Man—the missing team member? Can you show me where he is?"

Broxin cast a holomap display that tracked a single life form, surely this "Wild Man," in real time. "He's on his way, but there's a lot of Savages trying to stop him."

Keel's battle armor quickly synchronized with the map and then added it to its own overlay and removed Broxin's cast. The armor's version of the map showed a full schematic readout of the Savage hulk, including the decks below where the strand was supposed to be. Those decks were now showing a faded red and were not quite whole. They were just as gone as Leenah had said they were. The strand really was destroyed, then.

All the while the ancient battle armor fired the hand cannon and laid waste to what remained of the Savage reclaimers. They weren't dying, but they were falling injured in piles from the onslaught of the full-auto hand cannon. Keel became aware that the suit was also jumping him around on the jets, constantly repositioning. As he moved, Skrizz would wade into the pile of bodies he left behind and tear them asunder, or Pikkek would gleefully hop toward one and spray his own slug thrower into the mess. It was a mass execution of Savages even as Jack and the others still stood back, impotent.

"How do you kill these things?" Keel asked. He had meant to pose the question to Broxin, who was doing the job with a sleek blaster pistol that was firing a powerful mix of energy and projectile—much like the koob's rifle. But it was the armor that responded with a quick explanation of its own. An explanation that read like the crazed mumbo jumbo of the space wizard who had worn it before Keel. Never mind what they all saw Goth Sullus do at the end. Never mind seeing the things Prisma could do. And Ravi... never mind that either.

The armor said it came down to a matter of conviction. Belief. *Faith*. Channeling one's whole self into the act of killing. Shooting with your heart. Not the mechanical repetition built by relentless training, newly forged instincts embedded in muscle memory. Perfect trigger pulls. Physics. The biology of a well-placed shot. That wouldn't get it done, not by itself, even if that had been enough every day of Keel's life before today.

Intention was now important. Something decided what that intent was, something that felt outside of Keel's control.

It was all crazy. All of it.

What difference did it make *why* you killed something? It was dead either way.

And yet... there had been times in Keel's life when it was about more than orders, credits, or revenge. He had killed because it needed to be done, and not just so that he could live another day. He'd killed to save, and he'd killed because it was the right thing to do.

But it had been a long time since he'd thought about death in that way. Not since he'd left the Legion and shed those trappings to become Keel instead of Ford. It wasn't long after that when it all became a sort of meaningless dance. A way to survive, to achieve victory when someone else stood in your way and wouldn't move or back down. His mind flashed to Mallet Kline, the bounty hunter he'd killed when first acquiring Tyrus Rechs's armor. He hadn't even thought about it when the time came. Just put the man down. And if he had thought about it, if he'd hesitated at all, Kline would have killed him. There was no ill will in it. It was transactional. A part of being a professional. Keel almost liked the man, this fellow bounty hunter. Kline's last words—"I almost got you"—were endearing, even. Because they were true. If Klein had lived, Keel wouldn't have minded—so long as the man knew better than to come after him again.

But that wasn't the sort of killing that was needed here. And what the armor was telling Keel—telling him without words or text on screens but imparting it directly into his mind—was something at once more sophisticated and more primal.

The armor was proving full of surprises.

It conveyed the idea of a sort of righteous zeal of indignation. Something that came easily for the wobanki and the Kublaren.

It was a thing Ravi used to talk to him about. Even tease him about sometimes. "You kill because you are good at it, Captain Keel. And so you are. Of course we do the things we are good at. But when will you get good at something else? There are many things done in this galaxy which should not be so. And many of the things that should be done, even these are done in the wrong manner. Most men dwell lost in all of this. Yourself included. But, should you focus your skills, Captain... then you will be great."

Keel would usually thank the philosophy professor for next week's lecture and remind Ravi that everyone *he* killed deserved it. And these Savages... they deserved it, too.

Keel resumed control of the armor and attempted once more to put them down for good.

# 41

No "new deal" had been struck between the Wild Man and Archimedes. In fact, the only thing that had struck the Wild Man at all while he waited for Makaffie to return with Sergeant Fast and the opportunity to finish the simulation, get the strand, and nuke the hulk was... boredom. A dripping, constant dullness that came from too many cycles aboard a ship that had very little to offer the living except death. The gruel that Archimedes brought him was the only thing in sight that was an exception to that rule.

The Wild Man kept his large and powerful frame in shape, of course, preferring a regimen of calisthenics that for a man his size was every bit as effective as weight training. But there were only so many hours one could work out in a day. After spending time seeing which of the old captured ships were left unlocked, and poking around the memories of crews who'd died long ago, he asked Archimedes whether he could see the rest of the hulk. At this time Archimedes was still very much wanting the "impossible simulation" to be completed and agreed readily. Though not a tour guide, the Savage reclaimer gave the Wild Man full access to their current level.

There was very little to see. The simulation hangars partitioned by blast doors were all the same, save for the one containing the speedlift down. Eventually, the expanded space available to the Wild Man was used for runs, and then ruck marches in full kit. He needed to stay sharp, and though he dared not waste ammunition, he still packed it all in before the kilometers-long march from one end of the ship to the other and back again.

It was on one of these marches that Archimedes decided that the "impossible simulation" was no longer important.

It was a life-saving break that the Wild Man had been lugging his kit through the ship at the time.

He was proceeding through one of the simulation hangars when the blast doors closed, both ahead and behind, the mists swirled suddenly, and a simulation began. It was immediately clear to Wild Man that Archimedes had changed his mind—and that he would be sent through the crucible until he finally fell. He would be tested for as much data as he could provide before ultimately succumbing to the Savage ship's machinations... and then he would be re-processed for... other purposes.

Perhaps more of the thin gruel. Calories for the next soul damned to this vessel.

The type of simulation that rose from the mists swirling at his feet was another life-saving break. Had he been inserted into the tight confines of a ship, like the very first sim he'd encountered, Wild Man would have been in trouble. He was a large and powerful man, but that kind of action wasn't his strong suit. Instead he found himself in a sprawling and modern city. A city at war. Smoke rose steadily from burning buildings in all directions. Explosions punctuated the steady sound of blaster rifles and other small arms. Tanks crushed parked sleds and aircraft screamed overhead, drowning out the quiet, swishing hums of the various observation bots struggling to stay in runtime and complete their individual missions. This was brutal urban warfare, and it seemed to involve three factions: the Legion, some militant group of zhee, and Kimbrin, who Wild Man understood to be native to the planet, since the only noncombatants he came across were of that species.

Placing the Wild Man in a wide-open space would work to his advantage and against the Savage reclaimers' plans, for there was one thing the Wild Man could do exceptionally well in spite of his size... and that was hide.

He was known as a shooter. A sniper. He had been a good shot before his home planet was invaded and annihilated by the Savages; he became a much better shot afterward, when he'd follow the Savages wherever he could. Always moving from ship to ship, craft forever on their last power cells, never a guarantee that they'd be able to take him off-world once they crashed planetside. The Wild Man would follow every hint and rumor of a Savage sighting, and when he found them, he'd hide and kill as many as he could with his great, long rifle.

Savage patrols sent ahead of the hulks would go out undetected and reconnoiter the small sparsely populated worlds they'd selected to raid for resources. Or for calories. Worlds with a few hundred thousand people at most. The Wild Man would slip onto these worlds, just behind the Savages, and go to work. He'd learned early on not to bother trying to warn the inhabitants. No one ever believed that a Savage hulk was going to hit their insignificant back yard until it was much too late. The Wild Man had gotten himself into too many scrapes and been locked in too many jails for daring to disturb the peace on those back-edge worlds.

No one wanted to believe in those early days, before anyone even thought to call the Savage incursions a war, that *their* forgotten place in the galaxy would be of any interest to anyone but those who happened to descend from its original colonists—or wound up there unable to leave again. But those were *exactly* the sort of places the Savages hit first. Worlds of no account. Worlds like Stendahl's Bet.

At least until New Vega.

In those early days, the Wild Man would go and hide. Never in one spot, but always moving, hiding as he went. He'd set up ambushes and kill the Savages at long range and leave their bodies to bake under whatever star served as that world's sun. Sometimes the discovery of those terrible bodies would be enough to wake the populace up. Most times not.

He was always gone before they found him. He had a sixth sense about when they might be trying to lure him in. Occasionally he killed enough Savages to force them to focus on this hidden demon reducing their numbers and getting in the way of whatever groundwork they were supposed to be laying that would erase the planet's ability to defend itself and make the population's demise that much easier to accomplish. The Wild Man sensed when this focus changed. He'd stay two steps ahead, ambushing the ambushers and then taking his sweet time picking off the bait as they chittered and frantically wondered why things weren't going according to the plan. He enjoyed watching them die, even through the lens of his scope, so far away.

Time spent on any world could vary greatly. Sometimes weeks he would remain, killing Savages, lingering with the hope of doing just one more. Other times it was days. Occasionally he wiped the scouting parties out completely and then left the planet without anyone ever knowing he'd saved its unaware citizens. Or at least prolonged their lives.

It worked out best when he'd stay just long enough for the Savage hulk to land and let loose its armies. Those were the days when the Wild Man didn't bother to change his hide after each engagement. He'd pick a spot and allow himself a frenzied killing spree, shooting until all the ammunition he'd reloaded was spent. Savage marines would go down as they moved to their primary military objectives. Sometimes he'd wipe out an entire platoon.

It was never enough.

He could do that in the earliest parts of a planetary invasion, because the day one objectives were more important than he was. The losses were acceptable to whatever was running the particular Savage hulk. He was always gone before they went looking, before *he* became a priority. And he was also always gone before Tyrus Rechs could show up to burn the world clean with the fires of a trigger-nuke.

In those early days, the Wild Man was a shooter, a sniper... but not a soldier.

That would come later.

Now he was sniper and soldier both. A legionnaire, even. Aware that though there were targets everywhere, none of them were real. They could kill him, but they weren't real. There was no planet to save—even though it had always been about revenge and not saving in those early days for the Wild Man.

It wasn't real. There was no winning. Not for him. Not for the Wild Man. A victory over whatever objective was thrown at him was a victory for the Savage reclaimers.

Things the Wild Man hated with an intensity greater than that of any other member of Goth Sullus's special forces team. The men who were once Kill Team Ice. He would have already tried to blow the entire ship up because of the mere fact that it was Savage, except... he was a soldier now. He followed orders.

So until Makaffie told him otherwise, he'd stay alive and not jeopardize the mission.

In the simulation, the Legion was systematically moving through the city, taking it block by bloody block. The Kimbrin, quite possibly MCR, were intermixed with whatever Kimbrin civilians had decided their homes and possessions were too important to leave behind. Or, more often than not in a war, realized that they couldn't leave even if they wanted to. These MCR Kimbrin had been dutifully but unsuccessfully putting up a defense against a Legion that rolled right over them, or that's how it looked to the Wild Man's trained eyes.

But then, from another quarter of the city, a third force had entered the fray. This was the zhee. The MCR were placed between the hammer of the zhee and the anvil of the Legion. But Legion and zhee weren't working together, and wherever the hammer met the anvil, bitter fighting would briefly rage. The donks were tougher foes than the MCR and always had been—better fighters who contributed to the battlefield an unwavering zeal that could only be achieved through absolute moral certainty. But despite all that, the Legion was rolling them up as though warring against children. This was not the same weakened Legion the Wild Man had been told about when he woke up from cryo to see the admiral again... Goth Sullus.

As best the Wild Man could tell, the reclaimers wanted him to turn the tide of a small skirmish between Legion and zhee that played out in his vicinity. He was to assist in preventing the Legion from being flanked by a band of zhee raiders. Instead, the Wild Man disappeared. He could hide in a place like this. And he knew that to these reclaimers, the integrity of the data was paramount above all else. They wouldn't go searching for him, because that would change the whole simulation and the solution wouldn't be valid. They would have failed.

The Wild Man moved and hid and moved, living in the simulation. He ate food left in the blown-out apartment buildings, understanding it was likely the same gruel he'd been eating before, though it tasted—and smelled—different. Perhaps it was nothing at all. That was a possibility inside the Savage hulk, too.

What he was sure of was the fact that as long as he didn't die, and as long as he didn't show those kelhorns what they wanted to see, then it was the Wild Man and not the Savages who won. He knew how to hide. He could stay in that simulation indefinitely. And if the Savages ever grew tired of that, they could try to come and kill him.

But then the Wild Man would die knowing that he had defeated the Savages' plans one last time.

# 42

It was while the Wild Man was looking through his scope at a group of zhee congregating just beyond an apartment window a block away that she first appeared. The shooter had lost track of time, even though he'd promised himself he wouldn't. The days faded into one another and since the Wild Man wasn't engaging targets, he would simply watch them, like now. He was set up deep inside a vacated apartment high-rise, lying on a closet door that had been blown off its hinges, made level by a coffee table and a wooden chair.

It was there that she spoke to him. Unbidden... almost forgotten.

"These are Savages, aren't they, babe?"

The voice was soft and lilting—hers. She was in the room now, standing just behind him like she always had. It had been years—so many years—since the Wild Man had last been visited by her. Tormented by her. Although, hearing her voice now... it wasn't a torment. Had it ever really been?

The Wild Man didn't turn to look. To see if she'd be standing there like she used to. But it was her voice. He knew it. Her voice and not something conjured to draw him into completing the simulation.

"They're Savages," she said, answering her own question. "And those that you shot the other day, when you shot them all in a row, one after the other so they just lay there on the street... bleedin'... those were Savages too, weren't they?"

"Yeah." The Wild Man's voice was a croak, dry and parched, adding another layer of thickness to his already scraped and damaged vocal cords.

It wasn't true of course. They weren't Savages. They were phantoms, automatons that the Savages used for their research. He'd killed something that wasn't really even alive. At least no kind of life that the Wild Man recognized. So why did he lie to her and say that, yes, they were Savages?

*Because that's what she wants to hear. She... she was like that.*

He was afraid to turn around, afraid to look at her. Not because of what she might look like after all this time but because of what he knew he himself looked like without his helmet. Burnt. Disfigured. He'd once been handsome. She'd told him that. Used to tell him all the time when they were first together, and then told him some more once the baby came. The baby looked like him, she said. Handsome. And she... she was beautiful. More beautiful in death than she truly had been in life. He was sure that she'd still be beautiful now, if he turned to look.

But he couldn't stand the thought of seeing her recoil at his scarred and mangled face. So he kept his eyes forward, through the scope, to watch the zhee that weren't Savages, just like the ones he'd killed yesterday weren't Savages. He hoped she was pleased.

Yesterday had been the first time he'd fired his weapon. Whether it had been the simulation trying to flush him or just a case of picking the wrong hide at the wrong time, he didn't know. Up to that point, he hadn't stayed in a hide for more than a day. That seemed to be the limit of what worked. He kept himself in the sections of the city that were controlled by the Legion, because there was so much less foot traffic. Only the occasional rocket posed a threat, and that was just one of those things. If it happened, it happened. Also, the Wild Man figured his job involved taking down some zhee, and there were never any of those in the Legion-controlled areas of the city. Except for yesterday.

Below him had been a squad of legionnaires moving down the street, helmets off, looking for a place to rest after what looked like a hard fight at the city center. The battle had been raging for weeks, which had to be the simulation's doing, because the way Wild Man saw the engagements going, the real deal would've been over in days. The legionnaires were too fierce, their gains too swift. The city wasn't big enough to take weeks to conquer, barring a major counterassault.

The Wild Man was watching those legionnaires and wondering if they were pure artificial constructs, or if they were facial composites of real men. Before, when the team had been taken back to Sinasia... it had been all exactly as the Wild Man remembered it. Same for that fateful showdown with General Rex. So these legionnaires... were they really out there somewhere? And if so, who were they?

He could tell that their armor was new. An improvement over the shiny models the Legion had been stuck with when Goth Sullus woke up Kill Team Ice. Couldn't be an older version, because Wild Man knew those; he'd worn most of those on missions. Ice was always fitted with the latest and greatest when they were activated.

He spotted four zhee. They were moving quietly through the Legion-controlled territory and showed from their body language an intent to hit the squad of legionnaires resting up after the slog of a fight. Wild Man had been in this exact situation many times before, watching over the guys and keeping them alive. Call it force of instinct, call it training, but as he watched the zhee move with their subcompact blaster rifles at the ready, pushing themselves into position to murder those legionnaires... the Wild Man began to squeeze his trigger.

The big weapon boomed its fire and the first zhee's head disappeared into a mist that painted the snouts of its donk brothers. The carnage was so spectacular that even some of the legionnaires were sprinkled.

The second round hit the second donk before its brain had a chance to fully conceive what was happening. Then the other two raised their weapons and moved forward to engage their targets. The Wild Man dropped them in quick succession, each mammoth round ejecting a large piece of brass that more clunked than clattered on the apartment floor.

Wild Man got up and was out the door after that. He scrambled to a new hide, knowing there was no time to delay. He'd given himself up by helping the legionnaires, and he had no guarantees that they wouldn't seek him out and try to kill him. He was only guessing at what the simulation wanted. Maybe he was supposed to help the donks.

He found a building about six kilometers off and stayed for a night, ready for anything. Nothing more happened.

Now he was in his new hide and she was standing behind him and he could tell that she wanted him to waste these zhee, the same as the ones from yesterday. There were no legionnaires to protect, no friendlies needing support from sniper overwatch. In fact, shooting would only kill one zhee and would give away his position to the rest.

But still, he could feel the urge in his fingertips. It would please her so much if he squeezed the trigger.

"Do another one, babe," that haunted remnant of a long-dead wife said.

And then what? The supplies in his ruck were hardly exhaustive. His goal was to stay hidden and stay alive. Deny the Savages a win. Maybe Makaffie would come back. That was a possibility. He needed to at least stay alive until then. Perhaps he really would bring Fast, too.

Fast would know what to do. And once he told Wild Man how it had to be, Wild Man would be able to explain it to his wife. She always only ever wanted just one more dead Savage. Fast would say how it had to be, and the Wild Man would soothe her like he used to. Explain to her how many more Savages he could put down later by following orders now.

She usually listened when he explained it like that. When he told her the plan.

But right now Fast wasn't here. The husband had no excuse for his wife.

"Do another one, babe. For me. Do another."

He wanted to please her. He wanted to kill them for what they did. These weren't Savages. But that was starting to matter less and less in the Wild Man's mind. He wanted to kill. They might not even be real, but so what?

*One more. Do one more.*

For the first time in as long as he could remember the Wild Man was surprised when his rifle fired. That wasn't how a shooter did things. They *knew* when their weapon would discharge and were never surprised by it. That was something that happened to amateurs who were unfamiliar with their weapon. Guys who were still learning exactly what their triggers would yield. How much squeeze before the bang. The Wild Man could count on his weapon's discharge as sure as his own exhalations. You never surprised yourself by drawing a breath. But that trigger pull surprised the Wild Man.

He saw the carnage through his scope. Saw that his surprise had caused the shot to pull a little to the right. Not enough to make a difference; the zhee's neck and shoulders still disappeared in mist and then all of the donks in that apartment building dropped to the floor and out of sight, leaving only the red splatter of gore on the walls for the Wild Man to see.

"I love you, babe," she said.

The Wild Man pushed himself up and slid off his makeshift shooting platform. "I love you too, but now we've got to go." He grabbed his ruck where he'd left it and slung it onto his broad shoulders. But as he started to collapse the big rifle for transportation, his wife told him not to.

"Stay. There'll be more." It was a promise, one thick with the allure of future excitement. Spoken in the breathy voice usually reserved for lovers when alone. "If we stay here there'll be more. They know where you are now. They'll come running. Think of how many. Think of how many you can make pay for what they did to us. What they did to me. What they did to our child."

Fast would have known what to do. He would've given an order and the Wild Man would have obeyed. But no—he could *think* like Fast even if he didn't get an order from the man. And he knew this room wasn't the place to be if he wanted to keep the Savages from winning. Not with those zhee who'd dropped to the floor probably already calling in the direction of the shot.

But...

Maybe it would be best just to take on the whole lot and kill them until he couldn't do it any longer. He'd tried that once... and then woke up from a sleep he'd thought would be his last, burnt, scarred, disfigured... and inducted into Kill Team Ice.

He'd killed all those Savages that day on New Vega and then awakened to a paradise where still more needed to be killed. So maybe... maybe that would happen. Again.

"Stay here and do another one. No other way, babe."

The Wild Man decided that his wife was correct. He put his bag down and got his rifle ready. The weapon could do powerful, obscene damage up close. He'd made entire squads of men break and run when they saw what the big gun could do to just one of them. Nobody wanted to die like that. If he could lure them into someplace tight, like the hallway, he might be able to bring down... what? Five? Six? Seven? All with one trigger pull.

"Let's end it all now," he growled to her.

She giggled. Flirted with him just by that laugh. Made his blood run hot again.

But no such opportunity would come to the Wild Man, for as he looked about the room, trying to find that perfect spot, everything began to dissipate. Fell apart faster than he'd ever seen happen so that the mists hung low on his boots in the newly empty hangar. A pale mutant lay just ahead of him, dead. But this time... there were others still standing. They were spread about and shuffling aimlessly.

He looked for his wife, but she wasn't there. He couldn't hear her either. That was all right. She'd gone off to take care of the baby. That was good. That was what a mother did. And this was no place for a baby. No place for a child at all.

The Wild Man brought the big rifle up to his shoulder and held it there straight and true despite the immense weight of the barrel. He debated whether to shoot the shambling mutants. They seemed bereft of any purpose; didn't even seem to notice he was there. Without anything guiding them they seemed harmless, and the Wild Man began to wonder whether he ought to shoot them anyway, for pity's sake.

Howls came ahead of his decision. The raging, moaning terror of the reclaimers. He took a step back and watched as the ghouls emerged from the grates and fell upon the mutants, pulling them down, ripping them apart, recovering them back through the grating. This was something the Wild Man wouldn't interfere with. He'd seen what happened when you interfered with these things and had no desire to expose himself to the same fate.

Had Wild Man been wearing his bucket, he would have heard the voice of Praxus instructing the others. He missed all of that, but he did notice that the blast doors to his rear opened, giving him passage back to the docking bay. The reclaimers seemed to notice this as well. They turned and looked at him.

Wild Man rolled the powerful scope at the top of his rifle down to the side, bringing up smaller sights in preparation for an up-close engagement. The Savage reclaimers had taken what was theirs, yet they did not leave.

That was new. To the Wild Man they seemed lost, unsure what to do.

"They're Savages." His wife was again whispering in his ear, making the hairs on his neck and arms stand up. "They're Savages and you can kill them if you want to. You'd kill them if you loved me. Do it."

This time the Wild Man was *not* surprised by the report of his rifle. The heavy round struck one of the unsuspecting Savage reclaimers and... blew it apart. Banished it to another realm, because surely there was no trace of it left save a few spectral scraps that drifted like snow to the deck and then themselves disappeared.

Awoken, the other reclaimers hissed and roared, hurrying toward the Wild Man. The sniper stood his ground, ejected the cartridge by working the bolt, and brought a new round forward. He stepped to his side, urging them to come at him straight on as they sought to encircle him and perform their acts of barbarous terror.

He fired again and brought down five with one bullet.

Again he shifted his position. They were close now but were coming all together, seeking to overwhelm as a column of horror. He fired again. And again. And as the last of the spent cartridges hit the ground, so too were the last of those Savages destroyed.

The Wild Man ejected the big, heavy magazine and put in a replacement. His last. Then he turned for the open blast doors and fled the room, leaving ruck and helmet behind.

# 43

The onslaught of Savage reclaimers Keel faced was smaller than it had been and the incorporeal dead bodies stacked higher. That said, there were still too many to repulse, and those that remained showed no intentions of falling back. Not that it mattered. With what Praxus had said about the ship trying to blow itself up and the steady beating it was taking from the Interdictor outside, there was no point trying to hold ground. The concern now was getting Skrizz, Pikkek, and Jack—and anyone else who was unprotected against a sudden vacuum—safely aboard a ship in the hangar before it was too late.

"Jack!" Keel called above the din of weapons fire and the moans of their ghoulish attackers. "Get everyone who can't breathe in space back to the hangar. That includes you!"

Jack nodded. It was time. Although Skrizz was still deadly as ever, Pikkek had run out of ammunition and the koob's martial arts prowess paled in comparison to the wobanki. Andien's arrival had helped some, but mainly she just picked up the slack for Pikkek. Keel was still hit or miss, though he was now killing more of them than he had; he felt like he was getting close to figuring it out. And Jack hadn't fired his weapon in a long while. He was probably out of ammunition. All the more reason for him to depart.

Keel checked his own ammo levels; still plenty left drummed inside in the peculiar, armored pack that fed the hand cannon from the base of his tailbone.

"And let Zora know you're coming or she might shoot you!"

Jack nodded again. He believed it. "What are you gonna do?"

"Work on killing these until you get to the docking bay. I'll be right behind you."

It was as good a plan as any. The word was spread around and then a reluctant Skrizz and Pikkek moved toward the blast doors along with several much less reluctant Black Leaf mercs who'd taken too much damage to their armor to trust their seals against the vacuum of space.

Andien Broxin wasn't even wearing a helmet, but she stayed all the same, willing to risk certain death from a breach if it meant keeping the Savage reclaimers from catching those now fleeing. Keel was by no means introspective about what that might say about her character and commitment—the fight was still too heavy for such musing—but he was glad to have her around at that moment. Several Black Leaf mercs stayed as well, but were much less effective, and in some cases not effective at all.

Keel continued firing on the Savages. With each shot he tried to channel his mind into a sense of... of... he didn't even know what. It varied wildly. Anger, vengeance, justice, self-preservation, sometimes a mix of all of that along with the constant flow of adrenaline that the battle brought to him. Sometimes the reclaimers fell dead, other times they just fell and then crawled in an attempt to continue their destruction. It wasn't a matter of accuracy. Headshots would occasionally leave the Savages writhing like Archimedes had, whereas glancing hits to the stomach, or in one instance a shoulder, could kill outright. It was maddening.

"It's unfair," Keel muttered to himself after just having killed two Savages with hits to the neck only to see a third keep going after a round between its eyes.

"I'm not seeing a way through all this." Makaffie, in his shock trooper-like armor, had stayed. Not that it made a difference to the fight. "And I don't mean that in terms of survival. I mean through these Savages to reach our friend. Yours and mine, Sergeant Fast."

"Praxus," Andien called over the comm. "Do you still have readings on the separated humanoid still on the ship?"

"I do. With the simulations ending—"

Whatever Praxus was going to say was drowned out by the sudden cannon blast of the Wild Man's great sniper rifle. At once a whole section of the Savage reclaimers was incinerated by a ghostly, unseen fire.

"There you are!" shouted Makaffie. It was the happiest Keel had ever heard the man.

Seeing the damage that the big man could do with his rifle, Keel and Andien moved to wherever might give the shooter the clearest lines of fire. Makaffie hurried after them—after standing dumbstruck with joy for several seconds.

The Wild Man didn't hesitate to take any shot he deemed good. With each thundering boom of the rifle a large spent casing was ejected to fall at his feet as more Savage reclaimers—as many as were touched by the bullet—were destroyed.

Keel and Andien likewise kept firing, as did the Black Leaf mercenaries with their seemingly endless supply of charge packs. But that was all a mere holding pattern. The real cleanup work was the Wild Man's, and he performed it with relish.

At last the last of the hulk's supply of Savages was exhausted, and their howls were replaced by a long, ensuing silence that seemed somehow louder than the spectral moans. Across the cavernous simulation hangar that lay between where the Wild Man had emerged and where Keel and the others now stood, something was being said.

The Wild Man with shouting. But it was difficult to hear after so long a battle and with the steady thrumming blaster cannon bolts of the Interdictor still punishing the hull, even as that ship was punished by the *Battle Phoenix*.

"Makaffie!" Keel called. "Tell your man he needs to get over here or use his comm."

Makaffie smiled at the order. "Just like old times... *Captain* Fast."

The wiry man took several steps forward and put his hand on top of his head to indicate bucket-to-bucket communications were in order, then gave the hand signal indicating they couldn't understand the Wild Man's shouts.

The Wild Man gave a nod before hurrying back through the blast doors from which he'd just come. When he reemerged, he was setting his helmet on over his head. That simple act saved his life.

A moment later a direct hit to the hull above them caused a micro-breach. Air began to hiss in rapid escape and the blast doors behind the Wild Man closed shut. The blast doors leading back toward the docking bay also began to seal, with an additional set of emergency doors front and back to make up for the hole Garret had made.

Without thinking, Keel pushed Broxin hard in the chest, sending her tumbling backwards through the closing blast doors. She fell on her behind and could only watch as the others were sealed off in an instant.

No one had time for words as the micro-breach fractured into a full catastrophic rupture of the hull plating. At once the Black Leaf mercenaries were sucked through the newly formed split in the hull and out into the blackness of space, screaming the entire way. Some would wriggle and swim outside, trying to stabilize themselves in the void. Others, whose suits did not seal properly or quickly enough, floated motionless among the stars.

Keel, Makaffie, and the Wild Man kept their feet planted on the deck. All three had armor that automatically engaged magnetic boots to withstand the sudden tempest of the atmosphere violently leaving the ship. And what was now visible above them was breathtaking. A raging ship-to-ship battle at close range, with blaster cannons trading fire across the gap. The *Phoenix* was hammering the Interdictor; the Interdictor was doing its best to hit back while still focusing on wrecking the hulk. The massive bolts flying overhead lit up the three men's faces as though they were gazing up at a planetary independence celebration. And when a heavy blast struck the Savage hull nearby, it sent up a shower of sparks and molten metal that formed an iridescent ribbon as it cooled and trailed away from the vessel.

Keel sprang into action. "Makaffie, get me word on whether the others got to the docking bay. Tell them to abandon ship."

"Yes, sir."

"You—Wild Man." Keel pointed at the big man across the void.

"Good to see you again, Captain Ford," came the raspy, damaged voice of the Wild Man through the comm relay.

"Good to see you too," Keel said, not because he remembered the man but because it seemed the right thing to say. And in truth Keel *was* glad to see the sniper. Had it not been for him eliminating the last of the Savages, there was no telling what kind of mess they'd all be in now. Keel doubted those creatures would be slowed by a little thing like losing atmosphere. "Make your way over here and link up. I'm going to see about getting my ship to pull us out. Leenah—what's your status?"

"Oba's tears, you're alive!"

"It'll take more than that. Status?"

"Doing what I can to space this Interdictor, but it just doesn't want to go down!"

Keel gave a lopsided smile. "Go ahead and leave that to the *Battle Phoenix*. I need a ride." Although he didn't ask the armor to do it, a transponder signal was sent.

"Okay, I read you. Aeson... how are you not dead after that hit?"

"Just lucky, I guess. Hurry up, princess."

Keel turned to Makaffie, who was ready with his findings.

"Zora says that everyone's safe in the hangar. They're loading up ships and pulling out."

"Good. Our exfil is coming. We're gonna want to wait outside to get picked up."

And with that, Keel and the others pushed off the deck of the Savage hulk and drifted past the hull to open space. Keel used his jump jets to keep them all together, and they waited weightlessly beneath the gloriously blazing battle, eager to be far away from the cursed Savage vessel burning beneath their feet.

# 44

Keel burst out of the *Indelible VI*'s airlock, pulled off his helmet, and went straight to the cockpit, but not before telling Makaffie and the Wild Man, "Make yourselves at home."

The cockpit doors swished open and both Leenah and Nilo turned to see him arrive. "Musical chairs," Keel announced. "Everybody next one down."

When Nilo was slow in getting up, Keel grabbed him by his armor's drag handle, hoisted him up, and tossed him toward the back seats. "Move it, rich kid!"

Leenah quickly filled the navigator's chair as Keel dropped into the familiar pilot's seat to get the *Six* moving again. It felt almost exactly as it always had. A little newer, perhaps. Not quite as worn at the edges.

"Some of my men are still floating out there," Nilo said, sounding a bit bothered by his rough treatment. "We need to pick them up."

"We're likely to join 'em if we don't get going." Keel sent the *Indelible VI* racing ahead, and sure enough, a blaster cannon bolt sent by the Interdictor burned through the space where the vessel had held stationary for the airlock pickup a moment before.

"Any interceptors?" Keel asked as he pulled the freighter easily out of range, ignoring the latest in a series of close brushes with death.

"Not since the start," Leenah answered. "Think we took care of whatever they had."

"Good girl." Keel began adjusting the cockpit controls to his liking. "Now let's see what else we're up against."

"It's a Republic Interdictor," Nilo said, and missing was the smooth confidence of before. This entire operation had clearly shaken the man, or at least that was what Keel thought at the time. He would find out later that the weight of Sarai jumping without him and his father's recent message were much larger factors in Nilo's unease.

"Wasn't asking for an identification," Keel said. "I wanna know how much more she can take before going nova. She sure as hell doesn't look in any condition to jump."

"I've been doing what I can with a few torpedoes," Leenah explained. "Close-firing to get inside the PDCs and still veer off before impact. Ordnance that size isn't doing the job. We've got some bigger stuff, but... I wasn't sure if we should use them yet."

Keel was impressed by what he heard. "You were right not to. I'd say this Interdictor is hanging on just long enough to finish off that Savage hulk and then that'll be the end of them both. Looks like *Phoenix* already shot her up beyond the point of salvaging."

A simple look out the front viewport at the Interdictor showed exactly what Keel meant. Multiple decks were vented and exposed, the impervisteel twisted and torn away by some catastrophic blast. The main bridge cupola no longer existed at all, which meant the ship was now being controlled from the secondary bridge, where junior officers were intent on finishing their superiors' mission.

The Interdictor had just started to fire its escape pods. Evidently cracking the Savage hulk open had been the last order of the day before allowing at least some of the crew to escape while the others finished the job. The pods jettisoned in rapid succession from the Interdictor and burned initial thrusters to get some distance from the ship.

The *Battle Phoenix* immediately started to pick the pods off one by one, sending them up into miniature balls of flame.

Keel arched an eyebrow. "No way is the AI doing that..."

A comm transmission came from Zora. "Everyone is off the ship. I have Garret and Jack with me on the *Crow*... the others got out on the newcomers' shuttle."

"Roger. Keel out." The smuggler turned to Leenah. "Get G232 on comm, let him know we have three ships set to come into the *Phoenix* soon."

Leenah activated the comm, pausing long enough to say, "He's pinged the *Six* at least four times trying to find you."

Keel frowned. "What did he want?"

"Something about that psychotic little gunnery bot of yours. It's taken over the weapons system and won't give it up."

That explained the escape pod shooting gallery. Keel settled back into his chair and smiled. "Sounds like him."

"Capturing one of those pods might not be a bad idea," suggested Nilo. "I'd like to get whatever intel we can out of survivors before we commit to finding Earth."

Keel adjusted course and moved toward the nearest batch of pods. "Earth? Why don't we go ahead and waltz inside the temple of the Ancients while we're at it?"

"You don't understand. My father actually knows where it is. Or at least where we can start looking. New Vega. There are some leads we can follow."

"Uh-huh. And what's on Earth now, some kind of buried Savage treasure?"

"At the very least, another strand."

"I don't *care* about the strand. I've got other things that need doing after this."

Nilo sat back in his seat and chewed on his fist pensively. "There's got to be a way I can get you to reconsider."

"Not likely. Now quiet down back there or else we won't get those pods."

The ship got within range of a cluster of pods. The comm came alive with the chirping warnings of Death—they were getting too close to his shooting gallery.

"Yeah, sorry to spoil your fun," Keel replied, "but I need to try to take one of these pods alive."

The bot beeped a question.

"As long as at least one is left for us to take, I don't care what you do with the others. And don't shoot *us*."

Keel effortlessly looped the *Indelible VI* into an attack pattern that would bring him to the rear of the rapid-moving escape pods. A few of these pod models came equipped with a powerful single-shot torpedo just beneath the nose, and Keel didn't want to waste time having to outrun the weapon, which would give the pods time to escape.

"They're locking in their jump coordinates," Leenah warned.

"I'll try and disable all three in one pass," Keel said.

He brought the *Six* sweeping in and spat out a salvo of blaster cannons, promptly vaporizing all three pods.

"Whoops."

"Whoops?" Leenah parroted back.

Keel pressed his fingers into his chest. "It's not my fault. These guns are packing a bigger punch than before."

Nilo pointed through the viewport. "More pods jettisoning on the opposite side of the ship."

"Don't know if we can get around in time," said Leenah.

"We could wait here and see if more pods fire on this side," Nilo said. "Not all the bays have fired."

"Always take what the enemy gives you," Keel recited, repeating an oft-used phrase that a particular Legion instructor had once drilled into him during selection. He pushed the ship toward the Interdictor.

But even as fast as they were moving, he doubted he would reach the pods before they jumped—not if he had to go around the Nether Ops ship. Still, there was another option.

He pointed at a tiny patch of stars visible through the twisted and damaged hull. "Think that goes through?" he asked Leenah.

"Aeson, I don't know..."

"Eh, we'll fit."

Keel shot the *Indelible VI* inside the Interdictor and weaved through its ruined decks, making micro-adjustments as proximity alarms wailed their concern. Nilo and even Leenah shut their eyes against the spectacular collision that was sure to occur, but no sooner had they done so than Keel let out a triumphant laugh—"Ha-haa!"—and the *Six* screamed through the other side of the Interdictor and into the midst of the escape pods.

Now the modified Naseen light freighter was sitting like a venom shark dropped in a pool full of feeder fish. Keel gradually dialed back the weapons' intensity, vaporizing pod after pod with each new test. "Little less... Not quite... That one must've already been damaged... Almost there... Almost got it... Okay that one was just for fun... I think I got it... *now!*"

The *Six*'s blaster cannons raked the targeted pod's engines and caused a small explosion that didn't penetrate the hull. All around them, other little fish winked out of existence as they jumped away into the dark.

"Life forms inside," Leenah said. "Holding steady. Everything stable. No pressure loss detected. You did it, Aeson. We got them."

Keel smiled.

Nilo reached forward and placed an approving hand on Keel's shoulder. "Nice work."

Keel's smile disappeared. He turned his head and grumpily looked down at the hand until Nilo pulled it away.

"Sorry."

"Do you need us on these gun stations?" Makaffie called from deeper inside the ship. "Seems like we're in the thick of it. I'm not a particularly good hand, but the Wild Man can work miracles on anything that shoots."

Keel pressed the comm button. "I think we're out of it now, but be my guest. Better to be ready."

"Roger that, Sergeant Fast."

Being called "Sergeant Fast" *almost* didn't bother Keel, given the severity of recent events. And he forgot all about it the moment Leenah grabbed his head in her hands and kissed his cheek.

She rocked back in her chair, smiling. "It's nice to be back."

Keel nodded. "It is. You have comms with the other ships?"

Leenah checked. "Still showing green."

"Good. Tell them we're linking up on board the *Phoenix*. And tell Broxin she doesn't have to stay, but I'm not letting her take any of my crew again, either. She has to at least drop Skrizz off first."

Leenah relayed the message as Keel flew a tight protective pattern around the disabled escape pod. In the distance, the Savage hulk continued to break further and further apart, its pieces drifting across space in all directions. Whatever self-destruct Praxus had held off was now happening in earnest. The Interdictor wasn't in any better shape, and Keel wouldn't be surprised if it had its own self-destruct sequence now that the escape pods were done launching. If that was the case, they needed to be farther away from the ship than they were now.

"Affirmatives across the board," Leenah reported. "All craft reporting to the *Battle Phoenix*. Anything else?"

Keel arched an eyebrow. "These upgrades of yours—do they include a way for us to haul that escape pod before this whole damn sector of space explodes?"

Leenah grinned. "Of course."

# EPILOGUE

Prisma's room was as spacious as the entire *house* she and her father had inhabited in those blissful, last few days together on the planet Wayste. But whereas the Republic governor's mansion was, like most of the homes Prisma could remember, empty of life and only spartanly decorated, this room was luxuriant and lavish in style. Reina had pointed out the ornate tapestries that hung next to tower viewports; she'd named the furs, the fabrics, stones, woods, and even gems used. And even though this room was in a ship, and ships in deep space were always cold, Prisma felt cozy in this cavernous chamber. Before her was a grand horizon of crysteel that afforded a brilliant view of some swirling blue giant star in the distance. She had never been anywhere so beautiful, except those places in the galaxy not made by hands.

So why, then, did her room somehow also feel like a prison?

Prisma and her mother had used the same trick to travel across the stars as they had previously. Reina took them to a temple, worked her hands across the stellar map... and they both found themselves deposited directly into this ship. Into this very room.

Prisma had asked how it was that they'd come straight aboard the starship and not into another temple of the

Ancients like before. The temples had also done that for Ravi. When they'd come to save him, they'd appeared right before him. No stop at a temple first. How? Why?

Reina explained it all patiently. "There are some paths that you will learn well enough to only need the temple for a beginning or an end. In time, you may learn the way so expertly that no temple is needed at all."

"Like how Ravi does it?"

Her mother smiled, but the expression seemed without kindness. "Yes. Or... like us. Like I will be someday and you thereafter. I am close to mastery. You will catch up quickly."

"Now that we did what you said we needed to do," Prisma began, though she could tell then that her mother wanted to leave her in the room. "Maybe..."

Time passed. "Maybe what, Prisma?"

The girl knew her mother likely wouldn't want to hear what she had nearly suggested. She intended to keep quiet, but then the words came out all in a blur, practically connected to each other. "Maybe-Ravi-could-teach-both-of-us."

Another pause. "What Ravi knows... will surely stay with Ravi. For what he has done in destroying that creature was a terrible thing. I do not believe you will ever see him again, and I am asking you now, my daughter, to speak of him no more. I cannot forbid you to think about him, but do not speak to me of Ravi again, Prisma."

Prisma felt ashamed for some reason. "Oh... okay." She decided that she probably shouldn't mention Crash around her mother again either. Her mother had gotten the same look with Crash-talk earlier as she did with Ravi-talk now.

Now left alone in her quarters, Prisma wondered what the entire ship looked like on the outside. It must be huge given the size of her room. Her mother had parted with a promise that soon Prisma would be called for, but for now she should wait here.

So she did. She waited and she thought. Sometimes about Ravi, but mostly her mind drifted to Crash. She thought of all the times they'd spent together. It was hard to believe the war bot was really gone. Someday she would go back to that world, if only to recover him.

And what of his parting words to her? *The payment to Tyrus Rechs.* She remembered exactly what she'd paid the bounty hunter when she asked him to kill Goth Sullus on her behalf. She remembered it clearly. Tyrus Rechs had tried to talk her out of seeking vengeance. He spoke on and on about how it was a path that led to nothing but killing. But Prisma insisted. She offered credits, knowing that her father was rich but not exactly knowing how that might transfer to her or the bounty hunter's fees. Tyrus Rechs didn't want credits. He wouldn't accept them. He did the job without them.

Prisma remembered that.

When the doors to her chambers opened, Prisma didn't hear them. But she could sense her mother stepping inside, and so she reached out, trying to feel the other life on board in the way that she'd been taught. Back on that planet. Where they had left Crash, twisted, broken, and ruined. She would go there again—she would. If only to recover her bot. And then, eventually, when she was back aboard the *Indelible VI* with Leenah and Captain Keel, she would ask Garret to...

The thought took Prisma by surprise. It was the first time she'd pondered what it would be like going back to

Captain Keel and the others since... when? Perhaps the day she'd left Mother Ree's sanctuary.

Then Reina spoke, and the curious desire was gone almost as quickly as it had arrived. "This vessel shields itself from being known in such a way, Prisma."

For a moment Prisma was confused. "You mean when I tried to reach out and feel for the life aboard?"

"Precisely so." Reina sat down on a bed much too large for either of them; it would have been too large for a Drusic as well. She patted the red, velvety comforter and invited Prisma to sit at her side.

The young woman did as she was asked but said nothing.

"Don't you want to know *why* this is so?" Reina asked. "You're usually very inquisitive, Prisma. An excellent student."

"Sorry. I was just thinking." She looked out the viewport, then back to her mother. "Where are we?"

"Exactly where we are meant to be."

"And where is that? *Exactly.*"

"Far away. Impossibly far to explain. This ship, you see, can travel through the Quantum just like you or I, except it does not need a temple. Isn't that amazing?"

"Yeah. But... it's not your ship. How come?"

"It's not. We are guests."

"Whose guests?"

"Someone very important, Prisma." Reina looked at her expectantly.

Prisma wasn't sure what she was supposed to say. Her mother seemed to want something from her though, so she raised her eyebrows, hoping that would convey whatever expression her mother was after.

Reina smiled and rubbed Prisma's back. "I know my words don't mean anything to you right now, but if you knew who we will soon appear before, as I do, you would be excited." She leaned over and bumped Prisma's shoulder lovingly with her own. "The good news is, you'll see him soon. He is waiting for us now and sent me to bring you. One like him does not wait, Prisma. He is waited *upon*. So you see what an honor he shows us for our service."

"What service?"

Reina ignored the question.

"Do I need to do anything to get ready?" Prisma asked. "Daddy—*my father* always made me dress up and wash before we met anyone important."

"Fitting for those situations, such as they were. But Prisma, you must understand: there is nothing *you* can do that will make him think any higher or lower of you. What you are cannot be hidden from him." Reina stood. "Are you ready?"

Prisma jumped off the bed and immediately felt childish. She found herself physically too big for such things. She straightened her clothes. "I'm ready. Let's go."

The grand viewing bridge of the starship put Prisma's enormous bedroom to shame. It was almost entirely viewports, constructed more of crysteel than impervisteel as best Prisma could tell. The girl looked around in wonder, finding beautiful cosmic sights above her, below her, and especially in the great horizon before her.

A man, tall and broad-shouldered and wearing a regal cloak, stood elevated on a dais, enjoying that same view, watching the same blue-star nebula that Prisma had gazed at from her room.

Reina motioned for Prisma to follow her further into the vast chamber, then motioned again for her to stop after they'd walked some twenty meters. From there Reina continued on alone, before stopping ten meters short of the man.

Reina bowed, saying nothing. Then a golden and almost glowing hand came out from the man's side and waved her forward. Reina pulled up the tresses on her white gown and climbed the steps of the dais with grace and dignity, stopping just behind the man, on his left.

"Speak, Reina, my queen."

Reina bowed once more. "I present the girl. She has been trained in the ways. She has done all that we envisioned she could."

The man nodded and then turned his head to the side to look at Prisma for the first time from the corner of his eye. His face was shining and angelic. Handsome. The face of a young warrior but without blemish. It somehow also conveyed a wisdom and nobility far too advanced to be found in someone so young.

He turned back to his vigil, looking out through the massive horizontal viewport.

"Through many ages have I guided this vessel through the Quantum. And in the Quantum, I saw the failures of so many things I entrusted to others. To Maestro. Even, my queen, to you. For a very long time. But the Quantum brings about *all* things. The Quantum... has not failed us."

At each mention of the word "Quantum," Reina bowed her head.

"Long have I labored to bring about a reversal to this galaxy's fated end," the man continued. "And now it seems that you were right. These... unclean things. Primitives, even as you once were. They can become, like you, something more."

Reina gave a singular nod of her head, accepting the grace of these words.

"Do you still believe that, my queen?"

"Your Grace, as you said, they are as I once was. And..." She hesitated, as though about to say more, but then fell quiet.

"Yes. I remember. But the others. The warrior and the tactician. With them it was not so. And what of the girl you have brought me? Will your fate also be hers? Is it possible?"

"This one has served your purposes, Your Grace. Whatever befalls her now is not for me to say, but you alone, my king."

This seemed to please the man. The king. "You speak truth. So it must be of all in the galaxy. So it shall be here." He held out his right hand and almost imperceptibly twitched his finger forward.

Prisma saw the gesture but didn't know what to make of it. She hadn't heard any of the conversation. It wasn't until her mother turned around and made a more demonstrative motion, beckoning her forward, that Prisma began to move. Her father had once told her how to walk in the presence of House of Reason delegates, Republic senators, various dignitaries, and planetary royalty. Prisma tried to recall those lessons and put them to use. She remembered how her mother had stopped at the foot of the dais and halted there as well.

"She may come up," the man said to Reina. His voice was powerful and yet beautiful. Prisma had never heard the likes of it before. It at once made her want to love him. But also... it invoked fear.

Prisma realized that she'd taken a step prematurely. Apparently her mother was supposed to receive the order and usher her up. Prisma was halfway up the steps when that realization came. She continued to the top and stood beside her mother, still several feet behind the man.

Reina stepped around her and gently forced her down on her knees. In Prisma's head, she heard her mother say, *You are not yet worthy to stand before him.*

"No she is not," the man said aloud, as though he too had heard the inner-spoken words. "But for your service to me, girl, you have been granted the privilege of witnessing what will now come from it."

"What is to come?" Prisma asked.

Prisma knew she shouldn't have spoken when she saw the flash of horror cross her mother's face. But the man softly chuckled, and Reina's horror turned to mere annoyance.

"The greatest, most powerful army ever to have existed is now on its way to our galaxy. It has never failed to achieve its purposes. I will stop it."

"You are soon to be witness to history," Reina added. "The galaxy's ascendance is here."

But Prisma could think only of Crash. What had she paid to have Goth Sullus killed? What was she failing to remember?

THE END

# ABOUT THE MAKERS

**Jason Anspach** is the co-creator of Galaxy's Edge. He lives in the Pacific Northwest.

**Nick Cole** is the other co-creator of Galaxy's Edge. He lives in southern California with his wife, Nicole.

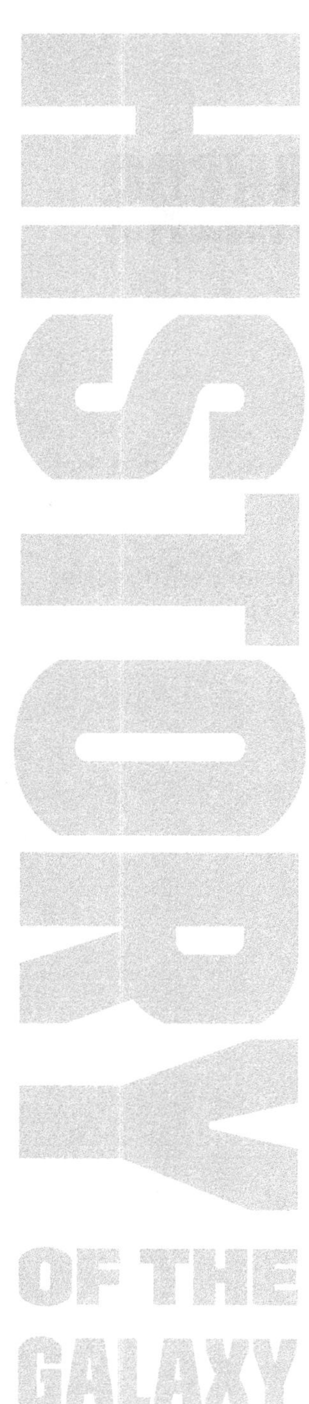

HISTORY
OF THE
GALAXY

Explore over 30+ Galaxy's Edge books and counting from the minds of Jason Anspach, Nick Cole, Doc Spears, Jonathan Yanez, Karen Traviss, and more.

# LAST BATTLE OF THE REPUBLIC

**OC**    **STRYKER'S WAR**

**OC**    **IRON WOLVES**

01    LEGIONNAIRE

02    GALACTIC OUTLAWS

03    KILL TEAM

**OC**    **THROUGH THE NETHER**

04    ATTACK OF SHADOWS

**OC**    **THE RESERVIST**

05    SWORD OF THE LEGION

06    PRISONERS OF DARKNESS

07    TURNING POINT

08    MESSAGE FOR THE DEAD

09    RETRIBUTION

10    TAKEOVER

# REBIRTH OF THE LEGION

01    LEGACIES

02    DARK VICTORY

03    CONVERGENCE

04    REMAINS

# Honor Roll

We would like to give our most sincere thanks and recognition to those who supported the creation of *Galaxy's Edge: Last Contact* by supporting us at GalaxysEdge.us.

| | |
|---|---|
| Cody Aalberg | Robert Anspach |
| Artis Aboltins | Melanie Apollo |
| Sam Abraham | Britton Archer |
| Guido Abreu | Benjamin Arguello |
| Chancellor Adams | Thomas Armona |
| Myron Adams | Daniel Armous |
| Garion Adkins | Linda Artman |
| Ryan Adwers | Jonathan Auerbach |
| Kyle Aguiar | Fritz Ausman |
| Elias Aguilar | Sean Averill |
| Neal Albritton | Albert Avilla |
| Jonathan Allain | Matthew Bagwell |
| Bill Allen | Marvin Bailey |
| Justin Allred | Sallie Baliunas |
| Jake Altman | Nathan Ball |
| Justin Altman | Kevin Bangert |
| Tony Alvarez | John Barber |
| Joachim Andersen | Logan Barker |
| Jarad Anderson | John Barley |
| Galen Anderson | Brian Barrows-Striker |
| Pat Andrews | Richard Bartle |

Austin Bartlett

Robert Battles

Eric Batzdorfer

John Baudoin

Adam Bear

Nahum Beard

Antonio Becerra

Mike Beeker

Randall Beem

Matt Beers

John Bell

Daniel Bendele

Royce Benford

Mark Bennett

Edward Benson

Cody Bente

Matthew Bergklint

Carl Berglund

Brian Berkley

Corey Berman

David Bernatski

Tim Berube

Michael Betz

Shannon Biggs

Brien Birge

Nathan Birt

Trevor Blasius

WJ Blood

David Blount

Evan Boldt

Rodney Bonner

Rodney Bonner

Thomas Seth Bouchard

William Boucher

Brandon Bowles

Alex Bowling

Chester Brads

Logan Brandon

Jordan Brann

Ernest Brant

Daniel Bratton

Dennis Bray

Christopher Brewster

Jacob Brinkman

Geoff Brisco

Wayne Brite

Spencer Bromley

Paul Brookins

Raymond Brooks

Zack Brown

Marion Buehring

Johncarlo Buitrago

Sean Bulman

Jim Burkhardt

Tyler Burnworth

Tyler Burnworth

Matthew Buzek

Noel Caddell

Daniel Cadwell

Brian Callahan

Joseph Calvey

Van Cammack

Chris Campbell

Danny Cannon

Zachary Cantwell

Brett Carden

Robert Cathey

Brian Cave

Shawn Cavitt
Brad Chenoweth
David Chor
Cooper Clark
Casey Clarkson
Ethan Clayton
Jonathan Clews
Beau Clifton
Sean Clifton
Jerremy Cobb
Morgan Cobb
William Coble
Robert Collins Sr.
Alex Collins-Gauweiler
Jerry Conard
Gayler Conlin
Michael Conn
James Connolly
Ryan Connolly
James Conyers
Brian Cook
Michael Corbin
Robert Cosler
Ryan Coulston
Seth Coussens
Andrew Craig
Adam Craig
Christopher Crowder
Phil Culpepper
Ben Curcio
Tommy Cutler
Thomas Cutler
Christopher Da Pra
John Dames

David Danz
Matthew Dare
Chad David
Alister Davidson
Peter Davies
Walter Davila
Ashton Davis
Brian Davis
Nathan Davis
Ivy Davis
Ben Davis
Joseph Dawson
Ron Deage
Anthony Del Villar
Tod Delaricheliere
Anerio (Wyatt)
Deorma (Dent)
Isaac Diamond
Alexander Dickson
Nicholas Dieter
Christopher DiNote
Matthew Dippel
Gregory Divis
Ellis Dobbins
Brian Dobson
Samuel Dodes
Graham Doering
Gerald Donovan
Dustyn Down
John Dryden
Josh DuBois
Garrett Dubois
Ray Duck
Marc-André Dufor

Trent Duncan
Christopher Durrant
Cami Dutton
Chris Dwyer
Virgil Dwyer
Brian Dye
Nick Edwards
Justin Eilenberger
William Ely
Michael Emes
Brian England
Andrew English
Stephane Escrig
Dakota Estepp
Benjamin Eugster
Jaeger Falco
Nicholas Fasanella
Christian Faulds
Steven Feily
Julie Fenimore
Meagan Ference
Brad Ferguson
Adolfo Fernandez
Rich Ferrante
Ashley Finnigan
Matthew Fiveson
Waren Fleming
Kath Flohrs
Daniel Flores
William Foley
Steve Forrester
Skyla Forster
Kenneth Foster
Timothy Foster

Chad Fox
Bryant Fox
Doug Foxford
Mark Franceschini
Greg Franz
Griffin Frendsdorff
Bob Fulsang
Jonathan Furney
Elizabeth Gafford
David Gaither
Seth Galarneau
Christopher Gallo
Richard Gallo
Kyle Gannon
Joshua Gardner
Michael Gardner
Alphonso Garner
Mackenzey Garrison
Cordell Gary
Brad Gatter
Tyler Gault
Angelo Gentile
Stephen George
Nick Gerlach
Eli Geroux
Christopher Gesell
Kevin Gilchrist
Dylan Giles
Oscar Gillott-Cain
Nathan Gioconda
John Giorgis
Johnny Glazebrooks
Martin Gleaton
James Glendenning

William Frank Godbold IV
Justin Godfrey
Luis Gomez
John Gooch
Tyler Goodman
Zack Gotsch
Justin Gottwaltz
George Gowland
Mitch Greathouse
Gordon Green
Matt Green
Shawn Greene
John Greenfield Jr.
Eric Griffin
Ronald Grisham
Paul Griz
Preston Groogan
Kyle Gudmundson
Harry Gurney
Levi Haas
Tyler Hagood
Tyler Hagood
Michael Hale
Brandon Handy
Erik Hansen
Greg Hanson
Jeffrey Hardy
Tyler Hardy
Adam Hargest
Ian Harper
Revan Harris
Jordan Harris
Brett Harrison
Brandon Hart

Matthew Hartmann
Adam Hartswick
Mohamed Hashem
Ronald Haulman
Joshua Hayes
Ryan Hays
Adam Hazen
Richard Heard
Colin Heavens
Jon Hedrick
Jesse Heidenreich
Brenton Held
Kyler Helker
Jason Henderson
Jason Henderson
John Henkel
Jonathan Herbst
Daniel Heron
Bradley Herren
Kyle Hetzer
Korrey Heyder
Matthew Hicks
Samuel Hillman
Victor Hipolito
Jonathan Hoehn
Aaron Holden
Clint Holmes
Jacob Honeter
Charles Hood
Garrett Hopkins
Tyson Hopkins
William Hopsicker
Jefferson Hotchkiss
Fred Houinato

| | |
|---|---|
| Ian House | Jason Jones |
| Jack House | David Jorgenson |
| Ken Houseal | John Josendale |
| Nathan Housley | Sunil Kakar |
| Jeff Howard | Ryan Kalle |
| Nicholas Howser | Chris Karabats |
| Mark Hoy | Ron Karroll |
| Kirstie Hudson | Timothy Keane |
| Mike Hull | Cody Keaton |
| Donald Humpal | Brian Keeter |
| Bradley Huntoon | Noah Kelly |
| Bobby Hurn | George Kelly |
| Charles Hurst | Jacob Kelly |
| James Hurtado | Caleb Kenner |
| Michael Hutchison | Daniel Kimm |
| Wayne Hutton | Kennith King |
| Gaetano Inglima | Zachary Kinsman |
| Antonio Iozzo | Rhet Klaahsen |
| Wendy Jacobson | Jesse Klein |
| Paul Jarman | William Knapp |
| James Jeffers | Marc Knapp |
| Tedman Jess | Robert Knox |
| Eric Jett | Andreas Kolb |
| Anthony Johnson | Steven Konecni |
| Josh Johnson | Ethan Koska |
| Eric Johnson | Evan Kowalski |
| James Johnson | Byl Kravetz |
| Cobra Johnson | John Kukovich |
| Nick Johnson | Mitchell Kusterer |
| Randolph Johnson | Brian Lambert |
| Nick Johnson | Clay Lambert |
| Tyler Jones | Jeremy Lambert |
| Tyler Jones | Andrew Langler |
| Paul Jones | Mikey Lanning |

Dave Lawrence
Alexander Le
Jacob Leake
David Leal
Andy Ledford
Nicholas Lee
Joseph Legacy
Ruel Lindsay
Eric Lindsey
Eron Lindsey
Paul Lizer
Kenneth Lizotte
Andre Locker
Maxwell Lombardi
Richard Long
Oliver Longchamps
Joseph Lopez
David Lopez
Kyle Lorenzi
David Losey
Doug Lower
Steven Ludtke
Andrew Luong
Jesse Lyon
Brooke Lyons
Taylo Lywood
David MacAlpine
Patrick Maclary
Daniel Magano
Richard Maier
Chris Malone
Adam Manlove
Andrew Mann
John Mannion

Brian Mansur
Brent Manzel
Robert Marchi
Jacob Margheim
Deven Marincovich
Cory Marko
Quinn Marquard
Logan Martin
Edward Martin
Jason Martin
Lucas Martin
Pawel Martin
Trevor Martin
Christopher P. Martin
Bill Martin
Alexander Martin
Tim Martindale
Joshua Martinez
Joseph Martinez
Phillip Martinez
Cory Masierowski
Tao Mason
Wills Masterson
Ashley Mateo
Michael Matsko
Justin Matsuoko
Ezekiel Matze
Mark Maurice
Simon Mayeski
Joseph Mazzara
Sean McCafferty
Logan McCallister
Kyle McCarley
Quinn McCusker

Alan McDonald
Caleb McDonald
Jeremy McElroy
Dennis McGriff
Hans McIlveen
Rachel McIntosh
Ryan McIntosh
Richard McKercher
Ryan McKracken
Jason McMarrow
Colin McPherson
Christopher Menkhaus
Jim Mern
Robert Mertz
Jacob Meushaw
Brady Meyer
Pete Micale
Christopher Miel
Mike Mieszcak
Ted Milker
Daniel Miller
Corrigan Miller
Patrick Millon
Reimar Moeller
Ryan Mongeau
Jacob Montagne
Ramon Montijo
Mitchell Moore
Matteo Morelli
Joe Morgan
Todd Moriarty
Matthew Morley
Daniel Morris
William Morris

Christian Morrison
Alex Morstadt
Nicholas Mukanos
Bob Murray
Jeff Murri
Joseph Nahas
Vinesh Narayan
Colby Neal
James Needham
Ray Neel
Merle Neer
Adam Nelson
Tyler Neuschwanger
Travis Nichols
Bennett Nickels
Trevor Nielsen
Andrew Niesent
Sean Noble
Otto (Mario) Noda
Greg Nugent
Christina Nymeyer
Brian O'Connor
Matthew O'Connor
Timothy O'Connor
Sean O'Hara
Colin O'neill
Ryan O'neill
Patrick O'Rourke
Jacob Odell
Grant Odom
Conor Oehler
Quinn Oehler
Nolan Oglesby
Tyler Ornelas

Gareth Ortiz-Timpson

James Owens

Will Page

John Park

David Parker

Matthew Parker

Shawn Parrish

Eric Pastorek

Andrew Patterson

Wesley Patteson

Joshua Pena

Thomas Pennington

Kevin Perkins

Zac Petersen

Trevor Petersen

Marcus Peterson

Chad Peyton

Jon Phillips

Dupres Pina

Jared Plathe

Luke Plummer

Paul Polanski

Matthew Pommerening

Stephen Pompeo

Jason Pond

Nathan Poplawski

Chancey Porter

Rodney Posey

Brian Potts

Jonathaon Poulter

Chris Pourteau

Daniel Powderly

Chris Prats

Matt Prescott

Thomas Preston

Matthew Print

Aleksander Purcell

Joshua Purvis

Max Quezada

Scott Raff

Joe Ralston

Frederick Ramlow

Jason Randolph

Aindriu Ratliff

Beverly Raymond

T.J. Recio

Ryan Aguiar

Cannon Renfro

John Resch

Nathaniel Reyes

Jacob Reynolds

Cody Richards

Dalton Richards

Eric Ritenour

John Robertson

Walt Robillard

Brian Robinson

Joshua Robinson

Daniel Robitaille

John Roche

Paul Roder

Zack Roeleveld

Thomas Rogneby

Thomas Roman

Elias Rostad

Joyce Roth

Rob Rudkin

Arthur Ruiz

| | |
|---|---|
| Jim Rumford | Dylan Sexton |
| John RunningWolf | Austin Shafer |
| John Runyan | Mitch Shami |
| Chad Rushing | Timothy Sharkey |
| Sterling Rutherford | Christopher Shaw |
| RW | Charles Sheehan |
| Mark Ryan | Wendell Shelton |
| Justin Ryan | Lawrence Shewark |
| Greg S | Ian Short |
| Lawrence Sanchez | Glenn Shotton |
| Dustin Sanders | Emaleigh Shriver |
| David Sanford | Dave Simmons |
| Chris Sapero | Joshua Sipin |
| Jaysn Schaener | Chris Sizelove |
| Shayne Schettler | Andrew Skaines |
| Jason Schilling | Scott Sloan |
| Andrew Schmidt | Steven Smead |
| Brian Schmidt | Anthony Smith |
| Ray Schmidt | Daniel Smith |
| Thomas Schmidt | Lawrence Smith |
| Kurt Schneider | Sharroll Smith |
| Peter Scholtes | Tyler Smith |
| Theodore Schott | Michael Smith |
| Kevin Schroeder | Michael Smith |
| William Schweisthal | Timothy Smith |
| Anthony Scimeca | Neal Smith |
| Cullen Scism | Ian Smith |
| Connor Scott | Tom Snapp |
| Preston Scott | David Snowden |
| Robert Sealey | Alexander Snyder |
| Aaron Seaman | Robert Speanburgh |
| Dan Searle | John Spears |
| Phillip Seek | Thomas Spencer |
| Kevin Serpa | Troy Spencer |

Peter Spitzer
Dustin Sprick
George Srutkowski
Cooper Stafford
Travis Stair
Graham Stanton
Paul Starck
Ethan Step
John Stephenson
Thomas Stewardson
Tanner Stewart
Maggie Stewart-Grant
John Stockley
Rob Strachan
James Street
Joshua Strickland
William Strickler
Shayla Striffler
John Stuhl
Brad Stumpp
Kevin Summers
Ernest Sumner
Randall Surles
Sonny Suttles
Andrew Suy
David Swantek
Aaron Sweeney
Shayne Sweetland
Tiffany Swindle
Lloyd Swistara
Carol Szpara
Travis TadeWaldt
Daniel Tanner
Blake Tate

Lawrence Tate
Kyler Tatsch
Justin Taylor
Robert Taylor
Tim Taylor
Jonathan Terry
Stavros Theohary
Vernetta Thomas
Marc Thomas
David P. Thomas
Chris Thompson
Steven Thompson
Jonathan Thompson
William Joseph Thorpe
Beverly Tierney
Daniel Torres
Matthew Townsend
Jameson Trauger
Dimitrios Tsaousis
Scott Tucker
Oliver Tunnicliffe
Eric Turnbull
Ryan Turner
Brandon Turton
John Tuttle
Dylan Tuxhorn
Nerissa Umanzor
Jalen Underwood
Barrett Utz
Paul Van Dop
Andrew Van Winkle
Patrick Van Winkle
Paden VanBuskirk
Patrick Varrassi

Daniel Vatamaniuck
Jason Vaughn
Jose Vazquez
Stephen Vea
Brian Veit
Daniel Venema
Marshall Verkler
Cole Vineyard
Ralph Vloemans
Anthony Wagnon
Wes "Gingy" Wahl
Humberto Waldheim
Christopher Walker
David Wall
Joshua Wallace
Justin Wang
Andrew Ward
Wedge Warford
Scot Washam
Tyler Washburn
Quentin Washington
Christopher Waters
Zachary Waters
John Watson
William Webb
Bill Webb
Hiram Wells
Jack Weston

William Westphal
Ben Wheeler
Paul White
Paul Wierzchowski
Grant Wiggins
Jack Williams
Justin Wilson
Scott Winters
Evan Wisniewski
Matthew Wittmann
Reese Wood
Tripp Wood
Robert Woodward
John Wooten
John Work
Bonnie Wright
Jason Wright
Ethan Yerigan
Matthew Young
John Zack
Phillip Zaragoza
Brandt Zeeh
Kevin Zhang
David Zimmerman
Jordan Ziroli
Nathan Zoss

www.ingramcontent.com/pod-product-compliance
Lightning Source LLC
Chambersburg PA
CBHW070813190726
48292CB00006B/1997